KARTOGRAPHY

KARTOGRAPHY

kamila shamsie

BLOOMSBURY

First published in Great Britain 2002

Copyright © 2002 by Kamila Shamsie

Map reproduced by permission of Lonely Planet Publications
Karachi and Central Karachi maps, *Pakistan, ed. 5*, © Lonely Planet, 1998

The moral right of the author has been asserted

Bloomsbury Publishing Plc, 38 Soho Square, London WID 3HB

A CIP catalogue record is available from the British Library

ISBN 0 7475 5730 6

10 9 8 7 6 5 4 3 2 1

Typeset by Hewer Text Ltd, Edinburgh
Printed in Great Britain by Clays Ltd, St Ives plc

ACKNOWLEDGEMENTS

I'd like to thank all the usual suspects. In addition, I must mention:

Agha Shahid Ali, for insisting I 'do something' with the image of the spinning globe.
Zain Mustafa, for drives through Karachi, and lunar streets.
Rehana Hakim, for giving me access to the *Newsline* archives.
Zerxes Spencer, for the stream of post-midnight e-mails which kept me company while I was at work on the first draft of this novel.
Aisha Rahman and Deepak Sathe, for the sofa-bed.
Marian McCarthy, for understanding where this book could go, and insisting I take it there.

It would be impossible to mention all the books, articles and websites I consulted while working on this novel. But I would like to mention the following, which were of particular help.

Ali, Tariq. *Can Pakistan Survive?* Verso, 1983.
Baillie, Alexander F. *Kurrachee Past, Present and Future.* Oxford, 1975.
Cosgrove, Denis (ed.), *Mappings.* Reaktion Books, 1999.
Lari, Yasmeen and Mihail S. *The Dual City: Karachi During the Raj.* Oxford, 1996.

For all my Karachi friends,

All over the world –

In particular,

Asad Haider and Tushna Kandawalla.

The globe spins. Mountain ranges skim my fingers; there is static above the Arabian Sea. Pakistan is split in two, but undivided. This world is out of date.

Rain outside. If it reaches Karachi, the waves will swell further. The airport, though, is inland. From there to here is no distance at all if you look at the map of the world. But distance is not about miles and kilometres, it is about fear. Who said that? Someone who wasn't married to a pilot, I'd guess. I unscrew a jar of ink. Scent of smudged words and metal fills the air.

Do all tentacled creatures produce ink, Raheen? Does the cuttlefish? Can you write on the waves with cuttleink?

I close my eyes, and wrap my fingers around a diamond-shaped bone. I still hear the world spinning. I spin with it, spin into a garden. At dusk. And yes, those are shoulder pads stitched into my shirt.

1986.

• • •

Of course the garden is located where all our beginnings, Karim's and mine, are located: Karachi. That spider-plant city where, if you know what to look for and some higher power is feeling indulgent, you might find a fossilized footprint of Alexander. The Great. He led his army through Karachi, long, long before the spider-plant effect took hold, when Karachi was a harbour named Krokola. Perhaps Alexander's was the first army that stirred up the sand along the eastern coast of the Arabian Sea.

That's an interesting thought.

Though, really, it's never been proved that Karachi is Krokola, and even if it is Alexander probably never stepped foot on its shores; so any ancient Macedonian footprints with heelstamps of authority in Karachi's rocks must belong to Alexander's admiral, Nearchus, who wasn't even Macedonian. He was a Cretan and that sounds rude.

I don't know if Karim and I were actually looking for ancient footsteps in the rockery of Karim's garden that October evening, the day all boxes were unpacked and the move from Karim's old house finally completed, but I do know that we were more than happy with our discovery of a fossilized cuttlefish.

'You sure it's a cuttlefish?' I said, turning the diamond-shaped fossil over in my hands. We were sitting cross-legged, side by side, on the grass that bordered the triangle of soil on which the rockery had been set out. Mud on his knees and chlorophyll on mine, though as we sat close, swaying back with laughter and forward with curiosity, the colours were mingling, dun shot through with emerald.

' 'Course it is. Well, cuttlebone. No sign of fish flesh on that thing.'

'So flesh is what makes a fish a fish?'

'Interesting question. Is a sole without flesh still a sole? Either way, a cuttlefish isn't a fish at all.' Karim waved his arms about like someone trying to breakdance. 'It's got tentacles.'

He fell back on his elbows, nearly flattening an ant, which, impervious, did not waver from its path but crawled over his arm and proceeded along through the short-cropped grass. 'Imagine it.' He looked around. 'This used to be an ocean. If you squint, can't you almost see Mai Kolachi rowing a boat through the hibiscus in search of her husband, and look! over there, through the bougainvillaea you can see a wave made up of the tears Alexander wept for Bucephalus.'

' "Bucephalus" is an anagram for "a puce blush". When I squint, I see only a blur.'

Karim rolled his eyes. 'You know, if I wasn't me, you wouldn't be you.'

Odd. No matter where I begin, that line finds its way into my narrative so very early on, and forces linearity to give way to a ramble of hindsight. This is the worst of our ways of remembering, this tendency to prod the crust of anecdote in the hope of releasing a gush of piping-hot symbolism.

Stop, Karim would say. Go and eat something. And look up 'symbolism' in the dictionary while you're at it. Symbolism is an anagram for 'Miss my lob'. The summer we played tennis together there was such symbolism in your game.

Karim, shut up. While you weren't looking I've melded the memories into a story beginningmiddlend, and don't you dare interrupt with your version of what-really-came-first and that-was-cause-not-effect.

Goodness, girlio, wouldn't dream of it. Chronology is all about effect. Which is why you should have started at the point . . .

Karim!

Proceed.

All right. Dusk . . . shoulder pads . . . cuttlefish . . . My parents pulling up in the driveway, and Karim's father – Uncle Ali – coming out to join them for tea, his tie immaculately knotted and the creases of his trousers so sharp they would have mowed the grass if he had rolled across the garden. That's a ridiculous thing to say, though. Imagine Uncle Ali deigning to roll.

'Oh, you really look like someone who's been unpacking boxes all day,' my mother said with a laugh, sitting down on a cane chair, her palm outstretched towards Uncle Ali as though proffering him a tray of teacups. 'Hanh, I know. The house is a mess, but your dressing room is tiptop and shipshape.'

Uncle Ali didn't smile. 'Such an optimistic move, buying a house.'

I caught my parents exchanging worried glances. 'What a silly remark, Ali,' my mother said.

'What's silly about it? The factory area is still under curfew. No sign of it lifting.'

'Oh, optimistic that way,' my father said, and then shut up because my mother kicked him.

I looked across at Karim to see if he knew what was going on, but he was gripping the cuttlebone tight, trying to imprint his palm with its scarred surface.

'Things are just so awful,' Uncle Ali went on. 'God only knows when the kids' school will open again.'

Karim and I tried to look sombre, but my father caught us touching toe to toe in delight.

'You're more than happy that the riots are continuing, right?' Aba said.

'Well, it's not . . .' I said.

'That we want more people to die or anything,' Karim went on. 'But . . .'

'But it wouldn't hurt if things remained . . .'

'Tense.'

'Just long enough for exams to be cancelled.'

'Quickly make as many idiotic statements like that as are necessary for a lifetime,' my father said. 'You're getting close to being old enough to know better. What is it? October? By January we're going to start expecting moral responsibility of you both.' Aba shifted sideways as he spoke and looped his legs over the arm of the chair, his every muscle conveying the indolence of a well-satisfied man. He could probably drape himself over a barbed-wire fence and still look entirely at ease.

Ami crooked a finger through the hole near the cuff of Aba's jeans. I had asked her once if she ever minded the absence of romance in her life, and she replied that her definition of romance was absent-minded intimacy, the way someone else's hands stray to your plate of food. I replied: no, that's just friendship; romance is always knowing exactly where that someone else's hands are. She smiled and said, there was a time I thought that way, too. But at the heart of romance is the knowledge that those hands may wander off elsewhere, but somehow through luck or destiny or plain blind groping they'll find their way back to you, and maybe you'll be smart enough then to be grateful for everything that's still possible, in spite of your own weaknesses – and his. I scrunched up my eyes at her and shook my head, confused, and she said, one day I'll sit down and tell you the whole story. But I hadn't been confused by an absence of narrative. I just wanted to know what she meant by 'his weaknesses'.

I looked at my parents for a moment. My father was pushing at Ami's chair with his bare foot, pretending he was about to tip it over, and she gave him a look – one of those officious looks of hers – and he winked at me and subsided. I winked back with my smaller, darker version of his cat eyes ('Tiger eyes', he and I would always insist. 'Panther eyes.'). We were co-conspirators, my father and I, though it was never entirely clear to me what we were conspiring about. Beside me, Karim started humming under his breath, so I turned back to the conversation to figure out what objectionable thing Uncle Ali was saying.

'What am I more afraid of: that one day my son will get caught up in the troubles, or that he'll never get caught up in it at all?

You know, I seriously think sometimes that I should just write to my brother and . . .'

Karim lay back and locked the tips of his fingers in a cradle for his head, but despite his attempt at nonchalance I could see the palms of his hands pressed tight against his ears, and I could hear the humming grow louder.

'Hey!' I prodded him. 'Dekho!'

Karim's mother stepped out through the sliding glass doors of the TV room, and Karim and I exchanged raised-eyebrow looks because her hair was a shade lighter than it had been an hour earlier, bringing it to almost-chestnut. Ever since she'd found those magazines under Karim's bed she had taken to dyeing her hair every time she tried to make an important decision regarding her son, and now she was blinking rapidly and clearing her throat, signalling that she was about to say something that she wasn't sure she should.

'Laila called a little while ago, just back from her honeymoon, says it was the best of the three so far. But she's feeling a little aisay-waisay, you know, trying to settle down to life on Asif's farm. So, and, darlings' – she turned to my parents here – 'I didn't give an answer, because I said we must all consult, though I know what my vote is and I'm prepared to get assertive about it, but what she said was we should all come to the farm to keep her company, which is, of course, ridiculous because ad agencies and linen factories and newspaper magazines don't just run themselves and you've both taken more than enough time off this year what with the trek up North and I have to be here for my cousin's wedding, but she also said, and here's the part that we need to talk about, she said that over the winter holidays we should send the kids to her.'

Karim and I curled our lips at each other. A farm! For God's sake, a farm! For two smogsniffers. Karachiites, damn it, who had things planned in the city for the winter holidays. Going crabbing and hanging out at Baleji Beach and driving to the airport for coffee, the world full of possibilities now that one of our crowd – Zia – drove, and the rest of us had chipped in with birthday and Eid money to buy him a driver's licence that claimed he was born in 1967, before the moon landing, before the Civil War of '71, before my mother and Karim's mother swapped fiancés and wondered why they hadn't earlier.

'I don't think that's a good idea, Maheen.' Ami absent-mindedly pulled petals of Raat-ki-Rani off the string of white buds that held her hair in a bun, rubbed the petals between her palms and spread her hands, releasing a musky scent which would hover around her for hours. My father once swore that Ami could climb into a vat of rotting rubbish and, if there were a single gladiolus amid the mess of eggshells, mould, mango peel, chicken gizzards and last week's dinner, Ami would emerge smelling as though she'd just sprayed on a perfume with a sense of humour.

'Well, I think it's a wonderful idea,' Aunty Maheen said, drawing her tiny frame to its full height. 'And it's my turn to be right.'

'But, sadly, she keeps missing her turn,' Uncle Ali said to my father.

I started to laugh, but stopped when I saw Aba kick Uncle Ali's chair and incline his head towards Karim. Karim was resolutely looking away from his parents. Perhaps he hadn't even heard his father's comment. But then he put his hand up to his cheek and I knew he did it to hide his clenched jaw. I wanted to tell him acerbity was just Uncle Ali's manner; it didn't mean anything. So I pulled a fistful of grass out of the ground and blew the green blades in his direction. He turned towards me when he heard me exhale, and caught a scattering of grass on his palm. I moved closer to him and started to rearrange the grass strands into a grid for noughts and crosses.

'Oho.' Ami clicked her tongue against the roof of her mouth. 'You can afford to think it's wonderful, Maheen, because you have a son, and now you're going to force me to use the dreaded phrase "what will people say?" Suno, yaar, Karim and Raheen are almost . . . no, oh khuda, they are teenagers. To send the two of them alone . . . buss, now don't give me that look!'

I thought she was talking to me, but it was Uncle Ali who answered. 'Don't be absurd, Yasmin. They're virtually cousins. In fact, they *are* cousins. You and I are third cousins, so that means our children are related, too. Tell that to the gossip-mongers.'

'Hey, cuz,' Karim said. He blew on the grass strands and they flew on to my face.

'We're third cousins-in-law,' Ami said. 'No actual blood relation. I thought you'd be on my side, Ali.'

'I have to sit down,' Aunty Maheen said. 'The husband is agreeing with me.'

'I don't think it'll do Karim much good to be here, the way things are now.' Uncle Ali sipped his tea and didn't look at his wife. I looked at Karim again. He was staring up at the sky, slipping away.

'He's having one of his Doomsday visions,' Ami cut in quickly. 'He wants the kids away from Karachi.'

'We can't afford to do that,' Aba said. 'If you send them away because it's too dangerous, how do you justify bringing them back?'

'It's only for the holidays,' Uncle Ali said. 'They run wild during the holidays. It just won't be much fun for them if we say they can't go anywhere, do anything. And it'll be a nice break for them to have all Asif's vast acreage to frolic in.'

'But we want to frolic at the beach,' I objected.

'Much too dangerous driving out all that way,' Ami said. 'Ali, you may have a point. There's a lot of fun to be had at Asif's farm. Well, there was fifteen years ago.'

When Ami said that, it seemed to me Aunty Maheen started to look at my father, then looked away and sighed. 'Maybe things will get better by December.' She rested her head on my mother's shoulder. 'When will this country learn?'

Uncle Ali leaned sideways in his chair and looked at his wife.

9

'This is not history repeating itself, Maheen. A military government such as ours can never rule a country that's united. Not for any length of time. They can't afford to allow any group to get powerful enough to instigate a mass movement. That's what it's about this time.'

'You choose to believe that all the trouble is artificially created, don't you, Ali?' Aunty Maheen sat up and glared at her husband. 'That makes things much easier for all of us in our civilized drawing rooms, doesn't it, because then it's only about the government, or the intelligence agencies, or even the Hidden Palm —'

'Hand,' Uncle Ali said.

'Oh, be quiet.'

'I think he was trying to reassure you, Maheen,' Aba said.

'Ali, she has a point,' Ami said, at the same time.

'I don't need reassuring. Why can't he understand that? Why do the two of you always have to explain my husband and me to each other?'

Karim was in another world, watching the clouds wisp past. Was he more of a dreamer than I was because his parents fought all the time? For a second I was almost jealous of the clouds. Why was he looking to them for escape when I was right here beside him? I twitched his sleeve, and he turned instantly to me, something close to relief on his face when I motioned him to follow me.

We crawled away from our parents and I squeezed myself into the narrow space between the boundary wall and the spreading hibiscus plant. Karim had to suck in his stomach to follow. The sun had trouble reaching this patch in which we crouched, knees drawn up to chin, and the mud was still damp from the mali's round with the garden hose earlier in the evening. I wondered if Karim was also recalling that long-ago monsoon day when we had hidden in the bushes of my grandmother's house; I had pointed out that my mother said that if you stand around in wet clothes you'll catch a chill, so in the interests of good health we had thrown all our clothing in a pile and: 'That's so funny-looking, Karim. Can I hold it? Can you make it move?' 'No, but I can wiggle my ears.'

Karim cleared his throat, and I shifted slightly away from him, watching his bare toes curl around a twig in the mud.

'We're really sick, aren't we?' he said. 'Wanting riots to continue just so school can remain closed.'

I scratched my knee and tried to look repentant, but really I was thinking that the riots had to stop, they absolutely had to, else we'd be sent away over the holidays. None of what was going on in Karachi made much sense to me – not since last year when that girl was killed by a speeding bus and you'd think that was a domestic tragedy, her poor family, and also, I wondered, what must go on in the head of the driver, who certainly didn't intend to kill a girl but now had to live with the ghastly consequences of his recklessness, but instead of being a family tragedy it all ignited a terrible ethnic fight. The girl Muhajir, the bus driver Pathan, and somehow, somehow, that became the issue, though my mother said 'a catalyst, no more' and Uncle Ali said, 'all being orchestrated to create divisions and factions', and my father responded, 'Don't the fools know these things can't be contained', while Aunty Maheen kept talking about 'the perils of amnesia'. Lots of people looked at her strangely when she said that. But Karim and I were thirteen; there was nothing we could do about the nation's problems, so why not stick to issues that perhaps we did have some control over?

I poked Karim in the stomach. 'We need a p.o.a.' I said. 'To stop them from sending us off to milk feudal cows.'

Karim adopted the voice of our maths teacher. 'The probability of success regarding a plan of action employed by two thirteen-year-olds against their parents is what? (a) one in one thousand; (b) two in three thousand; (c) too small to bother calculating.'

'Oh, come on, Karimazov. Forget maths and come up with a plan.' From between the hibiscus branches I saw Uncle Ali flick an insect out of his wife's hair. Aunty Maheen looked startled, and then smiled, and they regarded each other curiously, as though they hadn't seen one another in a very long time. For no reason at all, I felt suddenly gleeful, and I punched Karim's shoulder. 'Come on! Think of Miandad hitting that six off Sharma. If he could do that, you can do this.'

'Miandad wasn't thirteen, and Chetan Sharma wasn't his mother.'

'Final ball of the innings, Karim! Four runs needed to win! And Miandad at bat. Six runs the moment that ball left the willow. Come on, Karim. Think.'

'Why don't *you* think?'

'I'm the brawn.'

Which was true. At the time, I was about four inches taller than Karim and, just weeks earlier, in front of our whole class, I had lifted him off his feet and deposited him in the waste-paper basket during one of his bouts of recalcitrance. Of course, he had rescued himself from embarrassment by refusing to step out until Mr Ansari, our science teacher, walked in, whereupon Karim said, 'You were right, sir, last week when you said I am rubbish. Please pray for me so that I might be spared the destiny of pencil shavings.' Poor Mr Ansari stood speechless while the class dissolved into laughter around him.

But even as I was laughing I knew Karim was not playing for attention, but for justice. Mr Ansari really had called Karim 'rubbish' the week before, after finding Karim in the library looking at 'a dirty picture'. That is to say, Botticelli's *The Birth of Venus.*

So when the school principal walked past our class *en route* to teaching mathematics to Class 9-K, and saw Mr Ansari standing red-faced and ineffectual amid thirty-one laughing students, I knew it wasn't coincidence, but timing. Only afterwards did it occur to me that Karim couldn't have timed the whole thing, because he didn't know I was going to deposit him in the waste-paper basket. Or did he?

Three days later Karim apologized to Mr Ansari. He told me his sense of justice had evolved beyond revenge.

At thirteen we were all given to saying things that sounded as if we were trying too hard to grow up.

But that October day in the garden, when Karim said, 'Nope, sorry, no p.o.a. comes to mind', we were forced to face our status as children and accede to the tyranny of adults. Our only hope was that Ami's sense of propriety – which we regarded as rubbish – would win the day.

'You're going,' Aba said, nearly an hour later.

Karim and I looked round at the four grown-ups, trying to find some sign of relenting, but they had that look of solidarity which can only belong to four people who have switched partners without missing a step or treading on a toe.

'Do we have to call Aunty Laila's new husband "Uncle" even though he is a decadent feudal?' I asked.

My parents blanched.

My sense of justice was not as evolved as Karim's.

Less than two months later Karim and I boarded a train bound for farmland, with the decadent feudal's brother along as an 'in-charge', though I swear I heard my mother refer to him as a chaperon. Of course, when I confronted her about this she said, 'Don't be a silly-billy, I didn't say chaperon. I sneezed.' And for weeks afterwards she made her sneezes sound like 'a-chaperoo', to the point when it became normal and she couldn't sneeze in any other way even if she tried.

The journey to Rahim Yar Khan was an overnight one, and we were booked into two adjoining compartments, though each compartment slept four. Decadent Feudal's brother pretended to insist that Karim sleep within the same four walls as him, but when Karim slipped next door – ostensibly to borrow a book to read – Uncle Chaperoo (as we had already named him) pretended not to notice the length of his absence until the next morning.

What is it about a train charging down the tracks? Buses,

planes, cars, boats – I was blasé about all of them before I even knew what blasé meant. But that evening when the train pulled out of the station, I leaned out of the window like someone in a film and waved madly to anyone who cared to look. And I sang! I wanted a song appropriate to the moment but only 'Feed the World' came to mind, so I sang that and didn't care that the coolies laughed at me and a beggar flung a handful of peanuts in my direction.

Maybe I'd been watching too many movies.

'No,' Karim said, flinging himself on the lower bunk and rolling up the blinds. 'It's not Hollywood association that sets your heart racing. It's the sound of the train. Dhug-*dhug*. Dhug-*dhug*.'

'Ker-*chug*. Ker-*chug*,' I argued.

'Well, something iambic.'

Mr Intellectual.

I lay down on the top bunk. The black vinyl stuck to my skin and I imagined how it would feel if the boy on the lower bunk opposite me were Zia, not Karim. Zia with his fake driver's licence, Marlboro cool, thick lashes and curly hair. Zia who said that the point of smoking was to draw attention to your lips. Which I was quite happy to do, except Karim said he'd tell my parents.

I blew imaginary smoke rings in the air and said, 'Why do you have to be so annoying sometimes?'

Karim continued to look out of the train window. 'Can't help it. It's the company I keep.'

I propped myself up on my elbow, trying not to imagine to whom or what else the vinyl had clung in the past. The bed-sheets that Ami had packed for the journey were in Uncle Chaperoo's compartment, but I could hear him singing wedding songs through the wall that separated his bed from mine, and it seemed impolite to intrude. So instead I turned off the overhead light and watched Karim's reflection in the window while shadows of trees and tracks and rural stations passed over his face and the moon glowed in his hair. All the while, his finger traced station names on to his arm, left to right and right to left, impossible to say if he was writing Urdu or inverted-English, English or reflected Urdu. I thought, no, there's no one I would rather be here with than my best friend, my one-time crib companion, my blood-brother (or spit-brother; sputum being the fluid we chose to mingle in a cup and ingest), no one else who will catch me if I fall out of this top bunk, catch me not because of quick reflexes but because of anticipation.

When I finally slept, I dreamt I was on a train.

• • •

'Sugar cane thataway, kinoos thisaway, cotton everywhichaway.'
The decadent feudal, Uncle Asif, pointed his walking-stick in
the direction of his crops, all of which were hidden from us by
the wall of trees and bushes that separated the creeper-covered
house and its garden from the rest of the farm. 'I suggest a walk.
If you get lost, we'll launch a dramatic rescue operation
complete with local police, hunting dogs and a few snake
charmers for added rural colour.'

'We've got snake charmers in Karachi.' Karim's tone was sulky.
This I had not anticipated, though I was usually so in tune with his
moods that I would often claim emotions and realize, hours later,
that really they belonged to him. But all the way from the railway
station to the house I had been so captivated by Uncle Asif's
charm that it didn't occur to me that Karim's reaction might differ
from mine. How could anyone fail to be won over by raccoon-
eyed, pillow-bellied, pear-headed Uncle Asif?

'Oh, those snake and mongoose fights at the beach! All fakes!
The snakes are defanged, poor buggers, so that the cute little
mongooses – mongeese? mongii? – can win every time.'

'Everyone knows that,' Karim said. I stepped on his foot and
smiled at Uncle Asif, my mouth barely bearing up under the
pressure of being charming for two. My lips were already
beginning to chap in the cold, dry air, and I was afraid if I
smiled with any greater force my lips would split open.

'Is Aunty Laila here?' I said.

Uncle Asif lowered his voice to a whisper. 'The snake charmer
came and spirited her away in the dead of night.' He straightened
up and grinned at me. 'But he'll bring her back by lunch. She left
instructions that you should eat, shower and call your parents
the second you arrive, but since the second has passed and we're

still out on the veranda you're free to stretch your legs and other body parts also. Just be back in an hour, OK?' He waggled his cane at someone I couldn't see, and walked off towards the sugar-cane fields.

'Well, he's an oddity,' Karim said, as we turned away from the house and cut through the long, manicured garden with its beds of chrysanthemums and roses.

'And you, as Sonia might say, are an idioddity. What are you being so moody about?' I had the longer legs, but I was struggling to keep up with him as he strode from the garden on to the surrounding path and from there charged, head down, into the bushes.

There was, just feet away, a two-person-wide opening in the bushes to allow for easy access between house and crops but I was just old enough to worry that I might be turning ladylike, so I ignored the opening and followed Karim. He must have known I was behind him but this didn't stop him from pushing aside a pliant bit of foliage, stepping forward and letting go. The green and prickly thing lurched towards me and I had to put my arms up to fend it off. 'What the hell, Karim?'

'Walking, not talking, is a good idea.' He stepped out from the bushes and didn't even stop to take in the sight of those acres of crops rolling towards a distant shroud of mist, but merely continued walking along the mud-path that bordered the cotton, head still down.

This was all very strange. Surliness was *my* thing in those days. I could summon it up over an egg. All because of the tyranny of bras, I now believe. I had yet to reconcile myself to a lifetime of being so strapped in at the chest. But, my point being, Karim was the peacemaker, the even-tempered one, the joker who dared me to stay sullen in the face of his wit. *Look*, he'd said once, holding up a five-rupee mask of Sly Stallone in Rambo head-band looking peculiarly Pakistani, *it's the face of my wit.* He slipped it over my head. *Stay sullen in it. I dare you! Rambo Rehman. Rambunctious. Ram Boloo Pehlvan.*

In the middle of the path he came to a stop and closed his eyes. There was a faint roar of farm equipment in the distance. 'That's the sound of waves breaking,' Karim said, with an extraordinary leap of imagination. He raised an arm and started jabbing at the air. 'There's Zia's beach hut, and there's Runty's hut. There's the cave where Zia goes to smoke, there's the place where we saw the baby turtle, there's the steep cliff we thought we'd never be able to climb, there's Portal Karim and Portal Raheen, and Sonia Rock is almost lost in the gloom, and there's where my parents built a sand castle together two years ago.' He dropped his arm, his eyes scrunched tight.

Well, I decided, whatever's bothering him, either he'll tell me about it or he'll forget about it. I quickened my step and edged past him. For a few seconds the distance between us widened, and then somehow we were side by side again, our feet stepping in time to 'Left, right, left right, pyjama dheela, topi tight.' We walked past cottonfields, past buffaloes wallowing in pools of water, past goats, past chickens, past grass greener than any green in Karachi, past more cottonfields, always more cotton-fields, and I thought for the first time how strange it was that we never walked in Karachi, not from Karim's house to mine, not from Sind Club to the Gymkhana, not from anywhere to anywhere except at the beach, and even there you could walk only so far before water or rocks or crabs indicated, Enough now. Go back.

On our return to the house, Karim picked a chicken claw off the ground. 'This could be a starfish,' he said. 'It should be. We should be home. Planning a trip to the beach. We should be home. Doesn't it bother you that we're not?'

'Home is an anagram of "oh, me!" Such a dramatic cry. Speaking of which, why are you being the one-minute version of Drama Hour for no reason? This is a holiday; it's cool. We can wander around and explore and stuff. Besides, no one's going to get permission to go to the beach these days, not with all the violence and stuff.'

'Karachi is an anagram of "hack air".' He pulled a penknife out of his pocket and slashed at the wind. Women in bright clothes with makeshift cloth bags full of cotton slung over their shoulders walked past and pointed towards us, giggling. I felt oddly foreign.

'Karimazov?'

'Just mindless violence,' he said, snapping the blade closed. 'Doesn't it bother you that we're here because our parents don't feel we're safe at home?'

I shrugged. Our first time away from our parents, and he had to go and do the whole concerned-citizen-of-a-city-in-turmoil bit on me. Imagine if in *The Lion, the Witch and the Wardrobe* the four children sat around saying, 'We're here because there are air-raids in London. How terrible!' They'd never even make it up the stairs, let alone into the wardrobe, with that kind of attitude. I thought of mentioning this to Karim, but we'd decided that it was time to grow out of the Narnia books the previous year, and he might have laughed at my childishness had I invoked them. So instead I said, 'There's nothing wrong with spending a few days in this place.'

He looked at me as though I were very stupid. 'He thinks changing locations can alter things,' he said.

'He *who*? Your father? Well, so what? It can, can't it? Sometimes. Depending on the things.' I began to feel I had no idea what he was talking about.

'But when we go back nothing will have changed.' He tossed the claw away from him with a jerk, as though just realizing it was part of a dead animal. 'What does he think he's protecting me from?'

'Bullets and bombs. Come on, Cream, it's not so bad here.'

He turned away from me and rubbed his hands across his eyes. Probably tired from the journey, I told myself. But he'd fallen asleep before me on the train and woken up only when I woke him up. I knew I should ask him what really was the matter, not just today, but nearly every day for the last few weeks, or was it months? We were all beginning to surprise ourselves with our reactions to the world in those days, anger flaring up for no reason and solitude becoming a sought-after state in which we'd find ourselves thinking about things that formerly would have made us clump together in groups to giggle. So it would have been easy to dismiss Karim's moments of rage towards his father as nothing more than a manifestation of adolescence, and it seemed almost everyone did dismiss it as exactly that – Sonia and Zia did, and so did my parents, and even Uncle Ali was wont to respond to Karim's scowls with some exasperated comment about 'boys at that age', while Aunty Maheen sighed. But there was a gravity to Karim's anger, a sense of cause and effect, some terrible notion of consequence. Did no one but me see that? While the rest of us were still just changing, Karim was maturing, looking out at imaginable futures and facing up to the possibility that he would inhabit a less pleasant one. As he looked, face turned away from the rest of us, he held out a hand to me, and I don't know if I resisted because I lacked the courage to stare down at the precipice on which his life verged or because I was straining every sinew to pull him alongside me on a midnight shore adorned with phosphorescent starfish, the tide lifetimes away from submerging all that beauty.

'When we drove into the farm I thought I was seeing snow for the first time,' I said, leaning forward and speaking softly into his ear as he looked out at a distant point in the cottonfields. 'But really it's tired clouds, coming to rest on the ground.'

He turned away from whatever he was staring at to smile at me, and encircled my wrist with his thumb and forefinger. He was much smaller than I was in those days, but my wrist fitted perfectly into the 'O' created by his clasp. Then he cut across to the cottonfield, his feet squelching in the mud. He pulled a cotton boll out of its pod and walked back to where I was standing. 'Here. I found you an angel in disguise.' Sitting on the top of the cotton was a ladybird. Karim touched the cotton to my hand and the ladybird crawled off on to my palm. I wanted to hug Karim then, but was surprised to find myself imagining my breasts pressing against his chest, and so instead I just looked down at the ladybird and wondered out loud, if I touch its back will my finger come away red? The back became wings and the ladybird swooped off my hand.

There was more swooping a few hours later when Aunty Laila found Karim and me sitting at one end of the long dining table pulling faces at our reflections in the polished wood surface. 'Darlings!' she cried, descending upon us with arms outstretched, and coming to rest in a crouch between our intricately carved chairs. Her arms locked themselves around our necks and she pulled us close in a sudden gesture so that our faces almost bounced off her cheekbones. She pursed her Lancôme-enhanced lips into kisses that were presumably intended to ricochet off the opposite wall and on to our cheeks. Ami once said that no one, least of all Aunty Laila, knew where the boundaries existed between Aunty Laila's parody of Karachi high society and her genuine embodiment of the characteristics of a Karachi Knee.

Have I not mentioned the Knees yet? The Ghutnas, rather, in local lingo. This narrative demands tangents, but, for the moment, remain befuddled. Aunty Laila is on centre stage, and deserves her spotlight.

'Send word back to Karachi that I am bilkul a farmer's wife,' she said, twirling into her chair. 'Who needs parties? I'm happy to pick cotton and feed goats.'

'You're out every day with your scythe, cutting down the sugar cane,' Karim said, his mood sufficiently improved to allow him to smile at Uncle Asif who had just entered the room.

'Standing knee-deep in keechar to birth a buffalo,' Aunty Laila whooped.

'Every morning, you're up with the cock,' I said.

And regretted it immediately.

Karim covered his face with a napkin. Aunty Laila – beautiful, elegant, coiffed and manicured Aunty Laila – snorted with laughter. I glanced over at Uncle Asif, but he had the decency to pretend to be too engrossed in piling his plate high with food to realize what was going on. Or so I thought.

'A history lesson,' he said, a few seconds later, cutting through Aunty Laila's chatter and turning his plate towards Karim and me. 'In 1947, East and West Pakistan were created, providing a pair of testicles for the phallus of India.' He had moulded his rice into the subcontinent.

'Honestly, Asif,' Aunty Laila said. 'No genitalia in the dining room.'

I blushed. Karim crossed his legs.

'We're thirteen,' I said. 'Maybe you should wait another five years or so before having this kind of conversation in front of us.'

Aunty Laila laughed. 'Your mothers and I became friends at the age of ten when I told them about the facts of life.'

Karim retreated behind his napkin again.

'You needn't act so coy.' Aunty Laila pulled the napkin away from his face and slapped his shoulder with it. 'Your mother told me about the magazines under your bed.'

'They weren't mine! Zia brought them over. I can't believe she told . . . I can't believe you're bringing this up.'

'So to speak,' Aunty Laila said.

'Look.' Uncle Asif poured daal on to his plate. The liquid suffused and flowed off the rice. 'The Indus flooding the land and spilling into the Arabian Sea. See, here, the Oyster Rocks and there Manora lighthouse disguised as a carrot. Look at those tributaries engorged. Jhelum, Sutlej, Ravi, Chenab, and whatever that fifth one is. Guddu Barrage overflowing. See, now, I'm crumbling the Himalayas beneath my fork. Nanga Parbat goes down shrouded in lentils.'

I know what I was thinking. I was thinking, is this how people are forced to entertain themselves in Ruralistan? But Karim, when I looked at him for the raised eyebrow that would confirm our synchrony of thought, was staring down at his plate, shifting his rice around with his fork as though he, too, were trying to construct a rice-mould but the picture in his mind kept changing shape, stymieing all efforts to reconstruct it in rice.

Although, to be honest, I just made that up.

But I'm not making anything up when I recall Uncle Asif's friend, whatshisname, the diplomat who stopped at the farm after lunch to drop off a dead quail and, before departing, shook Karim's hand and said, 'So you're Ali's son? I suppose on meeting a young man your age it's customary to ask what you're going to be when you grow up, but no need for that with you, is there? I expect Ali's already preparing you to take over the linen industry. For three generations your family has kept my family's dining tables looking so elegant.'

'No,' Karim said. 'I'm not joining the family business.'

'Oh! What, then?'

Karim looked around, saw a dribble of daal on Uncle Asif's kameez. 'I'm going to be a map-maker.'

• • •

We were without obsessions at the time, a rare occurrence in our lives. A few months earlier it had been birds. We became buyers of bird books, spouters of bird facts ('the hummingbird eats fifty or sixty meals a day', 'the Gila woodpecker lives in the desert and never sees wood, only cactus'), imitators of bird walks (moving through the world on our toes, heels in the air), though the fascination with feathered creatures was necessarily short-lived since all we could see in our gardens were crows and sparrows, and what's the point of being bird-obsessed if you can't bird-watch. Prior to that, we'd filled our lives with disguises. We would wander around with cotton balls lodged in our cheeks, sling towels across our shoulders under loose shirts, stick black paper over our teeth, and we even collected hair clippings from Aunty Runty's beauty parlour and attempted to glue straight, long tresses to the ends of our own hair.

How each of our obsessions started and how they ended, and who instigated their beginnings and ends, we never remembered or cared about. But I cared deeply when Karim started pulling atlases out of Uncle Asif's bookshelf, the day after we arrived in Rahim Yar Khan, and traced distances and routes with his index finger, without any regard or concern for my lack of interest in the relationship of one place to another.

'You can't be a map-maker anyway,' I said to him one morning when I found him in Uncle Asif's desk poring over a large map of Pakistan that had creases where it had been folded and refolded into a neat rectangle. 'Because all the maps have been made already, right? What are you going to do? Discover a new continent and map it?' I hoisted myself on to the desk and sat down in the 'disputed territory' of Jammu and Kashmir. 'Better way to occupy yourself is to come outside and lose a game of badminton to me. Or we could walk to the dunes. Or leap around the cotton mountain.'

He took the glass of orange juice I held out to him, and gulped it down. Bits of pulp clung to the inside of the glass and to his upper lip. 'If you had to give someone directions to Zia's beach hut, what would you say?'

I looked out of the window. It was a beautiful day; winter sun was beckoning us outside. 'I don't know. I'd say, go towards the beach, and when you come to the turtle sign take a right and—'

'No, idiot.' He wiped his mouth on his sleeve. 'How would you give directions to someone who didn't know the way to the beach? Maybe someone who'd left Karachi years ago and couldn't remember the way there any more.'

'Oh.' I considered this. 'Well, I'd just say, "Don't worry, we'll meet somewhere and go to the beach together." '

Karim glared at me. 'That's not helpful.'

I glared back at him. 'There's something you need to know.'

'What?'

I lifted him up by the collar and slammed him against the chair back. 'You hate geography!'

'Yeah, so? Every map-maker has his quirks.'

I couldn't help laughing. 'Fine. By the way, map-makers are called cartographers.'

'Cartographers.' He wrote down the word, forming a circle with the letters, and we both bent our heads over the paper.

'Go rap her carts,' I suggested, rearranging letters in my head. 'Strap her cargo? Crop rag hearts?'

Karim grinned. 'Chop Ra's garter.'

'Listen,' I said. 'We're adolescents. We're supposed to be rebellious for the sake of it. So if you just want something that has nothing to do with making linen, that's really fine and in keeping with this stage of life and all that. But there are more interesting options than latitudes and longitudes. How about flea-trainer? Or bear-wrestler?'

'Bare wrestler? *Please*! Let's promise never to imagine each other naked. Oh, sorry, no. Too late for that.'

'What?'

'I've seen your baby pictures.'

I crossed my arms and gave him one of my that-is-so-pre-teen looks, attempting an air of superiority, but he waggled his ears at me in return and I couldn't help laughing.

'OK, but truthfully, Karim, what's so interesting about this stuff?' I picked up the atlas and placed it on his head; you'd never know how flat the top of his head was until you tried balancing something on it. 'I don't understand the fascination.'

He tilted his head forward and let the book fall on to the desk. 'It's like a giant jigsaw, the world. All these places connecting.' He opened the atlas to one of the first pages, where all the continents were spread out. 'See: Pakistan connects to Iran which connects to Turkey which connects to Bulgaria which connects to Yugoslavia which connects to Austria which connects to France. But then there's the sea. And after that, England. It doesn't quite connect, England.' He stared gloomily at the page.

'But we like seas,' I reminded him, before either of us could start thinking about the increasing frequency of Uncle Ali's threats to move to London. I traced a sea route with my finger from the coast of Karachi to Plymouth. 'If it were possible to walk on the sea bed, we could step into the water at Baleji Beach and just start walking. And everyone would see us go, and we'd wave back at them and we'd carry on waving at them and walking, even when we couldn't see them any more and just *knew* they were there, and we'd walk and walk and walk, and never know when we crossed out of Karachi's water and were surrounded by some other country's seaweed. And then, look, all of a sudden, there's England. And maybe the sea's colder now, but it's still the sea, you know.'

But he wouldn't be drawn into that vision of things. 'Even seas have boundaries,' he said. 'You'd be arrested by the coastguard.'

You?

'Can't turn everything into a game,' he muttered.

I swung my legs off the table, and shrugged. I wasn't going to let him see how much that stung. 'You started with the jigsaw puzzle.'

He pushed back his chair and stood up. 'True. Guilty. But may I say something in my defence?'

'Nope. You are dismissed as incontinent, irreverent and immaterialistic.' I kicked his shin. 'Come on. Let's go and find a nonexistent ghost.'

He saluted me, and all was forgiven. I never knew how to stay angry with Karim. We climbed out of the window and wandered to the back lawn, past the slightly sagging badminton net and towards the ancient tree that dominated the garden, thin, ropy strands falling like veils from its outstretched limbs. A ghost lived in this tree. Ghosts appeared to live in almost all the old trees near and around the farm, but they smelled citydwellers' disbelief emanating from both of us, and hid in protest. The least amount of courtesy you should extend to someone is acknowledgement that they exist, and Karim and I were horribly discourteous towards ghosts. The one in this tree was a nomad, but she'd stayed put here all her afterlife. She had belonged to one of the nomadic tribes that passed through the sand dunes bordering the farm – strange to look around Uncle Asif's land and consider that such a verdant place was reclaimed desert. The people of the town didn't mix with the nomads and whenever two peoples don't mix with each other it means Romeo and Juliet is about to happen. And so it was with the nomad girl and a boy from the village; they were in love, they swore they would die before they allowed themselves to be parted, and before the drama could develop further she died of pneumonia, which wasn't terribly romantic, and he married someone else, which was worse, and she had been sulking in the tree in the back yard ever since. Or, at least, that was Uncle Asif's version of things.

'How long do they remain nomads?' Karim climbed from one branch to another until he was high enough to see the silver-grey dunes, less than a ten-minute walk from where we were, on which the 'settled nomads' had built mud huts. 'They've been in one place for over twenty years now,' Uncle Asif said. 'When do they stop being called nomads?'

I put my arms around the tree trunk, and Karim clambered on to the branch growing out of the other side of the trunk and did the same. Tree-huggers before we'd ever heard the term. The trunk so wide (or we so small?) that even the tips of our fingers didn't reach. The sun's rays were piercing through narrow gaps between the leaves, and it almost seemed possible to grasp a shaft of sunlight and wield it like a lightsabre. 'Luke, I am your father,' I rasped in my best Darth Vader impersonation. Karim jumped up from a branch and, with his feet dangling, hooked his arm over the branch above. I looked down. We weren't very high up, but high enough that you wouldn't want to slip. I looked down again. The branch I was standing on seemed narrower than I had thought. Narrower, and flimsier.

'Karim, I'm stuck.'

Faster than I had thought possible, he was on the tree limb right below me, ready to climb up.

'No,' I yelled, when he put his hand up to take hold of the branch. 'No, don't. It can't take your weight.' I pressed my body against the tree trunk, willing it to absorb my body mass so that the branch would not give way beneath me.

'Don't panic,' he said. 'Just let go of the trunk and step back.'

I looked down again. The grass seemed to rise up towards me. Or was I falling and unaware of it? I gripped the trunk tighter. I knew I mustn't faint whatever happened, mustn't faint.

'Don't look down. Look up. *Look up!*'

I raised my head and looked out towards the dunes. One of the nomad women was sweeping the square of earthen ground outside the cluster of huts. Another was stirring a pot on the outdoor stove. Purple stain on the ground near the fire. Same colour as the woman's clothes. I wanted to point out to Karim that the dye had spread in a boot-shaped pattern. Like Italy.

How do you build a hut on a dune? Surely the sands must shift continually. My shirt was drenched in sweat. Would it be enough to suction me to the tree trunk when the branch broke?

'Ra, let go of the trunk and step back.'

'I'll fall.'

'You won't fall.'

'I'll fall. I'll fall and I'll die.' As I said it, I could see it happening. The foot stepping on air, pulling the rest of my body with it, tree limbs breaking as I plummeted down.

'No,' he said, his voice assured. 'You'd never do that to me.'

I let go of the tree trunk, turned, and sat down. The branch was wide and strong. I placed my palm on the branch and pushed down with the full weight of my body. It didn't even quiver. I could jump off the branch and I'd land in mud, entirely unharmed.

Karim touched my knee and then was gone, clambering back to the other side of the tree. I stretched out and lay down. Would it be so terrible to live here? In Karachi we never had this freedom, this space to wander in. Too dangerous to walk around, and too humid to want to walk most of the time. Besides, walk to where? Life compressed into houses and cars and private clubs and school and gardens too small to properly hide in. Zia was in Karachi, I had to remind myself. That was hardly inconsequential. I could hear Karim moving from branch to branch. We had never once talked about my feelings for Zia, and I had only realized that Karim knew how I felt when he backed up my insistence, in front of our whole gang, that there was no picture of Zia in my bedside-table drawer, despite Sonia's claims to the contrary. He backed me up on that, even though I had started keeping the drawer under lock and key and would not tell him why. He backed me up even though Sonia was the new girl in school and she was beautiful. That had been in August, at the beginning of the term, and now Sonia and I were fast friends ('I'm not fast; I'm fully modest,' Sonia had said, the day I let her look in my bedside drawer again. 'But you're a real Carl Lewis. Except, where Zia is concerned you're Legcramps-e-Azam'). But Karim still hadn't said another word to me about the picture. Or was it I who hadn't said another word to him? My eyebrows drew closer to each other. How would I feel if he had pictures of a girl in his drawer and never talked to me about it? Not good. In fact, I'd probably walk up to him and kick him hard for such an attempt at secrecy. But Karim didn't kick. Perhaps it was because he knew that he had only to wait and I would tell him everything.

'Hey, come and look at this,' he called out.

Without hesitation or even the slightest lurch of fear, I walked round to the branch just below the one on which Karim was standing, and stood up on my toes, resting my chin just inches from his feet. On the tree trunk someone had written 'Z+M', the letters biting deep into the bark.

Zia, I stupidly thought. Who's this 'M'?

Karim sat down, straddling the branch, and ran his thumb through the thick grooves of the letter 'M'. 'Mama told me Asif was a regular member of their gang back then. They all spent one New Year here. Must have been 1970, though she didn't tell me that part of it.'

Oh.

I looped my arm around the branch above me, and looked at my father's flamboyant 'Z'. He must have sat on the branch that Karim was now astride, leaning towards the tree trunk, hammer and chisel in hand. How long had it taken to gouge so deep a mark of devotion to Karim's mother? I pulled myself up so that I was sitting just behind Karim, and reached out to cover the 'Z' with my palm, pressing harder until I could feel the letter leave its mark on my skin. Karim did the same with the 'M', our hands separated by a +.

Oh.

I couldn't even begin to imagine them together – my father and Aunty Maheen. The only pairing that made less sense was my mother and Uncle Ali. Although perhaps it was just that I couldn't imagine my parents and Karim's parents as anything other than my parents and Karim's parents.

I pulled my hand away, and then pulled Karim's hand away. We had first heard about the fiancée swap when we were ten and our mothers told us they hadn't mentioned it before because it might have seemed too weird. They knew, they said, how sensitive kids can be about their parents. On the contrary Karim and I saw the news as thrilling proof that our friendship was destined, and spent many hours, over the years, drawing up lists of the foibles and the talents the other possessed, under the heading 'Those Genes Could Have Been Mine' – though for a long time we used 'Things' instead of 'Genes'. Until that moment on the tree, it had never bothered me at all to consider the way things might have been, the way things once were. But that he should have chiselled the letters so deeply, my father who hated exertion, that he should have done that for someone, and for that someone to not be my mother, was nothing less than an abomination.

I scrambled off the branch. 'Come on,' I said to Karim. 'Let's go somewhere else.' But he stayed where he was, running his fingers over the letters, again and again. 'Stop it,' I called out from the base of the tree. 'Stop doing that.' But he ignored me, and I could not stay to argue for the queasiness in my stomach.

• • •

Uncle Chaperoo was supposed to accompany us back to Karachi when our three weeks in RYK were up, but he decided to elope instead. At least, that's what he wanted everyone to believe, but Uncle Asif saw things a little differently. I was having tea with Uncle Asif in front of the fireplace when Uncle Chaperoo called with the news, and Uncle Asif put the call on his newly acquired speaker-phone.

'Bhai, Umber and I have eloped,' Uncle Chaperoo said.

'What? You've married her! Wonderful. And about time.'

'We've eloped!'

'Let me speak to her. I want to welcome her to the family.'

'We love each other. We don't care what anyone else says.'

'Excellent. Where's the honeymoon? When you return we'll throw a huge reception for the two of you.'

'We're prepared to live on love!'

'I'll get Laila on the line right away. She'll be so happy.'

'*We've eloped, damn you!*'

Uncle Asif hung up, and shook his head. 'Such assumptions, such assumptions! From my own brother.' He threw another log on to the fire and watched the sparks fly. 'At a time like this, Raheen, should I care about anything other than whether he's happy? Have I not always said that I wish to be the most unfeudal feudal in this country?'

'You don't seem very decadent to me,' I said by way of comfort. 'Though it's true you live in luxury and don't seem to spend a lot of time doing anything that looks even a little bit like work.' I tilted my head and looked at him sideways. 'I could see you lying on a couch in a toga, eating peeled grapes. Uncle Ali said that's the real definition of decadence.'

He threw back his head and laughed. 'You are your father's

daughter, aren't you? It requires a certain genetic disposition to say something like that at the age of thirteen and yet manage to be utterly charming.'

'I'm not the charming one,' I said, putting my feet up on the coffee table. 'That's Karim. He's got natural charm. I mean, you see him across a room and you know you'll like him.'

'And you?' Uncle Ali said. 'What do people think when they see you across a room?'

'I don't know,' I said slowly. 'But usually if I'm in a room I'm with Karim, Sonia, Zia. One or all of them. And then you'd notice Sonia, because she's gorgeous, and you'd notice Zia because he's completely cool, and you'd notice Karim because you can't help but notice Karim even though, or because, he never demands that you notice him. Me, I guess you'd notice that all three of them choose to be my friends. And that must say something.' It was true; I knew quite well that there was nothing remarkable about me. This is not to say I suffered insecurities because of everything I lacked. There wasn't a great deal that I did lack. I was intelligent enough, attractive enough, witty enough, cool enough. On sports day I won silver medals and even, occasionally, a gold; in school concerts I got speaking parts rather than being relegated to 'a rock' or 'crowd scene'; when teams were picked for anything, anything at all, I was never, ever, the last to be chosen; I knew all the words to all the songs on Wham!'s 'Make It Big' album, and had been the one to inform a group of sixteen-year-olds that the line from 'Wake Me Up' was not 'You make the sun shine brighter than the darkest day', which made no sense at all, but rather 'You make the sun shine brighter than Doris Day'. I could do a dead-on imitation of Qabacha from 'Tanhaiyan'; Qadir, not Imran, was my favourite bowler. And perhaps all this might have meant that I was remarkable for being a perfect blend of admirable traits, except for the fact that there were other things blended in, colder things. I didn't know how to embrace the world, the way Karim did; I didn't know how to make strangers feel at home, the way Sonia

33

did; and I didn't know how to embody a loyalty so fierce it meant putting myself at risk for others in any fight, even the fights that seemed absurd, the way Zia did.

'Hmmm . . .' Uncle Asif stared down at his toes and made them wiggle. 'But I notice you, even when there's no one else around.'

I smiled at him. 'That's because I really like you, and you know it.'

'Ah, there's that charm again.' He picked up a poker and smiled at me. 'I liked all my parents' friends when I was your age. Then I grew up and began to understand what kind of people they were and, you know, a lot of them just weren't very nice. Maybe one day, when you're old enough to see beneath the smiling veneer, you won't like me any more.'

Unsure if he was serious or not, I curled on to the sofa and looked at the framed black-and-white photograph on the coffee table of Uncle Asif baring his teeth in half-grimace, half-leer, at a camel which had pushed its snout to within inches of his face. 'Doubt it,' I said.

He waved the poker in my direction. 'An aphorism from the middle-aged to the extremely youthful: you can only know how you feel in the here and now, not how you'll feel years, months or even days down the line.'

The tree carving hadn't been far from my mind since I'd seen it; the memory of it gave rise to an uneasiness in my stomach that ruined my appetite all day. 'Why didn't my father marry Karim's mother?'

Uncle Asif turned away and poked the fire with vigour. Sparks flew up and leapt over the grate. 'That's not my story to tell.'

'In other words,' I said to Karim later that night, as I sat in the bay seat of his bedroom window, 'there is a story there.'

He nodded and brought two bowls over to the window from his bedside, liquid sloshing against the sides as he walked. Green dye in one and purple in the other. 'I got them from one of the nomad boys. In exchange for my marbles. Because green and purple seemed like map colours. But now I don't know what to do with them.'

I looked down at the ceramic bowls uneasily. I had the strong suspicion they were expensive items of art; I had a stronger suspicion the dye might not wash off very easily. 'Good you got rid of the marbles. They were beginning to give me the creeps.' They really were. They looked too much like the eyes of the nomads' mad goat with its twisted horns that resembled dried leaves curling in on themselves.

Karim tore a piece of paper out of a legal pad and sat down across from me. Jackals howled in the distance. I dipped my hand in green dye and pressed it against the paper. Karim dipped his hand in purple dye and pressed it over my palm print. Karim's hand was smaller but his fingers were broader. Some of the lines of our hands ran together for a while in purple–green, then veered off in different directions. I half-expected the letters 'Z' and 'M' to appear on the paper.

'How do you think it happened?' he asked.

'I think the mad goat's father came untethered and chased your mother around the dunes, and your father came by and saved her. And over on the other side of the farm a crazy bull was chasing my father and my mother waved her red sari at it to make it change course and, *olé*! Love swap!'

Karim laughed shortly. 'My father's not the kind of guy to walk out into the dunes. Sand in his shoes. He wouldn't like that.' He pushed his hair off his face, leaving a purple smudge, like a bruise, on his forehead.

'OK, so what's your version?' I wiped my hands on his jeans.

'I don't know. I can't think of any reason why someone would marry my father rather than yours.' He furrowed his brow and I ran my thumb over the creases that appeared between his eyes, leaving green streaks that dribbled down his nose. 'Maybe your mother saw she was getting the bad end of the bargain and whisked your father away.'

'Don't be silly.' I walked over to the bathroom to wash my

hands. 'My mother would never do a thing like that to your mother. And if she had, they wouldn't still be friends, would they?'

We dropped the topic then, but I couldn't get his words out of my mind and later that night I crept down to the drawing room in search of old photographs. Or, rather, one old photograph, which was framed and prominently displayed in both Karim's house and mine. A few days earlier I had come upon a copy of it, along with stacks of other pictures, in the rosewood cabinet in Laila and Asif's drawing room.

I switched on the table lamp, trying to suppress the feeling that I was doing something sneaky, and rummaged through the images of my parents and their friends, partying and holidaying and hamming it up in black-and-white. Picture of my father planting a kiss on Uncle Ali's cheek, as Uncle Ali – looking unexpectedly like Karim, with his wide grin – held up an aubergine to the camera. Age had made them more restrained. Towards the world, or towards each other? I found the photograph I was looking for, and sat on the sofa with it in my hand, first tilting the lampshade slightly so that light fell directly on the picture.

Taken at Karim's parents' wedding, it showed my parents flanking the bride and groom, all four of them laughing. There was no such photograph at my parents' wedding, which had taken place just months earlier, because Aunty Maheen hadn't been present. She'd been in the newly created nation of Bangladesh, spending her last weeks as a single woman with her family there. At least, that was the version I'd always been told.

As I looked at the photograph, I began to distrust their laughter. Were they laughing together, as a foursome? Or had the photographer said something amusing to make each of them, as individuals, laugh? They were not looking at one another, not at all; Aunty Maheen was not resting a hand on my mother's wrist to say 'I get it, I get it. Too funny, darling', and Aba was not half-turning towards Uncle Ali to see his own laughter mirrored in his best friend's face, and though Aunty Maheen was leaning towards Uncle Ali in what I had always taken as a sign of intimacy, perhaps she was really just leaning away from my mother.

The next morning, I went looking for Karim to show him the photograph. I found him in Uncle Asif's study, looking at the atlas again.

'Karimazov, where've you been?' I shut the door behind me with what I hoped was a conspiratorial air. 'We have to talk. I've been wondering about your parents' marriage.'

He looked up at me, blew out air from his cheeks, nodded, gulped, nodded again. 'OK,' he said, putting the atlas down and clutching the edge of the desk with both hands. 'OK.'

'Their wedding, I mean.' I held up the photograph, then put it down again. I felt I should say something other than what I had planned to say. He was looking at me as though there was something he wanted me to say. 'The photograph . . .' I put it down in front of him. 'I just wondered, you know, why it's the only one of the four of them together at the wedding.'

He didn't even look at it. He picked up the atlas, cutting off our view of each other, and then swivelled round in the leather chair so that I couldn't see him at all. 'Bet you don't know how many countries border the Soviet Union.'

'Bet you think everyone's going to be impressed that you do know,' I said and walked out. Knowledge had never been something we used against each other. The previous year when Ami's cousin visited from France and taught me foreign words, five new ones every day, I always called Karim at the end of the day to share the words with him. You could put Karim's brain in my skull, I believed at the time, and I wouldn't even notice the swap. Why ruin that over the number of countries bordering the Soviet Union? I suspected the real reason for his new interest in maps was the need to feel superior to me. But I couldn't say that. Couldn't say, 'You just like knowing things that I don't know,' because then he'd look even more superior and say, 'Who said

37

everything I do has to be about you?' And, I had to admit it, he'd have a point.

I didn't mention the photograph again that day or the next day, or the day after, but I kept it in my room and whenever I found I'd lost Karim to those infernal maps I'd climb up the nomad girl's tree, lean against my father's carving and examine the photograph, searching for clues to the past. That was how Uncle Ali found me, when he came to Rahim Yar Khan to take us home at the end of the winter holidays.

'What are you doing up there?' he shouted up to me. I stuffed the photograph into the pocket of my jacket, and climbed down.

'Nothing.' I took him by the hand to lead him away from the tree, but after a few paces he stopped and looked back, up to the branch where I had been sitting, his eyes sliding over to the tree trunk. Surely from this angle and this distance he couldn't see what was written there? He sighed, and then looked at me curiously.

'What? Why are you looking at me like that?' he said.

'Do you mind getting sand in your shoes?'

'Yes.'

We stood and looked at each other for a few seconds, his eyes grave. Uncle Ali always took me seriously, and I loved him for that.

'I was looking at old pictures,' I said. 'Karim has your smile. But you don't have it any more.'

He looked taken aback for a moment, then laughed without much humour. 'You're growing into a perceptive young woman, aren't you?' He put an arm round me. 'Karim has it mainly when you're around. It's a moonsmile. No light of its own unless there's a sun for it to reflect off.'

'I'm no sun. The sun is stationary, and I can't stay still for even five minutes. Karim can be the sun. I'll do the orbiting.' I pirouetted around Uncle Ali. He took my hand in his and twirled me as though we were dancing.

'You're a cool guy, Uncle Ali.'

'Thank you, sweetheart. If only my son were as easy to convince as you are.'

When I repeated that comment to Karim, as we were preparing to go to the train station later that day, he snorted in disdain. Of late, that had become his standard reaction to anything to do with his father, regardless of the context.

'Yeah, he's so cool he's frozen,' Karim said. He lifted his suitcase off his bed and carried it to the landing outside, where my suitcase was already waiting for one of Uncle Asif's innumerable servants to carry it to the car.

Uncle Asif, Aunty Laila and Uncle Ali were all in the drawing room on the ground floor, and as we made our way down the stairs we heard their voices through the wide-open door.

'But really, Ali, you must all come and stay,' Aunty Laila was saying. 'The kids are divine, but we'd quite like to have divinity's parents' with us, too. Asif, tell him.'

Karim and I stopped, hoping to overhear more about our sterling qualities as house guests.

Uncle Asif grunted. 'Of course you must all come. And tell Zafar that this time I won't take him for a walk and get him lost in the kinoo orchards if he starts his ranting about the need for land reforms.'

'God, I had forgotten about that. Asif, really, how could you have?'

Uncle Asif laughed. 'Laila, it was sixteen years ago, and before your civilizing influence. Besides, Zaf wasn't acting the polite guest himself. Still, I understand why he said those things. I mean, Muhajirs will never understand the way we feel about land. They all left their homes at Partition. No understanding of ties to a place.'

I put out my hand and gripped Karim's shoulder, stopping him as he was starting to walk, whether towards the drawing room or away from it I couldn't tell. When my father spoke of the need for land reforms to break the power of the feudals, he lost his customary languid posture and his soft voice took on an edge of urgency. Even at thirteen, I could link his fervour to a myriad reasons. The socialist professor who set his mind ablaze when he was at university; the capitalist profession he had entered when he started his own advertising agency; the novels he read (my mother always cringed when he referred to Hugo as 'Old Vic'); the stories he'd heard, firsthand, from employees and prospective employees who left their villages to come to the city, and were willing to do anything at all to earn a living in Karachi, anything but go back to 'that life'; his analysis of economic reports; his mistrust of humanity's capacity to be uncorrupted by power. Some reasons were contradictory and some were contradicted by other parts of his life, but all of them, *all*, were part of the mesh that made up his character. Yet Uncle Asif had summarily dismissed all that with one word: muhajir. Immigrant.

I heard a plate – or was it a saucer? – placed firmly on a table, and Uncle Ali said, 'I share Zafar's views on land reform. And I'm not a Muhajir.'

'Yes, but you've lived all those years in Karachi,' Uncle Asif said, never losing his jolly tone. 'It's made you so urban. Don't get uptight, Ali. I love Zafar, you know I do. And when the revolution comes, I'll take refuge in his house and he'll welcome me with open arms and guard me with his life. You, on the other hand, I'm not entirely sure about. Oh, for heaven's sake, yaar, smile.'

'What is it with people today and my smile?' Uncle Ali asked. 'Listen, Asif. Let's put aside the old feudal argument. Tell me what's going on in Karachi. What do your contacts in the government say?'

'That it's all going to hell. More tea?'

'Asif, this isn't a joke,' Aunty Laila said, her voice exploding as though it had been held captive somewhere for a long time. 'Karachi's my home, you know. Why did those bloody Muhajirs have to go and form a political group? Once they're united they'll do God knows what. Demanding this, demanding that. Thinking just because they're a majority in Karachi they can trample over everyone else. Like they did in '47. Coming across the border thinking we should be grateful for their presence.' I could see her shadow move across the wall as she paced across the room. 'Do you hear the way people like Zafar and Yasmin talk about "their Karachi"? My family lived there for generations. Who the hell are these Muhajirs to pretend it's their city!'

'Laila, Laila,' Uncle Ali said. 'Do you hear yourself?'

I must have said or done something then, or maybe it was just that I was so motionless that made Karim touch my shoulder. 'You OK?'

I nodded and pushed past him. 'Just going to the loo.'

In the downstairs bathroom, I locked the door behind me and climbed out of the window and into the garden. Ducking low beneath window frames, I stole away from the house and sat in the dark on the swing, my hands clenched around the linked chain that moored it to the red metal frame.

What kind of immigrant is born in a city and spends his whole life there, and gets married there, and raises his daughter there? And I, an immigrant's daughter, was an immigrant too. I had spent three weeks living in Uncle Asif and Aunty Laila's house; I'd told her about Zia; I'd sat on his shoulder to untangle a kite from the limb of a tree. If I went back to the house and told them I agreed with my father about land reforms, if I told them Karachi was my home just as much as it was anyone else's, would they look at me and think: another Muhajir.

But worse than what Uncle Asif and Aunty Laila had said, far worse than that, was Uncle Ali's remark: 'I'm not a Muhajir.' I had never stopped to think what Uncle Ali was or wasn't. Aunty Maheen was Bengali, I knew, because every so often aunts or cousins would arrive from Bangladesh to visit, bearing gift-wrapped saris and a reminder that Aunty Maheen grew up in another language. After the relatives left, stray words of Bengali would stay clustered around her tongue, falling off in ones and twos, un-understood and untranslated. And there was another reason, also, why I knew and had known for a long time where Aunty Maheen's family was from. I kicked at the ground and the swing jerked forward and back . . .

Forward and back, Zia marched up and down from the tree to the wall of the school building. I didn't like Zia, even though he and Karim sat together in class and were friends, but I wanted to know why he was moving his arms in that strange way and clenching his little fists – he was so small he could be mistaken for a Prep-E student; not like me, the tallest girl in kindergarten, and should have been the tallest person but wasn't because of that Ghous boy who had failed Class II and so had to repeat the year.

'It's marching,' he said, when I told Karim to ask him what he was doing. 'Because there's going to be a war and then I'll become a soldier.'

'Why will you become a soldier?' I pushed Karim aside.

'To fight for my country. Then if I die, I'll go to heaven. You can't, because you're a girl.'

'You're too little to fight. And I don't want to be a soldier, so . . . so . . . Karim do you want to be a soldier?'

'What war?' Karim said.

'There'll be war with India,' Zia said. 'There always is. There was one only two years before we were born.'

'That was because of Bangladesh,' Karim said. 'That's where my mother's from. She's Bengali. That means I'm half-Bengali.'

Zia pushed Karim. He fell over without a sound. No one knew it had happened, except the three of us.

'Donkey!' I yelled and kicked Zia.

'Tell him not to lie,' Zia yelled back. 'He's not Bengali, he's not. He's my friend. Why is he lying?' and he raised his foot to kick Karim, raised it back and forward . . .

Back and forward, higher and higher, the swing hurtled me through the air and I thought, I can do this with no hands, and then I was sprawled in the dirt, the swing thudding to a halt against my shoulder blade.

It had been easy for me to ignore Zia, but Karim's eyes kept filling with tears for the rest of the day and I didn't quite believe it was because of the dirt he'd got in his eyes when Zia kicked him to the ground. Because it had seemed to be a big deal to Karim, I repeated Zia's remark to my parents that afternoon. That's when everything went a little crazy. Zia's parents had come over, and Karim's parents, too, and voices were raised, though I'd been told to stay in my room and so I don't know who said what to whom and why. It was the first time I used the telephone. I called Karim and said, 'Why are they so angry?' and Karim said he really didn't know, but it just felt to him like Zia had said something really bad. And then Aba and Uncle Ali and Zia's parents all got into cars and went to Zia's house, where they called Zia out of his room and asked him why he'd said what he'd said to Karim. Zia told us the next day that it was so strange, they all looked so strange. When Zia said he thought Bengali was a bad word, his father went straight into his room and fired his ayah. But I don't even remember if she was the one who told me that, Zia said, and his mother yelled at him to be quiet. Talking about it made Karim and Zia friends once more, and when Zia said to me, admiringly, 'You kick like a boy,' instead of being angry that I'd ratted on him, I decided that maybe he wasn't so bad after all. We never mentioned the incident again. To tell the truth, it had all seemed like a fairly minor event in our lives back then when our reactions to anything more earth-shattering than the rules of playground games were merely parroted versions of our parents' attitudes, with no real understanding or conviction behind them other than the firm belief that our parents were always right.

But now, years later, I was forced to consider that Karim and I were separate in some way that seemed to matter terribly to people old enough to understand where significance lay. I wrapped my arms around the seat of the swing and rested my head on it. I was Muhajir with a trace of Pathan, and he was Bengali and . . . Punjabi? Sindhi? what? I considered. Probably Punjabi, I decided. He had relatives in Lahore. These days, with the Civil War treated as a long-distant memory that had nothing to do with our present lives, his Punjabiness would probably be more of an issue on the nation's ethnic battle-ground than his Bengaliness. But did any of it really have anything to do with Karim and me? Did differing ethnicities mean that there was something fundamentally disparate about us at the core?

Despite our closeness from the time of our births, I never made the claim that Karim was like a brother to me. I knew too many brothers to say a thing like that. But I believed that somewhere beneath skin and blood and bone, somewhere beyond personality and reflex, somewhere deep within the marrow of our marrow, we were the same. And so nothing in either of our lives needed to be inexplicable to the other; it was just laziness or stubbornness that created occasional baffled moments between us. But supposing that wasn't true . . . supposing there was something standing between us that neither of us could bulldoze our way through. I looked out into the gathering darkness and tried to imagine what I would feel if I ever lost Karim.

Utter, irreversible loneliness.

I stood up and shook my head to clear away those unasked-for thoughts. The breeze rustled through branches and I had the strong desire to put my arms around each haunted tree and weep for the ice-cold existence of ghosts I didn't, even at that moment, really believe in. But what if, as I embraced a tree, a ghost was to make its presence known to me? There would be no stepping back then from the knowledge that this lonely limbo might await.

I turned and ran towards the house. The door opened and Karim stepped out, his hand seizing my wrist as I tried to push past him.

'Don't listen to them,' he said fiercely. His hand gripped me tight. 'If we believed grown-ups really meant everything they said, we'd go mad.'

I turned my wrist in his grip and caught his arm, the buckle of his watchstrap cutting into my palm, as though we were two anachronistic legionnaires.

'What?' he said. 'Tell me.'

'No, nothing.'

'Rubbish.' He put his hand on my shoulder. 'Don't do that. You've started doing that. You disappear. One moment you're with me, and then next you've gone off somewhere and I don't know where your mind is taking you.'

'I thought you were too busy looking at maps to notice.'

He gave me one of his exasperated looks. 'No one's ever too busy to know when their foot has gone to sleep or their throat is itching.'

'Our friendship is an itchy throat?' I didn't know whether to be amused, annoyed or touched.

'Don't disappear on me,' he said it more softly. 'Please don't.'

I let go of his wrist and sat down, leaning against the brick exterior of the house. Karim had, of late, developed a taste for the dramatic. As if I could ever disappear on him when he knew me as well as he did, when he knew me well enough to finish almost any sentence that I started constructing in my head. I wanted to say that to him, but it seemed almost embarrassing; no, it seemed almost a betrayal of the trust we had in each other's friendship to have to articulate such a thing. So I said it indirectly, in a way I knew he'd understand. 'You're such an idiot,' I said, and didn't need to look at him to know he was smiling.

When we boarded the train back to Karachi – after I hugged Uncle Asif and Aunty Laila goodbye with affection (I had meant to be more distant, but he grinned at me and she spread her arms wide and I forgot) – Karim, for once, didn't retreat into the glowering silence that usually marked his physical propinquity to his father.

'We had such a great time,' he said, throwing himself on to the lower bunk of the compartment, having conveniently developed

45

selective amnesia about the fuss he'd kicked up about going to stay on the farm in the first place. 'Long walks, amazing climbing trees, the most succulent kinoos picked right off the branches. Look at my teeth! Chewing sugar cane has strengthened them. I saw a goat born. We climbed the cotton mountain but then we started sneezing. Tell him about dinner in the desert, Raheen.'

'We had dinner in the desert,' I said. And then I couldn't resist. 'Karim thought he heard a churail shrieking, ready to come and spirit us away, but then we ate the sand witch, crust and all.'

Uncle Ali rolled his eyes, but he was smiling too. 'That reminds me. Raheen, your parents are having a party tomorrow. You kids can help with the hors-d'œuvres.'

'Hello, Begum Ooh-de-la dripping diamonds in your *nouveau riche* way, would you like some horsed ovaries?' I said, with a curtsy. 'How's that, Uncle Ali?'

'I think the curtsy needs a little practice. But, Raheen, if anyone asks you anything about Asif's brother's wedding, just say Asif was very pleased with the news. And don't elaborate.'

'What's with the *nouveau riche* line?' Karim said. 'Sonia's parents fall into that category, according to our parents.'

'And they have the solid gold taps in their bathroom to prove it. Don't they?' I turned to Uncle Ali for confirmation.

'Well at least Sonia's father doesn't make fun of her mother all the time,' Karim said. 'At least he doesn't think he can make decisions that will change all their lives without worrying about what anyone else in his family thinks.'

'Karimazov, sshhhh!'

'Karim, you're making Raheen feel uncomfortable,' Uncle Ali said. 'So save it for later. Now go to sleep. Both of you.'

Uncle Ali turned off the light above Karim and my bunk bed and lay down to read his newspaper under the remaining light. When my father read the papers it was a noisy affair; paper rustled and crinkled, supplements fell out, the most interesting columns concluded on pages which could not be found until Aba lost interest and moved on to the next article. But with Uncle

Ali, all was silent and orderly, and newsprint never smudged on to his fingers.

My leg dangled over the edge of the top bunk but Karim did not kick up his foot to protest the presence of my limb in his airspace. One of the women from the village had waxed my legs and massaged them with coconut oil that morning. I withdrew my leg from Karim's line of sight and wondered how I could get Zia to see me bare-legged before the ugly stubble appeared.

'We should go to the beach in the next day or two,' Karim said.

'Certes, my lord,' I whispered down to him. Certes. An anagram for secret. I swung myself off the top bunk and lay down on his mattress, my body turned towards him, head propped on elbow, so that Uncle Ali wouldn't be able to see the shapes of the words leaving my mouth. Something unfamiliar – confusion? incomprehension? – flashed in his eyes, and I found we were both shifting backward, widening the space between us. No, no, no, I thought. Karim and I can't be awkward with each other.

'You're about to fall off, aren't you?' Karim said.

The bed was absurdly narrow. I nodded, considered getting up, realized that would only make things more awkward, and started laughing instead; I would have fallen off then if Karim hadn't shot his hand forward and pulled me away from the brink.

'What's the secret?' he said, releasing my wrist. As strangely as it appeared, the constraint between us had gone and we were now just lying beside each other as we had done all our lives.

'What does Zia say about me?'

Karim rested his head on the pillow and folded his arms across his chest. 'God, I'm sleepy,' he said and closed his eyes.

'In other words, Zia couldn't be less interested and there's no way you're going to be the one to tell me that. Breathe if I've guessed correctly.'

He kicked me and turned his face to the wall. I poked him in the spine and he started snoring.

'Raheen, I think my son's trying to tell you to leave him alone.'

I kicked Karim in one final attempt to get a reaction, and then turned to face Uncle Ali. 'So why didn't you marry my mother?' I said.

Uncle Ali looked at me the way someone wearing half-moon reading glasses might peer at something in the distance. I once heard Ami teasing him about that look, saying he only did it to draw attention to the fact that his eyesight was superb. Aunty Maheen never teased her husband, but Ami teased him all the time.

'The music changed,' he said.

I think the four of them chose that bit of imagery – the waltzing couples changing partners – long ago to avoid having to answer the kind of question I'd just asked. It was obvious why, though I hadn't given it much thought before. Off the dance floor, synchrony cannot exist. What I really wanted Uncle Ali to tell me – what he really wasn't going to tell me – was who was the first. Of the four of them, who was the first to decide to twirl away; who was the first, and who was the last?

'Good thing the record got stuck on "repeat play" after that?' It was meant to be a statement, but it came out as a question.

Uncle Ali folded up his newspaper – rather hastily, it seemed – and switched off the light. 'Very good thing. Otherwise you and Karim wouldn't be. 'Night, sweetheart.'

I wanted to ask him what made them think everything had worked out for the best before Karim and I came along and proved justification enough, but I was suddenly too drowsy to speak. I pulled Karim's pillow slightly closer to me and put my head down, grateful for being able to sleep spine to spine with Karim as I had done in the days when cameras in the hands of our parents formed the only memories we were ever to have of those earliest gestures of intimacy. Why grateful? Because sometimes you know you're standing on a cusp, and you know that in knowing it you've gone past the cusp over to the other

48

side, or at least almost entirely so, entirely except for one toe that still hangs on to childhood; one toe or one finger or one shoulder blade curving back to meet another shoulder blade which curves forward to meet yours in a reminder that, if you had wings, this, right here, is where they would sprout.

Can angels lie spine to spine?

If not, how they must envy us humans.

He watched the donkey kicking up red-brown earth between the cottonfields, the fury of its hoofs most likely an expression of disdain for the laughing, twittering creatures behind it, but no matter how fast it ran, spraying wet mud on the cotton-pickers, it could not outpace the cart attached to it, the laughter and shrieks getting louder and more high-pitched as the animal gathered speed. Ears laid flat against its skull, and mouth foaming. Such a fine line between laughter and braying.

Ali clicked his tongue, and turned away. It was ignoble to think of one's friends in that manner. Ignoble. Zafar would laugh if he heard him use the word. And Maheen would laugh, too, because these days Zafar's laughter made Maheen laugh, no matter what the cause. He stared gloomily down at the bruise on his thumb. Purple-yellow smudge beneath his nail.

When he looked up again Asif was emerging from the kinoo orchards and walking towards the dunes, the farm manager by his side gesticulating wildly. Asif barely seemed to notice the man as he took a long drag on his cigarette and surveyed his property from behind dark glasses with an air of satisfaction. Who would have thought Asif Marx of Oxford would turn into quite so contented a landowner within three years of returning home? Men who worked on the farm stepped off the path as he approached, their feet sinking in the wet soil of the cottonfields, eyes cast down. Ali wondered if New Year's Eve meant anything to them.

He followed Asif's progress through the field and to the sand dunes, where the old nomad woman raised her arms in greeting at his approach and called out to him in a dialect Ali couldn't understand. But Asif took off his glasses and called back to her, and the nomad woman put her hand on her broad hips and laughed. Ali knew that Asif was going to tell her that, yes, it was all right for her tribe to stay on the dune which belonged to him by law and belonged to her tribe by the laws of tradition. For longer than anyone knew, Asif had told him the night before, the nomad tribe had made this dune part of their migratory patterns. And now some of them wanted to build mud huts and settle, but the villagers and the farm hands considered them untouchables. To tell them that Islam had no concept of untouchables would have been futile, Asif insisted. So instead he had chosen compromise: the nomads could stay as long as they drank water from their own wells, and did not mix with the villagers.

How many walls can one nation erect and sustain, Ali wondered. Is it possible to circumnavigate one wall without crashing into another? How many fires do we light, how much rosewood do we turn to ash, to keep our dreamworlds aglow? How many fireflies do we turn away from, mistaking them for burning sparks? He squinted up at the sun, and pressed his thumbnail to test the level of pain.

Panes of glass reflected blinding sunlight, but Maheen knew there were faces pressed against the windows of the house, watching Zafar following her into the back garden, hoping for an indiscretion that could enliven coffee parties in its retelling.

'Hey, gorgeous.' Zafar caught the pulloo of her sari and tugged. She twirled towards him, the train of the white sari diaphanous between them. Her hands pressed against his shoulders, and pushed. Zafar fell back against the grass, laughing. Maheen looked up at the windows again.

'There's no one there.' Zafar's bare feet drummed against her ankles. 'Come here, come on.'

'No, darling, don't be silly. Someone could be watching.'

Zafar lit up a cigarette. He looked like a panther after a rainstorm, with his black turtleneck, catlike eyes, hair slicked down to gleaming, and the assurance with which he reclined on the grass. 'We're engaged. We're allowed to be slightly indiscreet.'

Maheen kicked off her shoes and sat opposite Zafar, her feet pressed against his. 'There's enough talk about me as it is, jaanoo, so why add impropriety to the list of my failings?'

Zafar raised himself slightly from his supine position. 'What are you talking about?'

'Last week, at the Sind Club. Rukhsana heard your boss singing your praises. Born to be an ad man, he said. Pity about his fiancée. Number of our clients won't like working with someone who has a Bengali wife. Still, months to go before the wedding. Maybe he'll see the light by then.'

Zafar pivoted round so that he was sitting beside Maheen. He put an arm around her shoulder, a cigarette dangling between his fingers. 'So, I'll change jobs.'

'You'll find that attitude everywhere, Zaf.'

'OK, so I'll change fiancées.' He laughed and buried his face in her hair. His hand touched her midriff, between sari and skin, and Maheen covered it with her own hand, pressing his fingers to her flesh for a moment before pulling his hand away, and slapping it lightly. He made a sound of mock exasperation, the fingers of his other hand brushing lightly against her neck as he brought his cigarette to her mouth so she could inhale the headrush. 'Silly girl. Why do we need the rest of the world?'

Maheen leaned against him. It was this she loved most in him: he could say everything but love was irrelevant, and come so close to making it seem true that when she looked up at the shifting clouds she almost did not see them pulling apart, rending into pieces, wisps of smoke spiralling . . .

. . . round the dining table cries of 'Happy New Year' stilled as Asif stood up, clinking a fork against his glass.

'I'm too drunk,' he said. 'And I've been an appalling host. Plus, I'm a decadent feudal, as Zafar so eloquently reminded us all last night. I will now pause so that you can all contradict me.'

There was silence from the eleven guests around the table, save for muffled sounds behind hands clamped over lips to prevent laughter.

'Well, if that's your attitude, none of you are invited back for New Year's Eve next year,' Asif said, grandly, waving one arm in the air and tangling it among the streamers that trailed down from the chandelier. 'Oh, hell. Zaf, you do the toast.' He fell back into his chair, ripping streamers in two.

Zafar stood up, and held up a glass. 'Ladies and gentlemen and Laila . . .' Cheers and catcalls rang from the crowd around the table, and Laila stood up imperiously and blew a raspberry at him.

Zafar winked at her, and continued. 'Before we move on to dessert—'

'Ice cream,' Rukhsana shouted, leaning across Asif to prong a fork into Zafar's arm. 'I want ice cream.'

'Isn't ice cream a sign of sexual frustration?' Laila said.

'Nonsense,' Yasmin said expansively. 'That's just a rumour started by those polygamous diabetics.'

'Bastards, the lot of them!' Maheen yelled.

'Maheen's drunk!' Yasmin said gleefully, putting an arm around her best friend's shoulder.

'Everyone's drunk,' Asif said, ripping up streamers and aiming them into wine glasses around the table.

'I want to get more drunk,' Laila's fiancé said. 'Hurry up with your toast, Zafar.'

'Well, if Rukhsana wouldn't interrupt . . .' Zafar said.

'Rukhsana's a teetotaller,' Yasmin said. 'She must be ignored.'

'Guess who's been doing everything but ignoring Rukhsana? Bunty!'

Whistles all around the table.

'Come on, Rukhsana, grab him quick,' Maheen said. 'I would, if I wasn't engaged to Thing here.'

'Please, Rukhsana, grab him quick.' Zafar clasped his hands together. 'Else she'll leave me for him.'

'Rukhsana and Bunty. Sounds good together.'

'Sounds awful,' Ali said, finally catching the mood of the party after three days of near-silence. 'We'll have to call him Bukhsana. He looks like a Bukhsana. Rukhsana and Bukhsana.'

'Or Runty and Bunty,' Maheen said.

'I'm no runt!' Rukhsana objected.

'Yes, she is.'

Everyone started thumping on the table. 'Runty! Runty!'

'Oh shut up and let Zafar propose the toast.'

'Right.' Zafar cleared his throat. 'I'd like to formally welcome 1971 to our homeland of Pakistan. This will be the year that signals the end of bachelorhood for me. And the end of divorceehood for Laila. Thank God she got rid of that first guy; we can all say it now. Maheen – I'm a lucky bastard, and I know you won't let me forget that. And if any of the beautiful single women around this table want to join the wedding bandwagon, allow me to recommend my friend Ali.'

Ali used his fork to catapult an olive at Zafar.

Zafar caught the olive in his mouth, and continued: 'So, 1971, these are the favours we ask of you: may the miniskirt get more mini, may long sideburns go out of fashion, and may something else happen that I'm really not sober enough to think of. Anyone, we need a third thing that we want to happen. May . . . may . . .'

'May we not have civil war,' someone shouted.

'He mentioned politics.' Laila pointed an accusing finger at the offending party. 'Into the buffalo swamp with him.'

Nine people stood up, and ran after the fleeing man.

Yasmin and Maheen were left at the table.

'May we not have civil war,' Yasmin said, and moved to clink glasses with Maheen. Maheen's glass tilted over and red wine streamed down both women's arms.

Streamers still wrapped around his arm, Asif pointed up at the bark of the gnarled tree in the back garden. 'Well, look at that. Zafar, you old romantic.'

The house guests pressed around him, peering up through the dark, buffalo swamps quite forgotten. 'Oh, that's so sweet!' Laila said. She slapped her fiancée's arm. 'You've never done anything like that for me.'

Zafar shook his head. 'As if it wasn't bad enough that you abandon me in the orchards at night, Asif, now you have to embarrass me in front of all our friends. Which of your poor minions had to do that?'

'You're denying it's your handiwork?' Asif roared with laughter. 'No weaseling out of this one, Romeo. Oh, and here comes the much-loved Maheen.'

Maheen and Yasmin walked arm in arm through the grass, and the crowd parted to let Maheen see the initials carved into the tree's bark.

'Zafar!' Something so intimate in the way she said his name that all their friends smiled at one another, not without a trace of wistfulness, and drew away.

'It wasn't . . .' Zafar started to say, looking at Asif.

But Maheen's arms were around his neck, and Asif was walking away, so Zafar never finished the sentence.

Is this a life sentence, or will I wake up one day and find I'm free of her? Ali twirled the stem of his glass between his fingers and tried not to think of that look in Maheen's eyes when she put her arms around Zafar's neck.

'I know you want to be alone, but I'm joining you all the same,' Yasmin said, coming to stand beside Ali on the balcony, which overlooked the back garden. She took his hand in hers, and inspected the bruise beneath his thumb. 'Must have hurt,' she said. 'Hammer?'

Ali nodded. 'It was dark. Missed the chisel, caught my thumb. How did you know it was me?'

Yasmin shivered in the cold, and put her hands into Ali's jacket pocket. 'Zafar's too lazy. And I saw the look on your face when Maheen put her arms around Zaf. What made you do it?'

Ali took off his jacket and placed it around her shoulders. 'Don't know. Anger, love, frustration, all of the above. I hate emotions I can't control. Hacking away at a bit of wood seemed a good way to release all that bottled-up stuff.'

'You should have told me you were doing it,' Yasmin said. 'I would have helped.'

Ali raised an eyebrow. 'Why?'

'Were you thinking of making some kind of amorous advances towards me about three months ago?'

'No . . . I mean, it's not to say I would have any objection . . . I mean, you are . . . What? What's wrong?'

Yasmin leaned a head against his shoulder. 'Bugger,' she said.

Ali regarded her bowed head with curiosity. Among all the women he knew, Yasmin was the only one he would really call a friend. More than that, she knew him in ways that constantly surprised him. She was probably the only person who would even consider it possible that controlled, aloof Ali could love Maheen enough to gouge her initial, and that of his best friend, into a tree. But why she was leaning her head against his shoulder and releasing a long stream of expletives he could not begin to fathom.

If she stopped cursing, Yasmin knew she'd start crying. *The bastard, the bastard,* she said, losing the words in the folds of Ali's shirt. No one else but Ali whose shirt she'd feel so comfortable weeping into. *Zafar, you bastard.* He had pulled her on to the dance floor at the Nasreen Room, just as summer was ending and Karachi's evenings began to invite dancing and festivities again. Pulled her on to the dance floor, black shirt moulded tight to his chest, and said, 'Don't you think it would be nice if sometimes we saw each other without seventeen dozen other people around?' A 'yes' seemed too simple an answer, too girlish, so instead Yasmin went the unfamiliar route of coquetry, fluttered her eyelashes, which he couldn't see in the dark, and said, 'I don't know that my parents would approve,' the laugh in her voice meant to convey what he should have already known: Yasmin was so in the habit of making her parents disapprove that to conform to their expectation would almost constitute filial betrayal. But Zafar's face went still when he heard her and he nodded curtly and led her off the floor. 'Good. Good answer. It's just that I think Ali might put that kind of question to you, and I wanted to make sure you knew how to handle the situation. Reputation, Yasmin, can't toy around with your reputation.'

'Are you crying?' Ali said. 'It's not that I object, but there's a handkerchief in my breast pocket which might come in handy.'

Yasmin stepped back and blew her nose vigorously on the piece of cloth Ali proffered. 'No one will ever marry me,' she declared.

Ali looked out towards the garden. He could hear Maheen's laughter, though Maheen was somewhere just out of sight. 'I was thinking the very thing.'

Without warning, Yasmin's hand stung across his cheekbone.

Ali put a hand to his cheek, and smiled. 'I meant, I was thinking it about myself.'

'Oh,' said Yasmin, mortified. 'Oh.' The pause that followed seemed to require her to say something further, so she said, 'I'd marry you.'

And somehow, as they stood and looked at each other, Zafar and Maheen's laughter floating up from an unseen part of the garden below, they knew they'd re-tell this mad, fumbled, impossible, tear-filled, bruised, cold, miraculous non-proposal scene to their children and grandchildren, and the most absurd part of the story would be how easily it might never have happened.

• • •

Karachi's air was heavy. I could feel it press down on me as I alighted on to the platform, and I had to open my mouth and imagine there was a Hoover in my lungs in order to inhale the amount of oxygen that had flowed through my nasal passages with one swift sniff in the rural atmosphere of Rahim Yar Khan. So the way we breathe is habit, I thought, and paused to wonder what was not habit. What, in my life, would I never forget, never unlearn, never attempt to do without?

'Home,' Karim said, jumping out of the compartment doorway with no regard for the steps.

When we were children, Karim always disregarded steps, or disregarded as many of them as he could. He leapt through the world, and not always cleanly. There were twisted ankles, bruised knees and, once, exposed bone, but none of these deterred him from throwing himself at the wind. When I try to understand how memories happen, Karim's leaps confound me. By which I mean, I cannot remember faces as they used to be before becoming what they were when I last saw them. When, for instance, I remember Sonia at thirteen I do not see a long-haired girl whose body is just beginning to curve into breath-taking beauty. I do not see her at all. But I sense her, I know – I remember – what it is like to be thirteen and angular and standing beside her. When I try harder for a visual image, old photographs come to mind. Sonia leaning on my shoulder as I lean against the orange shutters of the tuck shop; Sonia's face a scream as Zia holds up a lizard to her face; Sonia and Karim playing tug-of-war with her dupatta. But I cannot move those images forward even one second in time. How Sonia looked when the shutters opened without warning and we both tumbled back; how she looked when she realized the lizard was plastic; how she looked when the dupatta tore. I remember these things happening, I know they happened, but I cannot bring her face, or any of our faces, into focus as I recall the moment. So I want to say, visual memories overwrite themselves. The part of my brain that stores memories of Sonia keeps updating her face so that I can recall it clearly only as it was when we last met. And yet, I know exactly how Karim looked when wheeling through the air. I know how he looked doing it at seven, at ten, at fourteen.

And, yes, I know how he looked jumping on to the platform at thirteen. Not beautiful, though the notion of a leaping boy is beautiful. Some growth that still hadn't earned the right to be called a moustache had started to occupy the place between his nose and lip; his face and stomach still clung on to the previous year's puppy fat but his limbs were beginning to go gangly; his ears . . . at any age, Karim's ears were unfortunate. Don't get the idea that Karim stood out by virtue of his awkward looks; most of the boys I was in class with were going through a similar phase at the time.

Except Zia, you might expect me to say.

I keep forgetting how crazy I was about him then. I forget that, and I remember other things which surely can't be real memories. For instance, the drive home from the train station. I seem to think I remember Karim looking out of the window as we snaked through the congested parts of Karachi with its colourful buses maniacally racing one another, men selling fruit and vegetables from wooden carts on the side of the road, deformed beggars dextrously making their way through traffic, laundry flapping from washing lines on the latticed balconies of low-rise apartment buildings. But I can't really remember that, can I, because even if Karim had already started imagining what it would be like to be a stranger in Karachi, even if he were jumping ahead of his own life and seeing the city with the eyes of someone who views Karachi as contrast rather than norm, I had no inkling of it at all. And so I would not have paid any attention to buses or beggars or balconies, and I would not have paid any attention to Karim paying attention to them. I would, I'm quite sure, have been thinking of Zia instead.

He was waiting for us at my house, when Uncle Ali's driver dropped me off. Something wobbly happened to my knees when I saw his car parked outside. He was waiting at *my* house, not Karim's. He was waiting for me.

'Oh yes, I forgot to tell you. Zia's whisking the two of you off for breakfast. I told him we'd stop at your house first, Raheen, on our way back from the train station. I'll call your parents at work and tell them we've arrived safely. But promise you won't go too far away. Things have got better, but they're not OK yet.'

Karim and Zia greeted each other with whoops of delight and high-fives while I struggled to pull my suitcase out of the trunk of the car. Uncle Ali rolled down his car window and yelled at the boys and they both came running to give me a hand. Zia smelled of Drakkar Noir. He hoisted my suitcase up on to his head and held it there with one hand while swaying up the driveway as though he were a village woman bearing an earthenware matka full of water. He was so absorbed in being entertaining he had quite forgotten to say hello, let alone that it was good to see me. Uncle Ali gave me a look that seemed almost sympathetic, and then his car drove off.

'Zia, I'll take that inside. I need to use the Louvre in any case.' Karim took the suitcase and disappeared indoors, and I was left alone with Zia.

'Hi, Raheen. Suno, if you want to take a shower or something before we go for halva puri, no problem. Karim and I can hang about for a few minutes.'

I looked down at my crumpled shirt and the caked farm mud that clung to the hem of my jeans.

Zia laughed. 'No, I don't mean you look as though you need to. You look fine. Really good, in fact. Your parents are at work, aren't they?'

'Yeah,' I said, a voice in my head shouting *ohmygodohmygodohmygod*. 'Why?'

He pulled a packet of cigarettes out of the pocket of his denim jacket. 'Don't want them to see me smoking.'

I watched him unwrap the cellophane sheath, flip the packet open with his thumb and turn one cigarette upside down in the pack, for good luck. He took a box of matches out of his pocket, attempted to strike the flint against his shoe, and then realized he was wearing sneakers. He grinned, embarrassed. 'Good thing you're the only one around to see that. Which do you think is cooler? A box of matches or a lighter? I mean, obviously if the lighter is a Zippo, that wins. But if your choice is those transparent, brightly coloured lighters or a box of matches with a Ferrari pictured on the box, then which?'

'Vole,' I said. 'Damn vole.'

'Huh?'

'Nothing.'

'Karim, our friend's gone mad,' Zia shouted over my shoulder. 'She's talking about voles.'

'Get in the car and drive, Zia.' Karim came up to me and brought his fist down on my shoulder. 'Vole, huh? I thought you'd say "I rush cats".'

It's a crush? Lord, no, I thought. If it's a crush and nothing more, what must love feel like?

'So are we picking up Sonia?' I got into the passenger seat and passed a bunch of tapes back to Karim. He rejected tapes labelled 'Grooooves', 'Selexions' and 'Mewzic Micks' in favour of one marked 'Vybs'.

Zia snorted. 'Her father's gone mad. Won't let her out of the house because he knows someone who died recently in Korangi or Orangi or some such area, and that's made him completely paranoid about his darling daughter's safety.'

'It's not that absurd, Zia,' Karim said. 'I mean, our parents made us leave the city, and they don't even know anyone directly affected by what happened.'

Zia made another dismissive sound and threw his cigarette butt out of the window. I could see it spark as it hit the asphalt. 'Yeah, they made you leave because otherwise both of you would have kept wanting to go to the beach or the twins' farm or some far-flung place and they just didn't want to deal with the headache of always saying no. Believe me, I've driven my parents crazy the last few weeks with driving off for hours and not telling them where I'm going. But Sonia's father's not even letting her go as far as Boat Basin. And the really funny part of it is, this guy he knew who died, he fell off a bus. What the hell does that have to do with anything?'

'Fell off a bus?'

'That's what I'm saying. He was going home from work, and he lived in some area that's under curfew so there's a window of about an hour or so in the evening when the curfew is lifted so that everyone can come home, right?'

'If you say so.'

'I say so, Raheen. So, obviously, the buses at that hour are so full they almost topple over and this guy sees his bus and leaps on to it, except there's no place to even hang on to outside, forget managing to get a foot inside, so he ends up hanging on to this guy who's hanging on to the wide-open bus door which is flapping back and forth as the bus hurtles on and at one point the door swings and the guy holding on to the guy holding on to the door knocks his head against someone else and loses his grip and there's another bus speeding past and dhuzhook! next thing you know Sonia's father doesn't want her leaving the house.'

I couldn't help laughing at the incongruity of it all, even though I knew that Sonia's father didn't like any of Sonia's friends except Karim and me, so our absence must have been the real reason he forbade his daughter from hanging out with what he considered a 'fast, precocious crowd'.

Karim saw it similarly, but articulated it differently. 'Someone died. Someone he knew. And I bet you never even thought of telling him you were sorry.'

'Of course not. He'd just think I was trying to get into his good books.'

'I don't know.' Karim opened and closed a cassette cover repeatedly. 'Don't you think maybe there's something wrong in us having such fun all the time when people are being killed every day in the poorer parts of town?'

Zia rolled his eyes at Karim. 'This is Karachi. We have a good time while we can, 'cause tomorrow we might not be so lucky.'

But he couldn't have said that back in January '87, could he? Did we already know that something had begun that perhaps none of us would live to see the end of? Perhaps. Although the ethnic fighting had broken out for the first time in my life in 1985, I cannot remember Karachi being a safe city even before that. When Alexander's admiral, the Cretan Nearchus, reached Krokola he had to quell a mutiny among Alexander's Krokolan subjects, who had killed the satrap appointed by Alexander to gather supplies for his forces. If Karachi and Krokola are one and the same, recorded instances of violence on its soil go back over twenty-three hundred years. And yet, it is the only place where I have ever felt utterly safe. Who among us has never been moved to tears, or to tears' invisible counterparts, by mention of the word 'home'? Is there any other word that can feel so heavy as you hold it in your mouth?

I am trying to pass, like a needle, through the thread of narrative but my eye is distracted by what lies ahead.

'Everything looks different,' Karim said, leaning forward between the passenger's seat and the driver's, and looking out through the windscreen. 'It should seem cold. By Karachi standards it's cold, but compared with RYK it's not. And arid. Everything looks arid, even the trees.'

Everything did look different. I'm sure. Maybe my memory of Karim on the drive home from the train station isn't false after all. Three weeks away from Karachi and I was noticing things that were generally just so much background: the plastic buckets in which flower-sellers stored bouquets of roses encircling the roundabout near the graveyard; the sign on Sunset Boulevard that said 'Avoid Accidents Here'; the squat-walking street cleaners dodging traffic while sweeping dust and rubbish to the sides of the road; the carpet-sellers who spread their wares on pavements, with the choicest rugs draped above on the boughs of trees; on billboards, the Urdu letters spelling out English words; the illegal tinted glass fitted in cars with government licence plates. And, yes, Karim was right, the trees that looked so arid. I should have told him I agreed, but Zia was smirking at his remark.

'Go and write a poem, Karim,' I said, pushing him back so that he wouldn't obstruct my view of Zia any longer. 'Zee, where are we going?'

'For halva puri. You know, that place we went that time when it rained.'

'Oh. We promised Uncle Ali we wouldn't go too far.'

'Yeah, but he didn't define what he meant by too far, did he?' Zia winked. He had amazing eyelashes.

'Well, fine, but you turned off too early from the road leading to the airport.'

'No, I didn't. I turned after the petrol pump.'

'I don't know about the petrol pump, but we should have passed the Chinese restaurant. Remember last time we went past there and Sonia started craving chicken corn soup even though it was six in the morning?'

'Yes, but last time we got lost.'

'We got lost after the Chinese restaurant. We worked that out on the way home.'

Zia slowed the car and we looked up and down the road, which looked so wide after the little streets of RYK, and tried to find something familiar in the large, and largely hideous, houses behind their high boundary walls.

'You're right. OK, we're lost again. Now what, Raheen?'

'What did we do last time?'

'Sonia asked for directions.'

'So ask for directions.'

'OK. What's the name of the place?'

'Don't you know?'

'Shit.'

Zia drove on, frowning, and I watched him chew his lip.

'Wasn't it something beginning with a "T"?' he ventured after a few seconds.

'Yes. It was. And with two syllables.'

'Tata's? Tito's? Toto's?'

'Toto sounds familiar.'

'It does. It does sound familiar. Toto's. It's Toto's.'

'Or maybe we're just thinking of *The Wizard of Oz*.'

'Shit.'

Karim finally decided to join the conversation. 'It's Shahrah-e-Faisal.'

'I'm sure it's not.' Zia shook his head.

'The road leading to the airport. I just remembered. Its name is Shahrah-e-Faisal. How could we forget that?'

'I didn't forget,' I said. '*I* haven't forgotten.' Hadn't forgotten we always called it 'the road leading to the airport'. And the year before, stuck in a traffic jam, we had come up with: the road leading to the oar trip; the road lead gin to the rapt roi; O, I dare thee, old gnat, hit parrot; pin the aorta or glide to death.

And how do you glide to death, Karim?

If you don't pin my aorta we might find out.

So what need was there for him to call the road by its official name, when he'd had no part in the naming, when he had no memories stored in the curves of its official consonants? We should have stories in common, I found myself thinking. We should have stories, and jokes no one understands, and memories that we know will stay alive because neither of us will let the other forget; we should have all that when we've just spent so much time together in a context unfamiliar to all our friends, and to some extent we do, but over and above the jokes and stories and memories, he has maps and I don't. He has maps and I don't understand why.

'Zia, Karim's decided he's going to be a cartographer.'

'What's that?'

'Map-maker,' Karim said. 'A Karachi map-maker. Have you ever seen a proper map of this city? Not just one of those two-page things that you see in tourist books, but a real, proper map of the whole city?'

'No.' Zia shrugged. 'But why would I have looked for one?'

'Well, one might have come in handy right now,' Karim said. 'You have no idea where you are, do you?'

Zia swung the car around. 'There are really only two places you can ever be. Lost or not. When lost you do a youee until you're not. Which is what we're about to do. How about ditching halva puri and going to the airport for coffee instead?'

'What's a youee?'

'U-turn, Ra, U-turn. Arré, yaar, two weeks on a farm and you've fallen behind on the local ling.'

That stung, whether he intended it to or not. I felt desperately uncool and out of step.

'Strap her cargo,' Karim said. 'Crop rag hearts.'

'Huh?' Zia frowned.

'Go rap her carts.' I smiled at Karim.

'Chop Ra's garter.'

'What the hell . . .?' Zia said. 'What? Is this another one of your . . . what's that word thing called?'

'Anagram,' Karim said.

'Nag a ram,' I shot back. We grinned, enjoying the sound of that.

'Nag a ram. Nag-nag-nag nag-nagaram. Nag-a-ra-a-am,' Karim sang, drumming his hands on my shoulder.

And, just like that, life was cool again.

• • •

My litany of Karachi winter characteristics runs something like this: dry skin; socks; peanuts roasted in their shells and bought by the pao in bags made of newspaper; peaches that you twist just so to separate them into halves, flesh falling cleanly off seed; the silence of no fan and no air conditioner; hibiscus flowers; shawls; days at the beach (which involve a litany of their own: salted fish air; turtle tracks; shouts of warning from the fishermen just before toes tangle with their near-invisible lines; fishermen's baskets full of dead fish; fishermen's nets drawn in to shore; warm sand; wet sand; feet slippery on rock moss; jeans rolled up as we wade, and rolled down again heavy with salt and sea; shells; sparks from the barbecue; the concentrated colours of sunset; stars; the rings of sand on the bathtub; the fog of mirrors in the bathroom; the smell of salt on skin as we fall asleep, despite the earlier soap and scrubbing; the forgetting of every-thing that bothered us at the start of the day; the sheer childhood of it all). But, really, for Karachi high society, winter is about envelopes.

Or, rather, about the invitations inside the envelopes. They start to appear, in twos and threes, in early November, and by New Year every house has a shrunken mirror. That is absurdly oblique. I mean, the invitation cards get pushed into those crevices between the dressing-table mirror and its frame, en-croaching on the space that exists for reflection. This is true of invitations to parties; the wedding invitations are another matter entirely. Dholkis, mehndis, mayouns, milads, sham-e-rangs, ganas, shadi receptions, valimas – among the absurdly extra-vagant there is a card for each occasion (except the actual wedding ceremony itself, which hardly anyone attends) and the envelopes that arrive are so bloated with demands on your time that they cannot squeeze into cracks between wood and glass and must have their own space on the dressing-table top to lie back, engorged and insolent.

I have already invoked the Ghutnas; the Karachi Knees, remember? They are perennial creatures, but most in their element during the winter. It was during a winter wedding that my mother first named them, although really she deserves little credit herself; Aunty Runty all but presented Ami with the name on a platter.

'Oh Yaso, Yaso,' Aunty Runty sighed, coming upon my mother at a mehndi. 'Can't handle, darling, can't.'

My mother stepped back. Aunty Runty was swaying, and her cigarette was within dangerous proximity to my mother's heirloom sari. 'Can't what, Rukhsana?' My mother is the only person I know who refuses to make use of the nickname that was bestowed on her former classmate when she married the dipsomaniacal Bunty.

Aunty Runty took a deep breath and held one hand up as though silencing a gathered assembly. 'Can't take the social scene. Every night, people out drinking until three, four in the morning. Drinking, drinking, they fall on the street, ghutnay chhil gaye, yaar, yes, skin peels off knees and yet they drink on. Can't. And yet, what to do? Have to show up, be seen, let people know you're alive so they'll invite you to tomorrow's party. Yaar, can't take the scene, but have to peel knees, have to chhilo ghutnay, have to be seen to be invited.'

In the days and years after that, the term Ghutna became a euphemism used both as an adjective to describe a particularly social social 'do' and a noun to refer to the people who threw themselves into the socializing. For instance, 'And how was last night's party? Was it a Ghutna evening?' my mother might ask one of her friends.

'Oh, the Ghutnas were out in full force. Falling and peeling, falling and peeling, scrambling up the social ladder and falling and peeling. I tell you, the place was just awash with blood.'

'And how are your own knees?'

'Raw, darling, raw.'

Karim and I always encouraged our parents to go to as many parties as they could bear. We loved the morning-after parodies. But best of all were parties thrown by his parents or mine, because then we could watch the absurdity up close and, between laughs, pause to admire the elegance and the aplomb of it all while itching to grow up and have lives just like our parents' lives. The first time I reconsidered that aspiration was at the party my parents threw the day Karim and I got back from Rahim Yar Khan.

Karim and his parents were the first to arrive, both Aunty Maheen and Karim carrying buckets of roses. 'They were just so beautiful,' Aunty Maheen cried out, as she ascended the stairs to the 'upstairs study', where my mother was trying to unwind after the hectic party preparations and my father was gamely attempting to aid the process by playing 'Pack Up Your Troubles' on the hand-held, battery-powered organ he'd given me for my birthday. I was sitting on the arm of his chair, pulling each of his ear lobes in turn in time to the beat.

'And absurdly cheap,' Aunty Maheen continued, stepping into the room. 'So I bought them, buckets and all, from the phoolwalla by the roundabout.' She bent to place a bucket on the ground, and Uncle Ali whisked it out of her hand.

'Maheen, the bottom's muddy. You'll ruin the carpet.' He placed it outside on the marble floor, gesturing Karim to do the same with his bucket.

'Muddy bottom,' my father sang, plunking out the tune of 'Stormy Weather'.

'They're gorgeous, Maheen. Thanks,' Ami said. 'Ali, don't stand there looking cross. Pour yourself a drink. I refuse to start hosting duties until the proper guests arrive.'

Uncle Ali looked at the glass table in the centre of the room, with its vase overspilling with flowers, and frowned. 'You don't have nearly enough vases for that absurd amount of roses, do you?'

'Who needs vases?' My mother stood up, leaned outside and plucked a rose from the bucket. 'We'll make everyone do the tango.' She held the rose up horizontally. 'Like in *Some Like It Hot*.' She snipped off the thorns with Aba's pocketknife, and held the rose to Uncle Ali's mouth. For a moment he continued glaring and then, snap, his teeth closed around the rose stem.

'*Olé!*' Karim and I shouted.

'Duet, duet,' Aunty Maheen said, and sat down next to my father. 'One, two, three.' With more regard for volume than tune, they started bashing out 'Chopsticks' on the organ, while Ami and Uncle Ali twirled around the room in dance, Uncle Ali's feet nimbly avoiding the perils of dancing with a sari. The rose transferred itself from Uncle Ali's mouth to my mother's just as the tune ended, even though their cheeks didn't ever quite touch as they danced.

'Encore, encore,' Karim said when they finished.

'Absolutely not.' Ami collapsed on the sofa and slumped against Aba's shoulder. 'I'm exhausted. You're married to an old hag, Zaf.' She tucked the rose behind my father's ear.

'I've got the old hag on my hands,' Aba sang.

Aunty Maheen handed my mother the discarded thorns from the ashtray, and Ami jabbed Aba's neck with them. Uncle Ali cheered her on.

My analysis of the photograph at Ali and Maheen's wedding was clearly embarrassingly out of step with reality. I looked at my father's hands. Perilously close to being 'delicate'. Some other M, some other Z. Had to be. And if not, so what? Really, so what?

When the doorbell rang to signal the 'actual guests' had started to arrive, Ami said, 'Oh, can't we ignore them?' and I held my breath, hoping she would. But, of course, even as she said that she was already walking towards the door, stopping first to check with Aunty Maheen that the rose exchange hadn't smudged her lipstick.

Karim and I spent the next half-hour finding vases in different rooms and cupboards, and stuffing them full of roses. In between arranging roses, we did hors-d'œuvres twirls around the room, and by the time the first plate of devilled eggs was consumed everyone had arrived.

It wasn't a particularly large party, as Karachi parties go. Fifty people, or thereabouts, almost all of whom had known my parents longer than I had. Designer shalwar-kameezes were still relatively new in Karachi, but I'm quite sure that by then we were past those initial days of designer fever, when every experiment possible with form had been tried on the generic shalwar-kameez, resulting in such absurdities as the dhoti shalwar and the butterfly shalwar – but, let's admit it now, to those of us who had never known the swinging days of Karachi in the sixties there was an exuberance, a delight, in that revival of fashion right under the nose of the military government of the Islamic Republic of Pakistan.

Though I don't remember specifics about anyone's attire at the party it's safe to say that the person most expensively (though not necessarily most tastefully) dressed was Aunty Runty – Primo Ghutna, as Aunty Laila had once called her. Even while my parents had laughed at that remark, something in the way my father slid his glance around to me said that Aunty Laila was taking the easy option of parody. Easy to laugh at Aunty Runty; far harder to look at her and see, as my mother once said, 'a woman from whom loveliness has fled'. You only had to look at her once, and then look at photographs of her before she married, to know the difference between beauty and loveliness. For Aunty Runty, as long as I can remember and I can remember only after her marriage, has as much beauty as money can buy, with more than a little help from her genes, but there is something blasted and hollow about that beauty. When I was at university, a friend showed me a videotape of thousands and thousands of lights strung beneath a velvet-black starry sky; I murmured, 'Beautiful, that's so beautiful,' only to hear her say, 'Those are the lights of refugee camps,' and as I recoiled from the TV image I thought of Aunty Runty.

But back in 1987 refugees were still, to me, little more than a hassle that streamed across the Afghan border with guns and drugs, and Aunty Runty was a figure of fun as she sashayed her way across my parents' living room and clutched my arm. 'Raheenie, sweetie, why haven't you wished me a happy, happy, '87 yet?'

'Nappy Yew Hear,' I said, but it was lost on her.

'Now, darling . . .' Her voice lowered to a whisper. 'Tell all about Asif's brother's elopement. You were there, no?'

'Nothing to tell. Uncle Asif was very happy when he heard about it.'

Aunty Runty lowered her voice further. 'It's OK, you can trust me. Here . . .' She fumbled in her bag and pulled out a tube of lipstick. 'Boys will die for this colour. Take it, go on. Sign of friendship.'

I put my hands up and backed away. 'No, really, thank you.' I looked at the bright red stick that she was swivelling up and down before my eyes as though she intended to hypnotize me with it. 'I'm telling the truth. I was with Uncle Asif when his brother called, and he put it on speaker-phone, so I heard everything, and, really, he was very happy. Planning celebration parties.'

Aunty Runty looked over my shoulder at the mirror and applied a layer of lipstick to her mouth. The previous layer was on the rim of a whisky glass, as was the layer before that and the one before that and the one before that. 'Clever man, Asif,' she said. 'He knew we'd ask you what happened, so he put the call on speaker-phone and pretended he was happy.' She popped the lipstick back in her bag and snapped the clasp closed.

'Why shouldn't he be happy?' I couldn't help asking.

'The girl's a Shi'a.' When I looked confused, she added: 'Asif's Sunni.'

'Yes, but Uncle Asif doesn't seem religious.'

Aunty Runty laughed. 'What's that got to do with it? Every-one wants everyone in their family to marry same to same.' She looked across at her husband, the ghastly Bunty. 'And that doesn't mean same tastes in movies and books, OK. Just how they look on paper. The background. Class, sect, ethnic group: that's what a family looks at when considering who they are willing to be related to through marriage.' For a moment I thought I saw something in her that allowed me to understand how she and my mother had ever been friends, and then it was gone, and she said, 'Though, of course, that worked out for your parents.' She inclined her head to where Ami stood with her hand on Aba's shoulder, talking to Uncle Ali and Aunty Maheen. 'And Maheen no longer seems to mind that your father didn't want to marry her because she's Bengali. Although, I have to say, I was appalled when I first heard the engagement was broken. I said to your father, she's not even that dark, Zafar. Many people can't even tell where she's from.'

What an idiot, I thought. Does she really expect me to take her seriously?

'Excuse me,' I said. 'I have to help Karim with the hors-d'œuvres.'

'With Karim, you can't tell at all. That he's half-Bengali. Never guess it. But let's see – if one day you decide your friend Karim is husband material, what will Daddy say to that?'

'Daddy just wants me to be happy,' I said, and left her to her whisky.

'She's such a bitch,' I said, when I reached Karim.

'Raheen!'

'Well, she is. But I'm not going to tell you what she said, because it'll make you sick.' It was making me sick even though I knew it to be a lie. What prompted people to make up this kind of story? I looked around the room and, for a moment, for the first time, the room divided into two before my eyes, and in one group were people who were at the party because they were my parents' friends, and in the other group were people who were there because they wanted to drink, and they wanted to be seen, and they wanted most of all not to have to sit at home with themselves.

'Ali, yaar, Ali, mate, there you are.' Aunty Runty's husband slapped Uncle Ali on the back. 'Hear you're thinking of khisko-ing from the country, packing up in Paki-land.'

Beside me, Karim went very still.

Uncle Ali shrugged. 'Just a thought, Bunty. Nothing decided.'

'Oh, what's to think about? The place is going to hell. Might as well get out. And when you do, I'm buying your house. Don't even think of showing it to someone else, OK, mate?'

'Outside,' Karim said. We slipped past the guests to the garden and hoisted ourselves on to the boundary wall. I was content to sit on the wall, cross-legged, looking out at the pye-dogs padding across the quiet side street, but Karim stood up so that he could look down to the sea. It was too dark for him to see all the way to Clifton Beach, but he liked to believe he could discern tremors in the distant darkness, signifying waves.

'He's not really serious, Karimazov. He'll never leave Karachi. It's just talk. I mean, what would he do without my parents around? What would they do? Your parents without my parents is like . . . it's like . . . me and Zia and Sonia without you.' What I'd really meant was 'It's like me without you' but somehow it came out differently.

'I've already started thinking of Karachi as a place that I have to say goodbye to; every day I say goodbye to some part of it and then two days later I see that part again and I feel so relieved but also not, because then I have to say goodbye to it again. This must be what dying is like.'

That boy could really spoil the mood of an evening.

To change the subject I said, 'Aunty Runty says Aba didn't marry your mother because she's Bengali.'

Karim sat down. 'Well, it was 1971.'

'So?'

'The year of the Civil War. East Pakistan became Bangladesh.'

75

'Thanks for the history lesson. What are you trying to say about my father?'

Karim shrugged. 'Nothing. But of course people must have assumed that the ethnic thing was a factor.'

He's a muhajir.

He's *not Bengali, he's not.*

I wrapped my arms tight against my chest. 'Do you believe that?'

Karim pulled a leaf off a guava tree and bit off its tip. 'No.'

'Why are you eating a leaf?'

'I'm saying goodbye to it.'

He handed me the leaf. I looked down at the severed veins and ran my finger along Karim's tooth marks. 'It's easy to leave a leaf, Cream. But how do you say goodbye to the peepul tree? How do you eat your roots?'

He put his arm around me as he hadn't done since we were very young and not yet self-conscious about his boyarm and my girlshoulder. Spine to spine and foot to foot was fine, but this embrace we'd both cut out of our lives as soon as we were old enough to get embarrassed by the silliness of our peers and our elders who said: 'Oh, boyfriend girlfriend! Early starters, haina?'

He put his arm around me. That was all. He put his arm around me and we didn't say a word.

. . .

'Do you really think your father will decide you should move to London?'

It was break time, a few weeks into the start of the school term, and Sonia, Zia and Karim were sitting in our favourite spot, on the cement ground by the flagpole in the front yard, eating chilli chips. I had wandered off for a few minutes to find out from my house captain how soon netball practice would start – typically the netball season was in December, but because of the trouble in the city at the end of the previous year our entire sports calendar had been thrown into disarray. ('And they say the elite aren't affected by what's happening in the city,' I'd quipped to Karim a few weeks earlier when I found out softball had been cancelled altogether and my pitching arm would have to languish in mothballs until the following year; because he knew I was just trying to get his hackles up he calmly slid a piece of ice down the back of my shirt and paid my comment no further attention.) When I returned to join Sonia and the two boys, I found they'd somehow strayed on to that unmentionable matter of Uncle Ali's immigration plans.

'Of course he won't.' I answered Sonia before Karim could say anything. At that moment I believed it. The world was a joyful place that break-time because, minutes earlier, Zia had taken my dupatta off my shoulder where it hung like a limp rag and tied it on the sleeve of his blue blazer as an arm-band. Two evenings earlier we'd watched some awful adaptation of the Arthurian legends on TV – surely as he (with an air of absent-mindedness) knotted the dupatta above his elbow he must have thought of a knight wearing his true love's handkerchief into battle as a sign of her favour.

'Let's not even think about it,' Karim said, looking past us to the bowler charging down the concrete pitch of the playing field, his Imranesque run-up undisturbed by a football shooting past him from one of the competing games on the field. 'Things are better now than they were a few weeks ago, right? Maybe it'll keep getting better.'

Zia and I nodded, but Sonia shook her head. 'We don't know half the things that go on. My father won't let my mother go and visit all our relatives in other parts of town. He says there's too much they'll expect us to do, there's too little we can do or say without flaunting.' None of us knew what to say to that, and we all looked at one another uncomfortably, until Sonia relieved the moment of its awkwardness by speaking again. 'But if you do. Move to London, I mean.'

'Yes?' Karim prompted her.

'Well, it's just that, if you meet the Queen.'

'The Queen?' I said.

'Yes, the Queen. Will you ask her something for me?'

'Sonia.' Karim laid a hand on her arm. 'I'm not going to meet the Queen.'

'How do you know? Last year my neighbour was there. In London. Just walking in Hyde Park, taking a short cut from somewhere to somewhere else and she met Amitabh Bachhan. And' – triumphantly – 'he's not even English.'

'What!' Zia stood up and yelled, loudly enough to make a cat leap out of the bushes around the flagpole and scamper across the yard into the shade of the stone colonial building that housed our school: 'Amitabh Bachhan isn't English!'

The principal, who was English, as English as only an Englishman in Pakistan can be, walked past with a baleful look in Zia's direction. Zia saluted him and sat down.

'Ok, so, Sonia, what do you want me ask the Queen?'

'I just want to know if she got really depressed when they aged her on the coins.'

That statement could quite easily have come out of Karim's or my mouth; the difference was, Sonia wasn't trying to be funny.

'Coin-age. Ageing the head of a coin.' Sonia smiled at the addition to her list of compound words. 'Do you think they at least ask her before they do it?'

'Of course,' I replied. 'They write a letter. "Dear Queen, we would like to droop your jowls and thicken your neck. Is that OK?" '

'No, no,' Karim said, slapping my wrist with the end of his school tie and cutting in before I could develop the letter further. 'No one tells her. She doesn't know. After all, she has no use for money, so she never looks at coins. And anyone visiting her has to go through a metal detector; they check you aren't carrying any coins that show her looking old.'

'So avoid squeans,' Sonia said, taking a sip from my bottle of Coke. 'The squeals of a queen.'

'Yes,' Zia joined in. He started to take off his blazer, was impeded by my dupatta knotted round his sleeve, and just shrugged and sat back, his blazer half-off. I decided to interpret his unwillingness to unknot the dupatta as a good sign. 'Yes,' he said again. He affected a John Cleese accent: 'Are those all the coins you have? All right. Wait a minute. What's that stuck to the sole of your shoe? It's a 1986 coin! . . . What? That's the only one? Well, I'm sorry, sir, we simply can't take your word for it. Please step into that room with my associate. It's time to bring on the rubber gloves.'

Sonia furrowed her brow. 'Rubber gloves? Like for washing dishes with?'

Zia, Karim and I slapped our knees and laughed and laughed, and if Zia looked at Sonia in a way that neither Karim nor I looked at Sonia, I was simply too happy or too oblivious to notice it. Secret passions lurked in the breast of my boy Zia, but I was stupid enough to mistake the dupatta on his sleeve for his heart.

To sum up our little love triangle: I had a crush on Zia and Zia had a crush on Sonia and Sonia worried about hell. Hell is being a teenager worrying about hell, but Sonia exercised a steely grip on anything resembling a hormone and choked the life out of it. Once, soon after we had become friends, I tried convincing her to let her imagination run wild with some guy, any guy – there had to be someone out there – and she just smiled that wicked smile of hers that undercut her every dutiful utterance and said, 'When you know you're going to have an arranged marriage, you start preparing early on. I'm a lot happier than you, have you noticed?'

'So what do you think about to make yourself happy while I'm sitting here getting so blue I'm purple over Zia?'

'Heaven.' And then she looked so pious I knew she was joking.

Sonia was, we used to say, 'from a conservative family'. Or, at least, that's how Karim used to put it, though Zia was more apt to say, 'They're just not like us, yaar, though Sonia's got potential.' Conservative or not-like-us, put it however you want. The fact was, Sonia couldn't go to parties if boys were going to be there; she couldn't sit alone in a car with a boy for even a second, which is why Zia would always pick me up before picking her up even though that made no logistical sense; she couldn't speak to boys on the telephone unless the door was open and her parents could hear everything. There were plenty of girls at school with me who had much the same restrictions, but Sonia's family was the most 'not like us' of all because none of our parents knew her parents, none of our cousins were married to her cousins, none of our uncles had done business with her uncles. So naturally everyone concluded that it was shady, very shady, dealings that had enabled her father to move his family to the poshest part of town, enrol his daughter in the most elite school in the nation, and install those gold taps in his bathroom.

Zia was particularly scathing about the gold taps. And about the general décor of Sonia's house. 'Let's go over to Horror House,' he'd often say. 'I feel like a laugh. Let's go and see the latest acquisitions. What will they think of next? Leopard-print cushion covers made of real leopard skin? A reproduction of the Sistine Chapel ceiling? Diamond-encrusted calligraphy on the nameplate, with an armed guard employed to shoot on sight anyone who ventures too close to it? Any and all of the above are possible when there's enough money to buy everything except good taste. Come on, Raheen!' He never just said, 'Let's go and visit Sonia,' so perhaps I should have seen how hard he was trying to cover up his desire for her company, but I didn't. I didn't see anything at all in those days, least of all how strong a part Sonia's conservatism played in my friendship with her. If she had been willing to entertain romantic notions, surely she would have entertained them about Zia, and how would I have forgiven her that?

We were still laughing about the rubber gloves when someone called out my name. It was the fast bowler who had remained unfazed by the football. 'You want anything from the tuck shop, Raheen?' he called out. I had known him all my life; his parents used to live next door to us. But he was two years older than I, and when he entered the Senior School and I was left behind in the Junior School he'd stopped acknowledging my presence. Among some of my classmates, he was something of a heart-throb. Too surprised by this turnaround after four years of silence to decide whether I wanted another Coke or packet of chilli chips, I just shook my head and raised my hand in a gesture that might have been a 'thank you'.

Sonia poked me in the ribs. 'What was that?'

I shrugged. Zia was struggling back into his blazer, flipping up the collar and then smoothing it back down again. Nothing like a fifteen-year-old fast bowler to make a thirteen-year-old look like a novice in the game of cool. I had to bite back the urge to say to Zia, 'Oh, just give up.'

'I think he likes you,' Sonia whispered. The fast bowler had turned round to look at me again, and I swear he winked. 'He's really cute.'

I didn't agree with that latter assessment at all, but Zia was not looking happy so I said, with all the casualness at my disposal, 'Maybe I'll go out with him.'

'What?' Karim turned to me. 'Don't be so stupid.'

'What's your problem?' I said. He had turned quite red.

'He's right, though. It would be really dumb to go out with that guy,' Zia said. I almost didn't hear him; I was too busy trying to figure out what was making Karim so upset. Surely he knew I was joking? And if he didn't, that still didn't explain his attitude.

'He doesn't respect girls.' Karim was sounding positively huffy.

'Respect isn't what I want from him.' I tried to smile in a knowing way.

'Shut up, Raheen,' Karim shouted.

'Oho!' Sonia put a hand on both our wrists. 'Raheen's not that kind of girl, Karim. Don't worry about her.'

'What kind of girl am I not?'

'The kind of girl Betty is,' Zia said.

'Huh?' The three of us turned to stare at him.

'Yeah,' Zia said. He had tied my dupatta into a bandanna around his forehead, and was lying back on his elbow, lord of all he surveyed. 'Betty who I met in London last summer. I didn't mention it before because, you know, I do respect girls. I don't kiss-and-tell.'

'That's because you don't kiss,' Karim said. 'Where did this Betty suddenly come from?'

Zia raised an eyebrow. 'Don't get jealous, Karim. She was this girl I met last summer in London. We . . . well, a gentleman doesn't talk about that kind of stuff.'

He was really such a terrible liar that I couldn't even begin to feel jealous. Or was it that I didn't even begin to feel jealous and decided that was because he was a terrible liar?

'Zia!' Sonia said, appalled.

'Oh, rubbish, rubbish, rubbish.' Karim started laughing. 'OK, go on, describe her to us. What colour was her hair?'

'Golden.'

Karim and I shrieked with laughter. 'You could at least—' I said, and burst into laughter again.

'– At least say blonde,' Karim finished.

Sonia scrunched up her face and looked from Zia to Karim and me. 'Blonde Betty? Archie comics?'

'Archie comics!' Karim was bent double, his face almost touching my knee. 'Show some originality, man.'

Zia stood up, and flung my dupatta to the ground.

'Oh hey, Zia, come on,' Karim said. 'We're just joking around. Sit down, yaar, come on.'

Zia was looking at Sonia. I was looking at Zia and trying not to notice that I thought he was being ridiculous.

'Don't be angry,' Sonia reached a hand out and lightly touched his sleeve. 'I'm sure there really are blonde Bettys in London. Aren't there?' She turned to Karim and me, a fierce look on her face, daring us to contradict her.

Karim and I nodded. Karim nodded a little more fervently than I did. The bell rang, and so Zia was saved from having to decide whether to sit down again or not. Karim held out a hand, and Zia pulled him up. Karim turned towards me, and I started to hold my hand out to him, but found I was turning the gesture into something else, pretending I was only reaching up to pat the top of my own head. Sonia stood up and pulled me up, and we walked towards the school building, Sonia's arm around me, and the two boys close in conversation, a gap between them and us that seemed right somehow, seemed comfortable, and at the same time was quite new.

If Karim moved to London, would he meet Blonde Bettys?

• • •

It was probably soon after that conversation in the school yard that Zia called me up, late one evening, proposing a visit to Sonia's.

'I can't,' I said, rather feebly. 'There's school tomorrow and it's already after ten.'

'Come on,' he said. 'Your parents are at Runty and Bunty's beach party, aren't they? Mine are too. And, guess what, so are Sonia's parents. Aunty Runty told Mummy this morning that Bunty had invited them; he's such a loser, he'll invite anyone with a bank balance that goes into seven digits. OK, eight digits maybe.'

'I suppose I could call my parents and ask them . . .'

'Raheen! There aren't any phones at the beach. Besides, even if there were, you know your parents would say no. Come on, sneak out. Just once. I'll have you back within an hour.'

'Well . . .'

'I've got my neighbours' Merc.'

'What do you mean you've got it?'

'I have the keys. They're out of town for the next few days.'

'And they gave you the keys?'

'Details, details. I'll be there in ten minutes. Call Karim. Tell him we'll be at his place in thirteen minutes and tell Sonia we'll be there in eighteen.'

I dialled Karim's number and hung up after one ring. Then I did the same with Sonia's number. When Zia walked into my room, twirling unfamiliar car-keys, I said, 'Called the other two but no one answered their phones. I think Karim's at his cousin's place and maybe Sonia's gone to sleep already.'

'We'll stop at her place to check.'

Oh, great.

'Come on,' he said. 'This is going to be the ride of your life.'

He really did have his neighbour's Mercedes. It was red and it was cool. 'Wow!' I said out loud, forgetting that I had to be as quiet as possible so that none of the servants would know I was leaving and report me to my parents the next day.

Zia winked and flipped up the collar of his shirt. He opened the passenger side door for me and then slid across the bonnet to the driver's side. I thought I would faint with delirium.

We took the long route to Sonia's house via back roads, Zia gunning the engine for all it was worth. In those days that part of Defence was still comparatively uninhabited, so the back roads at night were deserted and Zia zigzagged from one side of the road to the other, weaving between street lamps, pretending to be out of control. I felt crazy enough to say or do anything, even to say, 'How's this for an idea, Zee? You and me. Is that an idea or is that an idea?' and I probably would have, except that the music was blaring too loudly, Springsteen singing 'No Surrender' and Zia lip-synching along, banging his palm against the steering wheel. When I hear that song today I'm almost-fourteen again and back in that car and nothing in the world is impossible except a broken heart.

We drove into a pitch-dark street and I said, 'Electricity's gone; yes, bye-bye, bijli.' A repair truck from the Karachi Electricity Supply Corporation rolled up and Zia said, 'KESC to the rescue . . . Oh, I know which song we have to listen to.' He rewound the tape all the way to the beginning and Status Quo's 'In the Army Now' blared through the speakers. 'Sing, girl,' he said, and together we drowned out Rick Parfitt and Francis Rossi's voices: 'Bijli fails in the dead of night/Won't help to call "I need a light"/You're in Karachi now/Oh, oh, you're in Karachi now.'

Volume turned up all the way, despite the fact we were now in a built-up residential neighbourhood with our windows wide open, we serenaded the streets: 'Night is falling and you just can't see/Is this illusion or KESC/You're in Karachi now.'

We didn't even hear the first shot. If Zia hadn't turned to look at me and seen through my window the gunman run out on to the street . . .

But he did. He yelled, 'Duck,' pushed me down, my hand on the volume knob jerked in surprise, the music disappeared, the rat-tat-tat-tat against the car, Zia so low in his seat he can't possibly see out of the windscreen, his foot on the accelerator, we fly over a speed bump, bang my head on the glove box, a thump against the front of the car, Zia mutters, 'Cat. Has to be. Cat.' I don't even look to check, he's zigzagging, taking turns so fast I swear all four wheels leave the ground. 'He was on foot, Zia, on foot,' I scream, but I'm still huddled, sweat all over, and finally he stops. 'We're OK,' he says. 'We're OK.'

He stepped out of the car before I did. We were on the main road, under a street light. A house a few doors down was festooned with fairy lights; the wedding season was at its height. The gate was wide open and girls holding rose garlands stood near the entrance, waiting for the imminent arrival of the baaraat. Music spilled out over the walls. Hé Jamalo. If we walked into that house we'd probably recognize someone there. But how would I explain being out with Zia, alone, at this hour? I tried to open the door but it was stuck, so I rolled down the window in time to see Zia in front of the car, wiping something off the mudguard. He held up his palm, plastered with bloodied fur. 'Cat,' he said. 'Told you. A silly-billy cat.' We both started laughing. I was half-in, half-out, of the car window, and as my hysteria grew I slapped my palm against the exterior of the door and felt something sharp bite into my skin.

'Zia, come here.' I slid out of the window, found my legs weren't working properly and sat down hard on the street. A wavy line of bullet holes ran all the way across the front and back door, just centimetres below the window. I bent forward at the waist and touched the tip of my finger to the jagged metal that marked a bullet's point of entrance. Hot. I jerked my finger away. What that thing could do to flesh. How my body would convulse. Thrown forward into the windshield. No pain, just burning. Seared.

And then this sentence, in these words exactly, came to mind: they cannot protect you against this.

I turned over, on to all fours, gasping when I expected to retch. Zia had walked over to stand next to me, and I saw him move his foot away as a line of spittle fell from my mouth. I knew I would never forget that gesture. I wiped my mouth against the back of my hand, and thought of rubbing my hand against his jeans, but when I turned my head to look at him, he was staring at the bullets in a kind of wonder that made me think of religious awe. 'It missed me,' he said, and flexed his shoulders, savouring the easy movement of his muscles. 'It's so easy to miss.' I pushed myself off the ground and stood next to him.

He switched on the torch attached to his key chain and shone it into a bullet hole. 'I can see it lodged there.' He leaned in through the open window. 'Yup,' he said.

I leaned in next to him. He was running his fingers along the protruding bumps in the car door. If the gun had been just a little more powerful, the bullets would have ripped through the door's inner sheet of steel.

'Man,' Zia said. 'They almost got you. Man. Your parents would have killed me. Karim, too. And Sonia. Man.'

I think I would have bashed his head against the car door if I hadn't seen the fingers of one hand gripping white on to the side mirror. Is this moment an exception, I somehow found the clarity to wonder, or is his cool demeanour always a mask? As he tried to light a cigarette, I looked away so that he wouldn't know I could see him snapping the heads off matches in his attempt to strike them against the flint.

'Damn wind's too strong to get a flame going,' he muttered, and tossed the matches back into the car.

I stepped back. 'Zia, the car,' I said.

He looked at the ravaged vehicle and this time he allowed stark terror to write itself across his face. I saw blood rush to his face and drain away as he slumped against the bonnet of the Mercedes. I put my hand on his shoulder, thinking that if he fell apart now he wouldn't be able to drive us home.

'The police. I have to go to the police,' he said, straightening up.

'Don't be stupid. What can they do?' We were both whispering.

'Have to register a complaint. The car. It's not my car. They never said I could . . . I stole the keys from my father; they gave him a spare set so he could run the engine every so often while they're away. They never said I could. He doesn't know. I have to be responsible. I have to be responsible. Insurance. I have to register a complaint with the police. When my cousin's car . . . He had to. Insurance purposes. I have to register.'

'Zia, I want to go home.'

He nodded. Blinked. Nodded again. 'Police station is no place for a girl. I'll drop you home and go. Won't mention your name. Your parents won't have to know.'

We drove home very slowly, stopping not just at the red lights but also at the amber ones. I can't remember a word Zia said but he could no more stop talking than I could start. When he dropped me off I said, 'Maybe I should come . . .' and was more than relieved when he shook his head.

'Call me when you get home. Promise, Zia.'

My first instinct when I stepped inside the house was to call my father. But there were no phones at the beach. Karim. I'd call Karim. But if it would have been hard to explain to the people at the wedding what I was doing out alone with Zia at that hour, it was somehow even more unthinkable to explain it to Karim, who would ask for no explanation, offer no comment. But my house was so silent, the gunshots still echoed so loudly in my head, and I needed to hear Karim's voice, I needed him to laugh and make me laugh. But no, I couldn't call Karim. I had to keep the line free in case Zia tried to call.

I sat down on the marble steps, unable to decide whether to go upstairs or down. If the gunman had aimed just a little higher, the bullet would have gone through the open window and hit me . . . *here*. I pressed a finger against the flesh halfway between elbow and shoulder. And if it had gone all the way through my arm it would have lodged itself here, between these two ribs. (The next morning I was to have two bruises exactly where I imagined the bullets would have hit. I didn't know whether to be terrified or exhilarated by my body's fidelity to recording the possible, and I briefly tried to imagine if I could turn into some kind of superhero if every morning my skin marked all the possible consequences of the previous night's follies. But then I remembered my fingers digging into my flesh, reassuring myself of its wholeness.)

'Damn you, Zia, call.' I curled up, my head resting uncomfortably on the edge of the step above me, and let hot tears spill on to my sleeve. 'Call, so I know you're OK. Call so that I can call Karim. Aba, come home. Please come home.'

Over an hour later Zia still hadn't called and no one answered his phone. No sign of my parents either. And again and again in my head: *they cannot protect you from this*. When I tried to force myself to think of something else, something silly that would mean nothing, I thought: *the hippo told the rhino piggledypoo and smartypants and what else?* But only part of that stuck. *They cannot protect you from this. And what else?* So I called Karim. All I said was, 'This is quick, in case Zia tries to call. But we went for a drive in his neighbour's car and someone shot at us and we're OK but he went to the police station and he should be home by now but he's not.'

An improbably short time after I hung up and went to the dining room to look out of the window, Karim climbed over the gate and jumped down into the driveway. I think that was the first real moment, the first inkling. If I had to start this story again, perhaps that would be the place to start. Stars, moon, blue-black sky, and a boy's head easing into the frame. He was not attractive, not well-proportioned, and he half fell over as he landed, but when I saw his head appear over the gate I clutched the curtains tight and said, 'Thank you, God, thank you.' And I thought, 'So that was loneliness, and this is loneliness ended.'

When I went out to meet him, he clutched my hands very tightly, and we just stood there, looking at each other, rocking back and forth on our toes, like birds. When he spoke it was to say, 'Which police thaanaa did he go to? Do you know?' I shook my head.

I got into the back seat of his car, and Karim sat in front with Altaf, his driver, who kept yawning as he drove, his eyes narrowing into squints, not yet reconciled to being awake. We spotted the Mercedes, after what seemed an interminable while, parked outside the third police station to which we drove. Karim had said only three things during our search for Zia: 'That fake driver's licence won't fool anyone', 'If only there was a map with police thaanaas marked on it, so we could do this efficiently' and 'You don't know how much money he had on him, do you?'

Outside the station, Karim and Altaf ran their hands along the pockmarked Mercedes door. Altaf inserted a finger into a bullet hole, just below the passenger side window. His finger disappeared almost down to the knuckle. I didn't feel anything when I saw that. I wondered if I was in shock. Karim knelt down by the mudguard and vanished from my line of sight. I walked around the car to see him staring down at his blood-streaked fingers. 'Cat,' I said.

'Did it die?'

I pictured a bloodied and bleeding feline dragging its shattered limbs along the road. 'We have to go back there.'

'Zia first, OK?'

'You go in,' Altaf told Karim. 'I'll stay here with her.'

Karim glanced at me, expecting an objection to this moment of 'Let's protect the girl from unpleasantness', but I felt only gratitude towards Altaf. 'Sack boon,' Karim said.

I don't know if he really was back soon or not. It could have been two minutes or twenty that I lay in the back of his car, trying to remember how to breathe evenly, before he opened the door and said, 'You've got to come inside.'

I thought, cat homicide. Fleeing the scene of an accident. I thought, it wasn't cat fur but human hair on the mudguard. I thought, I wasn't driving. I'm not responsible for anything.

'It's OK,' Karim said, taking my hand. 'They only want you to confirm you were in the car with him.

Then they'd say, what were you doing alone in a car late at night with a boy who is neither brother nor cousin nor husband?

'I've told them you're his cousin,' Karim said. 'And I'm your brother.'

He leaned to a side and the street lamp lit up the back of his head. 'You have a halo,' I said with a laugh and found myself able to step out of the car.

Inside the police station a grey-shirted, mustachioed policeman, whose resemblance to Pakistan's wicketkeeper, Saleem Yousuf, was immensely reassuring, asked me if I could confirm my brother's claim that I had been in the Mercedes with my cousin. I nodded and, laughing, he shouted to someone to bring the boy out. 'Sorry for this,' he said, spreading his hands. 'But he kept insisting he was alone in the car.'

A door opened and Zia emerged, his upturned collar looking absurd. When he saw us he tried to reassemble his expression into something approaching jauntiness, but it crumpled into relief instead. The Saleem Yousuf lookalike threw the Mercedes car-keys in his direction and gestured towards the door.

'What happened?' Zia and Karim said to each other in unison when we exited.

'You first,' Karim said. We got into the Mercedes – the front door was still jammed, so I climbed in through the window – and Karim signalled Altaf to follow us in his car.

'I don't know. I don't know what was going on. I went in, reported that someone had shot at my car, and they asked what colour the car was and where it happened. I said, "Near the Arab

Sheikh's palace, and it's a Mercedes." One of the cops looked out, saw the car and said, "It's red," and then they demanded to know who had been with me. Well, I didn't want to drag Raheen into it, so I said no one. Next thing I know, they've got me in this room and this big guy with really bad b.o. – who looks like Mike Gatting, there's some weird cricket thing going on there – is telling me I can't leave until I tell them who I was with. So now I'm completely confused and don't know if it'll make matters better or worse if I admit my original story wasn't true, so I decide just to wait. I knew you'd get worried, Raheen, when I didn't call, and that you guys or my parents would come in search of me.'

'They didn't hurt you or anything, did they?' I said.

Zia shrugged. 'Nah. I mentioned Uncle Wahab's name.'

'He's been suspended on corruption charges.'

'I know that, Karim. That's why they didn't let me out at the first mention of the first syllable of his name. But they're underlings, you know, and everyone knows the suspension won't last. They wouldn't let me sleep, though. Shook me awake when I tried heading into the land of Z. I tried mentioning another few names to them, of friends of my father's, but I think I overdid my list of connections and they were sure I was making it up.' He pulled up to Tony Paan Shop – which was not called Tony Paan Shop at all, but had somehow acquired the name even though no one named Tony worked there – and beeped his horn to signal for a packet of cigarettes.

A young boy standing outside the shop (more a cubbyhole with shutters than a shop) raised his hand to acknowledge the signal and Zia said to Karim, 'Pay him when he brings it, will you. I've left my wallet at home.'

Karim held out his empty wallet. 'Had to give Saleem Yousuf everything I had.'

'Why?'

'Because you're months away from turning fourteen and the minimum driving age is eighteen.'

'Oh, shit.' Zia leaned out and yelled to the paan shop boy: 'I don't have any money.'

The boy came over with a single cigarette. 'Take this.'

Zia looked at the brand name stamped on the cigarette. 'I can't smoke this.'

Karim made a noise of disgust and got out of the car. 'I'll borrow some money from Altaf.'

Seconds later, Zia lit up and sat back in his seat. 'Your turn, Karim. What really happened?'

'Can you drive us home?' I said. Tony who wasn't Tony was pulling down the shutters of his shop, and even the beggars had gone home – or gone away – for the night.

'Good thinking.' Zia smiled, and for the first time since the gun shots I remembered I was in love with him.

He started the car again and as we headed towards my house Karim told us why Zia had been treated like a criminal for having a bullet-marked car. There had been a series of burglaries in Phase V, where we all lived, in the preceding weeks, and the police had been unable to apprehend the perpetrators. (The Saleem Yousuf lookalike told Karim this in a mixture of Urdu and Punjabi but he said 'perpetrators' in English, pronouncing it as two words: perpa traitors.) Earlier that evening the dacoits had struck again, but this time their getaway car was spotted. The car was red. So the police alerted all the armed guards who were employed to protect the wealthiest houses in the neighbourhood.

'What exactly does "alerted" mean?' Karim asked the policeman.

The policeman smiled. 'We said, if you see a red car, going fast, with two people in the front seat, shoot them. We advised shooting at the tyres, so that the car would stall, but, you know, some of these guards don't have much skill at marksmanship. Also, they get quite bored, so any chance for excitement . . . Anyway, one of the guards told us he had shot a red car, near the Sheikh's palace, which had two people in the front seat. That's how we knew your cousin was lying to us about being alone. We couldn't let him go until we knew the truth, just in case he was involved with the thefts. But, of course, if you say a girl was with him . . . that explains things.'

'That's absurd,' Zia said, pulling up to my gate. 'It's a Mercedes. Since when do dacoits drive around in a Mercedes?'

. . .

When bullets have missed you by inches, you should assume you've expended your quota of good luck for the night. All the same, I was keeping my fingers crossed as we drove home, hoping my parents were still at the beach, or that they'd returned, exhausted, and gone to sleep without noticing my absence. But when Zia turned on to my street, there was no mistaking Aba standing on the boundary wall, binoculars trained on the Mercedes. Only when we pulled up in front of the gate, just inches away from him, did he lower the binoculars and call out in the direction of the house, 'It's them, Yasmin! Phone the others.'

'I'll take the blame,' Zia whispered to me. 'Get out and explain. Give whatever version you want.'

I was half-convinced he'd drive away instead, which is why I kept sitting in the car, forcing my father to lower himself from the wall and come over to us.

He walked around to Zia's side, and didn't lean down to look in, but stood straight, drumming his fingers on the roof of the car. Zia, Karim and I looked at one another, uncertain of how to proceed.

'Well, he's your father,' Zia whispered finally.

'You're sitting closer to him,' I replied.

In the end, I think it was the irritation of that drumming sound rather than any chivalric impulse that made Zia poke his head out of the window. 'Sorry, Uncle. Got excited about having this car. Mercedes, Uncle Zafar. Could you have resisted going for a spin when you were young?'

'Oh, very smooth, Zia,' Karim muttered from the back seat.

Zia tried again. 'Sorry, really. But back in one piece. If Raheen would just get out, I wouldn't hold you up any longer. Altaf's

95

behind us, see? He can drop Karim home and I'll drive back to my place and then we can all go to sleep, because it is late, I know, and we have school tomorrow and so if Raheen would just get out . . .'

Aba's hand reached in, pulled the key out of the ignition and pointed towards the house. 'Yes, sir, absolutely, Uncle. My parents aren't still at the beach, are they?'

By this time my mother had come outside, and walked around to my side of the car. Karim groaned. I suddenly realized why Zia had wanted me to get out so that he could drive off. I continued looking straight ahead, so I didn't see Ami's expression as she realized what the bullet holes were, but I heard her gasp.

'Where were you when this happened?' she asked me, pointing to the bullet holes.

'Right here,' I replied, from the passenger seat.

The looks we place on our parents' faces when we show them the jagged evidence that we are living in violent times, no escape from it. No mere fluke that it came our way, no, not a fluke but something closer to probability, something closer to the roll of a die. Those looks that we have never seen until that moment, but we know they've seen them in their imaginations, their dreams, in their mirrors that time last year when we were late coming home from school because there seemed no harm in loitering around the school yard and then there seemed no harm in stopping for sugar-cane juice halfway between departure point and destination. How do they forgive us every time, I wondered, as my father came round to my side of the car, his expression mirroring my mother's before he even saw the bullet holes; how have they forgiven us already?

Aba leaned through the window to hug me, one hand smacking the back of my head while the other one gripped my shoulder. 'My baby,' he said. 'My baby.'

'I'm fine, it's fine.' For the first time in my life I felt I needed to be the adult, reassuring my father that the world was still in order. But how could the world be in order if I was that one doing the reassuring? *Crack a joke, Aba. Issue a command. Tell me nothing like this will happen again.*

But he did none of these things, just held on to me, until Ami pulled him away and said, 'It's OK, darling.' I don't know which one of us she was speaking to, but it got my father to stand up straight and it got me to climb out of the car. When I explained what had happened Aba put one arm around me and another around Karim, reassuring rather than asking for reassurance this time, but Ami merely took Zia by the shoulder and said, 'Do you realize how lucky you are that I'm too relieved to be really angry?' I was completely mortified, of course, but Zia didn't hold it against me, just said, 'Yes, Aunty. Sorry, Aunty. Maybe I should call my parents.'

As we were walking towards the house, Ami put a hand on my shoulder and said, 'Why is it that the only thing you resemble me in is your wilfulness?'

I looked at Aba and then at Zia. 'And your weakness for gorgeous men,' I said.

She started to laugh, then forced a stern look on to her face. 'You're still in disgrace. Don't think this matter is over,' she said, in a voice that suggested terrible rules being prepared to curtail my freedom. I was hardly reassured when she put an arm around me and kissed me on the top of the head. My mother had been sufficiently wilful as a teenager to know exactly how wilful teenagers needed to be handled, and we both knew that a gentle word of admonishment would have as little effect on me as it would have had on her some twenty-five years ago. She left me to ponder the suffering I would have to endure and quickened her pace to catch up with Karim and whisper something that made him smile and look back at me.

Of course Karim wasn't in disgrace at all, but he was hardly the kind of boy to sit around looking chipper while his two friends were awaiting punishment, so when his parents and Zia's parents were called and all of us made to sit in the upstairs study to await their arrival, he didn't gloat or look satisfied but bit his lip and looked as nervous as Zia and I did. It wasn't long afterwards that we heard Aba open and close the front door, and then open and close it again. There was some conversation that was too soft for us to hear, and then Uncle Ali's voice demanded, in a raised but unnaturally even tone, 'For how long do we put up with this kind of thing?' I remember thinking that unfair. We'd never driven off at night in a stolen car and got shot at before.

Before anyone could answer Uncle Ali's question, Zia's father had barrelled into the study, where he picked Zia up by the collar and shook him wordlessly. Zia did nothing more than look down at the floor, but when I saw his father's face contorted in the manner of someone who's trying to remember how to cry I recalled that Zia's brother had been killed by a stray bullet when he was a toddler, back in the days when stray bullets made front-page news.

Zia turned red and extricated himself from his father's grip. 'Let's go, Dad. It's late,' he said, and with a final apology to my parents Zia left, his father two paces behind him.

'If they didn't spoil him so much,' said Ami, with a sigh. 'Still, I understand the impulse.'

Zia never talked about the brother he never knew and the only time I tried to bring up the subject, he said: 'Stray bullet. Funny expression. As though all that bullet needed was a good home and a bone to chew on.'

Karim went straight to his mother as she entered the room, and threw his arms around her, which seemed a little bit excessive considering he hadn't been anywhere near the bullets. Another one of his dramatic moments, I thought. I looked at my mother, and wondered if it would help to fling my arms around her. No, she'd see right through me. My father, on the other hand, would melt if I put my arms around his waist and started crying. How good it would be to put my arms around his waist and start crying. If my mother tried to speak strongly to me after that, he might just tell her I'd suffered enough. The question was: if Zia called me up next week and asked me to go for a drive late at night, just the two of us, would I say yes? Yes. And Ami knew it.

I squared my shoulder, ready to face what was to come, but my mother seemed determined to keep me in suspense, and continued some pointless conversation about the flaws in Zia's parents' child-rearing techniques. So I was almost grateful to Uncle Ali for saying, 'Bloody stupid, Raheen. Zero out of ten for responsibility and honesty. And anyway, as Mercedes go, that one's not very appealing.' I started to smile at him, but stopped when he turned to Karim and said, 'As for you, young man. Bribing police officers? Do you think that makes you a hero?'

'I think it got Zia out of jail.' Karim crossed one ankle over his knee in an exaggerated posture of adulthood.

'Shh, Karim, don't talk to your father like that.' Aunty Maheen sat down next to Karim and stroked his hair. He half-turned, rested his head on her shoulder, and linked his fingers through hers.

Uncle Ali switched the table lamp on and off and on again. 'So if you want to be a good friend, you bribe a policeman. If you stand on ethics, you're a lousy human being.' He looked at my parents. This was clearly a continuation of some other conversation. 'This is not about accepting grey areas any more; it's about a value system that's totally bankrupt.'

'And your solution?' Ami said, her face illuminating and disappearing into shadows by turn as Uncle Ali continued to fidget with the light switch.

'His solution is to leave,' Aba said. 'Isn't that the most bankrupt choice, Ali? To turn your back on something you love because it's grown unmanageable?'

'It's not as though you were never on the verge of doing the same,' Aunty Maheen said softly, still stroking Karim's hair.

What were they all talking about? For heaven's sake, I'd just been shot at.

Aba picked at something lodged beneath his fingernail. 'That was completely different: '71 was madness.'

'But perhaps it would have been best if you had left,' Uncle Ali said.

The reaction to that statement was baffling. Ami started plumping cushions into shape, muttering something about drycleaning; Aba leaned forward towards Uncle Ali and said, 'Have you gone mad, mate?' and Aunty Maheen's hand on Karim's hair started shaking. 'Oh, Ali,' she said. 'Ali, of all the things . . .'

Uncle Ali put up both his hands in a defensive gesture. 'I didn't mean it that way. God, Zaf, you know I wouldn't. Oh, for heaven's sake. You're all being ridiculous. I meant maybe we should all have left and . . . I mean, there is madness here now and it's getting worse, that's what I meant. I meant the country, I'm talking about the country, the government, the people. I don't mean . . . it wasn't personal.' I had never seen him so agitated. He stood up, sat down again, and resumed switching the lamp on and off. 'I need a drink, Zafar.'

'Sorry,' Aba said. 'Had to give Bunty my entire supply of the hard stuff. His bootlegger's gone on Hajj, and he was worried about running short for his party.'

'This is what I mean! What kind of country has this become?' Uncle Ali appeared unaware of my mother moving the lamp away from him. 'Bootleggers! No one in a civilized country should use that word except in jest.'

'Zia and Raheen get shot at and what's worrying him? The illegality of alcohol.' Aunty Maheen rolled her eyes. Precisely. 'Listen, baba, Prohibition happened in the dark distant past, back when I could eat three chocolate éclairs and still look good in a bathing suit the next day, back when you were still . . .' She stopped and looked at Karim, who hadn't moved at all during this whole exchange. That sick feeling I had begun getting whenever Uncle Ali and Aunty Maheen started on at each other in this manner crept over me now. I wanted to announce that I could still hear the gunshots echoing in my ears. I wanted to lean against Uncle Ali's shoulder and cry so that Aunty Maheen would sit down right next to him in order to put an arm around me and tell me it was OK. I wanted to stop thinking, as I looked at them, *And what else? And what else?* I wanted most of all never to mention any of this to Karim.

Uncle Ali turned to my mother. 'Poor Maheen. Stuck with a husband such as I. How long can any woman put up with such suffering? I think some of the Ghutnas are taking bets on that question. Do you think they'll let me place a wager?'

'Karim, Raheen, green tea,' Ami instructed. 'Oh, and call Sonia. I think we managed to make her panic about you.'

Glad to have a reason to leave the room, I accompanied Karim downstairs to the kitchen and called Sonia while he put the water on to boil.

'Oh, thanks God,' Sonia's mother said, when she heard my voice. 'Everything theek-thaak?'

'Everything's fine.' She told me to hang on while she called Sonia, but even after she had gone and there was no one on the line I continued to speak – 'Yes . . . umm hmmm . . . I'm sorry to have caused you concern' – just so Karim would think I was sufficiently distracted not to see his shoulders shake with weeping as he stood with his back to me.

'Who are you talking to and where were you guys?' Sonia shouted into the phone.

I ignored the first part of the question and answered the second, the words falling out of my mouth as though they were a recording. I was looking at Karim's shoulders and thinking how small they looked, how thin, and thinking that if he ever saw me crying he'd put his arms around me, and make me stop.

Sonia said, 'So did you go back? To find the cat?'

If I stayed put and did nothing, he would stop on his own, out of embarrassment. But if I went to comfort him, perhaps he'd start talking, perhaps he'd tell me what I never asked and he never mentioned: what it was like to live with his parents when my parents weren't around to re-channel the conversation. I suppose I had known it for a long while, but that evening was the first occasion I really allowed myself to think that Karim lived in sadness some of the time. The thought was so painful to me that I had to let go of it, had to tell myself that being shot at was making me melodramatic.

'No, idiot,' I said to Sonia, ducking my head so that I wouldn't have to look at Karim. 'We didn't go back for the cat.'

'Where did it happen exactly? I'll tell my father to drive me there. Poor cat could still be limping around.'

'Your father's car is red, Sonia.'

Karim turned around at that, and tried to smile. *Come on, Karimazov. Look, starfish!*

'You think we should just forget the cat?' Sonia's voice was uncertain.

'Put it out of your mind like last term's vocabulary list.' *Yes, like that, smile.* 'Which of our parents called you?'

Sonia laughed. 'All three sets. Ama got quite upset. Wanted to know if I minded that the three of you had gone on some joyride without inviting me round. Not that I'd have got permission on a school night.' She lowered her voice. 'I know you just wanted to be alone with Zia, but you should be careful. You could get a bad reputation.'

'Sonia, please. I'll see you in school, OK? 'Bye.'

I hung up, relieved that Karim was looking like himself again. And sounding like himself, too, as he walked around the kitchen pulling out teacups and spoons, and muttering: 'Is green tea popular in Greenland? When cannibals in Greenland tell their children to eat their greens are they referring to vegetable or meat? What do you call a cannibal who decides to become vegetarian?'

But when we returned upstairs, the atmosphere there hadn't improved at all.

'Things really are going to hell here,' Uncle Ali said, adding eleven grains of sugar to his green tea. 'How long can we just go on taking it? Don't you ever think of getting out, Zafar?'

Aba waved his hand dismissively. 'I can't imagine growing old anywhere but here.'

'Exactly,' Aunty Maheen said. 'I mean, London is fine, but I'll never get used to umbrellas, not to mention the way they talk.'

'The parrot-all parasol. Those talking umbrellas,' Karim whispered to me, but he was trying too hard.

'Really, those accents over there!' Aunty Maheen went on. 'Last time we were there, we had just stepped out of Heathrow and this man came up to us with a cigarette in his hand and said, 'Cu ah geh a lye fro you, plaiz,' so I thought, 'Oh, foreigner. Airport, after all,' but no, he was a local and he was asking if he could get a light from me, please. I thought, Henry Higgins, where are you now? But my point is, if we leave here I'll spend my whole time missing people in Karachi because there are so, so, many to miss that you can't just squeeze in all that missing during your morning cup of tea.'

'If one of those bullets had been aimed just a few inches higher . . .'

'Oh, shut up, Ali,' Ami said, managing not to make the rebuke personal. 'I hate it when you do this sort of thing. Just drink your tea and think calming thoughts. Think of dry-cleaning.'

Karim and I had got up and walked out by now, and Uncle Ali and Aunty Maheen must have seen us close the door and assumed we'd walked immediately away, away and out of hearing, but we hadn't because the string of my garnet necklace broke and Karim and I went down on hands and knees outside the TV room to pick up the fallen stones.

'Not this time, Yasmin,' Uncle Ali replied. 'Look, I know you don't want to think about it, but you've got to. This little incident has made up my mind, I'll tell you that. We're migrating.' At Aunty Maheen's noise of disbelief, he added, 'At least, I am. And I'm taking Karim with me.'

Karim's fist closed around a handful of garnets. My fist closed around Karim's wrist.

Aunty Maheen said, 'Ali, when did you become this person?'

'Stop it now, both of you,' Ami said.

But they didn't. 'I've become my reflection, dear wife. I've become the man I've seen reflected in your eyes for so long.'

'Ali, don't,' Aba pleaded. 'It's been a tense evening; best not to speak. We'll only say things we regret.'

'Regret is an emotion,' Aunty Maheen said. 'It doesn't apply to him.'

I tried pulling Karim away, but he shook me off. 'Karimazov, come on. Let's go to my room. You don't want to hear this.'

While I was speaking I drowned out whatever it was that my father said, but after Karim pushed me away again, the heel of his palm shoving my shoulder, we both heard Aunty Maheen's response. 'Please, Zafar. Don't you, of all people, try to tell me that feelings can't change. How dare you be the one to say that to me.'

Sometimes you hear the voices of people whose every cadence you think you know by heart. By *heart*. But then sounds emerge from their throats, sounds that you want to believe cannot belong to them, but it's worse than that because you know that they do; you hear the sound and you know that this grating cacophony belongs to them as much as does the music in their voices when they call you by nicknames that should sound utterly silly but instead are transformed by affection into something to cherish. I heard Aunty Maheen turn on my father, and I knew that one day, not today perhaps, not even next year, but one day people more familiar to me than the smell of sea air would become strangers and I would become a stranger to them.

'We live too near the surface of things,' I found myself thinking, and did not know what I meant by that. 'We live too near the surface of things,' I said to Karim, who was craning to hear my father's answer.

'The kids are still outside,' Ami said, and Karim and I turned and ran into my room.

'Now we'll listen to music and say nothing.' Karim headed straight for my stereo without waiting for a response. He popped in one of my parents' tapes and pressed PLAY and the room filled with the morose sounds of 'Seasons in the Sun'. Karim switched off the music and pulled a jigsaw puzzle out of my desk drawer. 'Let's assemble.'

He was so much his father's son, though I'd never seen that before (and maybe I didn't even see it quite then, but play along, play along). Both of them sought desperately for the imposition of order in their lives, though how anyone as adept at anagrams as Karim could fail to see the arbitrariness of order I'll never understand. I finally was ready to say, 'Let's talk, Karim,' but he was already placing all the border pieces into one pile and sorting the rest into piles of co-ordinating colour.

'You're putting the sky in the sea,' I said. 'And I think that branch is really an antler.'

He sat back and tapped his ankle bone, visible between jeans and sneakers. 'Where does that road go?' he asked.

I looked at the cover of the jigsaw box. 'What road? You mean this path?'

'No, the main road that cuts past the Sheikh's palace. Near where you were shot at. Khayaban-e-Shaheen. Where does it go? Does it keep going on to the sea?'

'Who knows?'

We heard his parents' voices rise up in anger from the study. I tapped Karim's clenched fist and when he didn't respond I prised open his fingers. He could become a hermit, I thought. I could see him alone on a mountain, spending hours observing his fingers' ability to flex and unflex, and tracing the bones that connected thumb to ankle in the jigsaw of his body. I shook my head. Karim on a mountain? He was such a city boy.

He looked up, suddenly concerned. 'Are you OK?'

'Me?'

'You were shot at.'

'Oh, yes.' I let go of his hand and sat back. Already that memory was fading, and I had started anticipating the social cachet I could enjoy in the school yard from having a story like tonight's under my belt. 'It's over,' I said.

He looked at me and shook his head. 'But the world is slightly different now, isn't it?'

They cannot protect you from this. And what else?

'Not as safe.' Inexplicably, I started crying. I drew my knees up against my chest, and looked down at the carpet. Tears landed on my jeans and sank into the fabric.

Karim rested his elbows on my knees and leaned forward, his forehead touching mine. 'Transmitting images into your brain,' he intoned. 'Images of teachers in red leather thongs.'

'Gross!' I pushed him away, laughing. He fell back, resting on his elbows, the toe of his sneaker pressing against the toe of mine.

'I almost wish you'd been there,' I said a little later, when silence had replaced the laughter.

'I wish I'd been there, too,' he said, turning a jigsaw piece over and over in his hand, looking at the precise irregularity of its edges. 'Because then I'd be thinking of how the bullets could have hit me, instead of sitting here imagining those bullets hitting you. All those bullets.' His face took on one of those expressions again: the one with which he receded away from me.

'You can't think things like that. I wish you'd never think things like that.'

'Tell me something funny, Raheen.'

I'd been saving this one up for him, for a moment when he'd really need it: 'One of the names the British used to refer to Karachi, in the days when it was little more than a fishing village, was Krotchy.'

'You're lying.'

'Nuh uh. We could all be Krotchians. Or Krotchyites.'

'Krotchyites! Sounds like a kinky communist party.'

I hadn't yet finished rolling my eyes about that when Uncle Ali opened the door. 'Let's go, son. Way past your bedtime.'

In the hallway, my parents stood awkwardly with Aunty Maheen, no one speaking. Ami and Uncle Ali exchanged 'what-just-happened-there?' and 'what-brought-that-on?' looks. Aunty Maheen started walking quickly towards the door, and Aba speeded up too and touched her lightly on the shoulder. At first I thought she was going to ignore him, but then she turned round and shrugged, half-apologetically, half-not. 'Forget about it,' we all heard her say. She looked over Aba's shoulder. 'Come on, Karim, let's go.'

Karim held my wrist for a moment, then followed his mother out.

'Talk to her,' Ami said to Uncle Ali.

'Yasmin, I've forgotten how.'

Then he left, too.

Later that night, unable to sleep, I went towards my parents' room, where I heard them through the part-opened door.

'Why after all these years?' Aba said.

'Given what's going on with her, why wouldn't she think of how else her life might have worked out? Why wouldn't she get angry that things didn't happen differently?'

'Do you think Ali knows? You know, about— . . .'

'I think that's part of the reason he wants them all to move to London.'

Whatever it was they were talking about, I knew they'd stop if I walked into the room. And, ordinarily, I would have turned and walked away, nothing more discomforting than lurking in shadows listening to conversations that weren't meant for you, but this had something to do with the possibility of Karim leaving Karachi, so I had to stay. I had to know.

'Has she said anything to you?' Aba said, after a hesitation that suggested he wasn't sure he wanted to take the conversation any further.

'No, of course not. She knows I'll feel I'm betraying Ali if I do anything except censure the situation.'

'You would?'

'Wouldn't you?'

Spell it out, I silently urged them on. S-P-E-L-L.

'I think I would be compassionate about the situation without feeling I'm betraying Ali. And, let's face it, if we portion out loyalties mine should belong with Ali and yours with Maheen.'

'Quite the reverse, if we're honest about it. Come on, Zafar: if Maheen told you she'd robbed an old woman you'd feel compassionate.' Her voice became accusing. 'You don't feel you're entitled to be anything but compassionate towards Maheen.'

I couldn't help lifting up my arms in exasperation. Why make compassion seem like a crime?

'Why so cold, Yasmin?'

'Because many years ago we decided to square our shoulders and say, this is what we have done; we will live with it. We will make it something less than a waste and an unmitigated cruelty. And you've backed out of that, Zafar. You look over your shoulder and squirm as if to say, what is past is past, all I can do is look abashed and change the subject as fast as possible. When Raheen was born we both promised ourselves that wouldn't happen.'

'Raheen has nothing to do with this.'

'Raheen has everything to do with this. Zafar, you were there when Ali told us Raheen's been asking questions about the past. You were there, but you were the only one of the four of us who seemed to think it's some passing curiosity that she'll soon forget about. You want to know what brought on Maheen's outburst? She knows that when Raheen asks questions, Karim asks them, too. She knows we're all going to have to start marshalling facts, making our cases. She knows we're all going to have to start thinking about it again.'

'Not yet. Yasmin, not yet. We can't tell Raheen yet.' His voice was desperate, pleading.

'Then when?'

'When she's old enough to know the impossibility of tracing backwards and saying, here, this is where love ends and this is where it begins. When she's old enough to understand that sometimes there is no understanding possible.'

'It's possible. It's always possible. It's just occasionally easier not to interrogate it too closely.'

'She doesn't have to know yet, Yasmin.'

'Zafar, sometimes I think I love you more than is good for either of us.'

'You mean, you acquiesce.' There was relief in his voice, and I exhaled deeply as if a hand had unclenched my own windpipe.

'That's only part of what I mean. But it's the only part you'll remember in the morning. Good-night.'

I made my way back to bed as noiselessly as possible. I had brought this on. Whatever it was that made Aunty Maheen use that terrible voice to Aba, whatever it was that made Uncle Ali and Ami exchange those looks of concern, almost fear, whatever it was that had my father near to tears in his need to protect me, I had brought it on.

I wouldn't ask any more questions, I swore silently. Not even to myself. Not even if it killed me. No truth was worth such upheaval. My heart was still racing and I found my lips moving in prayer, giving thanks that whatever it was they were talking about, I didn't know.

My bedroom door opened, and I heard Aba come in. He sat on the edge of my bed, and reached for my hand.

'Are they going to move to London?' I asked.

His grip tightened on mine. 'It isn't definite by any means,' he replied, and I knew he said it because he couldn't bear to tell me the truth.

. . .

Aba drove through the puddles left by the evening's monsoon shower, his headlights picking out steel billboards in a state of obeisance, bent over almost double by the weight of wind and rain, unable to return to an upright stance. Swish-swish of wheels traversing wet patches. Somewhere in front of us, almost out of hearing, a car with a burst silencer. Scent of a rinsed city.

'Nice of Bunty to lend us the Pajero. Couldn't manage six of us and luggage otherwise.'

'Probably wouldn't have made it this far in your car. That drain overflowing back there . . .'

'Yes. That poor Suzuki . . .'

'Remember the time your Foxy stalled and we had to wade home?'

'Your brand-new Italian shoes ruined.'

Something reassuring about Aba and Uncle Ali's voices from the front seat, engaged in meaningless talk as though there were no need to inject every statement with the weight of the occasion. Something reassuring also about Ami and Aunty Maheen silently holding hands, as though they were girls again; girls who no longer had pop stars and furtive smoking and shared crushes to bind them together, but who found that friendship was binding enough, even though there was little but friendship that now bound them to the school-yard twosome who broke every rule and got away with it.

But there was nothing reassuring about Karim. We were only inches apart, both swaying cross-legged on the suitcases in the back, but he was too busy looking at streets to pay attention to me. Looking at streets, and whispering street names when we drove past road signs, and drawing a map of the route we were taking from his house to the airport, his pen veering off course every time Aba braked or went over a speed bump or drove through a puddle.

At the airport, he handed me the map, our fingers barely touching. Then he swivelled round and threw his arms around my father and burst into tears. There was so much hugging goodbye between our parents, and between his parents and me, and my parents and him, that I pretended, even to myself, that it hadn't really registered that the brush of fingers had been Karim's and my goodbye.

On the drive home, I said, 'Who'll speak in anagrams with me now?'

'Poor Karim is the one who's left everyone. You'll still have Sonia.' My mother winked at me. 'And Zia.'

Yes, I'd still have Sonia. And Zia. And so many other things that Karim no longer had. I'd still have the Arabian Sea and Sindhri mangoes, and crabbing with Captain Saleem, who had the most popular boat of all because his business card promised 'Guaranteed no cockroach', and, yes, there'd still be those bottles of creamy, flavoured milk from Rahat Milk Corner and drives to the airport for coffee and warm sand at the beach and Thai soup at Yuan Tung; yes, Burns Road nihari; yes, student biryani; oh, yes, yes, yes, all that, and all that again. So why complain? Why contemplate words like 'longing'?

After all, it was just the ends of my sentences I was losing; it was just my antidote to loneliness that I had lost.

That night as I cried myself to sleep I knew that, somewhere in the sky, Karim was doing the same; and some of my tears were his tears, and some of his tears were mine.

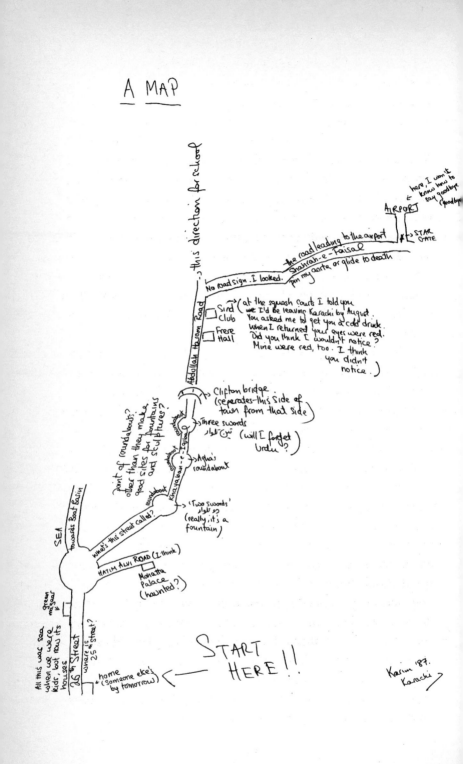

• • •

The rain had stopped. Water drops shimmered in the gossamer interstices of a spider's web outside my window. Not so much captured in the web as resting on it. I could, I thought, lift up that web, very carefully, and place it against my throat, where it would adhere, threads retreating into near invisibility and only rain drops remaining to glisten against my skin like some precious inheritance.

Jake's hand reached across me to close the window. 'It's freezing,' he said. 'I've been asking you for the last ten seconds to get rid of the draught.'

'Didn't hear you.' I swivelled my legs off the window ledge, making room for him to sit next to me, but he remained standing on my bed, head inches away from touching the ceiling.

'Of course you didn't. It's always Grand Central Station in here.' He jerked his head at all the people, seven or eight of them, crowded into my tiny dorm room.

When the downpour had started, less than an hour earlier, I had been attempting to read a supermarket romance for my 'Myths of Courtship' class, but the sudden ferocity of the rain made me set aside my herbal tea and rush outdoors. It was the closest thing to the monsoons I had encountered in the three years I'd been at university in America, rain ricocheting off the ground with the speed of bullets from a Kalashnikov. I half-expected to see little frogs and winged insects appear. People were running for shelter, the ones who knew me shouting as they charged past that I was crazy, 'Get inside, Raheen.' I looked down. Crazy I could handle, but crazy in a white shirt was probably not such a good idea. I pulled the clinging material away from my body, hearing with satisfaction the suction release of wet cotton from flesh, and ran up the stairs towards central heating.

'Study break. Ten minutes. My room. Who's going to make the hot chocolate?' I yelled down the hallway on my way into the shower.

Someone shouted, 'But I've just started *War and Peace*,' and someone else: 'We've been back from the dining hall less than half an hour.'

'Raheen says study break, ten minutes,' another of my hallmates declared. 'You want to argue with her?'

Less than fifteen minutes later, I had a crowd of people clustered in my room as, freshly showered and dressed in sweats and fleece jumper, I poured out hot chocolate with marshmallow bits from a large saucepan into mugs and plastic glasses bearing the university's crest. Tamara from next door held up my romance novel with a whoop of delight, and the rest of my friends chanted, 'Read, Raheen, read,' over and over until, with mock resignation, I took the book from Tamara, sat on the window ledge by my bed, cleared my throat and started reading out loud choice passages in breathy, emotive style.

She stared boldly into his piercing blue eyes, but he was not a man to be daunted by feminine fire and he stared right back, his gaze suggesting X-ray vision that could look right through her blouse and see the rapidly beating heart that lay beneath.

His jeans were so tight they could barely contain him, and she trembled with fear and ecstasy at the thought that he might burst out of them at any moment.

She tossed her head, and wished she could do the same with her emotions.

'Will you just come?' He impatiently pushed the door open and gestured her through.

'Make me,' she replied, saucily.

He had always been a man to rise to a challenge.

When I finally stopped reading, even Jake, who had come into the crowded room halfway through and was slouching in the door frame, was shaking his head in amusement, though the evening before I'd walked out on him in the dining hall while he was in the middle of yet another rant about how little time the two of us spent together, alone. I had told him he just didn't understand Pakistani attitudes towards friendship, and he'd sneered. That was, I had to admit to myself, entirely an appropriate reaction. I put the romance novel down. Between the body heat, central heating, cocoa and fleece I was beginning to feel a little hot. I turned to look outside, wondered exactly when it had stopped raining, and opened the window.

That smell in the air. The aftermath of rain. I let the book fall from my hands. Tawdry. Cheap and tawdry. I could hear Jake's voice, but I didn't want to have to deal with him, so I continued looking outside at the autumn leaves, vibrant reds and oranges, scattered across paths, plastered on to buildings. A breeze blew up and I came so close to telling everyone in the room to be quiet, just be quiet, so that I could hear the sound of leaves being blown about. Russet rustle. Almost the sound of waves breaking on pebbled sand.

In Karachi, I would never have been able to hold court for as long as I had just done. Hold court or play the jester, whatever it was that I had been doing. One or more of my friends would have sat down beside me, leaned an elbow on my shoulder, scanned ahead of where I was reading to some further point on the page and taken the book from my hands to read aloud the next absurd lines in exaggerated tones, at once competing and collaborating with me. I leaned my head against the window screen. Rain had tinged the mesh with the smell of rust. Not true, not true, that in Karachi I felt my world was perfect, although sometimes I deluded myself into thinking that when I was far from home. But even in Karachi I'd feel this need to turn away from people whose company, just seconds earlier, I had de-lighted in. Sonia sometimes told me off for my 'mood swings', in

Sonia's way of telling people off, which was not to rebuke or reprimand but merely to ask what was wrong. Once, not so long ago, I had finally said, 'Even when I'm with everyone whom I could possibly want to be with, I feel like something's absent,' and Sonia, showing no signs of being hurt by this remark, nodded, and asked, 'Absent or lost?'

There was a cobweb between the window and the ledge outside. Jake closed the window, and I turned back to my friends, wanting them gone, wanting him gone too.

'Break over,' I said.

Almost everyone stood up instantly, as though I had issued a military order, except for the guy who was supposed to be reading *War and Peace*. 'But we haven't even finished drinking our . . .' he said.

Tamara nudged him. 'Come on, finish it in my room.' Behind Jake's back she mouthed to me, 'Should I take him with me?' and I was about to nod, when Jake said, 'Tamara, I can see your reflection in the mirror. Goodbye.'

After everyone had left, Jake stepped off the bed, and leaned against my desk, hands stuffed in the pockets of his jeans. 'You know, after you walked out on me at dinner last night—'

'Oh, Jacob, for heaven's sake, I didn't walk out; I just said I had work to do and couldn't stay to watch you sip your coffee.'

He scuffed the carpet with the toe of his sneakers. 'Don't call me Jacob.'

I rolled my eyes. 'OK, after I walked out on you . . . what?'

'I decided it's over between us.' He was looking down at his hands. They were somewhat too soft, Jake's hands.

I nodded. 'I understand.'

He raised his head and looked at me. 'I was about to add, "but then I changed my mind".'

'Oh.'

We looked at each other for a few seconds, and then he said, 'It really makes no difference to you either way, does it?'

A spider was picking its way to the centre of the web,

sidestepping the drops of water. The sky cerulean once more. *Cerulean is an anagram of acne rule. Imagine a pimply, pustular sky, Ra!* I stood up so quickly I banged my head against the potted plant hanging from the ceiling near the foot of my bed. The pot tipped and loose soil showered down my jumper and on to my bed.

'You OK?' Jake moved forward, but I held my hands up to tell him to keep his distance. Tears in my eyes, and none of them because of him. I put my hand to my scalp and was almost disappointed to find no trickle of blood, nor even a bump. Jake stepped back and watched me scoop soil from the duvet into a cup and pour it back into the plant-holder.

'Soiled sheets. Dirt on your fingers. Talk about a break-up scene heavy in symbolism.' Jake made a sound that might have been laughter had it contained the slightest suggestion of amusement. 'You know, I finally figured out last night what all of us have in common. Ricardo, Amit, myself. Couldn't find any common denominator in all your boyfriends before. But it's this: we're the kind of guys you'll always stop short of loving. And that makes life easy, doesn't it?'

I didn't want to think too hard about what he had said, so I looked around for tissue to wipe my fingers with. Jake offered the sleeve of his shirt, but I brushed the dirt off against a corner of my duvet instead. *Don't touch him, and this will be easier.*

'Actually, the common denominator, Jake, is that you all have really sexy wrists. Call me shallow.'

I sat on the window ledge again, pressed the nib of my fountain pen through the mesh of the screen, and unscrewed the bottom of the pen. Jake came to stand beside me as I gently squeezed the ink cartridge and a rain drop turned blue.

'You really have this ability to find beauty in weird places.'

There was a tone of reconciliation in his voice, but when he had said it was over between us my heart had lurched ever so slightly, and if we were to stay together now perhaps it would lurch even more next week, next month or whenever that inevitable ending came. It would lurch especially if the ending didn't come until early next summer when we would graduate and I would head home to Karachi. What good would it do either Jake or me to allow such lurchings? What good would it do me to have a reason not to want to go home? So I didn't answer as I would have answered if I was unafraid of revealing too much of my heart. I didn't tell him that I grew up in an ugly city that taught me how to look between dust and rubbish and potholes to find a splinter of glass that looked like unmelting ice, beautiful in its defiance of the sun. I didn't tell him that he was right; I did stop short of loving him. I certainly didn't tell him, but that was getting a little bit harder as the days went on. I looked beyond him to the mirror. There was a crack in the glass, right at eye level, and for a second I half-fancied I saw that unmelting splinter lodged in one of my absurdly large eyes, slashing its darkness.

'I have work to do, Jake.'

'So do I. Can I stay?'

I shook my head, without turning to look at him.

He was all the way to the door before he stopped and said, 'Ever wonder how other people see you?'

I turned round. 'Is this the cruel parting blow, Jake? You going to – what's that funny expression? – hold up a mirror to my eyes?'

'I've never met anyone who knows how to be cruel to you, Raheen. You charm us all. And not, as you think, because you're the life of the party when you're in that partying mood. It's mainly because you'll always find something of worth in even the most useless among us, in even our most pathetic moments. People generally brush away a spider's web, Raheen, but not you.'

'Jake, don't talk rubbish. This is me, Raheen, the one who told you not to audition for Oberon in the college production of *A Midsummer Night's Dream* because as soon as you walked into that room everyone would throw up their hands in joy and say, we've found our Bottom! Kindness is not my greatest virtue.'

He stared down at the floor. 'I never told you this before . . . I did audition.'

'And?'

He looked gloomily at me. And made a braying sound.

'Oh God, Jake, I'm so sorry.' I tried hard not to laugh, but it was no good.

'Sometimes your honesty looks a lot like unkindness,' he said. 'But your intention is never to be hurtful.' He shook his head and smiled at me, as though I were a million miles away. 'And I'm taking a leaf out of your book now. Your friends adore you, Raheen, because at the end of the day you'll always forgive them no matter how hideously they've behaved. They adore you because they think you offer up your friendship and ask for nothing in return. But that's not true—' He took a deep breath. 'You do ask for something. You ask that we never expect you to need us.'

He blew a kiss at me, and left.

I drew my legs up to my body and rested my chin on my knees. Jake was right. Until then I had always thought my college friends saw me as the entertainer. And as the one who couldn't keep her opinions to herself. It was true, I supposed, that I didn't bear grudges or hold people accountable for every slip-up, though that had more to do with my father than with me. Aba had always said that it was easy to condemn people; condemnation was an act of smugness, wasn't it? Didn't it arise from the certainty that you would never do what you were condemning someone else for? But how could you say that unless you could slip into their soul, peer around and see what serpents fed there, what abysses gaped? How could you say anything unless you knew how the serpents and abysses had come to be, and what it meant to live with them every single day? Shouldn't we simply be grateful that our lives allow us to live with grace today? It came naturally to Aba – the ability to be grateful for his life, the ability to look at the Runtys of this world with understanding – but for me it sometimes felt as though I was forcing my nature into a mould I wanted to fit into rather than one that suited the contours of my personality.

I thought of everything Jake had just said, and looked at my watch. In Karachi, it was early in the morning, far too early to call my father without making him panic. But I needed to talk to someone – not just anyone, but someone who had always known me. I could call Zia, half an hour's drive away in the same time zone, but I rarely spoke to Zia about Jake since that time Zia had landed up on Jake's doorstep at midnight and announced that, although he had come to like Jake a great deal in the weeks since they'd first met, no white boy could lay hands on a Muslim girl and expect to live. Jake had leapt out of the second-floor window and broken his ankle. ('How was I supposed to know you'd be seeing someone moronic enough to take me seriously?' Zia had protested to me the next day. 'There are white Muslims in the world, for God's sake. Hasn't he heard of Cat Stevens?') No, I couldn't call Zia and so much as mention Jake's name without running the risk of him singing 'Moonshadow', which in Zia's rendition became 'Crescent Moonshadow'.

But Jake wasn't really the issue here. I looked at my watch again and added ten to establish Karachi time once more. In a couple of hours Sonia would wake up to say her morning prayers. I could call her then, and ask, 'Do you think I don't need you?' And however she answered, however tactfully, however generously, something in her response would remind me that we both knew I felt guilty about Sonia; if anyone asked who my closest friend in the world was I'd say her name without hesitation, but it was the lack of hesitation that comes from years of practice rather than conviction. In my heart, I still carried around the notion of a friendship that no reality could live up to.

I picked up my phone book. The last three years, every time I had been in Karachi packing to return to America, Ami would come into my room with a letter or package for Aunty Maheen, and every time she would say how much Maheen would appreciate it if I delivered it by hand next time I visited friends in Boston, or even if I just called from college to say 'hello', and every time I would say, 'Yes, sure, you gave me the number.

Meant to last semester, but things get so hectic,' and every time Ami looked at me with something so close to disappointment in her eyes that I had to pretend something was lost and busy myself in a flurry of searching for it.

Ami didn't know that in my first week as a foreigner, I had called that number, feeling excitement, even a touch of nervousness. It had been so long since I'd spoken to her. But it wasn't Aunty Maheen who answered. It was a man, and as he repeated, 'Hello? . . . Hello?' down the phone, I heard Aunty Maheen's voice in the background say, 'Who is it, darling?' and I thought of Uncle Ali in London, moving from one short-term affair to another, returning periodically to Karachi to tell my parents he didn't know why he left, he couldn't imagine returning, he was so afraid of old age. His life such sadness. I hung up, and cried all afternoon. I had never told anyone else about the call. Even now, I couldn't quite understand it. All these years later, why did it continue to affect me so much more than I could bear?

I opened the phone book to 'M'.

In my first days of college, I had gritted my teeth through freshman orientation with its attempts to create artificial bonds between everyone in the hall by getting us to share our most private pains, our most personal stories. I lied my way through it, of course, inventing broken hearts, ruined friendships, family disease, all in an attempt to keep up with the tragedies of the eighteen-year-old lives around me. But in my head I kept a chart of the real answers that came to mind to the questions: *What's the hardest thing you've had to deal with? What's your happiest memory? What's your biggest regret? Has there been one experience that changed your life? If you could pick up the phone and call one person now, who would it be?* The questions went on and on, and every one of my answers had to do with Karim leaving and Uncle Ali and Aunty Maheen divorcing.

Of the two events, the divorce had been the worse. The finality of it. I knew about divorced couples; I knew the way their friends divided into his friends and her friends. How to divide my parents between Ali and Maheen? It couldn't be done. That's when I really realized that Karim wouldn't be coming back. Before, some part of me had hoped that Uncle Ali would see the error of his ways. ('England, man. Mike Gatting, Graham Gooch, John Embury. Versus Pakistan. Wasim, Javed, Qadir. Imran, for God's sake, Imran! Of course they'll come back.' Zia logic, and I had more than half believed it.) But now they wouldn't come back, because that would mean the two of them living in the same city as my parents but the four of them never being a foursome again. How was that possible? It wasn't. It simply was not possible. More than Aunty Maheen's remarriage, or the worsening political situation in Pakistan, it was my belief in the impossibility of that quartet rearranging itself in any way that made my thoughts exile Ali and Maheen – and, by extension, Karim – from Karachi for ever. How I had resented Aunty Maheen then. Resented her so much that I had actually found myself agreeing with Aunty Runty, who came over to our house as soon as she heard news of the divorce and said, 'Who would have thought it? Maheen, an adulteress! Has she no considera-tion for her son?' My father had told Runty to get out of his house, and it was many months before either of my parents spoke to her again. Yes, I had almost hated Aunty Maheen then.

Then.

I put the phone book down. They were clawing at me now, those absurd memories and questions that should be long dead by now. I slipped off my bed, pulled on a pair of jeans and a jacket, grabbed my Walkman and headed out. The sky moved from sunset to twilight to something darker, something not quite night, as I walked from one end of campus to the other and then back, concentrating on the music, changing the radio frequency any time songs from the mid-eighties starting playing. But when I was just steps away from the dorm, I turned the Walkman off, veered away from the lamplit paths, and cut across rain-drenched fields, watching my feet step into the shoeprints of someone with wide toes, trusting to his purpose as he strode away from the dorms and towards the Observatory, then wavering in my faith as the moon disappeared behind a cloud, and turning to walk back towards the campus lights, forging my own path now, the hem of my jeans dark with wet.

To one side of the field was a patch of snow, the only remains of last week's early snowfall, protected against sun and rain by the overhang of a building's roof. I bent to pick up a fallen branch, and trailed its forked end behind me as I walked through the patch, the branch rising and falling as I took each step, leaving marks so faint it looked as though I had been walking alongside a sparrow. Or beside an angel that hovered above the ground, only the tips of its folded wings brushing against the snow.

Can angels lie spine to spine?

I closed my eyes, saw the snow before me transform into fields of white. *Tired clouds coming to rest on the ground.* My wrist remembered the pressure of a thumb and forefinger encircling it. A boy with ears too large and legs accustomed to leaping touched a cotton boll to my palm and tiny insect feet crawled across my skin.

It was an unexceptional moment, but, lord, how he smiled when he watched me watch a ladybird take flight.

Dear Uncle Ali,

It was lovely to see you in Karachi over the summer, although I have yet to recover from seeing you give the Ghutnas instructions in how to dance the 'Electric Slide'. This is what comes of dating Americans who run summer camps! I know, I know. It was a blind date, and you haven't seen her a second time, but I insist she's responsible.

It's good to be back at college again. Weather's bearable at the moment and there are still some gorgeous autumn (or, should I say, fall) leaves clinging to trees, but I'd appreciate the beauty of it a little more if it didn't serve to remind that another East Coast winter is about to begin. We've already had one round of snowfall. And yesterday there was a thunderstorm that was nothing short of a monsoon. Can't believe this is my last year up in the snowbelt of America. Although any regret at graduating is more than tempered by the joy of knowing no-more-dining-hall-food. Last night there was something call Noodle Sneeze on the menu. The pizza delivery man is my best friend, even though rumour has it he was once in jail for attempted murder. I'm a Karachiite. I can handle these things.

Just wrote a paper based on Calvino late last night (well, maybe early this morning would be more to the point) for my 'other (not Other) realisms' class. Please don't ask me to explain the course title – I just liked the reading list. Anyway, the point is, I'm enclosing the paper – could you forward it to Karim, whichever part of the world he's in on his Grand Tour (how nineteenth-century can you get! Or were you just pulling my leg about that?) And yes, you do still have to stick to your promise not to ask me any questions about your son and me.

Tons of love,
Raheen

Raheen Khan
Comp Lit 402
Fall 1994

Envisionable Cities

(a pastiche)

As the Imperial barge floated down the river the citydwellers gathered on the banks to look upon the Great Khan who reclined on his chair of gold talking to Marco Polo. Kublai affected not to notice them, but when one woman failed to gaze at the dazzle of his passing his eyebrows shot up, and he lost track of the tale Polo was telling him.

'Why is she so unmoved by my presence?' Kublai demanded.

Polo looked at the newborn child in the woman's arms and said, 'She is looking at the one person in the kingdom who can be believed to have a destiny greater than that of Kublai Khan. Why should she look anywhere else?'

A spider scuttled down from its web and hovered above the baby's face. The baby began to cry. Immediately the mother looked away from the child and bowed to the Great Khan.

'So,' said Kublai. 'Our moments of greatest potential occur in the moments just before we are born. The first time we cry, sneeze, or open our eyes to reveal the disproportion of our pupils we cease to be what we could have been.'

'It is even so with cities,' Polo replied. 'The greatest cities exist in the moments just before they become reality.'

'And if you could create the greatest city, here in conversation, what would it be?' Kublai said.

'That's easy,' Marco Polo replied. 'The greatest city is the one that exists away from all eyes, including its own. Because no one defines it or maps out its co-ordinates, it can be anything and everything we dream a city should be.'

Cities and Imagination

In Zytrow there is too much going on for anyone to pause long enough to name the streets. If you want to go somewhere you must ask the inhabitants of the city to take you there. On the way they'll point out the city's landmarks: the fruit seller whose fruits are always a season ahead of everyone else's; the street with the dry-cleaner's shop, where the two ghosts walked one summer; the airport where people begin to end friendships by simply failing to say goodbye.

By the time you reach your destination you'll be desperate to perform some bold or reckless action that no one can forget, so that you, too, may become part of Zytrow's landmarks. You'll leap a great distance, perhaps.

But if you leave Zytrow and forget its magic, you'll start listening to the poison of those who say all streets must have names. You'll join in the task of making directions easy for foreign travellers. And one by one, as you ink in your map, they disappear: the fruit seller, the ghosts, the friends you never said goodbye to.

When the map is nearly done the cartographers will gather to celebrate. They'll say there's only one street remaining that needs a name. As they write the name and complete the map, someone tells you: before this, the inhabitants of Zytrow referred to it as the street where that boy leapt an incredible leap.

Cities and Memory

It is the nature of Raya, city of cities, that it can only ever have two inhabitants. Others may visit, tour, speculate upon and write treatises about Raya, but only two can live there. I have seen them all, the different pairings in that city, but the pair I most remember is the 87th, who seemed to all who saw them the most perfect reflection of what the citymakers intended when they created Raya.

But one day they left. Turned in opposite directions and walked away, never imagining they would not return. When they went they took Raya with them. Cleft it in two and carried one half each on their backs, where it hid in pores, nestled between follicles, glistened beneath sweat. They traversed the earth with their half-Rayas and saw no city to match the one they would recreate when once more skin embraced skin.

But when they returned, met back at the starting point, Raya had disappeared and no amount of desperate embracing brought it back. And so once more they parted, each retracing the other's footprints, searching streets and deserts and seas for the other's cast-off skin.

And Raya smiles her sad, shifting smile, as she watches them retreat further and further away from each other, and her.

● ● ●

When I answered the phone he said, 'And?' as he always had, as he always did, as though our time apart had merely been a Karachi sunset: swift and startling.

I leaned back against the wall of my dorm room, and opened my desk drawer to look at the photograph of the four of us – Sonia, Zia, Karim and me – which lay, unframed, on top of a clutter of staples, paperclips, sticky tape, pens and drawing pins. 'The four of us' had never really ceased being 'the four of us' to me, despite all the intervening years, but it seemed somehow pathetic to frame a photograph taken at age thirteen when even the most nostalgic of my friends at college had reproductions of themselves going back no further than their penultimate year of school, so this picture which my father had taken the day before Karim left for London had stayed hidden yet within reach through all my years at college in upstate New York.

'Eratosthenes,' I said. That was the name with which I'd left off the last conversation I'd had in my head with him.

'What? Can't hear . . . sorry, it's Karim. I'm sorry, of course you don't recognize my voice, it's . . .'

'Broken,' I said. Why did he sound so formal? 'But instantly recognizable all the same.'

'And yours too.'

'My voice has not broken, thank you.' I'd intended flippancy, but I think I sounded annoyed.

'It's gone husky.'

'Not really. I've got a bit of a sore throat.'

'Sick as a dog?' he said.

'No, just a minor annoyance.'

'No, it was a joke. Your voice is husky. Huskie, like the dog. So you're sick as a—'

'Oh. Yeah. Got it.' I attempted a laugh but it came out wrong. The first rule of humour that Karim and I had always subscribed to: if the other person doesn't get the joke, just move on. I looked out of the window at my hallmates slinging snowballs at one another, the freshly fallen snow tinged blue in the moonlight. One of them, Tamara perhaps, looked up and saw me, threw a snowball at my window in an invitation to join the fun, and for a moment I wanted to end the phone call and run downstairs.

'I said Eratosthenes. Just now.'

'Can't hear properly. I'm at the airport and there are all these announcements and . . . oh hell, scary demon-baby has just started bawling. I'll find a quieter phone and call you back. Don't go away.'

I replaced the receiver on the phone base, and looked out of the window again. Two of my friends were lying next to each other in the snow, their arms fanning out away from their bodies, pushing aside the powdery snow. Watching them, I found I was raising my own arms, feeling remembered water currents tugging against my fingertips as I floated in Karachi's sea. I lowered my arms. What was I doing here? The two figures outside stood up and stepped out of their outlines, leaving behind a pair of snow angels, the wing of one overlapping with the wing of the other. Siamese twin angels.

I ran my fingers through my hair. Why had I sent him that essay? Of course he had called after receiving it. I sat down, cross-legged, beside my desk, and from the bottom drawer I pulled out four pieces of writing paper, neatly taped together, which constituted Karim's last communication with me, back in 1990. On one side was a map of Karachi. A useless, partial map of Karachi, which I had brought with me to America to see if they would bring me any kind of comfort, any kind of pain, on the days when I was most homesick. The answer to that question I quickly found was no, and no again. I laid the paper on the ground, map side up, smoothing it flat with the palm of my hand, reminding myself I needed to hoover – sorry, vacuum – my room. Streets leading to other streets, streets named, areas defined, places of interest clearly marked out. This map was Karachi's opposite. They could only exist through their disdain for the reality of the city: the jumble, the illogic, the self-definition, the quicksilver of the place. As usual, the maps did nothing but irritate me. I turned the taped sheet over, and flicked away the crumbs of chocolate-chip cookies that had been squashed between paper and carpet. I really needed to hoover.

Myriad pieces of paper taped together. What had hurt me most was that they were originals. If he'd wanted to make a point surely he could just have made photocopies of my letters and taken his scissors to them. But to cut up the originals . . . to have such certainty that nothing on those pages would ever make him want to take another look, make another assessment . . . to have such certainty, and not to hide it. He was never so cruel when I knew him.

He was certainly never so cruel that he unveiled my own cruelty to me, offered it up free of contrasts to make it appear all the harsher. I had written him letters full of laughter, letters in which I expressed how much I missed him. These fragments, which he pasted together, were only extracts, contextless; they did not – oh God, surely they did not – reflect anything but a partial truth of who I was, of who I had become in those defining years when he was in so many ways absent to me.

Dear Karim,
What do you expect me to do with a map of the route from Zia's house to the Club? You're a very odd boy. If you're going to send me something other than a letter, send me a Tom Cruise postcard. (Nadia's cousin just sent her one from London – bought it at HMV.) Or no, it might get lost in the post. So bring one when you come home for the holidays. And I really don't know what the road between Zamzama and Gizri is called. Completely forgot to check after I got your letter. We've all lived our lives quite happily without knowing the name of that street, and can continue to do so.

17th Aug '87

25th July '88 →

Can't believe I'm in London and you're in Boston. I wish we could stay here until you come back. I know school starts in less than a week, but Muhurram will begin in August and we all know that means Shia–Sunni fights and many deaths and then school will be closed until things return to normal. Aba got all upset when I pointed that out and told him we should just stay in London longer. I didn't say I want sectarian riots – I'm just being realistic.

Don't take this the wrong way but I'd much rather hear about your school friends, the movies you've seen, the girls you have crushes on, the funny things you've heard, I'd rather all that than read about your map-musings.

7th Nov '88 →

I don't know whether to say Happy New Year or not. I don't know how long things were going on between your mother and the Interloper. I only found out about him when your mother called to tell my mother about the divorce. Guess my parents already knew about him. If you have to spend all your holidays with your mother in Boston, when will you ever come home? When will I get my Tom Cruise postcard? Maybe you could just post it to me.

3rd Jan '88

8th Jan '89 →

Had so much fun over the winter holidays. I was out all the time – spent nights at the beach, went crabbing, lots of parties. Best winter ever! You really missed out.

Saw your father yesterday. He says the two of you are getting on pretty well these days. Good to hear it. I mean, I know the two of you will probably never have a relationship like me and Aba, but Uncle Ali's a cool guy in his way. How're things with you and your mother? I hear you were pretty angry with her in the beginning but we've got to allow our parents their imperfections, right?

19th June '89 →

Aba said I could place a trunk call to you. But it's so expensive and what could we say to each other in just a five- or ten-minute call?

10th Jan 88 ←

30th ... '89

You referred to the Boat Basin as Khayaban-e-Jami. Karim, it's the BOAT BASIN, OK? How much of an out-of-towner can you be?

No, until your last letter I didn't know the exact number of people reported killed in Karachi's violence so far this year. Thank you, Mr Reuters. I'm sure the dead feel much better about being dead now.

22nd March '88

1st April '90 ✓

Dear Karim,

April Fool's Day and nothing much to report.

OK, cards on the table. I was frankly a little annoyed by your last letter. Let me refresh your memory. You talked about cartography and wondered why you were interested in it, or some such thing, and then you said, and I quote: do you understand any of what I'm saying? Do you care? What's that supposed to mean? You think I'm both stupid and insensitive? Thanks, friend.

No, OK, that's not it either. When I started reading your letter I was predisposed to being annoyed and it didn't help that you started gushing on about what a good friend Zia is. He's a great friend when all that's required of his friendship is one overseas phone call and a little singing to cheer you up when you're in a bad mood.

I'm getting away from the point. The point is that I was predisposed to being annoyed at you. The reason: I read the letter you wrote to Sonia. The one when you start off on how terrible it is to hear about all the violence in Karachi, and how you can't understand how I can write to you while all that is going on and never even mention it, as though it isn't even worthy of ink. You wrote that when your uncle gets his weekly supply of *Dawn* you read through the articles detailing the dead and you go to your map and look up the places where they were killed, just as a way of taking a moment to think of them and mourn their deaths. Well, Mr Sitting-in-London, aren't you just so humane! Those of us who still live here don't have the luxury of being compassionate from a distance. We go on with our lives because we like the façade of maintaining a kind of sanity. When we laugh, that's defiance. So don't you tell me about the graves you mark on that map.

That map is what marks you as an ex-pat and not as a Karachiite. People here don't talk in street names. And you never did either. You know that U2 song, 'Where the streets have no name'. That's Karachi's song. Or, at least, the title is. What are the lyrics? Something about love burning down. I don't know, Karim. I never thought I'd write you this letter.

Love seems an odd word to use to sign this off, but everyone's a little odd now and then. Love.

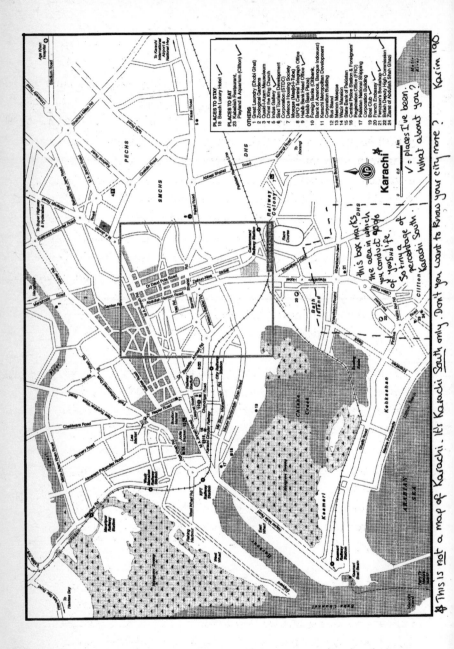

Karachi ★

PLACES TO STAY
18 Beach Luxury Hotel

PLACES TO EAT
23 Kabablah Restaurant, Playland & Aquarium (Clifton)

OTHERS
1 Great Laundry (Dhobi Ghat)
2 Zoological Gardens
3 Quaid-e-Azam Mausoleum
4 Christ the King Church
5 Indus Gallery
6 Sind Tourism Development Corporation (STDC)
7 Defence Housing Society
8 Mosque (Masjid-i-Tuba)
9 GPO & Central Telegraph Office
10 Habib Bank Head Office
   Habib Bank Plaza,
   Bank of America, Banque Indosuez)
11 Karachi Metropolitan Development Corporation Building
12 Bus Stand
13 Memon Mosque
14 Wazir Mansion
15 State Bank of Pakistan
16 Central Police Station & Foreigners' Registration Office (FRO)
17 Pakistan National Shipping Corporation Building
19 Boat Club
20 French Embassy
21 Ferozson's Bookshop
22 British Deputy High Commission
24 Ziarat of Abdullah Shah Ghazi

This box marks the area in which you conduct 90% of your life, so tiny a percentage of Karachi South.

✓ = places I've been.
What about you?

Karim '90

✗ This is not a map of Karachi. It's Karachi South only. Don't you want to know your city more?

I had never posted a response to that letter collage. Oh, it would have been easy to chop up his letters, paste together everything that had annoyed me in them, every question (and there were many) about maps and street names, which he knew I had no interest in, and which seemed to serve only as a reminder of the distance between us. I, too, could paste one side of a sheet with everything he'd said to irritate me. But, and here's the point I had never understood, Karim and I wrote so often, so copiously, to each other that one side of a sheet was nothing, just a tiny fraction of the whole, hardly indicative of anything at all. Yes, my final letter to him had been an explosion of irritation, but Karim should have known my flare-ups seldom lasted long. The Karim I thought I knew would have written back, his tone half-amused, half-sardonic, and said:

> Finally – you've let it all out. I could explain to you that YOU'RE NOT SUPPOSED TO READ LETTERS INTENDED FOR OTHER PEOPLE, STUPID! but we'll let your lack of etiquette pass this once. I've read between the lines of your letter, and I guess you really miss me, huh? Ra, that's a two-way street. Oops, I mentioned streets. Can you ever forgive me? All right, seriously though, since you've finally stopped making snippy little comments and seem willing to address the matter head-on, here's why I am the way I am about Karachi and maps and all that stuff . . .

That's the sort of letter I'd get from the Karim I thought I knew. But what had I done to set him off in such an unexpected and violent way? To take a pair of scissors to the letters I'd written, that was violence, nothing less. Why cut out the comment about Tom Cruise postcards, as though he really believed that was my greatest regret about his parents' divorce, when instead he could have cut out what I'd written further down in the letter – I could remember the exact words, I had spent so long composing them: 'Karimazov, you know I'm really saying I don't know what to say to you about this when you're so far away. But speak to me, and I'll answer.' And he'd written back: 'Ra, I have been speaking to you. Endlessly. It's all that's kept me sane.' To dismiss all that, to pretend those sorts of moments weren't the most significant ones in our letters was a betrayal so profound that I didn't even know how to respond to it. I could only assume that somehow the maps, the street names, the violence in Karachi, all that had become more real to Karim than our friendship and I had simply been too blind to see it happening. What else could explain the nature and extent of his reaction to my letter? And if my assumption was correct, how could I forgive him that?

That's what I had thought at the time, but in the years since I had come to realize that holding on to anger towards Karim was not an option I was physiologically capable of exercising. Not when my ears became more alert when his name was mentioned, not when my mouth broke into a smile when I thought I saw him walking down the street towards me.

But how could I expect things to revert to 1987, or even 1990?

I pushed aside the letter collage, stood up and reached for my gloves. I'd make snow angels and snowballs and snowmen, and that would be a far better way of spending the evening than—

The phone rang.

I stood and watched it.

The answering machine clicked on and my prerecorded voice started its Marlene Dietrich impersonation: Thank you. You have called. Leave a message. Darling.

'You are not seriously screening this call, Ra!'

Ra. No one had called me that in seven years. When I thought of her, of Ra, she was a fourteen-year-old who knew nothing about the empty spaces that can press against a person in the most crowded of rooms. I tossed the gloves on to the bed and picked up the phone. 'Congratulations,' I said, still in Dietrich mode. 'You have passed the screen test.'

'So who's Erin?' he said.

'Erin who?' I drew curvy lines in the dust on my bookcase. Grey dot on the tip of my fingers. I sucked it off, tasting dust in my mouth. What was he thinking right now? Was he only just realizing that somewhere inside he'd always known this conversation would happen? Was he wondering if the image he carried around of me was anything like the truth of who I had become? Was he terrified and was he unable to give the terror too much credence?

'When I called before. Sounded like you said Erin Toss The Knees. Like there was a bunch of Ghutnas standing around and muscle-bound Erin was going to throw them out.'

I walked over to my bed and lay down. So, gaps of years could close so fast we'd wonder if they had really existed; honestly, it was all so silly, because see how easily everything is restored. 'Remember that American girl called Erin who was at school with us for a term?'

'Yes, and made to sit in class next to Perin Mehta, just because Mrs H. loved the rhyme of Erin and Perin.'

'And Perin used to hum "By the rivers Of Babylon" all day, until Erin would yell at her and get thrown out of class because no one else could hear the humming and Perin insisted Erin was just making up stories . . .'

'. . . And of course we believed Perin because why would anyone hum a Boney M song in the mid-Eighties?'

'So poor Erin got a reputation for being a trouble-maker and no one hung out with her.'

'All those years she suffered torments because of it, always on the social fringes . . .'

'But now she's grown up into a body builder, and she's planning to return to Karachi to toss the Ghutnas! Piles of bodies, draped in designer silks, flying this way and that, whoosh, whoosh, as she makes her progress through town!'

'O hell,' he said.

'Hello yourself.'

Over four years since we'd written; longer since we'd had any kind of phone conversation. But some part of me had carried on talking to him, keeping up a dialogue about Ghutnas and anagrams, and perhaps I did that so we would never have to talk as strangers.

'God, Karimazov, it's good to hear your voice. Why the hell did it take you so long to call?'

'Didn't take me long at all. Calling-card number plus international code plus country code plus area code plus phone number all within four seconds. I am the king of speedy dialling.'

'You are the king of morons!' I was shouting now, for no reason, standing up on my bed, also for no reason except that I seemed to require elevation, my feet as many inches off the ground as possible. I jumped up and touched the ceiling and came down with cobwebs sticking to my fingers.

'I'm a marooned moron. Calling from Rome. I should be on a flight to London but the pilot can't find the keys to the plane. So I've been sitting here for the last hour, singing to myself to keep entertained.'

'Don't croon when marooned. Eat a macaroon, you goon.' I lay back on my bed, barely noticing the barrage of snowballs that thumped against my window, preceded by a carrot. 'So you're saying the only reason you're calling me after all these years is boredom?' I said, knowing the answer was no.

'Your essay finally caught up with me in Rome. Just got here, hours before I left for the airport. It's been all around the world trying to find me. Australia, Morocco, Lapland.'

'You went to Lapland?' I threw my hands up in mock incomprehension at my reflection in the mirror. I looked a lot better than I had when we'd last met – my hair shorter and combed back, not flopping over my face trying to cover the shape and size of my eyes; a little more flesh on my bones so elbows and knees weren't jutting out awkwardly; greater definition to my calf muscles after all those weeks of playing tennis with Jake. I rolled my eyes at myself. Such self-absorption.

'No, but it rounds off the sentence so nicely,' Karim said. It took me a moment to realize he was talking about Lapland. 'What *was* that thing you said?'

'Eratosthenes.'

A boot clunked against my window. I cranked the window open and stuck my head out. 'Stop ignoring us,' Tamara yelled up through a megaphone, waving one shoeless foot in the air. 'We want Chuck's nose back.' I leaned out, lifted the carrot – and the boot – off the ledge outside and threw them down.

'Now go away,' I yelled.

'Is that Mr Forehand bothering you again?' Tamara called up. I closed the window and lay down again.

'I had possession of a snowman's nose,' I explained to Karim. 'Who's Mr Forehand?'

'Oh, just this guy.' Strangely embarrassed.

'Jake?'

'How did you . . .?'

'My cousin, Omar, ran into Sonia in Karachi. She told him Jake's a tennis player. Is it love?'

'No, it's over. Has been for a while, though he keeps suffering memory lapses about that little detail.'

'Full story, please,' he said, in the tone of one who is entitled to know everything.

'He discovered his Hispanic roots. Decided to change the pronunciation of his name. I didn't take all this seriously enough.'

There was a pause, then laughter so dizzyingly contagious I knew it would have instantly healed my slightly aching heart if I'd heard it when the symptoms of break-up still persisted. 'Hake?' Karim spluttered. 'You were involved with a man who called himself Hake?'

'It's worse than that,' I said, laughing back. 'He's Hake Hunior.'

I could almost see Karim doubling over in the airport, oblivious to the stares of the jet-lagged and travel-weary. 'You're making up the Junior bit. Admit it!'

'But it rounds off the sentence so nicely.'

'God, it's good to laugh,' he said. 'Especially after I've been sitting here getting newsprint on my nose, reading about what's going on in Karachi.'

'What do you mean?'

'The violence flaring up. One hundred and thirty people killed in the first seventeen days of December. Have you see the new issue of *Newsline*? It says more people have been killed in Karachi this month than in Bosnia. Bosnia!'

'Oh, right.' I kept my voice as neutral as possible, but I was thinking: *Bloody, bloody hell.* Just when I thought all that rubbish between us had departed with the end of self-righteous adolescence. Why did he have to try so hard to let me know he still kept up with news from Karachi? Or was this an opening to get me to talk about that last letter I'd written him? Perhaps he expected me to apologize.

'I can hear you rolling your eyeballs.'

'Yeah, well. You know.' I looked out of the window again.

'No, I don't, and that's the problem, isn't it?'

'Whatever, Karim.' I felt sapped of all energy; I couldn't imagine ever having enough energy to fully engage in this conversation. I couldn't imagine having enough patience.

'"Whatever"? What is that little Americanism meant to signify?'

I do not know this man, I thought. I do not know him, but I cannot bear anything less than an intimacy that allows me to discern at ten paces whether the sheen on his skin is sweat or tears.

'Still searching for the comprehensive map of Karachi?' I said, knowing the remark to be cruel, though I couldn't have explained to anyone else why that was so.

'That essay you wrote . . . I thought it meant you were thinking about Karachi.'

I knew he couldn't see my eyebrows, but that didn't stop me raising them.

But he was going on: 'I mean, I've been trying for the last few years to come to grips with Karachi's nature, to face all these things that are so hard to face, and I'm just more glad than I can say that you've also started. Reading that essay, it was like you'd reached into my mind and pulled out all these thoughts from there. That cartographer in Zytrow, he was amazing. That you could write that was amazing. I mean, that you see he's willing to be unselfish – yes, because of the work he's doing people will stop talking about his great leap, and of course he's known that from the beginning, but he's willing to forgo that kind of self-glory in order to bring some order to the place.' I'd never heard anyone speak so fast or confuse me so much with what they were saying. 'And those two people in Raya, they have a kind of perfection, but it's in such a limited way because it's such a limited city, a city with only two inhabitants, and that's why they leave, isn't it? Because they have to see themselves in the context of something larger than just the two of them. It's like that Faiz poem, you know, *mujh say pehli si muhubat*, when you've seen the sorrows of the rest of the world you can't go on pretending none of it matters, you can't pretend two people can really live in isolation telling themselves their love is all that matters in the world. And the two of them, when they come back to the city, that's when they find out that their love was imperfect because it couldn't bear the knowledge of everything that lies outside and . . . Raheen, I see where you're going with it. I know what you're trying to say. Or beginning to. And I know it's not easy, but I'm here, Ra, I'm here.'

If he had been standing in front of me I would have hit him. 'You've been trying to come to grips with Karachi's nature and you're glad I've also *started*? I go home, Karim. Every bloody year. Twice a year. The day classes end. I get on that plane and I go back to Karachi. I'm going there in two weeks. And you, you'd rather go to Lapland!' I slammed my open palm against the side of my desk. 'Listen, do me a favour and burn that essay. Because it's obvious you haven't understood a word I've tried to say, and, frankly, right now I have no interest in pointing out all the places where you went wrong.'

There was silence from the other end. I could make out the noises of the airport, but from Karim I couldn't hear even a whisper of breath. It occurred to me that he'd simply walked away from the phone.

'When you go home do you ever catch a flight out of Boston?' he said at last.

I cranked open the window again and picked up a fistful of white from the ledge. When I opened my fist, my fingerprints were whorls of evidence in the tightly packed snow. I still remembered her number. I had only called it once, years ago, but I still remembered her number. 'Zia saw your mother over fall break. Went there for dinner while he was in Boston. I told him to give her my love.'

'What is Zia to my mother?' *His* voice tired now. 'You were the closest thing she had to a daughter. Over three years you've been on the East Coast, and not once have you bothered to call her. You really are your father's daughter.'

The mirror on the opposite wall showed my head jerking back in surprise, putting distance between myself and the words that came out of the handset. The only image that came to mind: my father putting an arm around Karim's shoulder at the airport, the last time our two families were together, and Karim turning one hundred and eighty degrees, wrapping his arms around Aba's waist and weeping. And I wondered again, as I'd so often wondered, of all those scraps of my letters that he'd chopped and pasted, why he had chosen the one in which I talked about parents and accepting their imperfections.

'I've got to go,' he said. 'They're calling my flight.'

'Karim ...' The thought that this was it, the attempt at reconciliation ended, was physically painful.

'What?'

'Why did you call?'

There was silence at the other end again, but I could hear him breathing. *Say it. Say, 'Because I missed you.'*

'Because I wanted to see ... if we could speak without noticing the palimpsest.'

'What?' He was receding, I could hear him drifting away, or was that me? Why had we ever thought it would be enough for us to speak to each other in fragments? What had we missed by finishing each other's sentences, assuming we'd always know the direction in which a thought was going? How many words had remained unspoken, misunderstood, between us at a time when we could so easily have set things right?

'Too many layers of words, Raheen, beneath and behind our sentences to each other.'

'Karim, don't, please, don't disappear.' Salty tracks curving beneath my eye and splashing on to the receiver.

'In that part of my mind that only remembers life before fourteen, Raheen, I'll love you for ever.'

He hung up so gently, I didn't even hear the click.

• • •

The boundary walls around Sonia's house were several feet higher than they had been in August when I was last in Karachi, and when Zia rang the bell no one opened the gate. Instead, a man I didn't recognize slid open a little flap in the gate and looked through. All I could see was one of his eyes and part of his nose. The eye darted from Zia to me, then back to Zia, where it stayed, narrowing slightly.

'We're here to see Sonia,' I said and waited for him to open the gate.

'Names?' he said.

Zia and I looked at each other, and Zia shrugged. 'I must look suspicious. Either that or unnecessary security measures are all the rage with the nouveau ri-chi-chi.'

'That's a Soniaism, right? Ri-chi-chi. I'd forgotten that one.' But now that he reminded me I wondered, as I had done when she first coined the term, if Sonia was aware of the way all of us regarded her parents, whose increased sophistication Aunty Laila dismissively compared to a thickening layer of make-up – merely drawing attention to how many blemishes there were and how much had to be done to hide them.

'Name?' the security guard said again.

'Where's Dost Mohommad? Where's Kalaam? They know who we are.' A part of me felt absurd for demanding the appearance of the cook and driver, but it seemed a point of pride to be admitted into Sonia's house without being forced to give my name to the guard.

He clicked his tongue and, stepping backwards, turned to speak to someone else. As his frame receded I was able to see that he had a gun slung over his shoulder and that there were two more armed guards, sitting on a charpai, between the driveway and the flower beds with their masses of canna lilies. A chill was beginning to seep from the cement driveway through my thin chapals, and my determination to win a stand-off with a guard who wasn't doing anything other than fulfilling the basic requirements of his job began to waver. I stepped away from the shadows.

'Serious weapons,' Zia said, drawing my attention to the guards' Kalashnikovs. 'You'd think this was some bigwig feudal household. Guess that's the idea.'

The guard pressed his eye against the flap again. 'Names?' he said.

Zia rolled his eyes and took his mobile phone out of his jeans pocket. He dialled a number and said, in Urdu for the guard's benefit, 'Uncle! Salaam! We're standing outside your house, talking to . . . just a second . . .' He looked up at the guard. 'Name?'

The guard closed the flap. There was the squeak of a lock unbolting. Zia put the phone back in his pocket and winked at me. 'Never mind, Uncle. We'll be right in,' he said to the air. I knew that he was behaving like a bit of a jerk, but I couldn't help thinking that it was so good to be home where we knew how everything worked and so know how to circumvent annoyances. In the air was a smell of something distant burning, which I always associated with Karachi winters.

We walked past the guards without a second glance, and went straight to the intricately carved front door. Locked. I turned back to the guards and made a gesture of irritation, and one of them went over to the little booth beside the charpai and spoke into the intercom. It was clear he was arguing with someone on the other side. I grabbed the branch of an almond tree and pulled down on it, relishing the weight of a branch without snow, no fear of something cold and wet sliding off and soaking your skin. The joy of breathing in deeply without teeth aching of cold. I heard footsteps inside approach. The tiniest of cracks appeared between the door frame and the door. I leaned close to the crack.

'Raheen and Zia,' I said, and Sonia's cook, Dost Mohommad, opened the door wide, beaming.

'Bored of America again?' he said. 'Come in, come in. These guards, they're useless. What will you eat? What will you drink? When did you get back?'

The marble floors were polished to a high gleam as always, and there was a new painting on the wall – a Chughtai watercolour of a beautiful woman, her glance poised between cruelty and sensuality – replacing the garish family portrait that used to form the first impression visitors had of the interior. The place had metamorphosed gradually over the years and it had been a long time since Zia had last made a snide comment about the Horror House and leopard-print carpets, though I was sure the gold taps still hadn't been replaced. On the table in the reception area was a photograph of Sonia's father standing next to the Pope. Rumour had it he'd paid a computer whiz huge amounts of money to have his image inserted next to that of the Pontiff. What, if not forgery, could explain the rabbit ears he'd formed with his fingers just behind the Pope's head? Although, if you were going to pay someone to digitally create a picture of you with someone famous, why would you choose the Pope?

'Just got back yesterday,' Zia said to Dost Mohommad. 'We'll call down from Sonia's room when we decide what we want for tea.' We both turned towards the stairs.

'Sit, sit in the drawing room. I'll tell her you're here.'

'No, no need. We'll go upstairs.'

Dost Mohammad made an apologetic sound. 'I'm sorry, Zia baba, you'll have to wait downstairs.'

Zia started to laugh, then saw that Dost Mohommad was serious. 'Me? Me specifically?'

Dost Mohommad looked down at his feet. 'Boys,' he said. 'No boys upstairs.'

'What? No, that must mean strangers. Or even friends of Sohail's. Obviously Sonia wouldn't want her brother's annoying seventeen-year-old friends barging into her room. It doesn't mean me.' Laughing again, Zia started to head towards the stairs, but Dost Mohommad's hand shot out and gripped Zia's arm.

'Last week, Cyrus baba said the same thing and I let him go upstairs. Almost got fired for it.'

'He's travelling to Egypt,' I mumbled.

'What?' Zia said, still looking at Dost Mohommad.

'Gone see-Nile. Look, why don't you wait down here, just to make him happy. I'll bring Sonia down.'

I took the stairs three at a time, and charged into Sonia's room without knocking. She wasn't there, but I heard the shower running so I thumped on the bathroom door and yelled, 'Come out or I'll un-alphabeticize your CDs.'

Sonia yelled with delight, 'I'm quickly, quickly rinsing.'

I sat down on her desk chair and picked up the magazine lying there, face down. It was the December issue of *Newsline*, the one that Karim had mentioned in our conversation two weeks earlier. I put it down and picked up the magazine next to it. The November issue of *Newsline*, with the words KARACHI: DEATH CITY running across the cover. I flipped it open and read an excerpted block:

Roaming the dark, death-haunted streets of Saddar where even the street lights were off, one would be confronted with the surreal glow of a flower shop not more than a thousand metres away from the troubled area of Jacob Lines. Asked why his shop was open late into the night when all others were closed, a flower-seller explained: 'This is the season not of marriage but of death. People come to buy floral wreaths for those who die in the riots.'

Shivering, I turned to the last page, which was guaranteed to bring comic relief with its round-up of the most absurd lines from Karachi's English-language press. Sure enough, there I read: 'Only the other day he was spotted lolloping into a famous disco which was a wee bit abnormal hangout for a bud like him. When interrogated he bleached.'

I was still laughing when the bathroom door opened and Sonia enveloped me in an embrace that was all softness.

'You hodious creature! When did you get back?' She pulled back and smiled at me, and I couldn't help thinking that if she were to walk down 5th Avenue just once, anorexic models would be pulled from the catwalk and a woman's beauty would no longer be judged by her success in obliterating flesh.

'Early this morning. You've put on weight since August. Looks good.'

'Hanh, well, happiness has a high calorie count.' She laughed and hugged me again. 'OK, sit, I have news to tell you so big that your eyes will pop out of their sockets and plop on to the floor; but don't worry: it was swept this morning.'

'First call down and tell Dost Mohommad to let Zia come up.'

'Zia's here?' She rolled down the sleeves of her kameez all the way to her wrists. 'Did you fly back together?' She bunched her wet hair together and squeezed out water, then reached behind me to the dupatta slung over the back of her chair and placed it on her head. 'Let's go down and sit with him.'

'Have I entered a parallel universe here?' I tugged at the dupatta, but she clapped one hand down to hold it in place. 'What's going on?'

She gave me one of her drop-the-topic looks. 'We are Muslim women,' she said.

I tried to find some sign that she was joking. 'We were Muslim women four months ago, too.'

'I thought we'd agreed to disagree about religion. Let's go downstairs. Poor Zia must be getting bored.'

The intercom beeped three times to indicate there was a phone call for her. She picked up the phone, listened to the voice on the other end, and made a gesture in my direction that said, 'Go down, I'll join you there.'

Thoroughly confused, and more than a little concerned, I

walked downstairs. Sonia's and my friendship had always existed against all probability, our ways of life so tangential that logic should dictate we could only look at each other across a wide gulf, and wave. The reason our friendship had survived and strengthened over the years was that Sonia succeeded in being so self-effacing in her beliefs, allowing nothing in her convictions to act as reproach, and I was well aware that I scarcely extended her the same courtesy.

As I reached the bottom of the stairs I could see Zia through the open door of the TV room, shuffling through a pile of CDs but not paying any attention to the jackets, his eyes fixed on a framed picture of Sonia instead.

In America I'd tell people that Zia and I had been friends for ever, but the truth was vastly more complicated than that. When we were both fifteen he became my first boyfriend, a title he managed to retain for less than seventy-two hours. Quite what happened to bring everything to a disastrous end neither of us could now remember, but when it happened, with no Karim around to laugh at us and listen to us and, in so doing, smooth the transition from relationship back to friendship, I had taken to making the lives of our mutual friends unnecessarily difficult by declaring I wanted nothing to do with Zia. Of our entire group only Sonia seemed not to mind, and blithely ripped the 'Z' page out of her phone book as a show of her support for my position. When she did that I was, I'll admit, dismayed; I wanted so much to have cause to dislike her, because it was clear that Zia had not, not for one moment, stopped being in love with her. Truth is, I missed his friendship, particularly since Karim was so far away and there was no one else with whom I could talk about Karim the way I talked about him with Zia. But I saw how much it hurt him to have Sonia put an arm around me and lead me away every time he approached, and so I continued pretending that I wanted to be lead away, my relationship with both Sonia and Zia a murky and tangled thing until Sonia finally let me yell at her, and the yells turned to tears which dissolved all my anger at her.

By that time Zia had found his own group of friends; a 'racy set', as Aunty Runty put it to everyone at her beauty parlour, and for over a year he disappeared in a haze of drugs and alcohol, and then he disappeared between the covers of textbooks, having decided he was getting out of Karachi even if it meant learning every word on the SAT word-list by heart and taking tuition lessons for every subject, not with the popular tuition teachers who we all went to post-school *en masse*, but one-on-one teachers whom Zia's father paid exorbitant amounts to aid Zia in racing to the top of the class, leaving his teachers no choice but to write letters of recommendation to US universities saying, for a while there he fell behind, but I have scarcely ever seen such a passion for learning as he has exhibited, blah, blah, blah.

America brought Zia and me together again – literally. At university, in the middle of New York state, nostalgic for things we'd never paid attention to, like Urdu music and basmati rice, Zia and I scoured the neighbouring towns and found each other at a moment when familiarity was ready to serve as a synonym for friendship. There was some initial tentativeness on both our parts when he first began to drive the half-hour from his college to mine on the feeblest of excuses, but it wasn't long before we slipped into our old habit of camaraderie and were even able to laugh at the melodrama of our break-up, which had occurred in the biology lab while we were both dissecting rabbits. 'I bet you're imagining that rabbit is me,' I had hissed to Zia, as he sped his way through the dissection at twice the speed everyone else was going. 'Impossible,' he had replied, stabbing a rabbit ventricle with his scalpel to send an arc of blood spurting at me. 'The bunny's got a heart!'

If sometimes in those first months of getting to know him again the whispers and suggestions of my college friends made me look at Zia and recollect first love, first kiss, and I found myself walking that line between remembering a past emotion and reawakening that feeling again, I had only to remind myself of the way Zia continued to look at photographs of Sonia to steel myself against further foolishness. Then Amit came along, then Ricardo, then Jake, and 'How do you do it, Zee? How do you love the same person at twenty-one as you did at thirteen?' I would ask, and Zia just shrugged and said, 'Desiring the unattainable; that's all this is about,' knowing I knew him too well to believe it. Every woman he dated at college had at least a touch of Sonia about her and when he was the one to break off the relationship it was always because 'she wasn't who I thought she was'.

I cleared my throat as I walked into the TV room and Zia turned away from the photograph. 'Just choosing some music to listen to.' He picked up the CD from the top of the pile – some Eighties compilation – and looked at the titles listed on the back. 'Remember when Sonia thought the lyrics to the Paul Young song were: "Every time you go away / You take a piece of meat with you"?'

'Yes!' Sonia walked into the room. 'And Karim dreamt up this video in which a guy announces he's running down to the supermarket, and his wife yells, "No! Don't take the venison!" '

Zia moved towards her, then stopped. He'd reacted the same way on first seeing her during our first winter back from college, unsure if the resumption of my friendship with him meant that he and Sonia could take their relationship back in time to 1988 as well. Sonia had laughed at his hesitation and reached out to hug him. But this time it was the covered head, and the sleeves she was tugging over her wrists, that made him pause and look to her for the first move. We heard the door to the drawing room open, and her father's voice came booming through; Sonia smiled at Zia and rested her fingers on the back of his hand. He blushed and, seeing that, she moved away from him, gesturing to us to sit down.

'Is it your father?' I asked. 'Is he making you do the hijab bit?'

'Raheen!' Zia's voice quavered. 'She does have a mind of her own.'

'Thanks, Zia. Raheen, stop asking bakwaasi questions. We have a lot to talk about that's more interesting than my wardrobe. Most importantly,' now it was her turn to blush, 'the seventh of January.'

'Birthday of Millard Fillmore, the thirteenth president of the USA?' I was thrilled to have the chance to display this piece of knowledge.

'Well, OK,' Sonia said. 'But now you have even another reason to burn it into your memory.'

'What, you getting married?' I laughed.

'Engaged.'

I did not dare look at Zia. I wanted to reach over and put my arms around him, but I knew the only thing I could do to demonstrate my friendship was to cover up his silence, which was so complete I wasn't sure he was even breathing.

'You're getting engaged? Sneaky thing! You never told me there was anyone . . .' I reached out to embrace her, but pulled back before we made contact. 'Is it arranged?'

'I really, really like him, Raheen. He's twenty-six, his name's Adel, good family, works with his father in the textile industry, really smart, good sense of humour, two sisters who adore him, we talk for ages on the phone every day, that was him just now calling from the office, and I'm happier than you've ever seen, admit it.'

'Who could deny it? You're radiant.' Zia sounded like a child of seven, utterly lost, but trying to repeat a formula that his mother had taught him to get out of trouble.

Sonia looked sideways and down, and I wondered if she finally saw that I hadn't been inventing things all those times in the last three years that I told her Zia would still walk on hot coals and eat them afterwards if she asked him to.

'Is Adel the reason Zia is being treated like a potential rapist in your house?'

'Raheen!' Zia rose to his feet in an instant. 'If she's observing customs of proper behaviour . . .'

'Proper behaviour? You can't see her hair, can't see her arms, can't make more than minimal physical contact, can't enter her bedroom. What does that say about you? As though you won't be able to restrain yourself if . . .' I faltered before the look on his face.

'Oh, sit down, both of you. You're such a drama queen, Raheen. And "customs of proper behaviour" . . . which rubbish-wallah sold you that line, Zia? I know you don't see the point in any of it. Now sit down and tell me if you want Dost Mo-hommad to bring tea or coffee.'

I sat down and put my arms around her. 'When do I meet him?'

'Not for a couple of weeks. In about an hour he's leaving for London on work. And to buy me an engagement ring.'

'Well, when I do meet him if he isn't completely gaga about you I'll have to punch him.'

'Not his nose,' Sonia said. 'He has a lovely straight nose. Don't ruin it.'

'I'll make sure to aim my punch well below the nose.'

'Not too much below.' She giggled. I started laughing too, and she turned red and pulled her dupatta down so it covered her face. 'Tobah! You are such a bad influence. Zia, promise to keep an eye on her during the mangni; I'm fully nervous she'll do something to embarrass me.'

'When have I ever been able to keep her in check?' Zia was smiling now, fooling Sonia into believing he was all right.

'True. Only one person ever could. Good thing he's also going to be here, flying in the day after and staying until after the mangni. No way I'd let him miss my engagement.'

'Seriously?' Zia said, leaning forward but keeping his knees just a few millimetres apart from Sonia's. 'Karim's coming?'

Sonia nodded and both of them looked at me, Sonia slightly nervous, as though unsure if she'd said something that would delight or appal me, and Zia merely appraising. He'd been the one who had, quite by chance, knocked on my dorm-room door just minutes after I finished that phone call with Karim, and he'd made it clear he thought I was being melodramatic, crying over something that had ended long before the phone had started to ring.

I leaned back against the cushions and watched the thin branches of the bougainvillaea whip against the window. If I closed my eyes I'd still see the red flowers, bright against my cornea, surrounded by black. If I closed my eyes I'd see Karim gather up pruned branches that his gardener had been about to throw into the incinerator; I'd see myself, aged thirteen, lying on the grass, resting my head on a pillow of bougainvillaea flowers, watching Karim fashion a hopscotch grid out of denuded branches. Through all that seeing, I'd hear myself laugh for no reason, no reason at all, and I'd wonder where that particular laugh had gone and I'd wonder if he'd bring it back with him when he walked through the doors of the airport.

• • •

Whoever he was, he wasn't my Karimazov, my Cream, my hopscotch partner, my shadow-self, my alter ego.

Showing his passport to the airport officials, just feet away from the wide-open terminal door, he was a tall, very tall, stranger with close-cropped hair, perfectly arched eyebrows, and stylish round glasses, dressed in jeans, sneakers, and a collarless kurta with sleeves rolled up. If it wasn't for those absurd ears waggling out of the sides of his head, I might have mistaken him for a foreigner, dressed in a manner that announced both his foreignness and his desire to absorb the influences of the East. 'Just as I feared,' I muttered to Zia, as we leaned against the barriers that stood between the terminal door and the crowds waiting to receive foreigners and foreign-returned. 'He's become a gora.'

'What you talking about? He's darker than you are.' Zia was trying hard not to act too excited about seeing Karim again, but the casual air with which he held a cigarette between his fingers was more than offset by the frequency with which he shifted his weight from one foot to the other, pausing only to try and raise his entire body weight with his elbows, which were planted on the barrier.

'Not skin complexion, idiot. His mode of being. What's he arguing with the customs guy about?'

'They're probably giving him a hard time about his Angrez passport. Or is it Amreekan? He could at least look up and wave. Damn, he's tall. "Mode of being"?'

'I still don't know why he asked to stay with you, not me.' I tilted my head to one side, as though a change in angle would make him look more familiar.

'Propriety.'

'Rubbish. If he came to stay he'd be my parents' guest; staying with us because he's Ali and Maheen's son, not because he's my one-time best friend.' A man smelling as I imagined the inside of a local bus would smell tried to elbow me aside so that he could secure a spot right against the barrier, and I wondered how to push him away without actually making any physical contact with him.

'Here he comes. Stop being moody.'

A swarm of cabbies surrounded Karim as he walked past the barrier without seeing us, and as Zia and I battled our way through the jostling figures we heard Karim say, in Urdu without a trace of hesitancy or rustiness, 'I have friends coming to meet me,' and the cabbies saying, 'Where? Where are they? At this hour, they must be asleep. No one's coming.' And one enterprising fellow pulled out a phone card and gestured to the public telephone. 'Call your friends. If there's no answer, they're asleep and you come with me.' Karim turned the visiting card over in his hands. Strong hands, the kind that make you think instantly of massages. 'Maybe if they don't answer it means they're on their way to the airport.' But he didn't sound convinced. Zia and I were standing within touching distance of him now, arms crossed, laughing, but he still didn't look up and see us.

One of the cab drivers clapped the palm of his hand on the top of Karim's head and turned it towards us. 'There are your friends,' he said.

Zia was closer to him, so it was Zia whom he threw his arms around, and I thought, he still hugs men like a real Pakistani, none of this let's-pretend-there's-nothing-intimate-about-our-physical-contact that so many American boys, and also so many Karachi boys who'd been watching too much America and too little Pakistan, were guilty of when they slapped and punched each other in greeting.

When he let go of Zia there was a moment when we just looked at each other, neither quite sure what to do, and I couldn't say if that was because of the way our letter-writing ended or the way our phone conversation ended or the way some of the men around us seemed to be sizing us up, trying to determine the nature of our relationship, forcing us to wonder the same thing also. And in both our minds the soundtrack of our last phone call was playing. I half-smiled – there I went, thinking I could read his mind again. He laughed, that sudden self-conscious laugh of his, and put his hands on my shoulders, his thumbs resting on bare skin, either side of my neck.

'Idiot,' I said, and put my arms around his waist, everything forgotten except how easily we always forgave each other.

He disengaged almost immediately, spinning around and putting an arm out to catch a man walking past. 'I have something of yours,' he said, pulling his suitcase off the trolley. He twirled the combination lock and snapped the case open.

'No, that's OK, you can have it.'

'Please, no, you've been too generous.' He pulled a T-shirt out of his suitcase. 'If you were going to be in town any longer, I'd have it washed and . . .' The end of the sentence was muffled by cloth as Karim pulled the white kurta over his head.

Zia whispered to me, 'No ogling. You don't want to derail another friendship.'

I jammed my elbow into his ribs, never taking my eyes off Karim's torso. 'You were the derailer, not me. Rabbit-mutilator!'

'What's the conspiracy?' Karim smiled at us. He had handed his kurta to the man and was wearing a T-shirt and sleeveless cardigan. I had to admit to myself, the kurta had looked better.

Zia pointed to the man and then back to Karim's T-shirt and looked expectant.

'Flight attendant asked me where I was going, so I said "Karachi" and he replied, "Of course. Caracas!" and spilt a thermos of tea down my shirt. That man kindly gave me a spare kurta. Zia, is that a shaving cut on your chin?'

Zia punched him lightly in the ribs, and Karim grabbed Zia in a headlock and spun him around, both of them laughing. For a moment they weren't men just past the brink of adulthood any more, but the same two boys who had stood in front of a mirror and made their first attempts at shaving some seven or eight years ago, both of them arriving in school the next day with nicks and cuts all over their faces, even in places where bristles hadn't started to grow. We would all have laughed at them a lot more if they hadn't combined their talents and presented such a perfect balance of swagger and self-deprecation.

Karim finally let go of Zia, and looked around him in some surprise. 'I can't believe this airport! It's so spacious and so clean.'

'So all foreign visitors can have a good first impression of the city. It's all downhill from here.' Zia waved the porters away and said he'd bring the car round. Seconds later, it was Karim and me and a suitcase standing by the side of the road, waiting, the cab drivers and porters and onlookers no longer interested in our presence. Cars shimmered in the sunlight like a mirage. Karim's glasses shimmered, too; perhaps he was the mirage. If I were ever delusional or hallucinating it would make sense for me to conjure up Karim, and not just any Karim but a Karim who looked like this. I looked sideways at him, but didn't say anything; I wanted to see if we could still be comfortable in silence. He didn't say anything either; he was too busy looking around, learning the landscape, the squat shrubs and billboards and low-rise buildings just past the manicured airport grounds, and recalling that, yes, this is what Karachi feels like at five-thirty on a winter's morning; time to wake up to cram in that last round of studying for today's exam, which we should have finished preparing for last night. These last three years, Karachi nothing more than holiday for me, I'd slept through this early daylight time, awakening only when the sun had been out long enough to glaze over the chill in the air, so now even I couldn't help a prickle of nostalgia for those school mornings of sweaters and chapped lips and staticky hair. Karim shivered, and I wrapped one end of my shawl around him, without actually making any contact with his skin – that was not through accident and certainly not through disdain. Coyness – or was it self-consciousness? – entered my life as we stood there, and confounded me entirely.

'It's not cold,' he said.

'You've got goosebumps.'

'It's not cold.'

Zia pulled up and I told Karim to sit in the front seat. I sat behind the driver's seat and watched him watch Karachi as Zia drove us out of the airport ground and on to the road, which was free of congestion at this hour, giving us an unobstructed view of the billboards: MOD GIRL! CUTE! – an advertisement for talcum powder; HAIR STOP FACE – an ad for facial-hair remover; WESTMINSTER ABBEY – an upstart rival to the well-established BIG BEN underwear company, attempting to attract customers with its painting of a man in leopard-print Y-fronts swinging his hips and raising his arms in triumph.

Karim pointed at the hip-swinging man. 'Zia, he looks like you! So that's what's become of the heirloom leopard skin that used to hang in your TV room. Are there matching socks?'

'Oh, go to hell,' Zia said, but he was smiling along with me to see Karim being so Karim.

We were in view of the Star Gate, which heralded the turn-off to the old airport, the one from which Karim had departed with his parents more than seven years ago, the nuclear family still intact back then, though showing signs of exploding.

'All right, where are we headed?' Zia asked. 'Karim?'

'Come to my place for breakfast,' I suggested. 'My parents can't wait to see you.'

'How about visiting the bride-to-be?' Karim said quickly, so quickly he must not have heard me.

'She's in Dubai for the weekend, visiting some relatives. And besides, if she were here it wouldn't look right if we had her woken up,' Zia said.

'Arré.' Karim laughed. 'What rot are you on about?'

'Implies familiarity,' Zia muttered. 'Too much of it.'

I repeated the invitation to have breakfast with my parents. Karim looked out of the window. Was he too overwhelmed by the remembered sights and sounds to be able to concentrate on anything anyone was saying? What had he meant by that remark about my father when we'd spoken on the phone? Which of us was going to be the first to bring up all the things we'd said?

'Ask me directions from here to somewhere I used to know, Zia.'

'OK. Kindergarten.'

'That's easy. Straight down Shahrah-e-Faisal and right on to Abdullah Haroon Road, and the school's on your right just before Aiwan-e-Saddar Road.'

I couldn't refrain from adding, 'Or, in Karachispeak, go straight straight straight straight straight and then turn right just after the Metropole, and when you see a church, stop.'

'Straight straight straight straight straight, huh?' Hard to tell if Karim was amused or annoyed, his expression cut off from me as he stuck his head out of the window, taking in the street's mishmash of tall concrete office buildings, large houses, and the signs, at the entrance to plots of land enclosed by boundary walls, spelling out 'Hina Marriage Garden', 'Diamond Marriage Garden', 'Sindbad Marriage Garden'. Zia caught my eye in the rear-view mirror and gave me an exasperated look. I shrugged.

Karim retracted his head. 'So many new buildings, and the driving is crazier than I remember, even with early-morning traffic. Wait, isn't that the turn-off for Tariq Road and Mohommad Ali Society? Can we go to Kaybee's?'

'You want ice cream at this hour?'

He pulled his ear and looked at me thoughtfully. 'No, I suppose not. This is all so strange for me . . .' He stuck his head out of the window again.

A bus sped past, just inches away, and Zia reached over and pulled Karim back into the car. 'Look out of the windscreen, OK? You're no fun when you're decapitated. So talk to us, yaar, tell us things. What have you been doing since you graduated last year? And why do you have a girlfriend named Spa?'

I tried not to look too interested. Sonia had mentioned the girlfriend after she'd met Karim in London the previous year, though she had no details on how serious things were between them.

'Don't really know what I'm doing with life outside uni. So, I've put aside the year to travel before worrying about it. And her name's actually Grace, which is what I call her, but she got her nickname because her parents fell in love while watching "Spartacus".'

'That's about as romantic as it gets.' I laughed. He couldn't possibly be serious about someone who allowed herself to be called Spa.

'And besides, she's my ex-girlfriend.'

Ha!

Zia blew his horn at a legless beggar crossing the street in a wheeled contraption, just inches off the ground, and swerved away from him. Karim didn't react, though I had expected him to have a moment of tourist horror.

'Was it the 1960 version, or the 1967 reissue?' I asked. 'Because, you know, the 1967 version cut out that great moment of whatshername looking at Spartacus writhing on a cross and saying, "Oh, please die, my darling." If that's not dialogue to fall in love to, what is? I bet it was the 1960 version.'

'Still the Queen of Trivia,' Karim said. 'Hey, QT.'

'Hey, Bloody Damn Idiot. Can you spot that clever acronym, BD-I? But before we lose track of the conv, tell me, did you and Grace ever watch "Spartacus" together?'

'Oh, you didn't,' Zia said. 'That would be too weird. Who wants to re-create their parents' relationship, have to imagine when they were young and hormonal and . . .' He looked at Karim, went bright red and started cursing the beggar who was now barely visible in the rear-view mirror. Karim turned to look at me, his expression unfathomable, then looked hurriedly away.

I remembered something I'd been wondering about for a while. 'So, have you ever visited your mother in Boston in the last few years? While Zia and I were on the east coast? Were you there, too?'

'Don't start with the recriminations,' he said shortly and looked away.

How could I explain to him about Aunty Maheen, when I hadn't really explained it to myself? He probably suspected that I had flown out of Boston again on my way home and still hadn't called her, despite his rebuke to me on the phone. It's not as though I hadn't thought of it. It's not as though I hadn't picked up the telephone and started to dial the number, more than once, more than twice, more than that even. I wanted to lean across and shake Karim. Why did this have to be so difficult? Although Zia barely ever answered his letters, and hadn't had any kind of verbal communication with him since we all left school, aside from one phone call last week when Karim asked if he could stay at Zia's, they were chatting away in the front seat as though no time had passed and nothing had changed since 1987, pausing only to look at each other, still sizing up the changes time had wrought in their physical selves, then laughing, half-embarrassed, as boys do when they've been caught paying any kind of attention to the way other boys look. And when Sonia had met Karim in London she had come back and reported that he was the same, their friendship was the same, everything same-to-same, except that now he was gorgeous, but that's just superfacial change, right?

'I can't believe I'm back,' Karim said.

'The temptation is strong to say, there is no going back.'

'Resist it,' he advised.

Resistance was never my strong suit, so I tried to look only at his ears. They really were his least attractive feature, and I had to concentrate hard to avoid shifting my attention to the triangle of moles on the nape of his neck, and the FromHereToEternity length of his legs, and the supple fingers that were drumming snatches of REM's 'Nightswimming' on thigh, throat, clavicle, and all this I was managing quite well, but what was really getting to me were the veins that stood out on his wrist and forearms, even when his hands were relaxed, and one vein in particular that ran all the way from his wrist to his elbow.

'Where are we going?' I asked, as Zia turned off the airport road earlier than he would if going to my house or his.

'I've made a command decision. We're off to Mehmoodabad. Where I bet neither of you have ever been. This will be my second trip. I have to look at a billboard that has my face painted on it, and explain to the painters what they need to do to capture my soul.'

'Eh?' I said.

'Oh, I agreed to pose for this photograph for some ad. As a favour to Cyrus's cousin – you remember Cyrus from school, Karim? – who's just started up this ad agency. Your father must know him, Raheen. Khushroo something or other. Anyway, I thought it would be some print ad, but it turns out my long lashes are going to greet you as you ascend Clifton Bridge. I'm replacing the billboard for GUL'S JOLLY JELLIES; aren't I special? But according to Khushroo the painters have captured my features but missed my essence, so I have to go and radiate essence, while also giving them a lecture on the difference between copying an image and interpreting a soul.'

'(A) Why did you do this odd thing? (B) Why are we doing this odder thing at this hour? (C) What are you advertising?'

'(A) Because I couldn't think of a reason to say no. (B) Because the painters said they'd start work at dawn today so they'd be done in time for some neighbourhood cricket match. And (C) I didn't actually bother to ask.'

'Mehmoodabad,' Karim said. 'That'll be great.'

'Why?' I was instantly irritated. It wasn't my Karimazov but the foreign cartographer speaking – the one who had sent me maps of Karachi from London, informing me how limited my knowledge of the place was. 'Why will Mehmoodabad be great when you've probably never been there and this city is full of old haunts you haven't seen in years and should be dying to revisit?'

Zia turned up the volume of the music, and Nusrat's rendition of 'Mera Piya Ghar Aya' drowned out anything Karim might have thought to say in retaliation. *Mera Piya Ghar Aya . . .* My beloved came home.

We crossed Kala Pul, the Black Bridge that wasn't black, and turned into the residential streets of Defence Housing Authority (Phase II), just past the roundabout that displayed a model of a fighter-plane with a trail of fire shooting out of its rear (when Runty and Bunty provided a map to their house for one of their Ghutna parties, the roundabout was marked: 'jet with flaming ass'). I closed my eyes, overcome with sleepiness. When I looked out again the comparative order of Defence had given way to the narrow alleys and tiny store-fronts of Mehmoodabad. I had no idea how we'd got here, and Zia seemed a little surprised himself. I could hear him muttering, 'Left after the place where the goats were eating the antenna, then right . . . before or after the hubcap?'

A bus rumbled past and a man with a wool cap on his head and cracked sandals on his feet fumbled with the lock at the base of his shop's shutter. Further on, a man sat cross-legged in a shop with tyres hanging from hooks on the bright pink walls, closely examining the inner tube of a bicycle. Next door to him a fruit seller arranged pomegranates into triangular piles, stopping before he reached the apex to weigh apples for a customer who took the apples and handed him a red note. The fruit seller called to the vegetable man across the road, and the vegetable man sent a young boy scampering back to the fruit seller with change for the customer's hundred-rupee note. We passed a white-tiled, tube-lit 'hotel' where men seated around wooden tables huddled for warmth over cups of steaming tea, and Zia pointed triumphantly at the hubcap propped against a wall and turned into an alley so narrow he had to snap his side-view mirror against the car frame so that it wouldn't graze the wooden shutters of the houses. Houses! To me the word conjured up structures surrounded by gardens and surrounded further by boundary walls, but here you could look down the street and see rectangular, double-storeyed buildings squished together – or was it one building, one which changed colour here and there? – with doors and windows at regular intervals, each set of doors marking the entry to a house.

What is it that makes a place feel like home, even when it is entirely removed from the neighbourhood you've grown up in? Is it merely some trick of the mind, an illusion of connectedness? At college, when I threw away a flyer from the Career Centre and declared to Zia that I was going home, goddammit, as soon as I graduated, he accused me of missing the luxury of upper-middle-class living, that's all. And I had thought then, Karim would understand, Karim would know, that 'belonging' is a spider-plant-shaped, sea-bordering, dusty word. But now, looking at Karim, I wondered if I could really say any more what he knew or understood.

Zia turned into another alley, slightly wider than the first, and drew up to a gate that looked brown but turned out to be rusted. He parked his car half on the street, half on the narrow pavement that ran along one side of the road.

Karim and I stepped out of the car at the same time, and Karim stretched, his shirt rising up as he did so, revealing a raised chicken-pox scar just above the waistband of his jeans and a line of hair leading downwards from his navel. He caught me looking at the scar and glanced at it self-consciously.

'I have one,' I said, and showed him the discoloured scar on my elbow. He touched it.

'Mine's bumpier,' he said, and raised his shirt so I could see it again.

'Is it?' It obviously was. I ran my finger over the scar. He breathed in suddenly, just as I touched him, and a gap opened up between his flat stomach and his jeans.

I didn't move my hand away, and he smiled, stomach muscles still contracted. 'You're cold. Gave me a shock.'

'You have goldfish on your boxers,' I said, looking down, and he laughed and exhaled.

'Are you guys coming?' Zia called out. He was peering over the rusty gate, and holding up a hand in greeting to someone on the other side. A man with a white streak in his hair – paint or pigmentation? – opened the gate. We followed Zia in, and I found myself in a place such as I had never imagined I'd come across in such a cramped street, behind such a rusty gate. Not that I gave much time to imagining cramped streets, rusted gates.

The ground was all concrete, but that was the only uniform aspect of the place. As we entered I saw a covered garage to the left, with no cars inside, but steel poles, buckets, cans, instead. To the right was uncovered space, allowing us to see the unim- pressive diffusion of early-morning light across the sky. Two long steel poles with rungs running along their length lay on the ground, taking up much of the floor space. It took a moment to register that these poles normally held up billboards, the primary source of colour (buses aside) on Karachi's streets. A man was sitting between two rungs, sipping his tea and looking at a vast blank canvas propped against the outer wall of the garage. Two rooms constructed from brick took up space at opposite ends of the plot. One room housed a water pump and unmarked bags that looked heavy but didn't further reveal their nature to me. The other room had a desk, a cupboard, chairs and a poster of a Pakistani film actress, alongside a watercolour reproduction of the poster. The outer walls of the second room were covered in dabs of multicoloured paint. Electric wires extended out of both rooms, well above ground level, with light bulbs at their ends wrapped around tree limbs (there was a tree, in the posture of an exhausted scarecrow, growing in the compound, and another tree, far more hale, reaching in from the plot next door).

Further in, as we walked diagonally from the gate, rusted steel poles held up a makeshift roof, constructed of old billboards, which covered about a third of the compound. There were more canvases propped up against the walls in this section, some with pencil drawings, some half-painted, some nearing completion, and one, clearly used for doodling, covered in calligraphy, caricatures of politicians, and a painting of a goat sticking out its tongue, little lines indicating that the tongue was waggling in the direction of the Prime Minister's caricature. The various men who'd been sipping tea and talking in the compound stood up and drew near Zia as Bilal – the man who had opened the gate – called Zia's attention to a billboard standing flush against a wall.

'Oh!' I couldn't help exclaiming.

It was Zia. Or Zia's head, rather, ten times its usual size, looking with delight at Zia's ten-times too large hand squeezing white liquid out of an inflated pink glove into Zia's wide and fleshy mouth.

'Uh, Zia?'

'I have no idea, Raheen. I have no idea what that is.'

Karim had been wandering around the compound, examining brushes stiff with paint and pretending to make a feat of balancing on the wide, prone poles, but now he came up and looked at the painting and as soon as he started laughing I knew exactly what the pink glove was.

'Bet this is where the slogan goes,' I said, pointing to a blank patch of canvas.

'But what am I selling?' Zia said.

Karim and I grinned at each other.

'Some new brand of milk,' I said. 'Probably with a name like HUMAN KINDNESS.'

'And the slogan: UDDERLY FRESH!' Karim said.

Zia looked at the dripping pink glove, and turned white, as Karim and I exchanged high-fives.

Bilal, ignoring all of this, asked for Zia's opinion on the painting.

'There's something slightly stiff about the features,' Zia said, trying to regain his composure.

Karim pushed Zia aside, and spoke up. 'There's no poetry in it. No dazzle.' He was speaking in Urdu, couldn't find the word for 'dazzle', so made do with 'day-zle'. He pointed towards the room with its poster of the actress. 'That quality which makes Neeli Neeli, which makes Amitabh Amitabh, which makes Schwarznegger Schwarznegger, it just isn't in this painting. Hero quality, that's what we need. Jazbaa, joush, Razzmatazz.' His face lit up. 'Chutzpah!'

Bilal nodded and walked towards his co-workers, his shoulders shaking.

'You have to speak their language,' Karim whispered conspiratorially.

'Yiddish?'

We exchanged glances and burst into laughter, laughing so hard we had to hold on to each other for support. And then we weren't laughing any more, but his arms were around me, my chin on his shoulder, his neck just centimetres away from my mouth, and I thought, how easy it is, how easy it can be. Where have you been all these years, Karim? Where have I been?

At the periphery of my vision, I was aware of Zia looking at us, his mouth open, a look of surprise, almost wonder, in his eyes.

The painters emerged, giggling, from their huddle, and Bilal cleared his throat. I remembered propriety and pulled away from Karim, just as Zia explained, 'Cousins. Haven't seen each other in a long time.'

Bilal looked simultaneously amused and disbelieving, and went back to the topic of the billboard. 'We'll touch it up a little. Now that we've seen you we've got a clearer image of your . . . day-zle.'

'If you give us some tea we'll sit here a while and you can watch him,' Karim said. 'So that his image takes root in your memory.'

'Like a mango tree,' Bilal said. 'And soon it will bear fruit, and his face above Clifton Bridge will be a sun-gold mango with cheeks you want to devour. Washed down with a glass of milk.'

'I feel the onset of terror,' Zia said.

Bilal smiled, none too reassuringly, and disappeared back into the room, but this time it was to bring out tea in flower-patterned cups. He offered us chairs as well, but we all preferred to sit on the steel poles, open sky above our heads. Zia said he was going to his car to get a sweater for himself, even though it was now warmer than it had been when we stood at the airport, and he hadn't felt any need for a sweater then. It was quiet enough that when a rooster crowed next door we could hear the accompanying flap of wings.

Karim sat beside me, his legs crossed at the ankles. He didn't say anything, or even sit as close as I hoped he would, but my world shimmered at the languor with which he caressed the flower pattern on the teacup, tracing the petals with his index finger, sliding his thumb up and down the stem, just prior to raising the cup to his lips. It was enough to make me wish I was porcelain, hollow and filled with hot liquid. I pulled his ear lobe and he smiled and kicked me gently.

'So I'm sorry about that last letter to you,' I said. 'I pretty much harangued you, didn't I?'

'Yeah, well, I'm sorrier about mine. The cut-up letters.'

I bit my lip and turned my face towards the sun so that he couldn't see the tears that had rushed to my eyes. Until he said it, I'd had no idea how much I needed to hear that from him.

'I had only just found out,' he continued. 'I guess you must have known for quite a while by then. But I only found out the day before I got your letter, and when I read it I thought I heard certain traits echoing.' He stopped to look at my face as I struggled to remember. What must I have known for quite a while by then? Was there some mass carnage, or something along those lines, that made my comments about 'Mr Compassionate-Sitting-in-London' and 'when we laugh it's survival' particularly tasteless? What was going on in the country in 1990 when I had sent him that letter? And what traits echoing? The traits of a Karachiite who was choosing to survive the calamity rather than weeping about it? From a distance, I could see how that looked like callousness.

I ran one finger along his eyebrow, feeling the soft hairs ruffle against my skin. 'Things look different when you're living here, Karim. Now that you're back, you'll see that.'

Karim pulled back and caught me by the wrists. 'What are you saying? That none of it made you angry?'

'But what good would that have done?' Did he think my anger would terrify the city into stopping its crazed behaviour? Why couldn't I remember what had been happening in Karachi when I wrote that letter?

He leaned forward, his chest pressing against my palms. I thought he was going to kiss me, and I glanced around – a Karachi girl's instinctive move in such a situation – to ensure Bilal and the others weren't looking. But his face remained several inches away from mine. 'Ra, you can tell me the truth. We don't have to be on opposite sides.'

'I am telling you the truth.'

He let go of my wrists and stood up. 'Raheen, you wouldn't have sent me that essay if you didn't . . . The two people in that city, what's that damn name, Ray . . . Rye . . . Ray . . . ?'

'Raya? What does that have to do with this?'

'Raya. Yes, the ones who reflected the attitude of that Faiz poem. The selfishness, the weakness, of certain kinds of love.'

I shook my head. 'You've got it all wrong. I was trying to say . . . well, I was trying to say that I wish you hadn't left.'

Karim blinked once, twice, three times. He turned around, his back to me, and put his hand over his eyes. 'That's it? That was about you and me?'

'Isn't that enough?'

'No,' he said. It was a wounded sound.

I stood up and put my hands on his shoulder. 'Karim, I don't understand why that letter of mine made you so angry.'

He went completely still. 'You don't understand?' He looked around him as though trying to find his bearings. He faced me again and his lips moved, as though he were rehearsing words, but nothing came out.

I didn't know what to say or do, so I simply took his hand in mine.

He wrenched away from me. 'I'm tired. I should probably go to Zia's and sleep for a while.' He walked towards the gate without looking back, calling out to Zia that it was time to leave. On his way out, I saw him reach back to his shoulder blade. He brushed off the rooster feather that had fallen from the branch above, and continued walking.

. . .

Minutes later, Zia's car stalled.

We weren't out of Mehmoodabad yet; Zia had attempted a short cut which brought us into a narrow, deserted alley lined with shops that still had their shutters down. The painted sign above one of the shops said 'MATA HARI SCHOOL UNIFORMS', but although both Karim's eyes and mine turned towards it neither of us pointed it out to the other.

Zia and Karim got out of the car and Zia propped open the bonnet, but it was clear he did that only because people in movies always responded to breakdowns in that manner. I got out also and stood beside them, despite the internal voice that sounded a lot like Sonia warning me I'd only call attention to myself, and who knows what strange types were wandering around the deserted streets at this hour, and perhaps I should at least cover my bare arms with my dupatta.

'We're near Parsi colony,' Karim said. 'Uncle Zerxes – my father's friend from the linen industry – lives there. Ten-minute walk.' He was looking at Zia, assiduously avoiding my eye.

Ten minutes? That was how long it would take to walk from my house to Zia's and I'd never once done anything but drive over. And those were streets I knew. I looked down the alley. How dangerous a section of town was Mehmoodabad? I couldn't be sure. Was it one of those areas where people were regularly shot by gunmen who were never apprehended, who never left clues behind, causing people all over the city to speculate *it was such-and-such group, of course, avenging yesterday's shooting of X*, while someone else argued *no, no, it was done by people who want us to leap to that conclusion in order to make such-and-such look like a terrorist organisation, nothing else*. At which point, *well, they are a terrorist organisation* and *come on, every group has its militant wing, why single out?* leading to *it could be anyone, it could be a personal vendetta, or rogue elements, or ethnic fighting or sectarian, or in-fighting or drug wars or shadow-government organisations or* (my personal favourite) *the Foreign Hand.*

'Who do we know who lives closest to here? Nadia? Call her on your mobile,' I told Zia. 'Tell her to send her car over to pick us up. It's a five-minute drive. Her driver can drop us home and then bring a mechanic over.'

'I'm not leaving my Integra standing on the side of the road in this part of town,' Zia said. 'We'll tell Nadia's driver to pick up my mechanic on his way.'

'Your mechanic is not "on the way". And it's six in the morning.'

'I know where he lives. I can have him woken up.'

'Guys,' Karim said, softly, 'there's someone coming.'

Zia and I turned and saw a moustached man walking towards us.

'Having trouble?' he said. He was wearing sneakers with his shalwar-kameez. Nike. Undoubtedly fake.

'No, we're fine. Just waiting for some friends. Thank you.' Zia tried to look confident and relaxed as he spoke, and I reached into the car and pulled out Zia's mobile phone. Quite why I thought that should intimidate the man, I don't know, but it gave me a feeling of power.

The man laughed. 'It's all right. I mean no harm. But I just wanted to ask if you had any anti-theft devices in the car. That might be why you've stalled.'

I looked helplessly at the phone. I didn't even know what the number for the police was.

Zia smacked his hand to his forehead. 'Yes. Stupid of me. I forgot to press the thief switch.'

'The what?' Karim said.

'Thief switch. It's a little button. Can be placed anywhere in the car. See? Mine's next to the ignition.' Zia guided Karim's hand in through the open car window and made him feel the button. 'If you don't press it within a few seconds of starting the engine it cuts off the petrol supply and the car stalls. So if someone's trying to steal the car and they don't press the switch the car just stops, destroying their quick getaway. My father had mine put in only a few days ago; I'm still not used to it.'

Zia turned to the fake-Nike man. 'Thanks,' he said, and offered the man a cigarette. The man produced a match and the two of them lit up. I stepped on Zia's toe, trying to draw his attention to my unhappiness about standing around in the middle of a deserted road with some unknown man, but he just moved his foot away.

'Are you a mechanic?' Zia said.

The man shook his head. 'Car thief.'

I contemplated calling my father. But what on earth would I say to him?

'You going to steal my car?' Zia tried to sound casual.

The man looked offended. 'After I've taken a cigarette from you?' He shook his head again. 'I don't work without my tools. My gun, my partner. Besides, I wouldn't take your car and leave you stranded when you're in the company of a girl. These are unsafe times. And it's obvious you don't live around here.'

'That's very decent of you.' Zia regarded me triumphantly, as though he'd won a point. The man still hadn't acknowledged me, which allowed me to feel comfortable enough to continue standing there.

'Where do you think we live?' Karim said.

'Defence.'

Karim laughed. 'Right. That obvious, huh?'

The man nodded. 'Burgers,' he said. Karim look confused. When he'd left Karachi we were still unaware of this term that most of Karachi used to refer to the English-speaking elite.

'Have you been doing this long?' I asked.

I thought he'd address his answer to Zia, but instead he looked straight at me. 'I wanted to join the civil service. I'm an educated, literate person, you know. I sat for the exam, and I did all right. I mean, not top marks, but decent, good marks. But I sat the exams from Karachi. It's not enough to be just good.' He looked from Zia to Karim to me. 'You know?'

That was probably just a rhetorical question, but I felt compelled to respond. 'We're Karachiwallahs, too,' I said, the word stumbling on my tongue. It just seemed a bad idea to use the more Anglicized 'Karachiite'. And then, because I was annoyed with Karim, I added: 'At least, the two of us are. He –' jerking my head at Karim, '– hasn't been here in eight years. He lives in England and America. Both.'

The man whistled. 'What a hero! Do you understand why I'm a car thief instead of a civil servant, hero?'

'Yes,' Karim said softly. 'The quota system.'

The man spat on the side of the road. 'May those who set it up burn in every kind of fire that hell has to offer.'

I caught Zia's sleeve, my eyes begging *Let's get out of here.*

The man caught my look. 'Why are you afraid of me? I have sisters. I'm not one of those uncivilized men. But I get frustrated. Don't you? You live in this city, how can you not suffer with it?'

In my dreams there is a brash, glittering, laughing Karachi that makes me want to sleep for ever. I had said that in one of my imaginary conversations with Karim, but I could hardly say it to this man. There was nothing I could say to this man without it being condescension or a lie. Privilege erased the day-to-day struggles of ethnic politics, and however Karim might want me to feel about the matter I couldn't pretend I was sorry that I had been born on 'this side of Clifton Bridge' where class bound everyone together in an enveloping, suffocating embrace, with ethnicity only a secondary or even tertiary concern. So what if I walked around with a heaviness in my heart after reading about the accelerating cycle of violence, unemployment, divisiveness in Karachi? So what if I agreed with this man that the quota system in the province discriminated against Karachiites, particularly Muhajirs who had no family domicile outside the city that they could claim as their own when government jobs and government-run university places were being allocated according to an absurd urban–rural divide? So what if I thought the entire city was being pillaged by the central government, which was happy to take the large percentage of its revenue from Karachi but unwilling to put very much back? I didn't find myself picking up a gun because of it, or losing people I loved because of it, or feeling my sanity slip away because of it. So how could I look this man in the eye and tell him, yes, I suffer with the city? How could I pretend that guessing part of what he suffered didn't make me scared to stand in a deserted alley with him?

'You're Muhajir,' I heard Karim say to the man. For God's sake, what was he trying to do!

'Yes, hero. What are you?'

'Bengali.'

Zia and I both turned to look at him in surprise. I'd never once heard Karim identify himself that way. Of course, none of us ever used to feel the need to identify ourselves by ethnicity when we were younger but it still took me off-guard that he chose to identify himself with his mother's ethnicity rather than his father's. Was he trying to imply that he existed outside the landscape of post-Civil War ethnic politics? Or was it that he felt it wiser not to associate himself with an ethnic group that this man saw as competitor or oppressor – easier to say you belonged to those who had broken away twenty-five years earlier and who no one ever spoke of any more? I wondered if Zia even remembered that school-yard fight when he had pushed Karim over and kicked him. I wondered if Karim remembered it.

The man straightened up. 'We didn't learn anything, did we? From '71.'

Again, Karim gave me one of those looks I couldn't decipher. 'We learned to forget,' he said. 'Do you have a family to support?'

'Everyone has a family to support. If not your own, then someone else's, someone who can't support anyone any more.

My brother has five children. The choices my brother's made . . . soon I'll have his family to support. And then there'll be his widow – I'll have to marry his widow, who else will marry her with five children? – and she sings all day, so badly, like a goat.' He put his hands together in supplication. 'I say to my brother, change your life quickly because if I end up with her I'll chop my ears off and how will I listen to cricket commentary after that?'

'Now that's a tough situation,' said Zia, laughing.

'Put it in the papers,' the man said, flicking away his cigarette butt. 'QUOTA SYSTEM FORCES NICE MAN TO MARRY WOMAN WHO SINGS LIKE GOAT. It'll start a revolution.' Zia and the man both laughed, but the man's laugh had an edge of bitterness to it.

'I can't do anything about the quota system,' Karim said, 'but maybe we could help you find something better suited to your education than car theft.'

The man nodded, all traces of amusement gone. 'I think that would be good. The longer I do this, the angrier I get. And already I can imagine myself doing things that a few months ago would have been unthinkable. I own a gun, and I'm imagining things. That's not a good combination.' He grimaced. 'Make it quick. You'll probably leave here and do nothing, but if you can do something, do it quickly.'

'How will I find you?' Karim said.

'Come back here in this car. I'll tell my friends to look out for it, and make themselves known to you.' He shook Karim's hand, and walked away.

'Your father could get him a job, couldn't he?' Karim said, turning to Zia.

Zia looked ready to explode. 'Did you just miss what he said? His friends the car thieves will be looking out for my Integra. And now he knows where the thief switch is. You are behaving like such a fresh-off-the-boat, Karim. Don't buy his "I'm forced into crime because I have no options" story.'

'You laughed at his jokes,' Karim said, getting into the car.

'Con men can have a sense of humour, Karim.'

'Oh, come on, Zia, it's not as though his story was far-fetched.' I pointed towards the thief switch as Zia started the car and he nodded and pressed it.

'If it's true, that makes things worse,' Zia said, screeching off, clearly as keen to get out of Mehmoodabad as I was. 'He's probably with the MQM and you just don't want to get involved with someone who has anything to do with these political groups.'

'Why is he obviously with the MQM?' I said. 'He didn't mention political affiliations.'

'It's the Muhajir Qaumi Movement, isn't it? And he's a Muhajir with grievances. Two plus two equals four.'

'I'm a Muhajir, Zia.' I poked his shoulder.

'Oh, don't give me that. You're nothing. You're just a burger. And thank God for that.'

'You macho Sindhi ass,' I said with a yawn. It was too early in the morning for a full-length replay of this little exchange – one that Zia and I trotted out every so often almost as a set routine – which deflected the differences in our backgrounds.

'Only half my ass is Sindhi. The other half is Punjabi.'

Karim didn't join our laughter. When I turned to look at him, his eyes were wide, terrified. 'I shouldn't have come back,' he said.

Zia reached over and touched my knee then. He saw how hurt I was by the comment, but Karim was oblivious. I thought of another car ride, heading to, rather than from, the airport. Karim had sat opposite me and drawn a map and even the fact that he couldn't have known it was the last time we were to be together for the next seven years didn't temper the corrosiveness of that memory. *Look up*, I had wanted to say then. *I'm here.* But he hadn't looked at me then and he wasn't looking at me now.

'Well, then, go home,' I said. 'If you have a home to go to.'

'Raheen, cool it,' Zia said.

'Let her continue, Zia.' Karim crossed his arms and looked at me in the manner of an eagle staring down a sparrow.

'There's really nothing more to say. Why don't you turn around and leave, and I'll draw you a nice map of all the places you might have visited while you were here. I'm sure for you that'll be better than actually having to deal with the realities of this place and the people in it.'

'Why the hell do you keep harping on about maps?' he said.

I didn't have the first idea how to respond to that one. We continued to glare at each other, while Zia turned the music up again and started singing along boisterously, as though he were listening to hard rock rather than a qawaali. Why *did* I keep harping on about maps? How had they become the symbol of everything that had gone so wrong, so inexplicably, in my relationship with Karim? Was it because of that drive to the airport? Was it because he'd pasted those maps on the back of my shredded letters? Was it because his fascination with maps had created a gap between us in that visit to Rahim Yar Khan? Or was it because every time Karim wrote to me from London and mentioned something about maps of Karachi I heard in his tone both a rebuke and a challenge? As if he knew the city better than I did. As if distance gave him a bird's-eye view, while I was locked in the four walls of some elite members-only enclave. As if he had a right to say any of that, even if some of it were true, when year after year he simply stayed away. OK, so he didn't have a choice; he had to spend the holidays with his mother. OK, so I wouldn't have reacted so badly unless he'd touched some nerve. OK, so . . . OK, time to grow up.

'Strabo and Eratosthenes,' I said. 'That's what I was going to talk to you about on the phone the other day.'

'Yes?' He looked at me cautiously, as though he thought I was drawing him closer just so that I could hit him over the head with a mallet.

I had first encountered mention of the two of them while researching a paper on Homer at college, and that's really when I decided it was time to get in touch with Karim again, although I had to wait until I wrote that Calvino paper before I was able to decide how to make the first move. Eratosthenes, the grandfather of cartography, was the first man to make a distinction between scientific and literary mapping. Prior to Eratosthenes, no one ever said that cartography should concern itself with science and facts rather than stories; the distinction didn't really exist. *The Odyssey* was considered as valuable a tool of mapping as were the charts and eyewitness accounts of sailors and travellers. But Eratosthenes' decision removed Homer, and all other poets, from the corpus of cartography.

In the furore over this move, which lasted through generations, Eratosthenes' greatest critic was the cartographer Strabo, who said that Homer depicted geographical truths in the language of poetry, so it was absurd to deny him a role in the realm of cartography. I loved the idea of those early cartographers who thought Odysseus' voyage was as valid a source for map-making as the charts of travellers who had actually set sail themselves.

Karim was silent when I explained this, but Zia wasn't able to refrain from reducing the conversation to its most literal level. 'Uh, so if you were a sailor and you wanted to get from Troy to Greece you'd take Homer along as your navigator?'

'Not Greece, Ithaca. But back then, maps weren't used for travel. They were mainly used for illustrating stories. There stands Mount Olympus. That's where Theseus fought the Minotaur. That kind of stuff. So maps weren't about going from point A to point B; they were about helping someone hear the heartbeat of a place.' I reached for Karim's hand and held it at the very tips of his fingers. He didn't draw away. 'Seems to me like we're Strabo and Eratosthenes, Karimazov. I want you to pay attention to the stories that define Karachi, and you want to know what the name of the road connecting Gizri to Zamzama is, and how many people have died there in the last year.'

But even as I said all that, I wondered why any of it should have been anything more than a minor irritation in our friendship. Surely we didn't need to agree on everything? How had all of this become so vast it swallowed up a lifetime's intimacy? What was really going on here? And back, again, to the question I had asked so many times it even invaded my dreams: what did I do to make him cut up my letters? What did I say that was so unforgivable he couldn't even talk to me about it straight out? Nothing he'd said yet had helped clarify that at all. I knew he was angry that I hadn't gone to visit his mother, but that had happened after the letters. And then there was something about selfish love, but that was much too nebulous to try to pin down. And, all right, I hadn't dedicated my whole life to crying over Karachi's dead, but it wasn't as though he'd shut himself up in a dark room and bawled his eyes out for the last eight years. There had to be something that I was missing, but, if so, why didn't he just tell me what it was?

His grip closed on mine so tightly I almost cried out. 'You want to hear the heartbeat of a place? Do you know how hard your heart beats when you're lost? Do you know what it is to wander out of the comfort of your own streets and your own stories?' He drew a deep breath. 'Which stories do you want me to pay attention to? Or, more to the point, which stories have you deliberately turned away from, Ra, and why?'

I pulled away from him. There was a memory beginning to resurface, but my heart was beating so loud, so fast, telling me to keep it away. I turned away from him, and then away from Zia's uncertain, sympathetic, exasperated eyes, which were meant as much for Karim as for me. I cranked up the volume of the music as high as it would go, so that none of us could hear our own thoughts.

All around us, Karachi kept moving.

'Of course there won't be war,' said Asif, running his fingers through his luxurious mass of hair. 'Everyone's playing brink-manship, that's all. Here's what'll happen: Mujib will back down on his Six Points, give up the whole idea of a decentralized federal system of government in exchange for some political and economic concessions towards East Pakistan. Once he does that, Yahya will invite him to form the government, and at that point Bhutto will also take his place as leader of the opposition. It's the only sane, rational, not to mention cheerful, choice. Mujib's no zealous revolutionary, and, besides, whatever the Bengali masses might want, they're just rabble, and our army will decimate them if they try to make some kind of one-legged stand. No one wants to be slaughtered.' He snapped his fingers at the Ampi's waiter and asked for more ice.

'No one wants to be enslaved either,' Maheen said, waving down at Laila and her new husband, who had entered and taken a table on the ground floor. 'Yasmin, don't you love what she's wearing?'

'My God, she is so gorgeous. What does she see in him?' Asif shook his head. 'And come on, Maheen, isn't enslaved a little too dramatic a word?'

'Nothing dramatic about it,' Ali said. 'Just look at the statistics.'

'Oh, you and your statistics,' Asif said with a laugh.

'Well, but just think about it. East Pakistan is the majority wing of the country in terms of population, and yet . . .' He started to count off his fingers, 'It gets less than 30 per cent of foreign aid allocation, less than 20 per cent of civil service jobs, less than 10 per cent of military positions, fewer schools, fewer universities, it makes up near 70 per cent of the country's export earnings but receives the benefits of less than 30 per cent of our import expenditure.'

'All these stupid bloody politicians on their own power trips,' Zafar said, picking up the menu and looking at the dessert section. 'Why don't Mujib and Bhutto just have a duel to the death, pistols at dawn, and leave the rest of us out of it?'

'It's not that simple, Zafar,' Ali said, folding his napkin neatly into a little square.

'Well it's not the little numbers game you make it out to be either, Ali.'

Maheen put a hand on her fiancé's arm. 'Jaanoo, Ali's right. Look, Asif, I wish – really, really, I wish and pray – that everything could be easily resolved, but you're deluding yourself if you think the Bengali people's demands are going to go away, because I don't know if they'll even accept a federation at this point when the word Independence has gone around and it's such a more soul-stirring word than federation.'

'Ah, but you don't know what I know,' Asif said.

'And what's that?'

'That just today Yahya told newsmen that his talks with Mujib were satisfactory, and that Mujib will be the next Prime Minister of Pakistan. They've reached a compromise, Maheen; I'm sorry, but your soul will have to do with being a little less stirred.'

'God's sake, Asif, she's lived all her life in Karachi,' Yasmin said. 'She's not . . .'

'Not what?' Maheen turned to her friend. 'One of them?'

There was a yelp from below. The waiter had spilt a drink on Laila. Her husband stood up and cracked a slap across the waiter's cheek. 'Halfwit Bingo! Go back to your jungle.'

Zafar stood up. Ali and Asif pulled him down.

Laila grabbed her husband's arm and whispered something. He looked up at Maheen, and turned red. 'It's a new sari,' he called out in Maheen's direction, pointing at Laila's stained clothes. 'I got angry, can you blame me? No hard feelings, OK, Maheen?'

Maheen shrugged noncommittally, which seemed to satisfy him. He sat down and resumed eating. Laila continued looking up, but Maheen refused to meet her eye.

'It's going to get worse,' Yasmin said.

'How much worse can it get?' Zafar sighed. He slipped his hand into Maheen's palm beneath the table, but her fingers didn't curl around his in response. She was looking at the Bengali waiter. He walked past and caught her eye, and for a moment the barriers of class and gender became porous and something passed between them that Zafar couldn't quite identify. Maheen's hand slipped out of Zafar's. He turned his face away from her, and saw Yasmin and Ali looking at Maheen, their faces moulded into identical expressions of concern. It was so brief he was almost unsure it happened, but for an instant he felt a most alien and inexplicable sensation of jealousy.

'A lassi stand. I'm going to set one up right here,' Yasmin declared. 'I'll mint millions.'

'Right here? In the middle of the racecourse stands? Excellent idea. And how do you think Ali will react to being married to the Lassi Lassie?' Zafar asked, fanning Yasmin with his newspaper.

'Oh, that's heaven, Zaf, thanks. Ali is not one of those Neanderthal men who expect their wives to stay at home. Done the crossword yet?'

'No. You like crosswords? Is that Neanderthal comment a swipe at me? What makes you think I'd want Maheen to stay at home?'

'It's not about what you want, Zafar, it's what Maheen wants that matters.'

Zafar tried to work out exactly what he'd said that was so objectionable. Hard to tell with Yasmin. Ever since that time she'd rebuffed him in the Nasreen Room he'd been too aware that he frequently misread her. For a moment he stopped to wonder how different things might have been if she had responded with more warmth to his suggestion. Impossible to imagine. Already it seemed a lifetime ago, and he honestly couldn't remember why it was that when Ali had reintroduced him to Maheen and Yasmin, both of whom he'd known only vaguely before Oxford, he'd looked longer and with more interest at Yasmin. 'I always manage to irritate you, don't I? Even when I'm in complete agreement with you. I really wish you liked me more.'

Yasmin looked at him, surprised. 'I don't dislike you. But you were a bastard to me once and I haven't quite forgotten it.'

'Me? When? I would never . . . What did I do?'

Yasmin shook her head. What was she doing? It could only do harm to revisit the past, particularly when he was wearing the same black shirt – why did he always have to wear black, even in the heat of Karachi's days, and why did he always have to look so good in it? She gripped her finger with its engagement ring. And more important than that, why did she still have to entertain these thoughts about this . . . boy, when every day she learnt something new about Ali, and every day felt more strongly than the day before how lucky the two of them were to have found themselves alone on that balcony on Asif's farm. 'Never mind. Nothing. I'm just joking. Oh look, there's Anwar.' She pointed out the curly-haired man on the other side of the racecourse stands. 'Poor Anwar and Dolly. There can't be anything worse than the death of a child.'

'Rumour is, it wasn't a stray bullet at all.' Zafar looked at his watch. 'Where are Maheen and Ali? The race is about to begin.' Below, the horses were being led on to the track.

'Oh, rumours are all the rage these days,' Yasmin replied, relieved he'd changed the subject. 'Just heard one that the fat cats are going to have the National Assembly building in East Pakistan bombed; that way work on it will never be completed and the National Assembly will never convene and Mujib will never become PM. You don't really believe what they say about the shooting, do you? How could Dolly and Anwar continue living where they do if that were true?

'Speaking of rumours, I think we're going to start one if the two of us are seen alone at the races.' He smiled at her, but she didn't smile back. Was that an inappropriate comment, Zafar wondered. He hastened to return to the earlier subject of conversation. 'I hear Dolly wants to move. But Anwar's been acting so strangely. They say he still hasn't shed a tear about the whole thing. And look who he's sitting down with. Here, look through the binoculars. See him? With a bunch of your afore-mentioned fat cats. He's been avoiding all his old friends since the . . . since. Only ever see him now with the kind of people who should make anyone sick.'

'Maybe they're all talking about bombing the National Assembly.'

'Probably talking about Bhutto's little speech yesterday.' He drummed his fingers on the newspaper headlines.

'Revolution from the Khyber to Karachi if the NA convenes without him. It would be nice to dismiss that as rhetoric. Some nights I can't sleep for terror.' If this is how I feel, Yasmin thought, how must Maheen feel, a Bengali living in West Pakistan? And every day someone new seemed to succumb to the madness that was sweeping the country, someone new said things that defied all understanding, and it was hard to say which were worse: the people who stopped dead, mid-sentence, as soon as Maheen entered the room, or the ones who kept on talking.

'The race really is about to begin now,' Zafar said. No escape from talk about it, not even here at the racecourse with Yasmin. It was a physical ache, this burden of trying to be some kind of refuge for Maheen; every day more comments to deflect, ignore, make light of. In the beginning it was easy enough: hell, it came naturally. But now, oh God, now . . . 'Where are they?' He looked at his watch again. 'Ali was supposed to pick her up half an hour ago.'

'Do you think there's been some kind of trouble?'

Don't think about it, don't start believing it. 'What, the start of revolution?'

'I'm serious, Zafar. Maheen should get out of the country. Something could happen.'

Zafar looked down at his hands. 'Any good at palmistry, Yasmin?'

Yasmin put a hand on his shoulder. This was not a voice she'd heard from him before. 'I don't believe in fate. Why?'

'I want to know if it'll tell me where I'm going to live.' After that day at Ampi's when Laila's husband slapped the waiter, he'd told Maheen they should leave. Get married straight away and move to London. He had wanted more than anything for her to say 'no', and she had, but he wasn't sure if that was because she meant it or because she saw how desperately he wanted that 'no'. Leave Karachi! Zafar shook his head at the thought. Leave home.

'Karachi's home to both of you,' Yasmin said.

Zafar felt nauseous. Of course it was. And yet, when he mentioned moving he'd thought that would mean leaving home for him, and leaving what was rapidly becoming enemy territory for Maheen. But this was her home, too. How could he have forgotten that? But he had. Not for a second, or an hour, but for days, for weeks. He hadn't even realized his own mistake until now. He covered his eyes with his hands. How insidiously this madness spread. God, when did things get so complicated?

'Race about to begin.' Yasmin nudged him.

Zafar sat up and tried to focus on the course below. 'My Two's looking jumpy.'

'Why can't racehorses have names like . . . Oh, false start!'

'Falstaff? For a racehorse? Oh, I see . . . No, listen, Maheen will be fine. We'll all be fine.' He said it again. 'We'll all be fine.'

'Unless rumours get around about the two of us spotted out in public without our fiancées.' She nudged him again, and laughed. 'What will my parents say?'

'As if you care. They're off!'

Hoofs pounded, jockeys' colours were misted in dust, and at the end of it all Zafar slumped back in disgust.

'I thought he was your favourite?'

'He is. That makes it more frustrating that I don't bet.' A thought was beginning to worm forward from the back of his mind. 'Hang on. That time I asked you out and you said your parents wouldn't approve.'

'Long time ago, Zaf.'

'Not that long. Just long enough that I didn't know you well enough to know the comment was absurd.'

'Bygones, Zaf.'

He scratched his head. 'You could just have said no straight out. I wouldn't have pushed.'

'Leave it, Zafar.'

'I'm just curious. Hang on, you weren't doing that woman thing of saying one thing and meaning another, were you?' As soon as he said it, he knew it was a mistake. Now she would narrow her eyes at him, or say something cutting, just when they were beginning to relax in each other's presence.

But she didn't say anything, just pretended not to hear him, and looked around through his binoculars. 'Here comes Ali! But where's Maheen?'

Zafar was out of his seat immediately. 'Where's Maheen, Ali? Where's Maheen?' He started running towards Ali, uncaring of the heads turning towards him. *Oh please, say she just wasn't in the mood to come out.*

Ali caught him by the shoulder. 'She's all right, don't panic. I dropped her home. You'd better go to her, Zaf. Some old beggar woman spat at her when she was walking to my car. You know, you've really got to get her out of here.'

'Hear that?' Maheen said, leaning against Zafar.

'What?'

'The sun setting into the sea. It's so quiet you can almost hear it sizzle as it touches the water.'

He put his arms around her, not caring that they were out in public. 'Peaceful, isn't it?'

She nodded. 'Hard to believe Civil War is actually here. It's almost as though it's happening in' – she laughed shakily – 'another country.' She continued to look at the sea gulls swooping impossibly close to the sea and rising up again without a single bead of water falling from their wings. 'Laila heard from some foreign journalist that the army's slaughtering my people by the thousands in Dhaka.'

My people. Zafar shivered. 'Maheen, listen to me.'

'No, Zaf, we're not leaving the country. I don't want to be a stranger among strangers. War does crazy things to people, but wars end. I'll lie low, I promise that. And when it's over – please, God, soon! – we'll get married and have children and one day, every day, we'll tell them how we survived this inferno.'

He shook his head. 'Right now, I can't think of any reason why you should feel an iota of loyalty for this country.'

'Treasonous? My views are treasonous?' Zafar turned and slammed his hand against the wall behind him.

'And that's only what your friends say.' Ali took a piece of ice out of his glass and held it against Zafar's reddening hand. 'This country's turned rabid – the soldiers are raping the women, Zaf, raping them, all over East Pakistan, and in drawing rooms around Karachi people applaud this attempt to improve the genes of the Bengalis.' Ali caught Zafar's hand to stop it shaking. 'If you and Maheen won't leave, then you've got to at least stay out of sight until it's over.'

'That shouldn't be too hard. You and Yasmin are about the only people who seek out our company these days.'

'The day breaks not, it is my heart.' Yasmin put an arm around Maheen as they watched the sun come up. 'John Donne, that was. We've been up talking for seven hours now, Maheen, and you've only talked about what Zafar says and how he feels. You've never once mentioned what you think of everything that's going on.'

The phone rang. 'Don't answer it,' Maheen said.

Yasmin looked at her watch, frowned and picked up the phone. 'Hello . . .' Her face went pale, and she slammed the phone down. 'Animals!' she swore.

'The worst are the ones whose voices I recognize. And, no, I'm not going to tell you who they are.' Maheen reached over and smoothed the creases on Yasmin's forehead with her palm. 'What do I think of everything that's going on? You're the only person in this city who's asked me that in a very long time. Yasmin, I think the end of the world will begin like this.'

'So it ends like this.' Yasmin put down the newspaper and reached across the table for Ali's hand. 'Surrender to the Indian forces.' She closed her eyes, and Ali came round the table to sit next to her.

'I think you need a wedding to cheer you up.'

Yasmin laughed. 'No one has ever uttered the word "wedding" more gloomily.'

'You know perfectly well I'm anything but gloomy at the thought of spending my life with you.'

Almost a year after that crazy night on the balcony, and this was probably the closest he'd come to saying he loved her. He was a man for whom such declarations were hard, but rather than making her insecure it had the effect of giving significance to even the tiniest admissions of affection. Yasmin leaned forward and kissed his ear, and watched with satisfaction as he turned red.

'I wonder how Maheen is taking the news,' Ali said.

'I wonder how Zafar is taking it. Perhaps there's a part of him that's even somewhat happy it might all be over now.'

'Happy? Why should I be happy?' Zafar stood in the squash courts, his racquet limp in his hand. 'Three days ago we surrendered to the Indian army. Of course I'm not happy. We've lost half the country and most of our soul. What the hell is there to be happy about? This whole year has been nothing but a nightmare.'

'Oh, come on, Zaf. You cheered a little when the Indian forces entered the war on the side of those Bengali bastards, didn't you?'

'Bunty, get your nose out of my face.'

'Get your face out of this club. And take the rest of you with it.'

'Go home, Bunty. I'm here for a game of squash. Who wants to play?' Zafar looked around. These men were his friends; he'd known them all his life. What was going on here? How much longer could he take this? What was he fighting about, he didn't even really know why he was locked in combat with his friends every day, every weary, soul-destroying day, even now that the war was over – especially now that the war was over – and every day, every damned day, he and Maheen slipped further and further from being the couple who walked so lightly through the world that the dew-wet grass barely registered their footprints.

'Yeah,' Bunty turned to the men. 'Who wants to play with the Bingo lover?'

As the first fist made contact with his body, Zafar closed his eyes and thought, I wasn't cut out for this role. I've stepped into someone else's story. Get me out. I want to get out.

Around him the men echoed his thoughts. 'Get out,' they snarled, their fists sticky with his blood. 'Get out.'

• • •

When I returned home, my parents were drinking tea and watching BBC World in the TV room, wearing their dressing gowns and unusually sunny morning faces.

'Where is he?' Ami said. 'Where's Karim?'

I tossed the newspaper in my father's direction. 'Asleep in Zia's car. I asked him over for breakfast when we picked him up, but I don't think he heard me.'

My mother handed me a cup of tea. 'Why didn't you ask again?'

'I did.' I sat down next to Aba, and leaned against his shoulder. 'Can't handle this early-morning stuff. I'm so glad I'm not a rooster.'

'Well . . . ?' Ami asked. 'How was it? How was he? Was it wonderful?'

'I don't know why you're making such a big deal out of it.' I picked up the bottle of jam from the breakfast tray and started reading the contents. 'We were just kids when we last met. Would you get excited meeting someone you hadn't seen since thirteen?'

'If that someone was Karim to my Raheen, yes, I would,' Ami said.

Aba rolled his eyes. 'Such a sentimentalist.'

Ami walked over to Aba and rapped the back of his hand with a teaspoon. 'You were the one getting all misty-eyed ten minutes ago remembering the two of them turning towards each other in their sleep the first time we put them in a crib together. And correct me if I'm wrong, but didn't you use the term "fated friendship"?'

'She's making all this up,' Aba said to me. 'She's a sentimentalist and a liar. And the day she loses her looks, I'm running off with a Scandinavian shot-putter.'

I had already sprawled out on the sofa Ami vacated, and now she sat down on the two-seater next to Aba and rolled the pink rubberband off the morning paper in such a way that it flew off the end of the bound paper and leapt through the air, contorting and braiding itself before landing on the bridge of Aba's nose. I watched my parents glance at the headlines and the back page, the rubber band falling off Aba's nose when he bent his head to read, and then move straight to the page with the crossword, which they always solved together in the mornings before going to work.

'Do you think there's such a thing as fated relationships?' I said.

Aba was concentrating on folding the crossword page into a neat rectangle, isolating the crossword and its clues, but Ami looked up and shook her head. 'Of course not. That implies the relationship will survive no matter what carelessness you're guilty of.'

'So who was guilty of carelessness? Uncle Ali or Aunty Maheen?'

Aba stopped folding the paper. 'Sometimes things just don't work out, Raheen. Ali and Maheen just couldn't . . .' He frowned. 'They weren't ever . . . Ali was always too cold for someone like Maheen.'

'Ali wasn't cold,' Ami said, very quietly, taking the paper from Aba.

'Yasmin, I'm not saying he's some heartless bum. I love Ali. But, you know, I've known the man all my life, and I've never really seen him show any kind of strong emotion, except anger on occasion.'

'You were never engaged to him either,' Ami said, still quiet, still looking down at the crossword.

Aba folded his arms and leaned back against the sofa cushions, clearly amused. 'As I recall, you told me the most romantic thing he ever said to you was "you can listen to that Barbra Streisand record if you really want to".'

'And when I did, he knew all the words.' Ami laughed. 'Eight-letter word for a kind of flower, beginning with "G". I'm not saying he was romantic; you're hardly romantic yourself. Obviously that doesn't bother me too much. But there are depths to his feelings that I don't think any of us really ever gave due credence to . . . All right, stop laughing at me, Zafar. You are so irritating sometimes. Guzmania?'

'Geranium, my love.'

For some reason my mind reached back over the years for a memory of Ami and Aba arguing about whether it was yet time to tell me something, something to do with things they had done in the past, though I couldn't remember the specifics of their argument or even what it might have related to. Ami had been ready to tell me, but that in itself was not an indicator to me that it was something I needed to hear. I once told Ami she was the sort of mother who would object to me spending the night at Sonia's place if there was school the next day, but would hardly raise an eyebrow if I told her I was going to the moon. To which she had responded, 'The moon might be good for you. Sometimes you have trouble leaving your own orbit.' When she said that I knew she was expressing her concern over my willingness to stay within my father's protective world. To someone who had been as rebellious a daughter as Ami once was, my lack of desire to break away from my family, dye my hair vivid shades of colour and join protest rallies against the government was a constant source of consternation. 'It's not as though you're any less wilful than I ever was,' she said. 'You just don't seem to use that wilfulness over anything larger than waking up one morning and declaring you'll never eat cabbage again. And it's not as though we even eat cabbage with any regularity in this house. But whatever you do, please don't tell me conformity is your form of rebellion against me. I'll commit suicide.'

The truth of the matter was, even now, Aba and I could sit with fingers on each other's pulses and feel our heartbeats synchronize. Why rebel against that? I pushed the memory down, as I did every time it bobbed up to the surface, which it did periodically for no discernible reason.

'I'm going to sleep,' I said. I rolled over and closed my eyes, but the room had become strangely silent. I waited for the silence to pass and when it didn't I opened my eyes and saw my parents looking at me.

'We want to hear about Karim,' Aba said.

'There's nothing to tell. He looks better, but I preferred him before. I haven't seen him since we were thirteen; it's no big deal, you know. Can I please go to sleep?' I walked out and went into my bedroom, closing the door firmly behind me. They had asked so many times over the years, *Why did you and Karim stop writing to each other? When you go to America won't you even try to get in touch?* and the more often I answered, *People grow apart, that's all*, the less convinced they looked. Both Karim's parents and mine always seemed to get such joy out of our friendship and, thinking about it, I had an inkling that the joy contained a strange sort of pride, as though our friendship proved their choices justified.

The door opened and my father walked in. 'What's the matter?'

'Nothing.' I sat on my bed and kicked out of view the album of pictures of Karim and me in Rahim Yar Khan which was lying by my bed. 'And if you keep asking, I'll get moody, and you'll get annoyed that I'm being moody, and that'll make me more moody and you more annoyed, so why go down that path?'

My father crossed his arms on his chest and looked down at me. 'I used to think we could talk about everything.'

'There's nothing I keep hidden from you that I would tell anyone else. Except maybe certain intimate details about boys and—'

Aba put one hand up and whistled sharply, placing tips of thumb and forefinger in his mouth, in imitation of a traffic cop. 'Red light. Red light. Don't need any of that.'

I took his hand in mine and squeezed it. He sat down and put his arm around me. 'My worry, kiddo, is about the things you don't tell anyone. Things mutate, thoughts and emotions, they mutate inside you in ways you aren't even aware of.'

My father, the court jester, in a serious moment.

'For instance?' I said.

He bit his lip and looked at me. 'For instance . . .' His voice trailed off. His foot kicked against the album lying just under the bed, and he pulled it out and looked at the cover. 'For instance, you and Karim. Have you ever spoken to anyone about why the two of you stopped writing to each other?'

How could I have shown him that final communication from Karim – he would have read my unkindest sentences and, however much I insisted that Karim had taken things out of context and the whole picture was very different from these scraps Karim had chosen to focus on, it would not have prevented him looking at me with disillusionment. I hadn't actually been able to show it to anyone, not even Sonia and Zia, though both of them knew the general gist of why Karim and I had stopped writing to each other. 'Aba, please. I really am tired.'

For a moment I thought he was going to say something else, but he only kissed my forehead and left. I felt strangely disappointed.

I lay down, convinced I would free-associate manically in that state between sleep and wakefulness when memories and dreams slipslide into each other, but instead I slept, almost instantly, and dreamt of wearing Nike shoes without soles in a rain-drenched park in Karachi that had ceased to be a park before I was born.

When I woke up the phone was ringing. It was afternoon, my parents were at work, and Zia was calling to say that he and Karim had both just woken up and were going over to visit the twins after they'd eaten something, so they'd come and pick me up in about an hour.

I put the phone down, and heard a tapping on the door. It was Naila, the maalishwali, doing a round of Defence to see which of her regular clients were home and wanted a massage to make up for the one they'd missed over the weekend, when Naila was unable to make it out of her part of town because of trouble in the city.

'Heaven,' I said, pulling off my clothes while Naila laid a white sheet on the carpet for me.

'Always asleep when I come. You miss the best part of the day,' she said, and then the scent of coconut oil filled the room as she unscrewed the cap of a plastic bottle and poured its contents into one hand. Massages on Saturday mornings in Karachi were one of life's great pleasures, and Naila was our yardstick for measuring the severity of violence in the city on Saturdays. The previous weekend, when she hadn't turned up by twelve, my mother had called around and told her friends, 'Don't leave the house today. Things are very bad.' Things in Karachi had gone from being very bad to very bad indeed of late, but in the last few days we'd entered a lull and though my parents and their friends sighed that it was just temporary, I was grateful that Karim had arrived after the start of the lull so I wouldn't have to hear his breast-beating about the grief he felt for his city every time he saw a newspaper headline.

Naila put the bottle of oil down by my head, and I caught a glimpse of her scarred elbow, reminder of the one time she had misjudged the situation and arrived at our house with her elbow bleeding. The bullet had only grazed her, she said, and if she didn't do her weekend rounds how would she pay her children's school fees, which were due at the end of next week?

When my mother mentioned to her friends that she was thinking of raising Naila's pay per session, many were horrified. 'But, sweetie, then she'll expect all of us to do the same,' Aunty Runty said. 'And if the servants hear of it, they'll all want salary increases. Please, darling, don't rock the apple-cart. Give an inch, they'll take a foot, and they'll take your best shoes along with it. If Naila's so concerned about her children's education, give her some books. You have so many at home and, really, though I scolded the person who said this to me at your dinner the other night, the bookshelves are beginning to look' – she dropped her voice dramatically – 'cluttered. Speaking of cluttered, guess who Chun-mun is sleeping with now.'

Naila massaged the oil into my shoulders, her thumbs rotating as they worked out the knots that I had felt forming the moment Sonia told me that Karim was arriving in Karachi. If only he had a hair-lip. If he'd had a hair-lip and I still felt this urge to touch, to taste, to nestle, I'd know it was a feeling I could trust. But I'd felt such urges before for a line of men – from Zia to Hake-Jake – stretching halfway around the world. So maybe this was just lust. Well, that was easy enough to deal with. No such thing as fated love, after all.

'Did you know your husband before you married him?' I asked Naila.

Her fingers paused for a moment, and then continued their kneading with more vigour than before. 'Three years I've been coming to your house every week, and this is the first time you've asked me a question. Are you planning on getting married?'

'No.'

'Good. Finish your education first. Learn from your mother's friend, Rukhsana – what do you people call her? Runty. Every week I massage her and she cries: "I was in university, studying law, and then I married this man and gave it all up and for what?" Every week, same thing. And uff! nowadays even in the morning her breath smells of alcohol. What you people all need are a few real problems. Like, should I leave the house to get medicines for my son even though I might get shot on the way? What are your problems in life, Raheen?'

'There's this boy . . .'

She laughed. 'And?'

'And I don't know what he thinks of me.'

She ran the tips of her fingers lightly down my back like spiders. 'Why don't you ever ask me any questions? About my life? Do you think my life is so uninteresting?'

'What would I do with the information if I had it?'

'What do your mother's friends all do with the information? They all ask questions. What do they do with the information?'

'Nothing. They treat shoe sales in London as more important topics of conversation.'

'You think this is the way you separate yourself from them? By not asking? Let me tell you something –' she stopped massaging, and sat back on her heels – 'you are not my god. I don't pray to you, I don't ask you for things. Don't treat me as though I'm someone who thinks you're important enough to take on my problems.' Before I could even register appropriate shame over this comment, she stood up. 'That's it for today. Bring my money. That's all I want from you. Soon I'll want a raise. But today, just bring my money.'

On her way out, she leaned close and whispered, 'The thing is to see what he says when he first walks into a room where he knows he'll find you. Because he'll have rehearsed that first sentence before entering the room. All you need to know about how he feels is in that first sentence.'

'You've changed the carpet,' Karim said in greeting, when he and Zia walked into the TV room, just minutes after I'd finished showering and changing after my maalish. *Thanks, Naila.* He was wrapped in a grey shawl. *Large enough for two*, I found myself thinking.

'My parents would really like to see you,' I said.

He sat down without responding, and picked up the framed photograph of our two sets of parents, and a group of their friends, including Runty and Asif and Laila, taken at Uncle Asif's farm in Rahim Yar Khan, before Karim and I were born.

'Ridiculous clothes,' Karim said, and put the photograph down.

The phone rang, and on the line was Sonia's brother sounding not-macho for the first time since his voice broke. He asked if it would be possible for me to meet Sonia at the airport and bring her home; her plane was due in thirty minutes.

'Of course I can. No biggie,' I said. 'But Sohail, what's wrong?'

'Mix-up, just a mix-up.'

'What? Did your mother take the second car and go off shopping like that time Sonia was supposed to pick me up for our A-level history exam?'

'We've got four cars now,' he said.

'Well, doesn't that make you special! So what's the problem?' I tried very hard to be fond of Sohail, but he was just such a generic spoilt adolescent. Like a younger Zia without spunk or humour or, to be blunt, intelligence. He didn't even have redeeming wrists.

'Some guys took my father away.'

'What guys? Took your father where?'

Zia and Karim stood up and Zia pointed to the extension in the hallway. I nodded and he and Karim were out of the room and had picked up the extension before Sohail stopped his ragged breathing and spoke again.

'Just . . . some guys. With guns. They said they're from the police. They said . . . drugs.'

'They wanted drugs?'

'Why did you say that?'

'Sohail, you just said . . .'

'You think my father is some kind of drug dealer.'

Zia had pulled the telephone cord as far as it would go, all the way to the doorway of the TV room, and I saw him lean his head against the door frame and close his eyes.

Karim, standing beside him, pulled the phone slightly closer to his own mouth and said, 'Sohail, it's Karim. Zia and I are on the extension. Just tell us what happened.'

'I don't know what happened. These guys came in, said they were from the police. Grabbed my father, said he had to come with them. He was so scared; I've never seen my father look like that. He grabbed the sofa and they prised his fingers off, one by one, and when it came to the last finger I heard . . . I heard a snap. Really clean. Like a wishbone breaking in two. I would have done something but I was holding my mother because she was going crazy, screaming, crying, would have attacked them, and they had guns, man, they had guns.'

'What about your guards?' I was trying to sound in control, digging my nails into my palms to fight the desire to lock all doors and think of places to hide. I looked at Karim, and he saw my panic, and just raised his palm slightly. *It's OK, it's OK.* My fingers unfurled. It was like that time when I saw his head appear over the gate, against the starry sky, before he was beautiful. That same sense of calm. *Hello, anchor. Where have you been? Welcome home.*

'What about my guards? Useless bastards,' Sohail said. 'I just fired them all. They said they couldn't take on the police, and I asked how they knew those men were the police. No uniforms, unmarked car. One of the guards said he was shown some identification. He's an illiterate Pathan: what kind of identification can he decipher? We've been calling around to different police thaanas and no one knows where he is. Listen, do any of you have contacts in the police?'

'Only Uncle Wahab,' I said. 'And he's on holiday in Florida. But he should be back in the next few days.'

'Few days? Oh, great! By the time he comes back wearing a cute little pair of Mickey Mouse ears who knows what could have happened . . . Raheen, what do you think they're doing to him? They wouldn't kill him, would they?'

'Don't be silly,' I said. 'If they wanted him dead they'd have killed him right there.'

'No, they wouldn't,' Sohail said. 'Not with our armed guards outside.'

'Oh yeah, I hadn't thought of that.'

Zia threw a pillow at me. Karim walked over and took the phone from my hand.

'Pull yourself together, Sohail. For your mother's sake, you have to stop talking this kind of rubbish.'

'Exactly,' Zia said. 'And for Sonia.'

Great macho moment. And why was I being treated like an outcast? As if anyone had ever taught us the etiquette for dealing with such situations. Oh God, Sonia.

Karim put an arm around me and pulled me close and for a moment I forgot all about Sonia. Then I realized he did it so that I could hear Sohail's voice coming through the receiver. 'They said – it was almost the only thing they said – that they were taking him away for . . .' his voice was breaking up and at first I thought there was something wrong with the phone line '. . . for questioning about drug smuggling.'

'Your father?' Karim said. 'Sohail, that's just absurd.' And then he looked at Zia's face, and then he looked at mine.

'We should leave if we're going to be at the airport in time,' Zia said.

None of us said anything in the car until we got to Zamzama, and then Karim said, 'What route are you taking?'

'Via the Club,' Zia said. 'My father's there. I have to ask him something.'

Zia's father, Uncle Anwar, was better-connected than anyone I knew. He kept politicians at arm's length, because they were too apt to fall from power, but the numbers stored in his phone's memory for single-touch dialling all belonged to bureaucrats, army generals, officials in the intelligence services and high-ranking police officers. No one knew quite how he acquired these people, or to what use he put them beyond the usual uses to which every successful businessman put people of influence, but his speed-dial meant he was right up there with Uncle Wahab on the list of those who the socialites called when their lives fell apart. For all that, he couldn't get his own son to string together two sentences in his company without turning hostile or contemptuous. Zia's jaw was clenched as he drove, and I had a feeling this signalled he was about to ask his father for a favour. He loved to boast that he'd never asked his father for anything, a claim I viewed with scepticism because I knew it only meant he asked his mother instead and she acted as intermediary, passing demands in one direction and college tuition money, new car, state-of-the-art computer in the other. I had once berated Zia for his attitude towards his father and he said, in one of those rare and excoriating moments of revelation about his family life, 'Do you have any idea what it feels like to know that every day of your life your father looks at you and thinks, "This one also could die at any second"?'

Zia drove through the Club gates and screeched to a halt on seeing his father walk under the covered archway that connected the 'No Ladies Beyond This Point' portion of the stone colonial building to the dining area. 'Raheen, deal with the car,' Zia said, getting out and striding after his father, who was now walking on to the veranda overlooking the Club gardens.

I hated watching Zia interact with his father, so even though there were no cars whose path we were blocking I drove on, parked by the tennis court and waited for Karim to start getting nostalgic about all the hours we had spent at the pool. I had ready an answer about the sexism of the Club, pedalling backwards into the nineteenth century with each new law and by-law, though perhaps that speech of mine was best avoided since Karim was bound to find out how much of my life I spent at the pool and squash courts.

'So you believe he's a drug smuggler,' Karim said.

I caught his eye in the rear-view mirror and raised my eyebrow in a manner meant to indicate I wasn't about to discount any possibility. 'No one makes that kind of money from manufacturing toothpicks. Certainly not in Pakistan.'

'It's not just toothpicks. He's got a number of business interests.'

'Yeah, because everyone used to say – to his face – "No one makes that kind of money from toothpicks." I mean, maybe he's gone legit now, but eight or ten years ago something was definitely black in the lentils. Did I tell you about that time some random Ghutna went up to him at a wedding and asked what he had to say about the allegations that his wealth was "ill-gotten"? And he replied, "Who has made these allegations? Who are the allegators?" Zia and I were standing there and almost died of laughter. Fortunately Sonia was at the other end of the room.'

Karim shook his head. 'I can't believe it.'

'Why? Because he always liked you? Come on, Karim. Remember Anis, that guy in kindergarten with us, whose father used to dress up as a magician at his birthday parties? Well, the father's a murderer. Had his brother-in-law bumped off over some inheritance chuker. But, oh, didn't we all wish we had fathers who would put on black capes and pull giraffe-shaped pencil sharpeners out of our ears?'

'Are you really as casual about this as you sound?' He was watching me intently. 'You really, truly, think people we've grown up respecting and loving can turn out to have these awful sides to them and it doesn't matter?'

I shrugged. 'Love and respect are somewhat extreme, aren't they? This is Sonia's father we're talking about. But obviously I don't want him to go to jail.'

'Not even if he's guilty?'

'No, of course not. Why, you want to see him in jail?'

'It would kill Sonia,' he said, as though that were an answer, and I suppose it was. 'But I don't understand how you can be so detached about this, as though it doesn't matter a bit what he's done, whose lives he's ruined – and don't you dare tell me I sound like a foreigner.'

'I was going to say you sound like your father.' Actually, I was going to say he sounded like a foreigner, but I hated being predictable.

I expected him to flare up in anger at the comparison to Uncle Ali, but instead he said, 'Yeah, well, you sound like your father a lot of the time. Think I'd rather have my set of genes, thanks.'

I reached back and grabbed him by the collar. 'Whatever your problem with me is, don't say a word about my father.'

'Wow,' Karim said. Without explaining what that meant, he

pulled my hand off his shirt and turned to stare out of the window.

Come back, Karim.

Zia opened the car door and I shifted over to the passenger seat. 'He's going to make inquiries,' he said. 'Hold on, Sonia's plane should have landed already; I'm going to drive like a maniac.'

A man of his word, my friend Zia. But when we got to the airport we didn't see Sonia, even though the arrival board informed us her plane had landed ahead of schedule. I called her house on Zia's mobile phone only to have Sohail tell me he hadn't heard from her and maybe she was still waiting by the conveyer belt for her luggage.

It was almost an hour before she finally emerged – an hour during which Zia carried on an almost relentlesss monologue to try to hide the silence between Karim and me. His voice was beginning to get hoarse by the time Sonia walked out of the terminal, her face bespeaking an anguish that went beyond bumpy landings and cold, greasy in-flight omelettes. But when she saw Karim she smiled and put her arms around him, unconcerned by her dupatta slipping off her head. I saw his arms tighten around her and thought, *Not Karim, too. Not this again*, and Zia winced and turned his face away.

'Why are you all here?' Sonia said, putting an arm around me, her other arm still around Karim, and nodding, merely nodding, at Zia, who waved away the porters and started to wheel her luggage trolley towards the car.

'All four of us together,' Karim said without missing a beat. We had decided not to say anything about her father until she got home; maybe, just maybe, everything would already have been cleared up by then. 'Couldn't wait any longer for it to happen. Here we are at last like four peas in a pod.'

'Keys in a cod,' I said.

'Bees in a bod,' said Zia.

'Seize in a sod,' said Sonia, with a smile. 'What? Why are you laughing? Tobah! Such filthy minds.'

We were still laughing when we reached the car even though it hadn't been that funny. Laughing because regardless of circumstances we were together at last, eight years down the line, all together, and despite everything that had changed and was changing we still found one another's laughter contagious.

'You remember that joke of Zia's?' Sonia said, as the boys finished loading her luggage into the boot. 'The one about Buckingham Palace and rubber gloves?'

'And you said, "Like the ones you wash dishes with." ' I started laughing again, but Karim put out an arm to stop me.

Sonia was trying to smile, but her face had turned lifeless, and her hands as she pulled her dupatta over her head were trembling. 'Yes,' she said, her voice without expression. 'Since about half an hour ago, I get the joke.'

A crow swooped by low, I remember, and I noticed two holes in its beak and wondered if they were nostrils. It swooped past Zia and I saw his face, the tears springing to his eyes, and wondered what my face looked like, because it felt like granite. The crow flew away, something red and glinting in its beak, and I remembered an airport official who had patted me down perfunctorily in the curtained-off area for women travellers the last time I had boarded a flight out of Karachi. Her red nail polish had been chipped at the nail-tips.

I watched myself put my arms around Sonia's neck. Karim had her hand in his, but I couldn't make out what he was saying. Her dupatta slipped off her head again and Zia cupped his palm against her head and stroked her hair. When I raised my head and saw him crying, I cried also.

It was only when Karim got a box of tissues out of the car and handed it to Zia, then me, that I realized Sonia was dry-eyed.

'How will I tell my fiancé?' she said to Karim above the sound of Zia and me blowing our noses. 'How will I tell Adel?'

Afterwards, I was to search my memory for any recollection of Zia's reaction to that, but I can only remember him seeing me look around for somewhere to throw the tissue and pointing to a flower-bed.

In the car, on the way to Sonia's we stopped at a traffic light where a man selling motia bracelets rapped on Zia's window and said, 'For pretty ladies.' Zia had only enough change for one bracelet, which he offered to Sonia, but she said the smell of the flowers was too cloying, though she appreciated the gesture. I slipped on the bracelet and felt the little white buds cool against my wrist. I can't recall if we drove to Sonia's house in silence, which must mean we didn't, but I know our conversation didn't touch on her father's situation or allude to the ordeal she had undergone. Round the corner from Sonia's house, another motiawallah approached our car at a traffic light and held up a row of bracelets.

Zia rolled down his window. 'No money. Besides, we've already bought. Raheen, show him.'

I held up my wrist.

The motiawallah turned to Sonia. 'And yours?'

She shook her head. 'I don't have one.'

The motiawallah's eyes widened. 'You must take this from me,' he said, slipping a bracelet off the wooden stick on which his wares were arrayed. 'No, you must. I am your brother; as a brother I'm giving this to you. See, I have three sisters myself. I understand these matters.' Here he gave Zia and Karim a look of disgust. 'Please, I won't sleep tonight if you don't.'

'That's so typical,' Sonia said, as Zia drove on. She had put the bracelet on and was leaning her cheek on her wrist, elbow propped on the window ledge, her nose almost buried in that cloying scent. 'It's so typical of our people. That generosity to strangers. I'm going to cry.'

She cried all the way to her house, tears mixing with flowers, the rest of us unsure what to do since she was in the front seat, which made it hard for Karim or me to put our arms around her. Zia signalled me frantically in the rear-view mirror. Should he pull over? And then what? Exchange positions with me so I could hug Sonia? Should he drive faster to get her quickly home, or slower to delay the inevitable knowledge that would greet her once she got there? I didn't know. How should I know?

'Just drive,' Karim mouthed to Zia. So Zia drove and Sonia cried and I felt utterly ineffectual. But, more than that, I felt guilty, because I couldn't stop thinking of how close Karim held Sonia at the airport and how beautiful she looked, even in pain, and now his hands were resting on her shoulders, and when she reached up to rest her hand on his I almost couldn't breathe for jealousy. So I was glad when we finally approached the road to Sonia's house; but when Zia turned the corner all four of us in the car were simply baffled – Sonia for reasons separate to ours – to see Sonia's father getting into a police car. Before we could react, the car drove away. No fuss, no fanfare.

. . .

If we had more reliable systems of law and governance, perhaps our friendships would be shallower. But with no one to rely on except one another, Karachiites come together in times of crises with attitudes which suggest that no matter what else we are in our lives – bankers, teachers, hypochondriacs, cynics, Marxists, feudals, vegetarians, divorcees, bigamists, anorexics, dyslexics, sexists – our real vocation is friendship.

So by the time Sonia's father was released by the first set of armed men, Sonia's house was already filling up with people dropping by to see how everyone was and what they could do to help. And shortly after the second set took him away in the police car, all chairs, sofas and floor cushions were in use, and a dozen different conversations were being conducted on mobile phones by people calling 'useful contacts' to try to find out what was going on. All anyone knew was that the first round of men had started questioning Sonia's father about his business affairs, when they were interrupted by a phone call, which involved a lot of 'yessirs' on the part of one of the interrogators, followed by a stream of curses when he hung up. Clearly, everyone surmised, two different agencies were after Sonia's father, and the first had been instructed by someone in a position of high authority to release their captive so that the other agency could deal with him.

I looked over at Sonia. She was sitting on the sofa in the downstairs study, our friend Nadia sitting to one side of her, clasping her hand, and Karim perched on the sofa arm on the other side of her, his hand on her shoulder. The room was filled with the hum of our friends talking, keeping the conversation light when Sonia seemed to need that, and discussing all the cases of people wrongfully arrested and soon released, when it seemed that would do her more good. Zia hovered in the doorway, trying to get in touch with his father, but every time he managed to get through to the Club – a difficult feat just days before the Winter Ball – and asked for the call to be transferred to his father he was put through to the bakery instead.

'God, Karim's looking gorgeous,' one of my friends whispered to me.

'Normally, we'd flip a coin and one of us would grab him,' her twin sister said. 'But you've got right of first refusal.'

'This is hardly the time,' I hissed back, and they exchanged meaningful looks and subsided.

I saw the front door open and more of Sohail's friends walked in, followed by one of Sonia's mother's cronies. That's when it struck me: none of Sonia's father's friends were here. In households like mine, and Nadia's and the twins' and – to some extent – Zia's, and – once upon a time – Karim's, there were no set boundaries between our mothers' friends and our fathers' friends. But Sonia's parents lived entirely separate lives, with Sonia and Sohail serving as the only links between them. So where now were Bunty and his cohorts, who for years had been spending their Friday nights drinking Sonia's father's whisky out of Sonia's father's glasses in Sonia's father's living room? I could picture them now, sitting back in their exaggeratedly regal postures, taking bets on whether he'd go to prison or not. And if he didn't, if he made it through this, they'd say, *yaar, of course we weren't at your house that day, mate; we were running all over town trying to find out what had happened to you. Pass the Black Label.* Well, that's what you get for trying to ingratiate yourself with high society on the sole basis of money so new the ink on it is barely dry.

I sunk my face into my hands. Why did I have to think this way? My palms smelt like steel. I didn't know why. There I'd been searching for specific reasons why Karim was so angry with me, and maybe it was just this: because he knew me. Maybe that was reason enough for disgust.

'Raheen?'

I looked up at Sonia. 'Are you OK?' she said.

Images flashed through my mind. Sonia watching her father accused of drug smuggling in court; Sonia hearing the verdict of 'guilty'; Sonia visiting her father in prison; Sonia sifting through the evidence and discovering it's all true; Sonia trying to find a way to still be herself, still be compassionate, forgiving, generous, when looking her father in the eye, knowing the truth of who he is. Then I saw Karim's hand, still resting on her shoulder, and I knew he would stand by her every moment she needed him. I thought, *Please, let the charges be dropped*, and I didn't know if I wanted it for Sonia's sake or for my own.

I lifted myself off the floor cushion. 'I'm fine. I just need some water.' I edged towards the door. Karim pointed at the jug of water and glasses on the trolley next to him, but I pretended to look distracted and turned away.

'Why would anyone do this to my father?' Sonia said.

I hoped it was a general question, and not one addressed to me. I didn't wait to find out, or turn around to see if she was looking at me. I just squeezed past Zia, who was yelling down the phone: 'No, I'm not calling about the quiche,' and went out of the front door, round to the back garden.

Zia came after me. 'So where's this wonderful fiancé of hers? Why hasn't he called? All of Karachi knows by now. Someone's bound to have got hold of him in London and told him. And why hasn't she called him?'

'Go and ask her,' I snapped.

'Oh, one of those moods,' he muttered, and stalked back to the house. Then he turned and strode back. 'What happened with you and Karim in Mehmoodabad when I went to get my sweater?'

'I wish I knew. I just seem to have this knack for saying the wrong things sometimes.'

'If there were prizes awarded for it, you'd win gold, baby.' He pulled an orange-gold flower out of a flowerpot and handed it to me.

I tucked the flower behind my ear. 'I can understand Sonia's friendship with me lasting through the years. She's a saint. But how the hell have I managed to keep you from slamming the door on your way out?'

'Well, to start with, we never actually have serious conversations about anything for more than twenty seconds. So there's a sort of beautiful superficiality to our relationship which sometimes gets covered up by all the genuine affection flowing back and forth.'

'That must be it.' I kicked his ankle. 'So if I actually ever bared my soul to you, it would all be over.'

'Could be. I know I would never subject you to my bare soul. Gorgeous outside, maggoty inside. That's me. You, I don't know. You can be the best person in the universe to hang out with a lot of the time – no, most of the time. I mean, whether I want to take a joyride in a stolen car, or drive two hundred miles across America to find the perfect milkshake, you're the girl I call, and you don't even hold it against me when someone shoots at you or the milkshake machine is broken. And there's, well, Raheen, people know they can count on you for the truth, about anything. And that's rare. But here's the thing: in your finest, sweetest, most generous moments, you always seems so suspicious of yourself.' He looked at his watch. 'Twenty seconds up. End of discussion. I have to try to get hold of my father again.'

I didn't follow him in, but walked over to the crescent-shaped fish pond, and sat cross-legged on the grass beside it, watching for streaks of gold to fin past between the green pond vegetation. If I seemed suspicious of my own kindness and generosity it was only because I knew my instinctive impulses were generally more selfish. Somewhere deep down I had always known that when Karim sent me that final letter he had held up a mirror to a side of me that I always turned away from, preferring to gaze at my more fetching profile. Rather than facing up to that, it had simply been easier to say Karim had overreacted and misunderstood and concentrated on the wrong details. A crow dropped a twig in my lap, and I dipped it beneath the surface of the water and watched the ripples. Give me something tiny to observe and I will clear my mind of everything else. Just leave me this pond, this twig, and that piece of algae, and do what you will with the rest of the world.

A Karim-shaped shadow cast itself over the surface of the water. 'Whatever your problems are at this moment, they're totally insignificant compared with Sonia's, so stop being so bloody selfish and get back inside and at least pretend to be a goddamn friend.'

A fish darted past, a streamlined streak through my reflection. 'I don't know how,' I said.

Karim dropped to his knees beside me. 'Rubbish.' But his tone was gentler now.

'I'm so sure her father's guilty, Karimazov. And she's going to know it. I'm such a damned awful liar.' I shook my head, and swooped my hand down to within millimetres of the water in a bird-of-prey imitation, terrifying the fish into zipping madly about. 'You know, everyone keeps going on about my wonderful trait of honesty. But it's only because I know I can't get away with lying. I squint, or I shift, or I scratch my nose, or I concentrate so much effort on not doing any of those things that I become a statue. It's pretty pathetic, really.'

'That is pathetic. And who says your honesty is wonderful? It can be brutal. And will you stop trying to give the fish a heart attack.' He slapped away my hand, which was still making diving motions towards the water. 'Maybe you need practice, that's all. Say something to me that's a blatant lie. Go on.'

'I haven't missed you at all.'

'Ah, but that's no good.' He crossed his legs, and we sat kneecap to kneecap. 'I would have to believe that's a lie, no matter how much conviction you put into saying it.'

'Why's that?'

'Because I've missed you too much to be able to bear the thought that it was all one-sided.' He linked his fingers through mine and we bounced our clasped hands from one knee to the other. We seemed to be encased in such a fragile moment of perfection that I hardly dared breathe for fear of destroying it.

'Something you want to ask me?' he said.

'When did it stop being awful, your parents' divorce?'

Never letting go of my hand, he pivoted round on his backside and lay down in the grass, resting his head on my knee. 'Never.' He held my hand against his chest, and I could feel his heart beat. 'But you kept telling me I needed to allow my mother to be happy.'

'When did I say that?'

'In my head, always. And you were right.'

I ran my fingers along his scalp, tracing the contours of his head beneath the soft, cropped hair. 'I think there's a better me inside your head than there is out here in the world. Is that why I make you so angry, Karim? Because I fail to live up to the person you thought I'd turn out to be?'

In those moments just before he answered I wondered how things might have been different had Karim never left. Perhaps we would have grown apart, the secrets between us multiplying as adolescence took over our bodies and our lives, his parents' marital woes placing a strain on their friendship with my parents, no one sure where loyalties should lie. But instead he left, and that allowed both of us to remember – or re-imagine – our friendship as something mythic, something fated, something waiting to be renewed and transfigured into a more adult version of itself.

He looked up at me and when he breathed out I could smell oranges on his breath. 'You turned out great,' he said.

What we both wanted then was impossible in Sonia's back garden, and would have been utterly foolish anywhere, and I was close enough to forgetting both those things to know we had to go back inside. But when we returned to the house, Sonia looked at the two of us walk in, and though she would never admit it I know it was something in our faces that made her tell everyone that she wanted to sit with her mother for a while, so could we come back later? I started to protest but Zia whispered, 'Go. Take my car. I'll stay here.' The twins nodded agreement and Nadia handed me her mobile and said someone would call if there was any news of Sonia's father.

I drove Karim to the Club, stopping at Zia's house and mine just long enough to pick up towels and swimming gear. I knew there'd be hardly anyone there at this hour, and I was right – the only other people in the pool area were a foreigner sunbathing, a father and his daughter playing ping-pong at the table to one end of the pool enclosure, and a man with the physique of a serious swimmer doing laps.

By the time I was out of the changing room, Karim was already standing under the shower at the edge of the pool, his back towards me; I stood on the hot cement strip outside the changing room, watching water stream down his bare limbs. I dug my nails into my palms, reminding myself how idiotic it would be to do anything that I was so close to doing that I could almost taste it.

Stop it, Raheen. I slapped my knuckles.

Karim called out to me, and I walked over to the deep end, laughing to see him walk away from the shower with tiny steps that tried to keep time with the tick-tick-tick sound of unbreakable eggshells bouncing which echoed from the ping-pong table.

'All right,' he said, when we stood side by side. 'So what are we doing, and do you mind if I put my glasses back on and just look at you for a few seconds?'

I smacked him on the back of the head, and lowered myself into the deep end. 'Just look? You wimp,' I said, and fitted my goggles over my eyes, the rubber around the eye-pieces pressing securely against my skin. The world was blue-tinged and smelled of chlorine.

'Do what I do,' I instructed him.

I turned on to my back and hooked my legs over the side of the pool to moor me in place, squinting against the glare of the sun. My back, bobbing up and down on the water, formed a ninety-degree angle with my upper legs. After checking Karim was following me, I filled my lungs with air, held my nose and sank beneath the water's surface, watching my breath bubble as its slow release pulled me down, the ninety-degree angle becoming increasingly obtuse. I continued exhaling until my back was flush against the wall of the pool. One hundred and eighty degrees. I was suspended upside down in water, like a sea-bat.

Karim was just inches away from me and he turned his head, his expression one of confusion. I gestured, *Don't look at me. Look around.* He did, and I watched him long enough to see his upside-down smile before looking around myself. It was like entering another world. Everything blue. The blue of the tiles turned the water into the colour of some Mediterranean dream. Bands of sunlight slid along the tiles. The surface of the water was whipped into activity by gusts of wind, and we saw the undulations on the underside of the water's surface. Troughs transformed into peaks. The swimmer was walking from one side of the pool to the other at the shallow end, and all we knew of him was his body, chest down, and the water cutting off the rest of him. We couldn't hear the ping-pong game any more. The shadow of a leaf moved along the bottom of the pool.

I could feel a pressure build up inside my lungs but I wasn't ready, not yet, to leave. I opened my mouth very slightly and exhaled just enough to buy me a little more time. Karim's hand reached through the water to try to catch the bubble of air as it escaped to the surface, but his limbs were in slow motion. His hand, attempting to grasp my breath, brushed against my thigh, and stayed there. Water bubbles attached themselves to every hair along Karim's arm. There was no world but this.

At last I could take it no more and I burst up to the surface, gasping for breath. But Karim stayed where he was. I took off my goggles, pulled myself out of the pool, lay by the edge in the sunshine, and ducked my face into the water. Without my goggles I couldn't see him clearly, but I knew he could see my face breaking through the calm surface of the water, and I knew he'd know I took my goggles off for vanity's sake. With a rush of bubbles he burst out of the water, his arms reaching for me and pulling me in. I pinched his nose shut and we ducked beneath the water's surface, exhaling again, our arms around each other as we twirled lower, no one in the pool now but us, so no one to see how my hands moved across his back and down, and his hands slid beneath my swimsuit, and legs tangled and muscles constricted and mouths forgot to exhale, and so we rose up and broke through the surface again to find a young girl at the side of the pool staring open-mouthed at us with a ping-pong ball in her hand.

But a little while later, when we lay side by side on the blue sunbeds, enough distance between us for propriety but no more, not one millimetre more, I watched his eyes flutter as he dreamt and I knew we were no closer to making peace with our pasts than we had been on the phone when he said he could not forget the palimpsest.

An insect walked across Karim's chest towards his stomach and I brushed it off, my fingers straying to trace the lower end of his rib cage. He smiled through his sleep. Was he dreaming of me? If so, did I understand him in dreams, did I understand why we had become so fragile together when once we'd thought our relationship could weather any maelstrom? Did I understand what I needed to do to prevent us from shattering apart irreparably? All our conversations rushed a headlong path towards pain unless, as in this last hour, we barely spoke, or allowed our thoughts to go only so far before veering to another course. I loved Karim, and I knew he loved me; there was no part of me that disputed that. But it was the kind of love that existed because it had always existed, because it didn't know how not to exist. It all sounded so romantic, but the truth was it frightened me; love wasn't going to be enough to keep us together for anything longer than an idyllic afternoon so long as he still had reason to look at me the way he'd looked at me more than once already since he got to Karachi. Disgust was not too strong a word for that look.

But why, goddammit? Why did he weave around the subject, jabbing accusations at me, then twirling away, and turning to glare when I looked baffled? I couldn't help but strike back, but I hit only his shadow, the blow passing through darkness and crumpling my fist against a wall.

Karim opened his eyes, and stood up with a sudden movement, quite ignoring my hand on his ribs. 'We really should go back to Sonia's. Wasn't very nice of us to leave her.'

I nodded, slipped my clothes on over my swimsuit and followed him out.

There were so many movies in which couples in love found that because of fate, circumstance, prior commitments or differing dreams they simply could not be together and, knowing that, they'd always have one last dance, one last kiss, one last here's-looking-at-you kid. Glancing back at the pool on my way out, I could not escape from the feeling that we'd just had that.

• • •

'Now, darlings, let me get this straight.' Aunty Laila rested a hand on my arm, fingers spread wide in order not to smudge her freshly applied nail polish. 'No, first help yourself to tea and then evaluate my recap.'

Aunty Laila and Uncle Asif had just got back to Karachi, after ten days on Uncle Asif's farm – which was about as long as Aunty Laila could spend there at a single stretch once the romance of being newlyweds living in isolation had departed – and Aunty Laila had phoned my house *en route* from the airport to say I must tell my parents to leave their respective places of work early, pick me up, and arrive promptly at her house. She wanted us waiting in her drawing room, ready to greet her with garlands of gossip when her car pulled in.

'All right, so—' Aunty Laila, tired of my vacillations over whether to take a sandwich or a slice of cake, put both on my plate, along with some pakoras, and pushed me back against the sofa cushions. Uncle Asif, more raccoon-eyed and pillow-bellied than ever, entered the room, his freshly washed hair plastered down in a manner that made his bald spot look like a crop circle. Aunty Laila motioned him to sit down silently and then pressed her fingertips against her temples and squeezed her eyes shut. 'Asif, I have the down-low on GoldTaps. Are you listening?'

Uncle Asif took advantage of his wife's closed eyes to whisk a piece of cake off the trolley, 'Yes, yes, go ahead. But don't break your concentration or you'll lose your thread.'

'OK. Sweetie,' she addressed my mother, eyes still closed, 'remove the trolley from his reach. I only married him for the agility of his limbs, and the mixture of age and weight is fast destroying the foundation of our union. Asif, stop chewing and listen.' She took a deep breath. 'Yesterday afternoon un-uniformed men claiming to be police showed some form of ID to GoldTaps' guards, who are illiterate Pathans and didn't know if they were being shown police IDs or library cards, so let the men in, and the men broke GoldTaps' finger and took him off somewhere. Begum and Baba GoldTaps called all the police stations, but . . . nothing, *nada*, zip. Hour or two later, call from GoldTaps saying he's at Boat Basin. Junior goes to get him, finds him eating kabab rolls, fit as a fiddler, though whether the same was true some hours later we don't know, because the last time I had kabab rolls at Boat Basin very unglamorous things happened to my insides. But, returning to plot, they return home, five minutes later the phone rings and it's some toothpick flunkey to say policemen are searching GoldTaps' office. Door bell rings and it's the police, with uniforms, and they arrest GoldTaps. Lawyer is called – JP, you know, Tahira's ex's brother, the one about whom there were all those rumours involving parrots and masks – and legal things go on. Now GoldTaps is home again, awaiting trial date; his name on the Exit Control List at airports and all border points – even the ones way up north where no one would travel at this time of year – and rumour has it there's evidence, in documents seized from his office, to link him to the finest poppy-growers of the region.'

Uncle Asif grunted, and eyed the oozing chocolate icing on the cake. 'Damn fool for leaving evidence lying round. Raheen, how's your friend Sonia?'

A hard question to answer. She was too busy (holding her mother's hand, massaging her father's head to bring him some relief from his blinding headaches, and stepping in to calm down her brother every time he flew into a rage over the tiniest grievance) to stop and think about herself, never mind articulate how she was feeling. That she believed the evidence was planted and that her father was as upright a man as had ever existed since evolution made bipeds of our species was not open to question. When I had dropped in this morning to see how she was, there had been only two instances when she had shown anything other than her customary serenity. The first was when I felt it my duty to prepare her for the inevitable revelation that her father was guilty; I did this by suggesting there seemed no reason for anyone to go through such trouble to frame him – after all, this was no slipshod, half-baked frame job but one that required forging his handwriting on dozens of incriminating documents, and doctoring his phone records to show frequent calls to well-known drug barons.

'No reason?' Sonia's hand gripped into a fist. 'He's richer and more successful than any of your lot with your old money and your generations-old friendships with the high and mighty. When a man gets too big for his boots, set them on fire, isn't that the way?'

She had apologized, as had I, within seconds of that comment, but we both knew that there was no taking back or forgetting her use of 'your lot'.

The second sign of stress getting to her had occurred shortly after that, when Karim and Zia dropped in, and Karim asked her if her fiancé was cutting short his London trip. Sonia wrapped the end of her dupatta round her hand and pulled the fabric so tight I could see the imprint of her veins against the block-printed material. 'I haven't spoken to him. So many people calling here, the line's always busy and it's impossible to get through. Also, I think he's visiting friends in one of those English towns with unnecessary letters in their names and I don't have the number. It's possible he hasn't even heard.'

'It must be strange to know what to say to him,' I said, haltingly, hoping that pauses between words would pass as tact. Tactful people never spoke as quickly as I generally did. 'I mean, since it's an arranged marriage—'

'Arrafection,' she said. 'Started as arranged, but ended up as affection. More than affection.'

About her airport ordeal, she hadn't said a thing.

If I'd been the sort of friend I wanted to be, I would be thinking only of Sonia, but my thoughts couldn't help returning to the awkwardness between Karim and me that had started on the drive from the pool back to Sonia's, both of us near mute the entire journey. I had hoped we were just overloaded from all the emotions of the day and everything would be a little better after a night's sleep, but if anything things were worse when we met at Sonia's this morning; he had hardly been able to meet my eye when he said hello and neither of us had directly addressed a question or comment to the other the entire time we sat, mere feet apart, in Sonia's TV room. My head still hurt from trying to understand what was going on.

Aunty Laila put a hand on my shoulder. 'Are you with us, darling? You're not upset about how I'm talking about your friend's father, are you? You know that's just the way I am. Don't you?'

Before I could answer, the phone rang and Aunty Laila's hand lifted off my shoulder, made the most graceful of arcs through the air without the slightest sign of haste, her rings catching the light at an angle that maximized their sparkle, and picked up the phone before it had completed its second ring.

'Runty, sweets!' Aunty Laila cooed down the phone, her voice entirely at odds with the exaggerated grimaces of distaste that contorted her face. I went to the kitchen to find some chutney for the pakoras, and when I came back Aunty Laila was recounting the tale of Sonia's father to Runty. '. . . But the guards were illiterate Pathans, so . . .'

I said, 'Why is the phrase "illiterate Pathan" the one constant in every variant of the story? As if he would have been any more capable of deciphering words if he were an illiterate Punjabi or Muhajir.' I threw it out as though it were a question about semantics, but really I wished I were old enough to talk to Aunty Laila as an equal and say, do you know what you reveal about yourself, and what you perpetuate with such stupidity? I've heard you talk about ethnicity, heard it when I was thirteen; it was you and Uncle Asif who first taught me how we can look at our friends and reduce them from individuals to members of some group that our group is at odds with. You made me learn how to derail or diffuse conversations when they headed down certain tracks just so I wouldn't have to feel that disgust, that disappointment, that still turns my stomach today.

'Well said, Raheen,' Aba applauded.

'Come on, Zafar,' said Uncle Asif, waggling his finger at Aba. 'I know what you want to say. If he were a Muhajir there's a far greater chance he would have been literate.'

My hand, reaching for another pakora, froze. What had I gone and started?

Aba shrugged. 'Well, yes, that's simple statistics. The literacy rate of Muhajirs is higher than that of other ethnic groups. I'm not saying this is the way it has to be because of some genetic reason, I'm just saying this is the way it is.'

Uncle Asif laughed. 'Poor Karachiites. Living in this spacious, clean, city in '47 when – whap! – Partition happens and all these immigrants come streaming across the new border, convinced of the superiority of their culture, and whisk away all the best jobs from Sindhis who'd been living here for generations. I'm speaking as a disinterested third party, of course.'

My father laughed even louder than Uncle Asif had. 'I'll let the disinterested bit go for the moment, Asif. But what I won't sit back and pretend to be unaware of is your obliviousness to the fact that Muhajirs came here leaving everything behind. Our homes, our families, our ways of life. We can't be blamed if some – mind you, *some* – of us came from areas with education systems that made us qualified for office jobs instead of latrine-cleaning, which is the kind of job you seem to think immigrants should be grateful for. And as for that term *immigrants . . .*'

He never attacked anyone else, but my father could defend his own with a startling fervour. If he wasn't Muhajir would he feel their grievances as strongly? If I wasn't his daughter, would I still believe that his views were justified? What did I really know about rural Sindh, after all? Nothing. Too confusing to accept that the aggrieved could also be the aggressors. Too difficult to untangle the mess of a situation in which there weren't clear-cut rights and wrongs.

'Oh, now who's forgetting history! Muhajirs loved being called Muhajirs. Loved the religious connotation of that word, linking them to the Muslims of Mecca who immigrated to Medina with the Prophet. It wasn't that you weren't welcome – it's just that you would have died rather than be absorbed.'

I could tell Aunty Laila was following this conversation closely, her eyes narrowing unpleasantly, though she still managed to continue her conversation with Aunty Runty at the same time.

My father nodded. 'I must have heard my parents say a thousand times "we came here to be Pakistani, not to be Sindhi". I won't deny there was an attitude of entitlement. I won't even deny there's still an attitude of cultural superiority, and I'm not defending that in any way. But, Asif, even if we put aside the political marginalization – I know you'll scoff at the term, so let's not go into that for the moment – this quota system is wreaking such havoc on the Muhajirs who have the education and the ambition . . .'

I thought of the car thief. Hundreds of thousands like him in Karachi.

'. . . and couple that with the police brutality, Asif, and you're driving people to the point when they'll pick up guns and detonate bombs.' He took a breath. 'I'm not denying that the rural parts of this province have their grievances . . .'

Aunty Laila put down the phone and turned to Aba. 'Aren't you? You really pretend to have an objective view of things, Zafar; but scratch the surface and that's one hundred per cent Muhajir blood that pours out, isn't it?'

'That's a pretty violent image,' Ami said. 'Friends don't scratch friends, Laila. And just in case you've forgotten, I'm not one hundred per cent anything. There's a good dose of illiterate Pathan blood zipping around my veins.'

Aunty Laila squeezed Ami's shoulder. 'You're right, darling.

I'm sorry.' She twirled towards the two men. 'Stop bickering and say something charming to me. Zafar, don't you think my hair colour is fetching? See, when I stand in the sunlight, it has an aubergine tint. Not eggplant or brinjal or baing'n. Aubergine, with that sexy "zh" sound in the last syllable.'

'Zzhhhhh,' Aba purred at her, and she threw him the burlesque of a kiss. In my relief, I stirred an extra spoon of sugar into my tea without really noticing what I was doing.

Uncle Asif poked me in the ribs. 'What do you think of all this, Raheen?'

'I think her hair looks great.'

'No, silly. What do you think about things in Karachi?'

I stirred my tea. No way was I going to get them started again. 'I think there's nothing I can do about the situation, Uncle Asif, so why waste brain cells thinking about it?'

'Raheen!' My father was staring at me, a look of shock on his face. My mother shook her head and leaned forward to say something, but before she could, Uncle Asif spoke.

'Oh, come on, Zaf. She's only twenty-one. Think back to your twenties. How concerned were you with—' He stopped, turned red, and looked down. My father bit his lip and looked at me. *What?*

The phone rang again, and we all turned to look at it gratefully, except for Ami, who was looking between Aba and me and shaking her head. But the call was for her – a mutual friend of hers and Aunty Laila's was phoning to say someone from the newspaper office had been calling around, trying to get hold of my mother.

'Odd,' Ami said. 'It's only midweek.' Ami worked on the paper's weekend magazine, and we were accustomed to her colleagues trying to track her down when last-minute crises occurred. The most notable of these calls happened a couple of years ago when the magazine was running a piece on some musical evening Aunty Runty was organizing as part of a cultural festival, and an assistant at the office received a message from Runty at the nth hour, saying it was imperative that the article mention she would not tolerate 'monkey business with toothpicks at the musical evening, so ne'er-do-wellers beware'. The assistant, terrified by this ominous statement, tracked down my mother, who advised him to ignore the call and proceeded to scatter toothpicks into Runty's letter box on her way to dinner that evening. Runty didn't speak to her for weeks after that, and still hadn't explained the connection between monkey business and toothpicks.

Ami dialled her office number and said, 'What's the toothpick? . . . Sonia Lohawalla? Yes, that's right, she's Raheen's best friend . . . in the main paper? . . . Can't you tell me what it is, I'm not home . . . oh, wait, there's a fax machine here too.'

When did the front door open without my hearing it? When exactly did the footsteps progress down the hall, and stop, as he realised my parents were inside and paused to decide: what next?

I didn't hear him, none of us did, because all our attention was focused on the drama within the room as Aunty Laila tore the paper out of the fax machine and handed it to my mother, unable to resist glancing at it first. She made a sound of disgust. 'Tacky, so tacky. She's best out of it if this is the kind of people they are.'

It was a paid announcement that was to appear in the next morning's paper. Ami read it out loud. *The Rana family wishes to announce that the engagement between Adel Rana and Sonia, daughter of Ehsan Lohawalla, will not take place. The Ranas hereby apologize to all those whose good counsel they did not heed earlier in this matter, and request that the Lohawalla family, and those associated with them, make no attempt to contact Adel Rana or anyone connected to him.'*

Ami shook her head. 'Oh, that poor girl. That poor, poor girl.'

Aunty Laila nodded agreement. 'No good family will want their son to marry her now – not after both the drug charges and this slap in the face.'

With an explosion of invective, Aba crumpled up the fax and flung it against the wall. The strength of his reaction shocked me out of my own fist-clenched fury. He was fond of Sonia, certainly, but this was entirely out of character. He saw me staring at him, and his eyes panicked. 'How dare he,' he said, as though he need to explain himself. 'How dare he think he was even good enough for that darling girl? If I ever see him I'll— Karim?'

Everyone's head turned towards the doorway, at which my father was staring in a mixture of disbelief and joy. I heard Ami get to her feet with a whispered, 'Oh, there he is. At last!' but as soon as I saw Karim's face I knew something horrible was going to happen, because nothing was moving in the unblinking, unsmiling mask that had settled on his face like a second skin.

'If you ever see him you'll what, Zafar?' He didn't just cut the appellation 'Uncle' from his form of address; he cut every tie to his past relationship with my father.

I caught Uncle Asif by the sleeve and whispered, 'Please do something. Get him out of here.'

'Karim.' My father held open his arms, though it should have been so obvious that Karim was not in an embracing mood.

'Is that what you'll do when you see Adel Rana, Zaf?'

I saw Ami flinch at the way he spat out that last syllable. But was that anxiety or a glimmer of excitement in Aunty Laila's eyes?

'Is it, Zaf? Will you, Zaf, when you see him, Zaf, hold your arms open, Zaf, and say, "Welcome, brother, welcome to the club"? The break-a-heart-too-good-for-you-you-cowardly-bastard club.'

'Karim.' Ami started walking towards him, he held his hand up.

'I don't want anything to do with you either, I'm sorry, Aunty Yasmin. Please stay away.'

Something in my life was about to be destroyed. I could feel it. 'Karimazov, go away.'

He turned to me. 'Are you going to stand by him, and call that loyalty?'

'Karim, can we go somewhere and talk?' My father took a step towards Karim, his arms still spread wide, though now it was in the manner of a man holding his arms away from his body to prove he's not about to reach for concealed weapons.

'We'll talk here!' Karim roared. He caught my father by the shoulder and pushed him down in a chair.

In sheer terror, I caught him by his ear lobe and yanked at it. He spun around, cursing. I watched my hand form into a fist and fly at his jaw. He sidestepped, and my fist smashed into a glass ornament on the shelf behind him. Explosion of glass. I turn my face away. Karim turns his face away. Scrunch shut my eyes. Impact against my cheekbone. Not glass. The tinkle of shards falling to the ground. I open my eyes and there is Karim's hand moving away from my face. Karim's hand, which slapped me.

Face stinging, hand miraculously unharmed, I stepped away from him. 'You bastard,' I said.

'He didn't slap you.' It was Aba. He took his shoes off his feet and handed them to me, as I stood barefoot amid the broken glass. 'He didn't slap you. He was shielding your eyes from glass splinters. He just moved a little too fast. Panic. But it was instinctive. He shielded your eyes before his own.' He ran his fingers through his hair, glanced at Ami, and then looked back at Karim. 'She doesn't know, Karim. Raheen doesn't know.'

Steel hooks latched on to the weightlessness of the air when he said that. A stillness infected everyone, even me, though I didn't understand the remark. Looking around, I saw I was the only one who didn't understand it. Uncle Asif and Aunty Laila were standing together, holding hands like little children. Ami just looked at my father and in the sadness of her expression I heard her voice echoing from years away. *Zafar, sometimes I think I love you more than I should.* And Karim had recoiled, his eyes moving all around the room, settling momentarily on every face except mine, his voice, staccato, saying 'but if' and 'that time' and 'how' and 'so why did' and, finally, as he turned to look at me, 'Oh God, what have I done?'

'*I* did this, not you,' Aba said. 'Raheen, look at me. It's time you heard the truth.'

I closed my eyes and, half-turning, leaned against the wall. The white paint was cool against my cheek and tongue. All my life I'd visited this house and never thought to taste the walls. What an odd and misleading thing familiarity is; so ready to disguise itself as intimacy.

'It was soon after the war ended,' Aba began. 'My neighbours, in those days, were the Mumtazes. A lovely couple, and their sons Bilal and Shafiq. Shafiq and I had been at school together. Bilal was a year younger. He was in East Pakistan, Bilal was, when the war broke out. His parents had been telling him for a long time to come home and he'd said he would but he kept delaying his return. Rumour was there was a girl there.' Aba's voice was strange, a monotone. I reached out to touch his sleeve, but something in Karim's glance made me drop my hand.

Aba continued speaking, without even noticing. 'Shafiq was alone at home when the telegram came. Pink. The telegrams were pink. He'd been stirring his tea, still had a spoon in his hand, and it dropped tea on to one corner of the telegram.' It was as though he was talking about a movie he had once seen.

'He looked across the street and saw my house. I wasn't directly opposite him, but close. Close enough that Bilal could hobble over to visit in the days when he had an injured ankle. He was always injuring himself playing some sport or other, and his ankle was so prone to fractures and swellings we were all convinced he'd end up permanently on crutches by the time he was middle-aged. Weren't we, Laila?' He'd been inspecting a piece of glass all this while, but he finally looked up and smiled at Aunty Laila.

'Zafar, don't,' she said.

I looked at Ami. She put a hand on my shoulder and gripped tight. I moved away from the contagion of fear in her fingertips, stepping closer to Karim as I did so.

'Middle age seemed very far away in those days.' Aba held the piece of glass between thumb and forefinger, his fingertip applying enough pressure to cause his skin to dimple but not to bleed. 'I saw Shafiq run up the driveway, something silver glinting in his hand, and then he was banging on the front door, so hard I thought he'd break it. I opened the door and he just started screaming, "Those bastards, those bastards, those Mukti Bahini bastards! They've won the war, let them have the country, let them have it. I never cared. Not the way everyone else did."

'I asked him what had happened. I'd seen the pink telegram, I'd half guessed already, but I couldn't accept it was true. He said, "You, I used to listen to you, and sometimes you made sense. I never said it, I'm no fool, but sometimes I listened to you. Those bastards, those bastards!" And still I couldn't, I couldn't believe it. I asked him again what had happened and he said—' There was blood now on his fingertip, but his voice was still that monotone, though speeded up, and now I felt as though I was the one watching a movie.

'Shafiq said, "My brother. My brother and all those other West Pakistanis stranded on the other side. The day we surrendered. Not even recognizable, his body. Not even recognizable, you bastard! My baby brother. What the hell do you have to say about your precious freedom fighters now?"'

For the first time I really wondered what it had been like for Aba to be engaged to a Bengali during those days. I knew he'd opposed the West Pakistani action prior to and through the war; I had never heard much about 1971, but I'd heard enough to allow me to know where his sympathies lay. It must have cost him a great deal, but even then, even when he was little older than I now was, he would not back down on his convictions for the sake of expediency. My father. His bravery, more than Shafiq's loss or Bilal's death, brought tears to my eyes.

'I still couldn't quite believe it. What do you say to someone at a time like that? I said, "Shafiq. I'm so . . . Not Bilal, oh God, not Bilal." And his face twisted into such rage as he answered,

"You say 'not Bilal' but I know what you're thinking. You're thinking, it's payback time. You're thinking, our soldiers did as much and worse. You're thinking, maybe Bilal did too. Isn't that it? You're thinking my brother did all those things people say the soldiers did." Really, I was thinking I would never again hear him turn every tale of an accident into some grand joke; I was thinking, even Bilal couldn't make any part of this seem anything less than horrific. And Shafiq said, "Don't even think of coming to the funeral, do you hear me? Don't even think of it." And then he rose up on his toes in fury and said, "How can you do it? *How?*" I asked him, what? do what? and he replied, "You're going to marry one of them. You're going to let her have your children. How?" '

The same way Aba had known the truth when he saw the pink telegram in Shafiq's hand yet had been unable to accept it, I knew, right then, the tenor of what was to come and I turned to leave, to run away, but Karim gripped me fast, thumb and forefinger squeezing my wrist bones, his childhood gesture of intimacy towards me transformed into a grim vice. I looked up at him. Tears mingled with the blood from a glass-cut, just centimetres from his eye.

'I heard Shafiq tell his version of what happened, months later,' Aba continued, his tone still unvarying. 'I was standing outside your living room, Laila, the day of your anniversary party. The one you thought we never came to. We were there. Both Yasmin and I were. About to enter, when I heard Shafiq. Yasmin wanted to walk right in and tell him to be quiet or say whatever he had to say to my face, but I said no, we'll stand here, and you listen to what he has to say.'

Ami was looking at him with such terrible sadness.

Aba looked straight at Karim. 'Shafiq said, "But then the kitchen door behind Zafar opened and she stepped out into the hall. Maheen. I had started to raise my hand to strike Zafar, but as soon as I saw her my arm just dropped to my side. Maheen. She had taught Bilal how to waltz; he had adored her. And with

231

good reason. I was half in love with her myself. Maheen. Beautiful Maheen, who was looking at me so sadly. Lovely, laughing Maheen. All I could think was, *don't let the war have destroyed her too*. The crazy roar in my head began to recede, and I turned to Zafar, ready to apologize, ready to fall into his arms, weeping." '

Aba turned from Karim to look at me. 'But Shafiq didn't do that. He was about to: I believe his version, I really do. But before he could do anything, I spoke. I said, "How can I marry one of them? How can I let one of them bear my children? Think of it as a civic duty. I'll be diluting her Bengali blood line." '

• • •

He had barely finished uttering the words 'blood line', his voice never varying from a robotic monotone, when Ami grabbed me by the shoulder and turned me to face her.

'Before you say or do anything, I want you to think about everything you know about this man. Think about the fact that Maheen forgave him. Ask Asif, ask Laila, the madness that existed in the country in '71, and how he never succumbed to it, not for an instant, until that final moment. These things have to count. The father, the husband, he's been all these years, that has to count.'

'Yasmin, stop it,' Aba said. 'For God's sake, stop it.'

'She deserves an explanation. Karim deserves an explanation. Zafar, you deserve an explanation.'

'I deserve? There was an animal inside me. Karim, I'm sorry. Raheen, I'm so sorry.'

'Stop it!' Ami slammed a fist on the tea trolley and sent cutlery flying. 'There is no animal inside you that made you do it; there is no animal inside you at all, goddammit. Why won't you accept that and look back at what you did, without feeling that looking back is an attempt at excusing yourself?'

I looked from one parent to the other. What did something that happened nearly a quarter of a century ago have to do with our lives? Why were my parents looking at me, so terrified, so grave, making me feel my lack of reaction was some sort of failure? Why were they being so . . . *irritating?* That was it, they were being irritating. As they so often could be, but that was the nature of parents and I hardly regarded it as unforgivable, so why stand around making a big deal of it? I opened my mouth to

233

say all this, but to my horror I found I got no further than 'You're both . . .' before my voice cracked and a sob constricted my throat.

My father's face crumpled up, as if I had sliced a blade through him. I turned, hands bunching into fists, and yelled at Karim: 'Who told you to come back, you outsider!'

I grabbed Aba's car-keys from the coffee table, pushed past Aunty Laila, who was crying on her husband's shoulder, and then I was off, fingers scraping against steel while opening the sliding door to the garden, feet pounding towards the car, Aba's too-large shoes slapping against my soles and against the ground, feet pressing down on the accelerator, down and down, turning the volume of the music up and up . . . one times two is two two times two is four three times two is six four times two is eight in but an hour it shall be ten and so from our house in the middle of the street where the streets have no *name the person you most admire* . . . my father . . . *why? because he's never given me reason not to . . . and your mother?* . . . yes, her too, but him first because . . . because I don't know why but because he laughs louder and sings more often and always has an answer to any question I ask when the world doesn't make sense to me and you'd think this sort of adoration wouldn't last past adolescence but here I am, and everyone says I'm like him, and that makes me proud, *but how will you react when you see his face in shadows for the first time?* I'll, I'll, I'll . . .

I kept driving, further out of my part of town than I had ever driven alone, but I knew where I was going as soon as I crossed Mai Kolachi, the road newly built to connect the Boat Basin to the street parallel to the Beach Luxury Hotel road. Traffic made way before me, lumbering trucks and gaudy buses and exhaust-spewing rickshaws moving in formations that allowed me to squeeze through, and even the barrier in front of the railway tracks rose at my approach. I suppose I was driving like a lunatic.

Then I was past the naval base, and past the abandoned toll stop; the road stretched before me, potholed but clear, with dusty land to either side on which boys in white played cricket. My eyes registered blurs that memory and expectation rather than visual cortex resolved into shapes: a cluster of shops, frying pakoras, Pepsi signs, fishermen's village, mad-eyed goats poking faces into heaps of polythene bags and rubbish, beach huts enclosed by walls, the hills of Balochistan grey-brown in the distance and soon, yes, soon, yes, now! between one beach hut and the next, that shimmer of blue.

I eased my foot a fraction off the accelerator. Sun glanced off the water, so still that last summer's glimpse of the monsoon seas seemed a nightmare of distortion. Since I had arrived back in Karachi I had been vociferous in my demands for making a beach plan, but when Sonia told me Karim was coming I thought, wait, let's see it together.

I turned the volume of the music up even further, my heart pounding with the bass.

When I finally pulled up in front of the gate to Zia's beach hut, almost an hour after I'd torn out of Aunty Laila's house, the fisherman who looked after all the huts on that strip of beach looked at me with a mixture of curiosity and concern, but opened the gate.

'Is Zia Sahib also coming?' Baba, the caretaker, asked when I got out of the car.

I shook my head. 'Just me.'

'Don't stay long. It's not safe driving back, particularly after dark. Particularly for a girl.'

I nodded and bent down to scratch the head of the yellow-brown mongrel who had come running towards me.

'Hey, Puppi. What happened here?' I inspected the caked black blood at the end of the dog's ear.

'Some men shot at him.'

'Shot Puppi? Why?'

Baba shrugged. 'Because they're Pakistani. Don't go on the second beach to the left.'

Baba wasn't given to explaining such pronouncements – which could mean 'bluebottles' or 'men roaring up and down the sand on motorbikes' or 'smugglers' or 'dolphin carcass' – and I didn't feel myself capable of forming another sentence, so I nodded, kicked off Aba's shoes, and made my way down to the beach via the natural footholds in the least sheer part of the dun-coloured cliffs. My feet sank in the warm sand when I jumped down from a height of a few feet. There was no one else on the beach. All mine. For a moment my mind actually cleared, and I stood, breathing in the sea air through my nose, closing my eyes to isolate the sound of waves so small they were just bands of water. The first time I had realized I was homesick at college was when I entered a friend's dorm room and saw a collection of shells arrayed on her desk. I picked each one up in turn and held it to my ear, desperate to hear the sounds of my sea, but most of the shells were too small and even the largest only carried the echo of an unfamiliar ocean. Aba and Uncle Ali, when they were the same age as I was, would routinely leave parties in the small hours of the morning and drive to the beach to smoke cigarettes and talk until dawn, and when the sun rose behind them Baba could always be prevailed upon to give them cups of sweet tea that both men would find unpalatable anywhere but here.

I started to walk towards the water, where the sand sloped down, slicked and shiny with the last inrush of tide. Away from the backshore. The dry part of the beach is called the backshore. I discovered that when flipping through a book about cartography some years ago. God knows why I even pulled it off the shelf.

The water was cold, but bearable. I rolled up my shalwar, and waded further in. My toe grazed submerged sharpness. There were times I had spent hours in the water during the afternoon, and when the tide went out in the evening I'd seen dozens of rocks scattered across the sea bed right where I'd allowed myself to be tossed about by the waves. Once, Aunty Maheen got swept out by the tide, and Baba had to tie a rope around his waist – Aba and Uncle Ali standing on the shore gripping one end of the rope – and swim out to rescue her. That was before I was born. How long before?

I turned and looked towards the cliffs. This stretch of beach was maybe a hundred feet long, bound on either side by cliff walls that jutted out to sea, though at low tide you could pick your way over rocks to the beaches on the other side of the cliff walls. There were six huts, including Zia's, standing side by side, which hadn't fallen into disrepair. But further along the cliffs there were only shells of what were once huts; rooms with three walls and no roof, a square formation of bricks, a single wall. Look towards that side of the cliff and you'd think you were looking at a one-time war zone, all inhabitants fled, nothing left worth reclaiming.

I splashed water over my face. Pulled my feet out of their own prints and watched water rush in to take their place. Stood on a rock that rose from the water, unbothered by its eroded un-evenness prickling my soles. Wished for a dolphin to leap out of the water. Wished again.

I tried to hear my father saying those words in a tone other than the one he'd used to re-tell it to me. I tried to see his face say those words and mean it. But I couldn't. So why were my fingers trembling as I held my hand out in front of me?

I closed my eyes to try to think of Karim's face as it must have been when someone told him why his mother broke off her engagement with my father. It all fell into place, then, all his moments of withdrawal, all those cryptic comments about my father and about the traits he heard echoing through me. Who told him? Which meddling, trouble-making, heartless, disgusting . . . may you suffer, whoever you are, may you suffer by losing everything you thought most important and most secure, may you love someone who doesn't love you back . . .

No, worse, may you love someone who loves you but cannot look at you without seeing . . . what? what?

And then I saw her. Aunty Maheen. Young, beautiful and in love, but with a heart that was daily further cleft by emotions more complicated than anything conjured up by the words 'politics', 'patriotism', 'loyalty'. Who every day heard the news, heard what was reported and what was not reported, heard things that I couldn't pretend to know because no one ever talked about it, no one ever talked about those days and told us what the people who raised us had to bear and what they made others bear, and what could not be borne. What could not be borne for her was obvious, so obvious: Zafar stepping into history, no more pretence at living outside the world around him (as I know he lived for so long, as he had told me he lived for so long, without explaining when he stopped), Zafar stepping into history, stepping where she could not go, and kicking her away as he stepped there, kicking her with blood-drenched boots.

I saw her face as she heard her finacé's words, saw her expression register betrayal and, then, register loss, and I sat down hard on the jagged rock, weeping until my throat ached, weeping until I was past tears, my body convulsing in shudders that I couldn't understand, couldn't stop. How would I ever get off this rock, how would I ever go back? How? Karim. How? Aba, Aba, Aba.

How did my father? How, my mother? How, all those memories I had of the four of them together? When did . . . ? What . . . ? What . . .

Why does it matter? I tried to prise a barnacle off the rock. Why does any of this matter now? But it did. It mattered in ways that crept into the blood stream, too diffused to locate and examine. Every heartbeat the sound of that infection pumping through the body. I bunched my fingernails around the barnacle and pulled. Two fingernails broke.

Near sunset, he found me.

'Zia said you'd probably be here.' He was holding the shoes I had left at Aunty Laila's.

I nodded. It seemed to require an extraordinary amount of effort.

'Uncle Asif gave me his mobile. I called Aunty Laila when I saw your car parked near the hut. She'll tell . . . she said she'd let your mother know.'

I just blinked in response. Why didn't he go away?

He put my shoes down on the sand and went away.

I turned to watch the gulls wheeling between sky and water, and when I looked back again he had gone. I drew my knees up to my chin and hated him.

I heard his footsteps slosh through the water towards me. He had only wandered off a little way, and now he came towards me, one hand filled with pebbles, the other holding something oblong and white. He pulled himself on to the rock beside me and, his feet dangling in the water, placed the pebbles between us. In silence, we took turns skipping the smooth, grey stones across the water. He threw with a flick of the wrist, and I threw with a hopelessly inadequate technique, but I still managed to make my stones skip more than his.

When there were only two pebbles left, we picked up one each and threw them out to sea at the same time. They clinked against each other in the air and spun back towards us. We turned our faces away, and this time it was my hand that moved by instinct, shielding the eye that had a glass-splinter scratch just beneath it. The pebbles splashed in the water, feet away from the rock.

'April 1987. Last time I was here. Remember?'

I remembered it well. Zia, Sonia and I were trying to put a positive spin on Karim's departure that summer ('you'll be able to eat MacDonald's Quarterpounder with Cheese *all the time*', 'while we're melting in the sun, you'll be wearing all those cool sweaters', 'concerts, Karim, concerts!' 'Lords, man,

Lords', 'Not the aristos, idiot, the cricket ground!'), and finally decided that the best thing about being in London was that you were likely to run into people who could give you a record deal. We'd form a band and make demo tapes and Karim would get us a contract. The name, Karim and I decided, was key. Once we had a name for our band, every-thing else would fall into place even though we couldn't play any instruments and the only one with a halfway decent singing voice was Zia, and he only sang when seated at a dining table, which might make for interesting concert ar-rangements. But all those concerns were just minor irritations as long as we had a name. Zia confessed he'd once stayed awake until four in the morning trying to find a suitably catchy name for a pop band.

'And?' I said. 'Didja?'

'That's it!' Karim whooped. He used the end of his cricket bat to write in the sand: DIDJA DJINNS. 'How's that for a name?' We decided that by the time Karim returned home in the winter with his parents we'd all have thought up a name for our first album, along with song titles.

'Did you ever think of any names? For our album?' Karim turned to me on the rock.

'Hundreds. Just the other day I came up with one: Exporting Exotica to the West.'

Karim smiled. 'That's good.' He pulled a notebook and tiny pencil out of his back pocket and wrote EXPORTING EXOTICA TO THE WEST *(buy quick and free samosa)* on top of the page.

'Now song titles,' he said. I looked at him, and he tapped the piece of paper with his pen. 'We need song titles. Come on, Raheen. Can't do this without you.' I went on looking at him, and he gestured to the note pad again, and wrote:

Kabobs and Nabobs

Id Mubarak, Mr Freud

I took the pen from his hand, and wrote:

You'll Find Us by the Indus

'That doesn't really rhyme,' Karim said.
I wrote:

Paki Up Your Troubles

Karim made a sound of amusement, and took the pen from me. He wrote:

By gum, Begum

And I wrote:

Saatchi and Saatchi in Karachi

And he wrote:

Don't make Whoopie, Save your Rupee

And I wrote:

(Kar)achi, nivals and ousing

'Except Carnival and Carousing are spelt with a "C",' Karim pointed out. Somehow, my cheek was resting against his shoulder.
'Not in Karachi. We worship at the alter of K. Haven't you noticed all the Ks in business names in Karachi: Karachi Kars, Karachi Karpets, Karachi Kards – not to mention Karat Jewellers, Kwick Kababs, Kleen Kleeners and Kweer Kween.'
'Kweer Kween?'
'Somewhere in Karachi there's got to be a Kweer Kween.'

Karim roared with laughter, rocking forward, slapping his thigh, bent almost double.

'Idi-oh, you'll fall off,' I said, catching him by his collar and pulling him upright. He straightened, turned to face me, and, just like that, all laughter was gone. I let go of his collar, and didn't know what to say.

Finally, Karim spoke. 'That essay you sent me. The last city was the City of Friendship. Raya is an anagram of yaar.'

'Yes.' I ran my finger over a piece of velvety moss that clung to the rock, just inches away from his hand.

'I should have seen that.' The oblong thing he'd been holding was the bone of a cuttlefish. He started to trace around my hand with its pointy edge.

'You drove over Mai Kolachi to get here,' I said. 'You wrote to me about it once, remember?'

I kept my hand planted on the rock while he traced around it, and reached down to the sea with the other hand to pick up a bit of seaweed. It was rubbery, with bubbles along one side filled with liquid. I handed him one end of the seaweed and we started bursting bubbles between thumb and forefinger, hands moving closer and closer together.

'Yes. I said if they made a road through the mangrove swamps it would cut down the drive to the beach by at least fifteen minutes.'

'Must have given you a thrill. Driving through the road you predicted.'

'I wasn't thinking about roads, Raheen.'

'Not even for a second?'

He smiled. 'Maybe half a second.'

'Mangrove swamps are an endangered species,' I said.

A wave lurched at us, soaking our lower bodies, washing the seaweed away.

'I don't want to see him again. My father. Not ever.' Karim didn't say anything. 'Well, that's what you want me to say, isn't it?' I leaned back on the rock, feeling physically sick. 'All this time I've been trying to understand what had gone wrong between us. I thought it had something to do with maps or my reaction to newspaper headlines or telling you that you've become a foreigner, and all along you just wanted me to say I hate my father. That's all.' I looked out at the waves curling into themselves and breaking, grey-white, and I felt an overwhelming sense of loss. 'That's all.'

'I thought you knew. I really thought you knew. You were asking questions before I left, Raheen. You were asking my father and Uncle Asif. In a place like Karachi where everyone knew, and plenty of people love breaking bad news, how could I know you'd never find anyone who'd tell you?'

'Well, a funny thing happened. I stopped asking.'

'Why?'

It was that gorgeous moment of sunset when the most vibrant colours in the world are pulled towards the sun, the sky shot through with every shade of purple and red and yellow, and everything else darkening. I could remember it all quite clearly now: Aunty Maheen saying to my father, 'Don't tell me that feelings can't change; don't you dare be the one to tell me that,' and my parents' argument afterwards, frightening enough to my sense of order that I had decided I would not ask about this again, not even if it killed me.

'Because I was smart.' I almost started crying again. 'Why did I have to know? What does it benefit us to know? He's been a good father, Karim, he's been better than that. You knew how much I idolize, how much I idolized – oh, fuck tenses! You thought I knew what he had done and you never bothered to say you were sorry.'

I jumped down to the sand, lost my footing and fell over in the cold water, my elbow gashing red against a jut of rock. When he reached down to help me, I pushed him away. 'You found out what he'd said, you thought I'd found out too, and instead of taking even half a second to think of how that would have made me feel you mutilated my letters and sent me maps.'

'Oh, come on, Ra.' He pushed himself off the rock. 'If you can't understand that instead of thinking about you I'd be thinking about my mother and what he put her through, then you really are the most self-absorbed person I've ever met.'

'Oh, no, you can't. You can't accuse me. I'm the perfect friend now.' I knew I was being absurd but I couldn't stop. 'You wanted me to hate my father. My one failure was my refusal to hate my father. Well, I've told you now: I want nothing more to do with him. You happy? You miserable bastard, haven't I just lived up to all your wildest expectations?'

'I didn't want you to hate him, Raheen. I wanted you to stop being him.' He grabbed my hands. 'He thought he could pretend the war and everything going on had nothing to do with him, or with her; he pretended and pretended that the outlines in which they lived didn't matter, until one day it was at his door and things inside him that he never acknowledged, never tried to deal with, came out.'

'We don't know that's how it happened.'

'And you're the same. You're the same, Raheen. The city is falling apart and you're the same. That's why I sent you those maps. Because I wanted you to find a way to see beyond the tiny circle you live in, I wanted you to acknowledge that you're part of something larger. Maps, Raheen, are amazing things. They define a city as a single territorial unit, they give a sense of connectedness, and you don't want to admit you're connected to anything that's painful or uncomfortable.

'Karim, my world is falling to pieces and you're still talking about maps!'

'I'm not, I'm not. I'm talking about why I look at you and see him and can't bear it or forgive you or be with you . . . Oh, God, why weren't we born orphans?'

Now all colour was leached from the day. We were shadows in a shadow world. The beach was always the one place I could go to and never stumble upon unpleasant memories, and now even that had been taken from me.

'I don't want anything more to do with either him or you. This friendship is over, Karim.'

He shook his head and walked past me. 'Well done. You've just made the circle you live in that much smaller.' No emotion was left in his voice. 'Come on, then. We have to go to Sonia's and tell her about the newspaper announcement. She's the one whose world is falling to pieces. We're just Punch and Judy by comparison.'

• • •

Karim followed me to Sonia's house, in Zia's car, the drive home excruciatingly long, involving traffic jams, an interminable wait at the railway crossing, and more red traffic lights than I normally encountered in a week of driving. Near the naval base, Rangers – the much-feared special police force deployed in Karachi to counter terrorism (so the official line had it) – were rounding up suspicious characters. Had Karim been in Zia's Integra he might have looked well-connected enough to be allowed through, but given that he had never driven in Karachi, Zia had entrusted him with only a second-rate Corolla, the car that Zia used when he first learned to drive. There were too many glorious memories associated with that car for Zia to countenance the thought of getting rid of it, even though the beige paint had turned to rust in many places and the axle was prone to snapping. The Rangers flagged down Karim ('young and male', a synonym for suspicious) but I reversed back before he even got out of the car, almost knocking over a uniformed man, and told them that he was my cousin, following me home to ensure I wasn't harassed by lafangas; surely they didn't expect me, a lone woman, to drive without escort while they questioned him? They apologized and let him go.

Karim raised his hand in a gesture of thanks, but I didn't acknowledge it. He thought I was capable of saying something as hurtful, as disgusting, as what my father had said to Aunty Maheen. *Aba, how could you? Karim, how could you think I would ever?* I wiped away my tears impatiently. Neither of them was worth crying over. But the traffic still blurred before my eyes all the way back to our part of town.

When we reached Sonia's house, Dost Mohommad, the cook,

was cycling out. Seeing us get out of our cars he hopped off the bicycle, beaming with delight.

'Allah ka shukar, Raheen Bibi, Karim Baba, Allah ka shukar!'

'What is it, Dost Mohommad?' Karim asked.

'That police nonsense is over. They came to say the case against Lohawalla Sahib has been dropped.'

'Who came? What do you mean?'

'The lawyers. They said they had a call from the police. No case. No charges. All over. The family has gone to give Lohawalla Sahib's parents the good news in person.' He clasped Karim's hand, and shook it with gusto before cycling off again.

Karim and I looked at each other. He must have seen how blotched and red my face was but all he said was, 'We still have to tell her about the newspaper announcement.'

'I don't see any need for you to be there when she's told. You know, you're pretty much a stranger in all our lives. I'll break the news to her.'

Karim raised his eyebrows, unbearably superior. 'With your customary tact and concern for others' feelings? Planning to ask her how much her father paid to the right people to get the charges dropped?'

I turned away. That *had* been the thought that ran through my mind when Dost Mohommad gave us the news. 'I'm going over to Zia's now. To tell him about Sonia. Why don't you go somewhere else? Go and draw a map.'

'Fine.'

'Fine.'

And we so left it.

At Zia's there was an eerie flickering from the window of the annexe above the garage which Zia's father had built to entice his son to return to Karachi for the summer and winter holidays during his years at college. His parent were denied entry to the annexe, though Zia often relaxed that rule for his mother. Among our friends, the annexe was known as Club Zia.

I walked up the stairs to the annexe door, and banged on it as loudly as I could. No response. I leaned over the banister, pulled a few almonds off the nearby tree, and threw them at the window from which the glow emanated.

Zia pushed open the window, waved, and came round to open the door. 'Hey!' he shouted.

I walked into his 'den' and switched off the LaserDisc player, which was relaying some action movie on to his widescreen TV, taking full advantage of the surround-sound speakers. 'Hey,' I replied without enthusiasm.

Zia slid behind the bar in the far corner of the vast room. 'Come on, then. Spill your woes to the bartender.'

I sat down on the bar stool and rested my head on the gleaming black marble of the bar. 'I just found out why my father's engagement to Aunty Maheen broke off. Karim made him tell me.'

'Oh, man. You really need a drink, then.'

I looked up at Zia, who was unscrewing the top of a bottle of Black Label. He poured a generous amount into a glass and topped it with ice and Coke.

'You knew?' I waved away the proffered glass.

'Can't let it go to waste. Not while people are dying of thirst.' Zia tilted and straightened the glass, listening with satisfaction to the tinkle of ice. 'Yeah, I've known for a while.'

'How?'

'The Anwar files.'

Everyone knew, though no one had ever seen them, that Zia's father, Uncle Anwar, had files on anyone who was anyone, and many besides, in Karachi, detailing their illicit, illiberal and ill-advised activities. Uncle Anwar said the reason he never employed guards to protect his house was that people of consequence in Karachi had such a fear of his files falling into their enemies' hands that they all deployed their trusted aides to keep a close watch on Anwar's house to ensure no one broke in and stole the files (and these people never attempted to steal the files themselves, because they knew there would be a hundred eyes watching them).

'There's a file on my father?'

Zia sipped his Black Label and nodded. 'I wasn't looking for it. But I got hold of the key to the filing cabinet one day, and thought I'd see what there was on Sonia's father. Don't know why. Just because he hated me and didn't want me near his darling daughter, I suppose. Anyway, I thought it would be good to have some dirt on him. You know, just so I could feel superior. I wasn't going to do anything with the information. I don't think. I must have been about fourteen or fifteen. And the end of "K" and the beginning of "L" were in the same cabinet, so while I was looking for "Lohawalla, Ehsan" I saw "Khan, Zafar" and I was so surprised I had to look. There was just one page. I think someone transcribed Shafiq's description of what happened.'

'And then?'

'And then I closed the filing cabinet, and told my father to find a new hiding place for his key.'

'Was there a "Khan, Yasmin" in there as well?'

Zia looked down into his drink and nodded. 'I looked at that. Couldn't help myself. It was just one line.'

'Something like "She married Zafar after what he said to her best friend"?'

'Yeah. Something like that.'

'So you've known. All these years.' I tried to fathom that. 'Didn't it change the way you felt about them?'

Zia unwrapped a packet of Marlboro Reds and turned one cigarette upside down, for luck. 'I didn't really think about it in terms of them.' He lit up and took a drag. 'They're supposed to be my father's friends. And he had files on them.' Zia shook his head. 'I didn't know much about '71 – that year's main significance for me is that it's when my brother died – but I knew a thing or two about friendship. Why are you looking at me like that?'

I caught his wrist and traced the veins on it with my thumb-nail. 'You've still got the sexiest wrists in the world.'

Zia took another drag, but didn't move his arm away. 'And if you weren't in love with Karim, and I wasn't besotted by Sonia, who knows?'

I let go of his wrist. 'Repeating patterns. We could end up together, and Sonia and Karim could end up together, and one pairing would work, and one wouldn't.'

Zia lifted a fifty-paisa coin from the ashtray and blew off the clinging ash. 'Heads, we divorce. Tails, we play marriage counsellors to Karim and Sonia.' He placed the coin on his thumb and flipped it.

My parents hadn't played marriage counsellors to Uncle Ali and Aunty Maheen, but I always half-believed that the divorce wouldn't have happened had Karim's parents stayed in Karachi, in the company of my parents. My mother had tried to convince Uncle Ali to change his mind about immigrating, right until the last minute, but he wouldn't listen to her. It was the only thing I ever saw her ask of him that he refused her. At the time, I had thought it was the worsening political situation that had driven him away, and it was only much later that I wondered if he wanted to put as much distance between Aunty Maheen and the Interloper as possible; but all he did was bring the situation to a head, and force Aunty Maheen to make that final, irrevocable choice.

It was the only really selfish day that I could point to in my parents' lives: the day Aunty Maheen called to say she was divorcing Uncle Ali and moving to Boston with the man my parents had already known about, though Aunty Maheen had never admitted anything about him to either of them.

I remember how quickly Ami's face lost its sparkle after she answered the phone and heard Aunty Maheen's voice. I re-member her saying, 'No, Maheen. Say you're not serious,' her hand reaching out for my father's hand as she spoke. When she hung up, they held each other in a way I wasn't accustomed to seeing, and he had tears in his eyes even as he told her not to cry. They left me alone that evening, and went out to dinner together. It's the only time I remember them going out to a restaurant and leaving me behind, and how angry I was with them for doing that. The tragedy wasn't theirs, it was mine. Karim would be dividing his time between his parents. School term in London and holidays in Boston. So when would he ever come home? When would I see him? How was I supposed to go from day to day without the thought at the back of my mind that soon Karim would return and I had to store up every memory worth storing just so that I could repeat it to him? How to see the world without seeing it as a world I would replay for Karim soon, very soon, just a few more weeks now? How could I bear to think of what he was having to bear?

The coin bounced off the edge of the bar, and fell somewhere on Zia's side. He shrugged. 'Guess we'll never know.'

I told him everything then. Starting with the conversation in Mehmoodabad and carrying on to the moment we left the beach. Zia listened without saying anything beyond the occasional 'uh-huh' or 'and then?' When I had finished he said something entirely unexpected. He said, 'At least it's all out in the open now.'

'Oh, please, Zia, don't talk rubbish. I don't want to have to fight with you as well.'

Zia crunched a piece of ice between his teeth and pressed PLAY on his CD remote control. Billie Holiday's voice filled the room. I laughed. He could have such incongruous tastes.

'I tried telling you once that you should talk to you father about why the engagement broke off.'

'You did?'

'Uh-huh. When we became friends again at college. Sonia and I sat down and talked about why Karim went so weird on you with that letter, and we sort of guessed that maybe he knew. Yeah, Sonia knows about it. Everyone knows about it. Both of us tried telling you to talk to your father. You really don't remember this, do you? Every time we tried to bring the conversation round to the topic you just deflected it or ducked it, and it looked to both of us like you guessed it was something painful and you were trying really hard not to have to face it. So the question is: now you know that you have to face it, what are you going to do? Avert your eyes? Coyness doesn't suit you, you know.'

'I'm not averting anything. I'm disgusted with my father for what he said. And I'm disgusted with Karim for saying I'm a reflection of my father.'

'You've always wanted to be a reflection of your father.'

'Of the man I thought he was, Zia. Not the man he is.'

'Rot,' Zia said succinctly.

'You think I could say something like that? Like what he said?'

'I think you want life to be easy. I think that's what worries Karim. Because it means imposing blindness on yourself.'

'Why should I care what Karim worries about?'

'Because there's something about the two of you that's almost magic.'

I looked at him to see if he was joking. 'Magic' was not the kind of word Zia was prone to using.

'Seriously, yaar. Still is. When you were laughing together in Mehmoodabad, about that painting of me, I felt so . . . I felt jealous, Raheen. Not jealous jealous; not really jealous,' he hastened to add, suddenly the cool guy again, refusing to admit any imperfections in his life. 'It was just that I see you two and I know *I'll never have that.*'

'Zia.' I put an arm on his shoulder.

'No, I won't. You said something to me a couple of years ago when I broke up with someone or other. You said, "There's a ghost of a dream that you don't even try to shake free of because you're too in love with the way she haunts you." That was a good line.' He was silent for a moment. 'But forget about me. My life's too messed up even to begin to sort out. But you can sort out this thing that you and Karim have together. I don't know exactly what's going on in his head, but I know you. I know you've never fought for anything. Always easier to pretend it doesn't matter enough to get bruised over. But, listen, if you have to bleed for Karim, bleed. Promise me you will.'

I loved him more in that moment than ever before. I stood up on the rung of the bar stool and reached over to hug him. 'Don't undersell yourself, sweetheart. You're worth bleeding over too.'

'But not by you.'

I kissed his cheek. 'I have news for you.'

I told him about the newspaper announcement. I think I expected him to show some satisfaction about the news that Sonia was no longer engaged, but I was shamed entirely to see that he swore and clenched his fist and said, 'When you tell her, you've got to force her to talk about it, Raheen. It's doing her no good, holding everything in. She'll fall ill. Can't you see she's already looking so run-down, she has to talk about it.' He ground out his cigarette, his scowl deepening. 'One touch of my father's speed dial, and when that Adel creature gets back to Karachi I could have him met at the airport and thrashed within an inch, or maybe even a millimeter, or maybe even less . . .'

'Zia! Stop talking like a goonda.'

Zia made a dismissive gesture in my direction. 'You're always so civilized, Raheen. People like the Ranas, they deserve to be treated like the animals they are. It's only because Sonia's father is in danger of losing all his money if he's found guilty, that's all there is to this.'

'And you're going to prove your great love by paying some-one to break Adel Rana's head with a hockey stick? Really macho, Zia.'

He banged the CD power button with the flat of his hand, switching off Billie's 'Strange Fruit'.

'And anyway, Zee, if the issue is the money, Adel Rana will be feeling sick enough tomorrow when he finds out that the charges have been dropped and Daddy Lohawalla's millions are intact.'

'What?'

'Yeah. Dost Mohommad told Karim and me. All charges dropped.' I paused to consider the strangeness of it. 'If it had happened just a few hours earlier, Sonia would probably still be engaged.'

'Oh God.' Zia sat down.

'What's the matter?'

'You'd better leave, Raheen.'

'What?'

'Raheen, go. You don't want to be in this house for what's about to happen.'

'Where do you want me to go?'

'Anywhere.' He looked up at me, arms wrapped around his stomach as if he was in severe pain. 'Go home, Raheen. Go home.'

● ● ●

To go home really wasn't an option I felt in any state to exercise, so I drove back to Sonia's house and sat outside in my car until one of the guards came out and told me I could wait inside. I had been sitting in the drawing room for only a few minutes when the front door opened and Karim walked in. We sat at opposite ends of the sofa in silence, leafing through coffee-table books. Easy for Zia to talk about magic, but once a spell is broken, pumpkins and rats appear.

At last Sonia and her family arrived home.

'Have you heard?' Sonia said, rushing forward to put her arms around me.

Karim stood up and shook Sonia's father's hand. 'I'm so sorry you had to go through that, Uncle, but at least it's over.'

'Yes, thank God. Over.' Sonia's father thumped Karim on the shoulder. 'But everyone's going to say I just paid off the police. Never mind. Memories are short in this part of town. Throw a few parties and everyone forgets your crimes. At least, everyone who's invited does.' He grinned at me.

'You aren't guilty of any crimes, Aboo,' Sonia said softly.

'Ama, you look exhausted. Go to sleep.' I hadn't even noticed her mother enter the room. No one ever did.

'Everyone's guilty of crimes,' Sonia's father said. 'Just not always the ones you're accused of.'

'And what are your crimes?' I asked.

I saw Karim glare at me, but I thought, *let all truths ring out tonight. Enough secrecy and innuendo.*

Sonia's father gestured around him. 'Look at this place. Look at where I live. Look at all I had to leave behind to be here. That's my crime. I left so much behind.'

'You did it for us,' Sonia said, in the manner of a second-rate

255

actress who has played a climactic scene so often she can't remember how to inject that quality of revelation into her voice. 'For Sohail and me.'

Her father kissed her forehead. 'Yes. I thought you'd be better off in this world. There was a time when I had certainty.' He put an arm around Karim's shoulder; he'd always been fond of Karim. 'Now that I don't have this on my mind, I'll sort out something for your car-thief friend.'

When had he told Sonia's father about the car thief? Had he been to visit Sonia at some point without telling me? How could anyone look at Sonia and not want to drown forever in her serene beauty? How could anyone look at Sonia and not see how easy it was to love her? I put my arms around her shoulders and kissed the side of her head. Karim looked surprised at that. Did he think I wasn't capable of a single genuine emotion? Did he expect me to say, 'Pity you won't be marrying Adel Rana. He would have purified your *nouveau riche* blood line.'

God, Aba, how could you have?

Dost Mohommad entered the room, with a tray bearing cups of green tea with mint and cardamom. Karim, Sonia and I each took a cup, and went outside. We sat in the garden, forgoing cane chairs for the sprawl of grass, and Sonia raised her cup. 'To the grey areas of our lives,' she said. 'To the slippery slopes, and the absence of signposts.'

What had she begun to suspect about her father?

Karim clinked cups with her and waved away swooping, bewinged insects. 'Raheen has something to tell you.'

I told her about the newspaper announcement.

She listened, without interrupting, as I spoke, and then laid a hand on my arm. 'Thank you. I'd rather hear it from you than anyone in the whole wide . . .' She closed her eyes, and looked away.

I held my cup against her cold cheek, and understood Zia's inclination to beat Adel Rana senseless. She didn't look at me, fidgeting instead with a long fleshy leaf that sprouted from a calla lilly bulb. She wrapped the leaf around her fisted hand and the leaf snapped, just centimetres above the bulb.

I took the leaf out of her hand and knotted it around her neck. She rested her head on my shoulder, and I put my arms around her, and wondered: how had we come to this, all four of us? How had the laughter gone out of our lives?

Karim stood up and walked around the garden, running his palms over the outline of flowers and shrubs. I closed my eyes for a long moment. When I looked again, he was out of the radius of the veranda light, transformed into shadow. When a moth veered past his shoulder I was almost surprised it didn't flit right through his dark form.

Sonia raised her head from my shoulder, and looked from me to Karim.

'I'm going in to tell my parents what's happened. Karim, you and Raheen wait for me.'

She went back inside, and Karim continued staring intently at a cluster of flowers, with more fascination than was necessary for what was just a pink clump of petals trying hard to assert resemblance to a rose. I lay back and tried to find something to focus all my attention on, but my mind simply would not clear of everything whirling around in it. It seemed so easy to curl up in a ball on the grass and never think of anyone or anything again.

At length, Sonia came back outside. 'Zia just rang. Sounded strange. He said he had to see me. Do you know what this is about?'

I shook my head.

'Well, he's driving aimlessly. Refused to come here. And I don't want to go anywhere we're likely to run into people we know. So I said the two of you would drive me to Kharadar to meet him. That's OK, isn't it?'

I looked at my watch. 'Your father won't let you leave the house at this hour. Why Kharadar? I've only ever driven through there on the way to the beach.'

'My father's feeling too bad about my broken engagement to say no to anything I ask. And you've answered "why Kharadar?" Because no one we know goes there.'

And so, for the second time in the day, I drove over Mai Kolachi, the road that cut through mangrove swamps. A few minutes later we were on I. I. Chundrigar Road, just past the Jubilee Insurance House, which, in the dark with some of its illuminated letters fused, spelt out the suggestive command: JUBILE IN RA HOUSE.

'Oh, I always Jubile in Raheen's house. Don't you?' Sonia said, turning to smile at me. I rolled my eyes and then smiled back. It was the only thing she'd said since we'd left her house. It was the only thing anyone had said. Zia's car streaked past us on I. I, and then reversed back when he realized it was my car he'd overtaken. Karim opened the door without a word and stepped into Zia's car.

'What's happened with the two of you?' Sonia said, but she didn't need my pain to add to hers, so I told her 'nothing serious'.

'You'll tell me when you're ready,' Sonia said, and touched my cheek, almost crumbling my resolve.

Before long we were in narrow gullies. Zia pulled alongside and asked Sonia if she could find her way around here.

'Is the map man lost?' Sonia said, smiling in at Karim.

Karim smiled back and said he'd never seen a map of Kharadar and no one he knew could verbally re-create its twists and turns. I knew nothing about Kharadar as it existed in the present, although somewhere in my head was the information that when Karachi was little more than a cluster of huts within a boundary wall surrounded by marshy ground, there were two points of entry to the town: Kharadar (the salt doorway) and Mithadar (the sweet doorway), named after the quality of water in the wells that stood by each door. So this was as Old Karachi as it got.

Sonia directed me through the narrow lanes, with Zia following behind. She was the only one among us not surprised to see that the shops were still open and the streets bustling with activity, though it was near midnight and most of Karachi had shut down for the night.

A woman was buying a plush animal from a shop that had dozens of toys, individually stored in plastic bags, hanging from hooks outside the store, forcing people walking along the narrow pavement to duck and weave out of the way of footballs, teddy bears, dolls and plastic cricket bats. Through the open door of a travel agency I saw a group of men sitting in a ragged circle with their feet up on a table; further ahead, a sheep poked its nose through the door that stood ajar to a video-game arcade, if arcade is not too elaborate a term for a tiny enclosure with space for only three games. A crowd of children stood around a man who fed long, yellowy sugar cane into a press on a rickety cart and filled old Coca-Cola and 7-Up bottles with sweet liquid. Piles of flattened canes were stacked on the road beside him.

I was moved, absurdly, to tears. A week or two ago people were wary of leaving their houses, particularly after dark, the violence in the city both unpredictable and terrifyingly ordered, causing some to speculate that the factional violence, ethnic violence, sectarian violence and random violence were not unconnected but fuelled by someone who wanted Karachi terrorized. But who? Why? No one was sure, though there was no shortage of theories. We all knew it would start up again – the shootings on a massive scale, the unnatural silence in the evenings, the siege mentality – but for the moment, for today, Karachi was getting back to its feet, as it had always been able to do, and that didn't just mean getting back to work, but getting back to play: friendship, chai, cricket on the street, conversation. It was a terribly self-involved thought, I knew, but I couldn't help feeling that, in the midst of everything that was happening, Karachi had decided to turn around and wink at me. And in that wink was serious intent: yes, the city said, I am a breeding ground for monsters, but don't think that is the full measure of what I am.

Sonia told me to pull over next to a paan shop; Zia parked next to me, and we walked together to a chai shop. There didn't appear to be any female customers, but no one gave us a second glance. The interior of the chai shop – confusingly called a 'hotel' – was fitted with white bathroom tiles and fluorescent lights, as was the norm with such establishments, and our collective aesthetic gave one long shudder and sat us down outdoors, on wooden backless benches around a laminated-top long table, with watery imprints of the bottoms of glasses on it. The owner (at least, he appeared to be the owner because he had a note pad and pencil in hand) snapped his fingers and a man in black shalwar-kameez appeared to wipe the table clean. When he was done, Karim, Sonia and I rested our elbows on the table top, though Zia first removed a handkerchief from his pocket and spread that on the table in front of him. When he saw we were about to laugh he whisked the handkerchief away, and planted his palms on the table with an air of nonchalance. Sonia ordered parathas and four cups of tea 'with malai'; Zia interrupted, 'No malai for me.' He couldn't bear even the tiniest speck of cream to mix with the milk in his tea.

A beggar girl came and stood by our table with a cupped palm extended towards us.

'Move away,' Zia said.

She stood her ground.

'Are you deaf? Move away. Can't we drink tea in peace?'

'Zia!' Karim remonstrated.

'Fine,' Zia said. He pointed at Karim. 'He's the one with the money.'

The girl turned to Karim. Sonia nudged him and pointed out the other beggars who were watching with interest to see if he was a soft touch. 'Come back when we've finished,' he said. The girl continued to stand her ground, blocking Karim's view of the street. I couldn't help getting some perverse pleasure from watching him so torn between the moral code that served him so well in the abstract and the terrible irritation of having someone standing so close, pushing her outstretched palm in front of him and mumbling, without conviction, phrases about her sick mother and sick brother and no money for medicine. These were the sort of things he could remain blithely unaware of when he sat in London or Boston, shaking his head in disgust at the tiny circles in which I lived my life.

'We're clearly the rich kids around here,' I said. 'She'd be a disgrace to her profession if she gave up on you so easily. Guess no one's ever shown her a map that lets her know her connectedness to you. Guess she isn't aware of your great, bleeding heart that sees your life in the context of her world.'

'Sonia, would you tell your friend to stop directing every conversation back to herself,' Karim said.

'What's going on?' Sonia said. Neither Karim nor I answered, and Zia seemed to be in another world.

The waiter came back to our table, shooing the girl away, and set down four pieces of paper as place mats. They were shipping schedules, detailing lists of Ships, Ports of Call, ETA and ETD, Voyage Number, Flag, Agents and other indecipherables such as: Line Advert, Service, Terminal and EGM. The last column was To Load For ('sort of like "to die for" but less intense', Karim said, and I couldn't believe how much I wanted to laugh at that) and there were a wealth of place names: Riga, Ashkabad, Fos, Beira, Abidjan, Leixões, Thessalaniki, Stavanger, Limassol, Monrovia, Lomé, Mouakchott, Port Gentile. I'd never before given thought to what it meant to be part of a port city, to leave the imprint of a tea-wet spoon on names of places that preferred coffee, to have these strange and foreign syllables intrinsically involved in the commerce of the place, to look at the man two tables from you and wonder if, for all his lack of external signs of affluence, he knew the word for 'ocean' in thirty different languages or the taste of fish cooked in a hundred different spices, and knew too, despite all his travelling, that home meant this alley and these place mats and those different dialects swirling around him. But to admit any of that out loud would be tantamount to saying Karim had a point about me, and I wasn't going to give him the satisfaction.

The parathas arrived, as did the tea, and I gulped when I saw it. The cream rose entire centimetres above the rim of the cup, more frothy than any cappuccino I'd ever seen, and as we watched it in awe it wobbled. 'The thing's alive,' I said.

Sonia, scooping it up with a spoon, smiled at me and said, 'What were you expecting? A dribble of single cream?' I continued to stare at the cup and she said, 'If you eat it up really fast like ice cream on a hot day with the car window open and wind whooshing through, you might get to the tea beneath; but if you leave it it'll just go on absorbing tea and expanding, expanding.'

Of course it was delicious, once I summoned up the courage to put it in my mouth. But Karim gave up after only a couple of spoons. Too rich, too sweet. If I'd been a little more convinced of my ability to finish the cup of tea-flavoured cream I'd have mocked his fragile foreign stomach.

The beggar girl returned and held out her palm again. Zia raised his hand threateningly. 'Go away!'

'Zia!' Even I was shocked by the violence in his voice.

Zia bit his lip. 'I hate them. Those beggars. All of them. Particularly the deformed ones.' He started tearing the place mat into little strips. 'I had this ayah when I was a kid. She said I should never trust strangers, because Karachi is full of people in the employ of the beggar master, and they kidnap children and lop off their limbs so that they can be effective beggars, pulling the heartstrings of passers-by.'

'We all heard variants of that,' I said. 'Why are you the only one who's traumatized by it?'

'I became convinced that my brother hadn't died, but was kidnapped and no one wanted to tell me that.'

'So you used to see these young beggars and think one of them might be your brother and no one would know it?' Sonia said.

Zia shook his head. 'I used to be terrified that one of them was my brother, and my parents would recognize him, so they'd take him home with us and then I'd have to share my room with this maimed, emaciated creature.'

Karim and I couldn't help but look at each other, for the first time without rancour that evening, neither of us able to think of any response to this statement, both of us confirming with each other the horror of what Zia had just said.

Sonia spoke up. 'Zia, I'm sure, I mean . . . he would have put on weight.'

It was the silliest thing anyone could have said. It was the only thing anyone could have said to make Zia smile. He reached forward as if to put his hand on hers, but drew back before making any kind of contact, and gestured to the beggar girl, who came forward hesitantly.

Zia took his wallet out of his pocket and pulled out a hundred-rupee note. The girl's eyes widened. 'If you stay away from us, and keep everyone else away from us until we leave, I'll give you this money after I've paid the bill,' Zia said. I'm not sure she believed him, but his tone of voice didn't leave room for any bargaining. The girl moved a few feet away.

'So why are we here?' I said.

Zia took a cigarette and a box of matches out of his pocket. He put the cigarette in his mouth and tried to light a match, but only snapped the matchstick in two. When he took out another match and struck it against the side of the box, there was a sound of friction – flint against flint – but no flame appeared. Karim borrowed a lighter from the man at the next table, and lit Zia's cigarette for him.

'Storytime,' Zia said. 'Let me tell you a story. True story. Once upon a time, it wasn't a stray bullet that killed my brother.'

My head jerked up.

'No, Raheen, don't interrupt. No one interrupt. There was a man who lived next door to us, a powerful man, one of those men who's in favour with every government. He and my father were friends, not close friends but friends enough that the man invited my parents to go, with my brother, to his beach hut one weekend. At the beach, only a handful of people there, the man pulled out a gun – he had a collection – and started shooting, no reason, just to impress some of the young kids, fishermen's children, who had heard that a government official with a new gun just bought from . . . I don't know where, this was before Afghanistan . . . but they heard, from the driver or someone, that there was this really cool gun around. So, this guy, he thinks he'll give them a bit of a thrill: he starts firing in the direction of the sea. My father tells him to stop because those are real bullets after all, and what if someone's swimming there whom they can't see? So the guy says, OK, I'll stop after one grand finale. See that sand castle? Bet I could shoot a hole straight through that flag on top, anyone want to lay bets, and my father says no but the guy's brother says yes and the guy shoots and loses the bet. It was a huge sand castle, really immense. Large enough that if you stood at a distance, at a certain angle, you couldn't see my mother and her one-year-old son making sand turtles and mudpies on the other side of the castle.'

I shivered and, reaching beneath the table, found Karim's hand reaching for mine. We both gripped hard, my thumb pressing down on the indentation between his knuckles. The smell of salt in the air was overpowering. I held my nose closed and breathed through my mouth.

'My father knew it would be pointless to press charges, because of the other man's position. Pointless to press charges and pointless to weep. Yes, no point to tears. My father is a man who believes in every action having a point. So he swore he'd build himself a list of contacts so long, so powerful, that he would never again feel helpless before another man's clout. And if he ever had another son, his son would not suffer at the hands of anyone, not if my father could help it. No one, no one, would make his son suffer.'

Fathers, again. I released Karim's hand just as he released

mine. Poor, messed-up Zia, who at fourteen could have looked up secret files on every grown-up he knew in Karachi and read about all their flaws and none of their redeeming qualities. Poor Zia, his house always full of people worth cultivating, rather than people worth having in your home. Poor, poor Zia, whose father tried to give him everything and, in so doing, turned him into a boy with whom Sonia could never contemplate being more than friends. As soon as I thought that, I knew.

Zia saw the change that came over my face, and nodded. But Sonia and Karim were still looking at him in pity and bewilderment, forcing him to spell it out.

'I yelled at him, Sonia. When I heard you were engaged. I asked him what could he do now, after he'd always sworn I could have anything I wanted . . . what could he do about . . .'

Sonia flushed, and looked down, seeing the declaration of his feelings towards her, but seeing nothing beyond it.

'But he proved me wrong. Dad to the rescue. He did something about it, didn't he? Of course the Ranas wouldn't let their son marry the daughter of an accused drug smuggler.'

Tears started rolling down Sonia's face.

'Helps to have friends in positions of power. Helps a great deal. Accuse and acquit at will. No need for a court of law. Dear Dad. He's got it all figured out. Was almost too efficient. Got two separate agencies involved. Bit of confusion, but in the end they did the trick. And once the engagement broke off, all charges dropped. No harm done, right? No harm.'

'At the airport. What they did to me . . .' Sonia buried her face in her hands.

Dear God, dear God, take me away from this place.

'He swears he didn't know. He swears he told them not to hurt you.' Zia started raking the skin of the back of his hands with his fingernails. 'I'm sorry, Sonia. I'm so sorry. Please, look at me. Sonia, please.'

But she kept her head buried in her hands.

All of us. Everyone who's been here long enough. My father,

yes. And my mother, who went ahead and married him despite that. And Zia's father. And Sonia's father, who – I don't care how manufactured the evidence this time round – was certainly guilty of something even if I didn't know what. Aunty Runty, once the sweetest, most light-hearted woman. Uncle Bunty, who borrowed money from Sonia's father but didn't spare a breath to defend him or commiserate when he was arrested. The list went on. Every one of my parents' friends, every one of my friends' parents, guilty. And we were no longer young enough simply to watch from the sidelines. How could any of us face up to the truth, and stay?

I put my arm around Sonia, wanting only to erase all the misery that her bent head and sagging shoulders conveyed. 'At least it's over now. And you don't want to marry someone who's so fickle. There'll be others, tons of proposals, all better than Adel Rana.'

She pulled away from me. 'It's not over. Things like this are never over.'

Karim stood up, pushing back the wooden bench. 'I can't stay here. I don't understand this place. I don't want to.' He looked at me sadly, almost apologetically. He turned to Sonia. 'I'm going to fly out tomorrow. But I want your permission to see your father first, Sonia.'

'My father?'

'Her father?'

'Karimazov, don't do this.'

'I'd like to ask his permission to marry you.'

A boy selling balloons moved towards us. The beggar girl knocked him to the ground. One balloon burst; another slipped out of his grasp and flew up, a white oval against the moon-empty sky. Karim and Zia rushed to separate the beggar and boy. I stayed seated on the wooden bench, and watched the balloon. It rose higher and higher and disappeared into a constellation.

'What's going on?' Sonia said. 'Will someone tell me what's going on?'

I could see Karim turning to say something to Zia, and Zia shaking his arm off. Sonia was saying, 'I thought you and Karim . . .' and I wanted to yell at her, 'He wants perfection, so he's choosing you.'

That was when it hit me for the first time: I had lost him.

Not to Sonia and not to maps. I had lost him to the past, and there was no changing that. Mine was still the hand he reached for under the table when the world turned awful, but that only made the loss more unbearable. It was as though our instincts to turn to each other, to want each other, remained as strong as ever, but when instinct stopped and thought took over we pulled away, each time with a little more disgust than the time before.

'Are you angry with me?' Sonia asked. 'I'm not going to marry him, you know that, don't you? He's yours, even if both of you don't see it.'

'You're a better woman than I am, Sonia. You're a better woman than my mother was.'

Karim and Zia had finally stopped the beggar girl and the balloon boy from striking out at each other. They started to walk towards us.

'I don't want to talk to Zia,' Sonia said.

'I don't want to talk to Karim.'

We turned, ran towards my car, despite the stares and exclamations of the men around us, and drove off. In my rear-view mirror I saw the boys watch us go. Neither of them attempted to stop us.

• • •

There are two kinds of blessed moments to which we can awake: the first, that moment of realizing a nightmare was unhinged from reality, no place in our lives for it save for those places in which we store memories that make us shudder even though they aren't true memories at all; the second, more elusive – for we don't fully recognize the peace of mind it brings until it's gone – is the moment of believing reality was a nightmare, nothing more. But the morning after Kharadar, covered in sweat despite the December breeze, I awoke to memory.

I looked at the clock. Early. Forty-eight hours ago, at this time, I was standing at the airport, waiting for Karim. I picked myself off the mattress quietly so as not to disturb Sonia, who was fast asleep in bed, just inches away from me.

I brushed my teeth using my finger as a toothbrush and changed from Sonia's T-shirt back into the clothes I had been wearing the night before. They were stiff with sea salt. I took them off again, and borrowed a shalwar-kameez from Sonia's wardrobe. I was unable to imagine how I would make my way through the coming day. Karim was leaving in a few hours. He had called Sonia's house last night to say he had used Uncle Asif's contacts at PIA to get himself a seat on today's flight to London. While he was speaking, Sonia had tried to hand the phone to me, but I refused to take it. He had clearly said something to her about coming to see her father, and Sonia said, 'Please, don't. Our friendship will be over if you do.'

Sonia and I spent the rest of the night watching tear-jerkers: *Beaches*, *Dead Poet's Society*, *The Outsiders*, a tissue box placed between us.

'C. Thomas Howell,' Sonia said, pointing at the screen as the credits rolled for *The Outsiders*. 'He must have thought he was going to be such a big star. What happened to him?'

'Playing Ponyboy was the zenith of his career,' I replied, and then we both had to laugh at how much that made us cry.

Halfway through *Beaches*, my mother had called looking for me. Sonia said I'd be spending the night at her place. She was too embarrassed to say I refused to talk to my mother so she told her I was already asleep.

I pushed the mattress under Sonia's bed and sat down at her desk. Now what? At some point I'd have to go home. What happens when you spend your life creating yourself in someone else's image and that image festers overnight? How can you point a finger without it turning right round and stabbing you in the throat? I pressed a fingernail against my gullet, ran to the bathroom and threw up all the chai and paratha and sandwiches and pakoras from the evening before.

Afterwards I lay on the bathroom tiles, concentrating on the expansion and deflation of my chest cavity as I breathed in and out. At length, I reached over for Sonia's make-up basket, took out her eyeliner, tore a length of loo paper off a roll and wrote:

(1)   Why did Zafar make that remark about Bengalis?
(2)   Why did Yasmin and Ali's engagement break off?
(3)   How did they all remain friends?
(4)   Who felt what for whom, and when?

I tore off another square and wrote:

(1)   What does 1971 have to do with now?

The blank whiteness of the loo paper below that question faced me like an accusation. I pressed the nib of the eyeliner against the paper, and a tiny prick of black spread into a wider and wider circle. I pulled the entire roll of paper off its holder, placed a magazine beneath it, and wrote:

> Days away from 1995, we are nearly forty-eight years old as a nation, young enough that there are people alive who have lived through our entire history and more, but too old to put our worries down to teething problems. Between our birth in 1947 and 1995, dead bang between our beginning and our present, is 1971, of which I know next to nothing except that there was a war and East Pakistan became Bangladesh, and what terrible things we must have done then to remain so silent about it. Is it shame at losing the war, or guilt about what we did to try to win that mutes us?

I put the eyeliner down, looked at the furious scribbling, much of which had torn through the paper and left black squiggles on the Prime Minister's face. Time to find my father.

When I walked into our house, he was pacing the hallway. He clearly hadn't slept all night. I didn't know what I was feeling as we looked at each other, but it wasn't anything I'd ever felt before.

'Come on,' he said to me.

I followed him outside, but when he got into his car, I hesitated.

'We're going for a drive,' he said.

'I think I might feel claustrophobic.'

'So open the window.'

'I don't really think you're in a position to tell me what to do.'

He started the engine without responding to that.

I opened the gate so that he could drive out. Our street was just beginning to awaken. The retired army officer down the road was taking his two German Shepherd dogs for a walk; the jamadaar was hosing down the driveway next door, sending bougainvillaea flowers flowing under the gate and on to the street in rivulets of oily water; the newspaperwallah was driving slowly along on his motorbike, tossing papers into houses – but on arriving at the house of the American chairman of some multinational, he had to veer his bike all the way to one side of the street in order to achieve a trajectory that would allow the paper to clear the absurdly high wall. When he reached the house next door, the paperwallah wavered, conscious of the wet driveway; then, seeing me looking at him, he smiled a huge smile and tossed the paper over the wall. The jamadaar stormed out, waving the wet newspaper over his head, and demanding a dry copy. The paperwallah said, 'Blow on it, it'll dry. If you can water a driveway, you can do that,' and zipped down the street on his motorbike.

Aba reversed out of the gate, and I got into the car. He drove towards Clifton, past the shrine of the Sufi, Shah Abdullah Ghazi, with its surrounding world of pavement fortune-tellers and heroin addicts and shops selling flower garlands, then up the incline from where we could see Mohatta Palace, that decaying pink building which, with its domes and its history and its amalgamation of British, Middle Eastern, Hindu and Mughal styles, had always been my favourite of Karachi's structures. Aba steered his car away from the palace and parked in the large circle overlooking Funland and a green field and, further out, the sea. I followed him down the graffiti-covered steps leading from the circle to the field, and we stopped just before the steps gave way to a stone walkway with carved archways cut into its underside, which ended in a covered stone structure, open on all four sides.

'The Lady Lloyd Pier,' he said, gesturing at the structure. 'That's where I proposed to your mother. It stood in the waves once.'

We walked along the stone approach to the pier, a sea of grass and polythene bags around us. The Ferris wheel and Pirate Ship and other Funland rides were motionless to our left, the white minaret of a mosque cleft the air between the pier and the sea wall in front of us, and the rock shaped like man metamorphosing out of stone rose from the water on the other side of the sea wall. The transparent polythene bags looked like balloons where inflated, sleeping giant jellyfish where not. It hits you in unexpected moments, this city's romance; everywhere, air pockets of loveliness just when your lungs can't take any more congestion or pollution or stifling newspaper headlines. A pier in the middle of a field that was clearly used on occasion as a rubbish dump should have been absurd, or sad, but instead was suggestive of both constancy and change.

I'll take constancy. Keep the change.

The rumble of buses behind us sounded as the ocean might sound to someone who had only heard it in imagination. The early morning sea not yet woken up to full colour.

I turned to Aba. 'Karim wants to marry Sonia.'

Aba tilted his head to one side. 'Marry! I still think of you as kids. Karim and Sonia? I didn't realize there was . . . well, to be honest I thought you and he . . .'

I looked away, rubbing my thumb in the pockmarked stone between my father and me. 'I thought so, too.'

'Oh God. Is it because of me . . . ?'

I nodded. I wanted to hit him and hug him all at once. He didn't say anything, and I imagined him thinking back to that day, nearly a quarter of a century ago, when he proposed to my mother. All I knew about the proposal was that when he popped the question she replied, 'Zaf, yesterday when I told you to give me a ring, I meant a phone call.' I had always thought of their courtship as being rife with humour.

'If I had told you earlier what I said to Shafiq, how would that have changed things with you and Karim?'

I raised my hands and dropped them, unable to answer. It would have changed everything. It would have changed nothing.

'People have always said how much I'm like you.' I stood up and put my arms around the stone pillar. 'I thought I knew what that meant. I thought I was your distilled self. Raheen's like a younger, female version of Zafar, but slightly less charming, slightly less intelligent, slightly less prone to singing tunelessly.' We both smiled at that. The same smile, mouth going up at one corner, head tilting forward slightly, something slightly sardonic about our eyebrows. 'Slightly less capable of putting aside all biases and prejudices for the sake of justice.'

'Is that how you see me?' He couldn't keep the pleasure from his voice. 'Champion of justice?'

'It was.' I shook my head. 'I don't know now. Something's changed, something's changed horribly, and I don't even know what it is. But I know this. We are alike. We are alike in this: we don't deserve the people who love us.'

'Oh, sweetheart.' He stood up and started to come towards me.

'I'll hit you. If you try and touch me, I'll hit you. I swear I will.'

Neither he nor I were prepared for the ferocity of my reaction. We both looked away from each other, tears running down our cheeks.

'What do you want me to say?' His voice was unrecognizable. 'If I knew what to say I'd have said it long ago. There was a moment when I thought that by the time you were old enough to know, I'd be old enough to know what to tell you. But what can I say?'

'Tell me why. Why did you say that to Shafiq?'

He looked at the sea, at the field, at the ships on the horizon.

'I swear to you, I don't know.' He clenched his hands. 'I don't think I even knew at the moment I said it. Raheen, how could I have said it? After everything we'd just lived through, after everything that she'd had to bear.' He leaned his face against a pillar and, as I watched his shoulders shake, a thought sprang to mind so hideous that I cried out loud.

He looked up at me.

'You've brought me up to forgive you, haven't you?' I backed away from him. 'Everything you've ever taught me about how to live my life. "Condemnation is an act of smugness . . . How can you blame a person unless you've slipped into their soul, seen the serpents and abysses that lie there? . . . Shouldn't we simply be grateful that our lives allow us to live with grace today?" Everything I thought was so damn noble of you, it was just a self-serving attempt to turn me into someone who would forgive you when this moment came.'

'Raheen, that's not true.'

'And when it came to ethnic politics, weren't you the great man? Never attacking anyone else, but also standing firm on your position, saying it wasn't ethnicity that mattered *per se* but questions of injustice. Zafar the Just. And what was that all about? So you could say to me, look at my track record, Raheen; see how I've evolved?'

'You're getting it all wrong. I wanted you to grow up to be someone who would never do what I did. I wanted you to be better than I am.' He reached for me, and I pushed him away, slamming him against a corner of the brick column. He choked in pain.

'If that's what you wanted you wouldn't have made it so easy for me to love you. You've destroyed our relationship; maybe I could forgive you that. But you've destroyed whatever hope Karim and I had together, and that, Aba, I will hold against you well past the day you die.'

I wrenched the keys from his hand and ran, faster than I had run with Sonia to get away from Karim. But Aba was following. Calling my name and running, his feet echoing in time with mine. Did I even have to run like he did? Men walking down the stairs saw us and called out to me as I drew near them, 'Is he bothering you? Should we stop him?'

'No,' I said, hearing his steps falter as age caught up with him. 'Get him a taxi.'

. . .

'Oh, here you are. I've just been looking for you.' Zia strode into his den later that morning, holding aloft a large quiche. 'You been here long?'

I shook my head and turned down Billie Holiday. 'Been driving aimlessly for a while. I needed a place of refuge.'

'So it would be stupid of me to ask if things are OK at home, since you obviously haven't been there since last night.' When I looked questioning he pointed to my clothes. 'Those are Sonia's,' he said. 'You don't own anything with full-length sleeves.'

'Well done, Sherlock. You're not entirely right, though. I walked through my front door this morning. Then walked back out. Don't plan to return in any hurry. Basically, I'm avoiding my mother and not speaking to my father. Why are you carrying a quiche?'

'You have to admit, I win the contest for unspeakable fathers.' He twirled the quiche dish on his fingertips. 'We always acted like Sonia was the one who had got unlucky when fathers were handed out, but you know what?'

'Yeah. Your father's some kind of Mafia don, and my father's just a few steps away from being an advocate of ethnic cleansing. Meanwhile, Sonia's father might not even be a drug smuggler for all we know. Why are you carrying a quiche?'

'Right. I mean, he could be an arms dealer.' Zia grinned, and placed the quiche next to me. 'I just felt like picking it up from the Club bakery on my way back from dropping Karim at the airport. But I hate quiche. So you can have it.'

'Such a gent.'

Zia sat on the floor next to the black leather sofa, resting his head against the sofa arm. 'You doing OK?' he said.

'No. You?'

'Not even close.'

I laid my hand on the top of his head. 'It's not your fault, Zia. You didn't know what he was going to do.'

'Doesn't stop me being partly responsible.' He pressed the CD remote control and Billie became Paul Simon. We listened in silence for a while until Paul started repeating *I don't want no part of this crazy love/I don't want no part of your love* again and again. I looked at Zia; he seemed oblivious to the lyrics, and to me, as he sat blowing smoke rings in the air, his expression mired in concentration. I prised the remote out of his hand and switched off the music.

Zia looked up at me. 'Raheen, I want you to do something for me. I've been thinking about this since last night. I want you to call Sonia and tell her you'll be perfectly happy if she marries Karim.'

'That's not funny, Zia.'

Zia got up and walked over to the bar. 'Nothing about this is funny.'

'You are not having a drink at this hour. Put that down.'

Zia set the Black Label back on the bar and lit up another cigarette. 'Rumours stick. No good family will want their son marrying her. Not after everyone who knows her father said "I told you so" when he was arrested. Not after she's been so publicly humiliated by those pillars of society, the Ranas. No, the only proposals she'll get now will be from money-grabbing scum. If she means anything to me, I can't let her marry anyone like that. I can't. She breaks my heart if she gets a splinter in her finger; how could I bear to see . . .' He shook his head. 'Far better she marry Karim.'

I walked over to the bar. 'Or you.'

Zia cradled the Black Label to him. 'It'll never happen. Even if I thought she'd agree, which I know she won't, I'll never do something that would allow my father to think his way of fixing things works. Please, Raheen. Be as true a friend as I know you can be. Let Karim go. You've lost him already, you know that. You lost him before any of us were born, back in 1971. Now let him go. It's not as though you believe they won't be happy together.'

He was being serious. If a gold sign with flashing light bulbs had appeared in front of me with the words HERE IS YOUR CHANCE AT REDEMPTION I don't think I would have been very surprised. I brushed Zia's hair off his forehead. I would not have thought him capable of such an act of love. In some way I had always been slightly condescending about his feelings for Sonia. I thought those feelings had a lot of breadth, but little depth. I think I liked seeing Zia as somewhat shallow; the party guy, the spoilt boy. I liked the absence of startling contrast when I stood next to him. Well, no more. I looked at Zia's framed photograph of Sonia, Karim, himself and me. Remarkable people, my friends. But did he really think he could see her with Karim and not resent them both, even if they were happy, particularly if they were happy? Perhaps resentment was a price he was willing to pay.

I slid off the bar stool. 'Zee, I have to go and talk to someone. I'll be back soon.'

He nodded, and as I turned to go he tugged my sleeve. 'Is love stronger when it lets go or when it holds on?'

I went to ask my mother.

I knew she hadn't gone to the office that morning, but was at Karachi's premier art gallery instead, interviewing Aunty Laila about her upcoming sculpture exhibit. The two of them were the only people at the gallery when I got there a few minutes later. I opened the door to hear Aunty Laila talking on the phone to someone at a plant nursery about getting a poinsettia to decorate her hallway for the party she was having that night. Aunty Laila was horrified to hear the price of the plant and said to the nurseryman, 'That's very expensive. I only want it for one night. Who's going to pay that much for a plant for one night? Can't I just borrow it for a few hours?' I rolled my eyes, but it seemed that the nurseryman agreed, because there was Aunty Laila saying, 'Oh, wonderful, but you don't really need it back in the morning, do you? Early afternoon all right instead? I'm very tired the morning after parties. You know how it is . . . Good . . . Well, I think we'll have to discuss what you mean by "in case of damages" when I come to pick it up. Surely you're not going to take an inventory of every leaf and check it for signs of discoloration the next morning? . . . I don't believe it . . . I don't believe it . . . Really? Who else? . . . No! . . . No! . . . *No!* . . . Well, I assure you I don't invite that sort of guest to my parties.'

She hung up and turned to my mother. 'You will not believe what he just told me certain politicians have been known to do to plants. Yick! Oh, sorry, sweetheart, you're really not in the mood for gossip, are you?' She looked up and saw me before my mother did. 'Oh. I'll just go and get something from downstairs.' She walked past me towards the door, stopping on her way to put her hand on my cheek. 'Darling, if you hold everyone accountable for what they said and did in '71 hardly anyone escapes whipping.'

The comfort of collective guilt.

I kicked off my shoes and walked across the cool beige floor towards my mother. She was standing at the far end of the gallery, looking down at the street below. I stood next to her, crossed my arms and leaned forward, pressing my forehead against the window. My breath misted an O in the glass.

With all windows closed we couldn't hear anything of the bustle and honking horns beneath, but we did see a gaudily painted bus, bright yellow with red calligraphy and multi-hued flowers, come within inches of ploughing into a lorry that had a portrait of an actress, gun in hand, painted on its rear end. The two large vehicles missed each other, but a car just behind them veered into another car in an effort to move out of the path of collision and, though there seemed no damage done beyond a cracked headlight, the occupants of both cars got out and passers-by gathered around in a knot to see if everyone was

OK, and if any assistance was required, and also to discuss who was to blame and what should be done about it.

There was a street sign right below the window and I pointed to it and said, 'So this is Khayaban-e-Jami.'

'What?'

'We always just refer to it as the road from Schon Circle to the submarine roundabout. Why is there a submarine in the middle of a roundabout?'

'When they first put it up Bunty said it was so that the Rangers and the army guys could hide inside and shoot out of the window thingies during showdowns between the law-enforcement agencies and political activists. But we all said he was being absurd. When do shoot-outs happen in our part of town? And why are we talking about streets and landmarks?'

I laughed shortly. A foot-high bronze man, poised to dive, stood at the edge of the desk beside me. I ran my thumb along his shoulder blades and wrapped my hand around his chest. 'How much did she love him? Aunty Maheen. How much did she love Aba when they were engaged?'

Ami looked me straight in the eyes. If she'd said love wasn't quantifiable, I might have stormed out of there. But she said, 'Very much. Very, very much.'

'That makes you pretty despicable, doesn't it?'

She drew herself up to her full height. A tall woman, my mother, and capable of great regality. 'I will not apologize for marrying your father.' She made a tiny self-deprecating sound. 'Would it help you if I said I loved him first? And that as long as I thought he and Maheen had a chance I never made one move towards him?'

'But didn't you think about what you were doing to her? You were her best friend, Ami, and you married the man who broke her heart.'

'I loved him more than her. Yes. I don't deny it. I'm not going to make this easy for you, Raheen. Your father may want to play the martyr and say, "Come, hate me, I deserve it," but I will show you so many shades of grey about this business it'll make your head spin.'

I backed away. 'God, you'd make a good tyrant.'

'I'm a mother. The boundary between the two is sometimes very blurry.'

I started to smile, but forced myself to stop. 'How could you want to spend your life with someone who said a thing like that?'

A tiny furrow of concentration appeared on her forehead, as though she were trying to remember something she hadn't thought about in a very long time. 'I didn't believe he meant it.'

'Oh, so it's that simple.'

'There was nothing simple about any of it.' She gazed out of the window again, then looked at me as though sizing me up. 'He only had one major fault, your father, when we were all young. One flaw. He lacked strength. But somewhere along the way he found it, and to this day I don't know if he found it when he was engaged to Maheen or just after. No, Raheen, I don't know why he said what he said, but I know that after he did it he was able to look the country straight in the eye. Until then he'd been looking from a height, a position of remove, and suddenly he was down there – or thought he was – with the rabid crowd, saying the kinds of things that came out of their mouths, believing that a part of him may have believed what he was saying, though I can tell you he didn't.'

'Or at least that's what you need to believe to justify marrying him.' I couldn't stop myself saying it, though I had already lost Aba and Karim and I didn't know how I could bear another loss. But Ami and I had always spoken straight to each other; maybe, just maybe, that would be enough to save us. I could have shown her Karim's last letter to me, all those years ago; I almost did, except I didn't know how to tell her not to tell Aba about it.

'If you choose to believe that, I can't dissuade you.'

I waited for her to continue, but she didn't. She gave me this look as though to say, you decide what questions you need to ask.

'What do you mean, he looked the country straight in the eye?'

'I mean, he didn't pretend it hadn't happened. He said, this is what we have done, these are the consequences we must live with, and these are all the ways in which we've got to learn from this. He developed incredible strength, Raheen; but then you came along and all his residual weakness became concentrated on you. Everything he promised he wouldn't do – like keep quiet about what he'd done, like turn his back on '71 – he did because he was afraid of the consequences of telling you the truth. It was the one thing I could never argue him out of. Didn't really try hard enough, I suppose.'

'He brought me up to be someone who'd forgive him.'

'You sure about that?'

'Yes.'

'Do you forgive him?'

'Never.'

She gave me a knowing look. 'Exactly.'

I dropped my gaze from hers.

'Tell me what's been happening with Karim,' she said. I looked at her and knew that she understood about love and friendships getting so tangled it seemed impossible to find your way clear except through following something in the gut that bypassed the brain entirely. If '71 had defined Aba, it had in some way defined her, too. She married my father and decided it was not something she would ever apologize for. So she became a women who held her head high, not in arrogance, or contempt, but because she knew that it was a form of cowardice to make a choice and then pretend you didn't really make it. And while my father was charming me, pulling me close to hear his heartbeat, teaching me how to look at the world, she taught me that you didn't have always to agree with your parents or want to emulate them in order to know they mean the world to you and you to them.

So I told her about Sonia, about Zia, about Karim, and when I had finished the telling, she said, 'There are no blueprints for love. But you want to know how things unfolded with the four of us?'

You couldn't escape from my mother's voice when she wanted it to hold you in place. It reached out to me – honey over gravel – and pulled me into the past, into 1970, to a Karachi before drugs, before guns, before Civil War, before the economy ran on foreign aid, before religion was wielded as the most powerful of political tools. A Karachi in which people stayed. There they all were, in the Nasreen Room – Zafar, Yasmin, Ali, Maheen and all their closest friends – many of them recently returned from university abroad as though it were the most natural thing in the world to come back, to return home, no reason not to. Zafar pulled Yasmin on to the floor, he asked her a question, she replied with coquetry, he thought it was refusal. Everyone's futures changed, right there.

She walked around the gallery, her hand alighting on this sculpture's head, that one's back, but always moving on, and looking in my direction less and less as the story moved to Rahim Yar Khan and then back to Karachi, to Ampi's, to the racetrack, to the Club. She reached up and swivelled a track light so that her aspect moved in and out of shadows, her voice getting hoarser and everything in my mind more jumbled.

When she had finished, the story taking me past Karim and my first meeting in the cradle, I was more confused than ever. How do you measure love? How do you separate it from selfishness? Think of all the futures that could have been, all the pasts we'd never understand, everything in the present we keep hidden from one another and ourselves, all the futures that still might be. Is love strongest when it holds on or lets go?

I closed my eyes. I imagined Karim walking into the room. All abstractions fled.

Sonia, I'm sorry.

Ali paused, hand on the door knob, and tried to identify the source of the noise from the other side of the door. *Plock! Thock! Crash! Plock! Thock! Plock! Thock! Plock! Thock! Crash!* He eased open the door and poked his head in, hesitantly, ready to withdraw it in a hurry.

Zafar stood at one end of his drawing room, whacking a tennis ball with his cricket bat – *plock!* The ball ricocheted off the opposite wall – *Thock!* Ali noticed the broken glass around the room, remnants of a rather expensive set of whiskey tumblers, of which only two now remained intact on the drinks cabinet.

Crash!

Or, rather, only one now remained.

Ali closed the door behind him and walked closer to Zafar, who still hadn't acknowledged his presence. There was a cut on Zafar's arm, with a shard of glass protruding from it. Ali took hold of Zafar's arm and pulled out the shard.

'Maheen's over at Yasmin's place,' he said.

'Thought she might be. I suppose you're here to ask why I said what I said.'

'No.' Ali took the tumbler from the drinks cabinet and poured himself a drink. Bits of glass swirled around in the amber liquid. 'Honestly, Zafar, this is so irritating,' he said, looking in disgust at the contents of the tumbler.

Zafar whacked the tennis ball. 'Well, then, find another bar.'

Ali dipped his handkerchief in the alcohol, carefully avoiding glass, and pressed the wet cloth against Zafar's gashed arm. Zafar yelled but didn't move away.

Ali said, 'I'm here to ask why you haven't yet attempted to make your apologies and try to patch things up with her.'

'After what I said? You want me to ask her to forgive that?'

'Try.'

'It's no use.' Zafar pushed Ali away. 'Go away, Ali. I don't want you here. Go back to Yasmin. You know, you're a lucky bastard to have her.'

Ali saw himself and Zafar reflected in the mirror. Zaf movie-star gorgeous with eyes that revealed every emotion, and he, Ali, fastidious and remote. He turned away and closed his eyes. *For how much longer do I have her, how much longer? How can I make her stay? How will I bear it if she leaves? Who would have thought, who would have thought . . .*

. . . That Zafar could say such a thing. Yasmin sat on the arm of the sofa, and stroked Maheen's hair as she slept. Tears still not dry on her cheeks. Who would have thought he could say it and then allow the days to slip away, no excuse, no explanation.

She heard someone push open the front door, and left the room to see who it was.

'Hi.' It was Ali. He was looking at her strangely. He'd been looking at her strangely since he'd first heard Maheen and Zafar's engagement was off. 'Is Maheen here?' he asked.

There was a hollowness in her stomach, the sudden realization of what it meant, what it meant for Ali, that Maheen was no longer engaged.

'Yes, she is,' she replied, holding her head up. She wasn't going to cry.

How coldly she looks at me.

'Zafar's at his house. I just came from there. He refused to discuss it with me, but maybe you . . .'

Can't you be more subtle, Ali, about getting me out of the house so you can be here to comfort her? After a year-long engagement, can't you care a little more?

'No point denying the obvious, I suppose,' she said. 'Things are no longer as they were that night on the balcony when I said I'd marry you.'

No longer the same at all, Ali.

No, no longer the same in any way. My darling, my love.

She took off her engagement ring and handed it to him. 'Well, thanks,' she said. 'You've been a thorough gentlemen.'

He bowed clumsily. What else to do?

When she closed the front door on her way out of her house, Maheen heard the sound and woke up.

'What's going on?' Maheen asked, coming out into the hall-way.

Ali's fist closed around the ring.

'Nothing,' he said, and set the tone for all their years together.

'To get him back must still be possible.' Maheen furrowed her brow, trying to understand why Yasmin wasn't engaged any longer.

If she knows the truth. If she suspects I let him go so he could go to her, she'll push him back to me with both hands. But I don't want him that way. I couldn't bear to have him that way.

'I don't want to get him back. He doesn't want to get me back.' She shrugged. 'It was never this big love thing with us, you know. I thought we could be happy together, that's all.'

'You were right. What's changed? Nothing's changed.'

No, she'll never even think of him that way. He's been engaged to me, how could she think of him that way? Unless, unless . . .

'Something has most certainly changed. There's a new bachelor in town, and he's not too shoddy.'

Maheen looked at Yasmin uncomprehendingly. Yasmin looked guiltily away. Maheen gasped.

'Love and war,' Yasmin shrugged.

'Yasmin, don't talk to me. I can't talk to you about this, I can't accept this. Not now, not ever.'

'Everest. Climbing Everest would be easier than understanding you women. Why did you call it off, Yasmin? You think you'll find anyone better than Ali?'

'I'm just sitting here, trying to drink my cup of tea and read my magazine in peace. I don't require polite conversation from the likes of you.'

Zafar's face fell. 'I'm sorry,' he said. 'I don't expect you to forgive me what I said.'

Yasmin squinted up at him, standing between her and the Club pool in the bright sunlight. 'Oh, please! I hardly for a second think you meant it. The unforgivable thing was your refusal to go running after her when she ran out of your house.'

He continued to stand in front of her, shifting awkwardly from foot to foot.

'Oh, sit down, Zaf. I can't see you properly against that sun.'

He sat down. They looked at each other, nothing to say.

'Can you see me properly now?'

'Yes. But you're not much to look at.'

His mouth curved into a smile. 'Liar.'

She poked him in the ribs, and he laughed and grabbed her hand. Ali's hand on hers had never had such an effect on her spine: warmth and chills radiated from it at the same time. She closed her eyes.

Maheen, I'm sorry.

'There's no call for apology, Zaf. I'm thrilled for both of you.'
What else can I say?

'But what about you, Ali?'

'Oh, someone else will come along.' *Yasmin. Yasmin. The sound of my heartbeat.*

'Have you seen Maheen lately?'

'This is not a waltz, Zafar. We can't just swap partners.'

'All this partner swapping. It's like a square dance.' Maheen pointed to the book she'd been reading when Ali walked into her garden and found her sitting there. 'I can hardly keep them all straight. Let's see . . . Hermia loves Lysander and Lysander loves Hermia, but Demetrius also loves Hermia though he used to love Helena, who still loves him and so hates Hermia because

Demetrius loves Hermia, not her. I mean Helena. Or do I mean Hermia?'

Ali opened his own copy of the same play. 'Do you? No, you've got it right. Let me try the next series of steps. Strike up the band, enter Puck, bearing love-juice. Now he pours love-juice on Lysander's eyes and Lysander finds he loves Helena and hates Hermia, but Helena hates Lysander because she thinks he's mocking her and Hermia doubtless hates Helena because Lysander loves Helena, not her. I mean Hermia.'

'Though, really, why blame Helena if Lysander's affections have changed? But now here comes Demetrius, also affected by love-juice, and now he too loves Helena, who believes he must also be mocking her, so declares she hates him too. And, for good measure, also hates Hermia, whom she blames for putting the men up to their acts of cruelty, a terrible thing to do since Hermia and Helena were friends before these two jokers appeared.'

'But wait, wait, all's well . . . Lysander's love-juice is negated by another potion, so once more he loves Hermia . . .'

'. . . Who you'd think might be a little concerned about how quickly he's been changing his affection . . .'

'. . . But love is love, so she's happy. And Demetrius still loves Helena, who still loves him, and who cares if his love is all the result of love-juice, love is love. And they all live happily for the next ten minutes, after which the play ends and no one knows anything further.'

Maheen leaned back in her chair, laughing. 'So the reason you told me to read *A Midsummer Night's Dream* and meet you for tea is . . . ?'

Ali raised an eyebrow. 'I didn't. You dropped a note off at my place with those very instructions.'

'Oh. Well, something here is strange.' She handed him a typewritten note with his name signed at the bottom. 'So you didn't write this?'

Ali laughed. 'We'll call whoever wrote it "Puck".' He straightened his tie and remembered the night he had chiselled her initial into a tree. Whatever had brought that out, surely it could be revived again. Not to that extent, perhaps, not enough to make him pick up hammer and chisel, but some echo of it. He watched her run her fingers along her eyebrows, smoothing down the hairs in that familiar gesture of hers which signified uncertainty, and he thought perhaps he heard an echo.

'How about it, Maheen? Are you in the mood for a wedding?'

'Invitation? For me?' Yasmin ran her fingers along the embossed surface of the card. 'I half-thought I wouldn't be invited. Zafar neither.'

'I half-thought you wouldn't either, Puck.' He smiled at her and she didn't pretend to be confused. 'But Maheen was in a gentle mood after she heard about Laila, so I took the opportunity to add to our invitation list.'

'I just heard about the miscarriage. Awful, it's so awful. Poor Laila.'

'She nearly died, you know. Loss of blood. But Dolly was at the hospital, visiting a relative, and she heard there was no blood matching Laila's type, so she called her husband and God knows what strings Anwar pulled but he managed to get hold of a match.'

'God bless Anwar. And we're always so snide about his newly-found connections.' *Strange how already it seems a dream or a part I once played, all those months I was engaged to you with no thought of wanting anything differently for the rest of my life.*

'Hmmm. There was some half-deranged guy at the hospital who almost attacked the doctors. Seemed to think those last available units of blood were earmarked for his brother, who died without them.'

'Good God.'

'Yes. Apparently the police were called to get rid of him. He was led off screaming about how one day he'll be rich and powerful and his house will have running water, twenty-four hours a day, gushing out of gold taps.' *Stay where you are. Don't move any closer. Don't let me smell that scent of jasmine and spice on your hands. At this distance, I can make myself believe you're only an old friend.*

'I am so glad I'm not poor. Particularly not in Pakistan.'

'I'm so glad I don't know anyone with gold taps.'

'Silver tea set? What do you think, Zafar? As a wedding present for Ali and Maheen.'

Zafar, when we send out wedding invitations, can we say: no silver, please. Show some originality.

Or we could just elope, Maheen. How about it? Today?

'Silver's fine, Yasmin.'

Yasmin raised her eyebrows at him across the Ampi's table. 'That was a joke. You know Maheen hates silver.'

'Oh.' He swirled ice cream around in its pewter bowl.

She had to say it. For all their sakes. 'Zafar, it's still not too late for you and Maheen.'

He found he didn't even have to pause an instant before taking Yasmin's hand and saying, 'Yes, it is.' Guilt had swallowed up everything else between him and Maheen, and for a while he had thought that regret would swallow him up too. But Yasmin had changed that. He suspected people thought him fickle, and if everyone wasn't so frantically busy trying to put the war and everything associated with it behind them he doubted his engagement to Yasmin would have met with such approval all around.

And Maheen was with Ali. Fine and upstanding Ali.

He didn't think very hard about Maheen and Ali together. He couldn't. Not yet.

His other hand closed around Yasmin's.

But soon.

'So soon? I thought you'd refuse to see me for at least another decade.' Yasmin drew Maheen into an embrace. 'Oh God, I've missed you more than a little.'

'Silly girl, as if you thought I could stay angry for ever. I've been picking up the phone to call you every day since Karim was born and twice a day since Raheen was. Did you really imagine I'd turn you away at my doorstep? Ali, what are you doing?'

'I'm smelling Yasmin's hands.'

'Is it a pleasant smell?' Yasmin smiled at him.

'Talcum powder.' *Now I know, we'll all be all right. We'll all be friends for ever. The echo stronger now than it was the day we got married, and surely it can only amplify as the years wear on.*

'Now all you have to do is convince that husband of yours that all is forgiven,' Maheen said. 'What does he want from me, Yasmin, an official letter of pardon?' *Zafar, when we talked of names for the children we were going to have, neither Karim nor Raheen were on the list. I miss you. I miss the way you made me laugh. Come back, in whatever form it is. I'd rather have you as my friend than watch you sulking in corners ashamed to meet my eye each time we meet.*

God, Zaf, why didn't you try even once to say you were sorry?

• • •

One more month, and the reprieve would be over. I lay down on the bed and looked out through the huge window at the lushness of early summer. Odd to think these paths that I'd walked, that glen in which I'd spotted deer, that student diner where I'd braved the most arctic of nights for a plate of curly fries, would soon only be memory.

'Out into the real world,' my classmates and I would chirp, when thinking of graduation and what lay beyond. To them the real world meant work, bills, the start of a road leading to a mortgage, children, a suburban house and a car in the driveway. But what my real world was, I still hadn't decided.

'You should stay,' Zia had said to me on the phone the night before, calling from New York, where he'd gone to talk to real-estate agents. 'You're entitled to a year of practical training with your student visa. You should definitely stay. This isn't about your father any more, Raheen; the way things are in Karachi, you'd be a fool to go home.'

It would be so easy to stay, and convince myself that it wasn't about my father any more. I hadn't seen him since that day on the pier. While I was still talking to Ami in the gallery, Aunty Laila had walked back in, and I told her I wanted Uncle Asif to get me on the next flight back to New York. My old school friend Cyrus was there, and I knew he'd put me up until the start of the semester without asking any questions. 'I just need to go away and clear my head,' I told Ami, expecting her to argue me out of it, but she had replied, 'As long as you promise to clear it rather than empty it.' I didn't tell her the main attraction of staying with Cyrus was that he could be counted on to envelop me in a whirlwind of activity that made it possible to live from one hour to the next without any thought of what lay beyond, or behind.

There had been a flight that evening. My only qualm was leaving Sonia, but when I called her she said her father was taking the family on Umra. I doubted any desire for religious pilgrimage lay behind her father's decision; he probably just wanted her out of Karachi so that she wouldn't have to face the scandal of the broken engagement.

There was a gentle tapping on my door. I ignored it. Probably Zia, back from New York, stopping off to see me on his way to his college. I wanted to lie here and wallow in nostalgia about my college days, not discuss the future and what I honestly thought lay in it for me if I went home. The tapping turned into a loud knocking.

'Oh, go away,' I said.

There was the sound of footsteps retreating from my door. I rolled my eyes. Sometimes he gave up so easily. Truth was, one of the things I already regretted most about graduation was that it meant moving out of a place where Zia was less than twenty minutes away by car; it meant Zia would no longer be within my local calling zone with his peculiar nocturnal hours that allowed me to wake from nightmare at four in the morning and call him without hesitation. I walked towards the door. The phone rang.

'Hello,' I said into the receiver.

'Hey, I've got an idea.'

'Zia? Who just knocked on my door?'

'Tooth fairy. Listen, I have an idea.'

'What?'

'Don't go.'

I covered my eyes with my hand and fell back on my bed. 'Zia, not this conversation.'

'No, I'm serious. Move to New York with me.'

'What do you mean "with me"?'

'You know. I mean, no strings or anything. Well, not too many of them. But what the hell, you know. Why not? One day at a time.'

I couldn't tell if he was serious or not. 'Why ruin a beautiful friendship, Zee?'

'Come on, Rasputin. Come on. Save me from myself.'

'Zia, I can't.'

'It's Karim, isn't it?'

'Yes.'

I waited for him to remind me that in four months Karim had made no attempt to get in touch with me, and to remind me further that Sonia had still not received any halfway decent proposals and didn't I see how selfish I was being? But instead he said, 'Abracadabra, baby. Guess there's a part of me that still believes in magic.'

'Thanks, sweetheart.' I hung up, and opened the door, hoping to find some clue to the identity of the person who had knocked.

'Ra!'

At first I thought I must have imagined it. The voice came from behind me, it came from inside my room.

'Open the window, I'm about to fall.'

I swivelled around. One foot on my window ledge, one foot on a tree, head tilted back to prevent the glasses balanced on the edge of his nose from falling off, he was Charlie Chaplin rather than the Romeo I'd imagined when I'd imagined him appearing outside my window.

'Karim, what are you doing?' I levered open the window, and fumbled with the clips that kept the screen in place.

'Attempting the splits, fifteen feet above ground. Could you remove that screen?'

'No, it's stuck. You'll have to go down and use the front door.'

'I don't think you appreciate my problem.' A gust of wind blew and Karim yelped, removed his foot from the ledge and wrapped himself around the tree limb. 'I can't get down.'

'Nice shorts, Cream. Have I mentioned you've got great thighs.'

'Raheen!'

I went next door to Tamara's room, which was empty but unlocked, and put a heavy hiking boot on to my right foot. Then I returned, stood on my bed and kicked the screen. My foot went through the wire mesh.

'What the hell are you doing?'

'I thought I'd kick the whole screen off.'

'Yeah, and then you'd have fallen out yourself.'

I looked at Karim, clutching on to the tree, head still tilted back, and then looked at myself, one foot in a large boot sticking out of the screen. 'One day we'll tell our children about this moment,' I said.

'Is that "our" as in your children and my children, or "our" as in our children?'

The wire mesh had left cuts all around my ankle, but I really didn't care. 'Is that a proposal or a proposition?'

'I'll take what I can get.'

'Raheen, what's going on?' Jake stood below, staring open-mouthed up at us.

'That's Jake,' I said to Karim. 'He called you a bastard a few weeks ago.' We'd briefly got back together, Jake and I, not so long ago, but he broke it off because I couldn't stop talking about Karim. Jake had conceived a violent dislike for Karim, not so much because of me, but because I told him Karim had spent much of his teenage life in Boston but still preferred cricket to baseball any day. *Red Sox is an anagram for Sex Rod* Karim had written in one of his letters to me during our adolescence, after the Interloper took him to a baseball game at Fenway Park in an attempt to achieve Hollywood-style father–son bonding. *Yikes!*

I retracted my foot, cutting myself further and feeling it this time.

'Hi, Jake,' Karim shouted down. To me he whispered, 'Hake Jake?'

'Are you stuck?' Jake asked Karim.

Karim looked at Jake, looked at me, looked at the ground, looked at the branches beneath him. 'Of course not,' he said, and leapt clear of the limbs and leaves, his arms spread wide, embracing the wind. He jumped up, not down. Lifted himself up, Daedalus for a moment, long enough for me to extend my arm through the jagged screen and feel the air that brushed his fingertips brush my fingertips also; then he was rolling on the grass, the gradient of that patch of lawn carrying him away from the concrete dorm and towards the gravel path. Jake stepped out of his way, and bent to see that he was OK.

By the time I made it outside, Karim was standing up, talking to Jake.

'Hi, boy,' I said, and put my arms around him, too conscious of Jake's look of hurt to greet Karim with the abandon I felt.

'So, it was nice to meet you,' Jake said, extending a hand to Karim. He started to pull my knapsack off his back, but thought better of it, and just shrugged. 'I'll bring your . . . books . . . by later. I was just cleaning up and found them. You left them in my room when . . . I don't know, sometime.' He started to walk away. After a few steps, he stopped and turned round. 'You know,' he said to Karim, 'the word "maps" is an anagram of "spam".' He raised a hand and jogged off.

'Funny guy,' Karim said.

I took his face in my hands. 'To hell with Jake. I can't believe you're here.'

He pulled away and bent to retrieve his fallen glasses, which had somehow managed not to break during his fall.

'Oh, for God's sake, Karim. Now what's the matter?'

'I couldn't see you.' He put his glasses on. 'Could you bear not to go back to Karachi?'

'What?'

'Let's walk.'

Walk? Who wanted to walk?

We walked. I led him away from the dorms and towards the glen, where I often stepped off the beaten path and headed towards the river, every tree looking like the one beside it, with neither stories nor signs to distinguish one from the other.

There should have been many questions in my mind, but I was suddenly so happy that all I could think of was something I'd wanted to ask him since he'd yawned and stretched and his shirt had lifted to reveal his stomach in Mehmoodabad.

'Does that chicken-pox scar on your stomach mark an erogenous zone? Tamara says her boyfriend's chicken-pox scar does.'

'Every part of me is an erogenous zone when you're around,' he said, as though remarking on the time of day. 'Now, behave yourself.' I was raising his T-shirt, and he caught my hand and smacked it lightly. 'I'm here on serious matters.' I felt myself grow tense, and he said, 'Because I've seriously discovered that I seriously don't want to believe that everything between us is over.'

Was this because things were too convoluted to reason out, so he just clutched on to that instinctive need we'd always had for each other? I was afraid to ask. 'Do you know what "erogenous" is an anagram of?'

'Rouge nose,' he said, after a pause.

'Neo-rogues,' I corrected him. 'OK, you have three minutes to be serious.'

He kissed me.

'That was not three minutes,' I protested.

'Raheen.' He took my hands in his, and sat me down on a bench at the edge of the glen. 'I can't go back to Karachi.'

'Are you having visa problems? I know someone in the embassy in DC who can sort that out.'

'No.' He shook his head. 'It's starting again. The same kind of stuff that went on in '71.'

'That's silly.' I cupped my hands around the back of his ears, forcing them to stick out even more than usual. I couldn't help it; just having him here was making me feel near delirious. 'Just because ethnic politics are involved doesn't mean it's the same thing.' Now he would mention my father and it would all start again.

'I don't mean the specifics.' He ran the tip of a leaf down my face. 'The desperation, the craziness. The stench from the newspapers. This is how it begins.'

'Is that a hickey on your neck?'

'No . . . well, now it is. So you'll come with me?'

'Where?'

'Anywhere but Karachi.'

I pulled back. 'Karim, you really are being silly.'

'Why do you even want to go back?'

Did I want to go back? Back to a city without glens, without places to sit in public with my arms round his neck, without the luxury of wandering among indistinguishable trees unmindful of the repercussions of getting lost. Back to a city that was feasting on its own blood, the violence so crazy now that all the earlier violence felt like mere pinpricks. Back to a city that bred monsters. Back to a city where I'd have to face my father. Why should I want to go back to any of that?

And yet. When I read the *Dawn* on-line and then looked around me to the pristine surroundings of campus life, I knew that every other city in the world only showed me its surface, but when I looked at Karachi I saw the blood running through and out of its veins; I knew that I understood the unspoken as much as the articulated among its inhabitants; I knew that there were so many reasons to fail to love it, to cease to love it, to be unable to love it, that it made love a fierce and unfathomable thing; I knew that I couldn't think of Karachi and find any easy answers, and I didn't know how to decide if that was reason to go back or reason to stay away. 'Because, Karim, you've shown me that it's not so simple to leave a city behind.'

'You have to see why I can't go back.'

I nodded. I saw that, for all his obsessing about the city, or perhaps because of his obsessing, Karachi was an abstraction to him, in the way the past is an abstraction, and he lacked the heart to make it a reality. And I saw that everything he had heard about 1971 gave him reason to fear that national politics would again force people he loved to reveal their narrow-mindedness and cowardice and rage, and those people might include Zafar's daughter, so like her father in so many ways.

'You were the one who said I needed to stop living in tiny circles.'

'I've found that doesn't matter to me as much as I thought. Or maybe it's just that you mean more to me that I knew.'

I stood up and walked away from him, twigs and dry leaves crunching beneath my feet. If Zia had walked through the opening in the trees, I think I might have said yes to New York City and made it all simple. But there was no one there except Karim and me and more ghosts than we could count. Ghosts of his parents' failed marriage, of Zafar and Maheen's failed engagement, of the years apart when we grew into people other than the people we would have been had he stayed in Karachi, of the Karachi we once thought we were living in and would always live in, of the imagined-other each of us kept up a conversation with long after our letters stopped.

'What about Sonia?'

He took a deep breath. 'She's the loveliest girl in the world. And to marry her because I think no one else will come along for her is such a supreme act of condescension. She said that to me on the phone just the other day.' He smiled. 'Except she called it an act of condemnescension.'

'Just a minute. Aren't *I* the loveliest girl in the world?'

'No, no. You're not. You're not, but that doesn't matter. Not one bit. Just say you won't go back to Karachi. We'll escape to the middle of nowhere, and eat roots and berries, and never read a newspaper.'

'When did love become so dependent on geography?'

'When personality started to change with location.'

I rubbed the palm of my hand against a tree, needing to feel the gnarled and knotty bark against my skin. 'I'm the same person here as in Karachi.'

'In Karachi I have to see your reactions to certain things. Amid the roots and berries there's no cause for those reactions.'

'I'm sorry if my imperfection makes life inconvenient.' I jammed my hands in my pocket and stepped further away from him. 'We can't all be godlike.'

A twig snapped in his grasp, and birds flew chirping madly out of the tree at the gun-like sound. 'No, but some of us could try not to be so stubborn and so stupid.'

'Why don't you just say whatever you want to say, Karim, before I get really bored? Is there something in my list of faults that you left out when we talked at the beach? You need to get another complaint off your chest?'

'You've had a happy life, haven't you?'

The shadows were reaching out from the tree trunks, and I shivered and moved into one of the remaining patches of light, but he didn't follow.

'You never stopped to consider that your happy family existed at the cost of mine. They should never have got married, my parents. They wouldn't have, except your father said the most unforgivable thing, and then your mother forgave him for it with such a magnificent show of compassion. Never mind how my mother felt. Never mind that my father might have had feelings about the whole thing. But you haven't considered that. How could you consider that, when the consideration would disrupt your happiness? How could you consider that if my mother had married him she would have been happy all the years I was growing up, and she wouldn't have had to cheat and lie and sneak around? You think it's hard becoming disillusioned with a parent when you're twenty-one, Raheen? Well, try it when you're fifteen. God, I was angry with her for over two years. Until I found out what your father said. He was the one who ruined her life, and my father's, and mine. And don't you dare look at me as if to say I'm transferring my anger on to your father. This is not transference. It's the real thing.'

I wasn't about to defend my father, or even point out how silly it was of him to attack my father and yet simultaneously assume he would have been the perfect husband. 'I don't know what this has to do with going back to Karachi. Karim, I don't understand what we're fighting about.'

'You're going to go back, aren't you? After everything that's happened you're going to go back, because all you really want is to go on the way you've been going on. Like your father, who could so easily transfer his affections simply because it was easier to love someone who wasn't Bengali, you arrange your life around everything that's easy, even though it means wrapping yourself in a little cocoon and deciding that things that happen away from the street where you live don't touch you. And then you pretend your street is the world.'

I stared at him, appalled. 'You're the one who started this conversation by saying you don't want to go back to Karachi.'

'You're the one who has no problems going back because nothing that happens there will really bother you. And what happens tomorrow when you decide that being with me is too hard, what happens then, Raheen? How dispensable will I prove to be? As dispensable as I was when I left Karachi, and all you could do was write letters about how much fun you were having, and how foreign I was becoming day by day, and how you really weren't interested in anything I had to say about how hard it was, how goddamn miserable it made me, to be away from Karachi, which meant being away from you.'

'That's not true, Karim.' I was pulling a leaf apart between my fingers, the fleshy part separating easily and falling off the veins. 'Go and read my letters again.'

'I can't. I cut them up, remember, and burnt what was left.'

'Well, I remember what I wrote. I remember I used to tell you everything that was going on in school, every little detail, so that when you came back you wouldn't have to feel like an outsider for even a second.'

'You made me feel like the outsider. You told me what was happening without telling me it would be so much better if I were there.'

This was turning into some twisted nightmare. 'I was only matching the tone you set in your letters, Karim. Your first letter to me, the first correspondence between either of us, started with you saying: Bet you're boiling in that deadly summer sun, and here it's cool enough for a sweater. Ha-ha!' I repeated it again to emphasize the lightness of the letter's tone. 'Ha-ha!'

'How could I use any other tone but "ha-ha!" when it was so obvious you didn't want to hear anything from me that wasn't a joke? Raheen, you used to see me crying, before I left Karachi, your best friend since we were born, you used to see me crying, because my parents were always yelling and my father was threatening to take me away and do you know how hard it is for a thirteen-year-old boy to cry in front of anyone? I cried in front of you, only in front of you, because I just needed you to ask what's wrong and you couldn't, you couldn't, you didn't even care enough to want to know. Go back to bloody Karachi. Go back and turn into Runty and see if I give a damn. Coming here was the stupidest thing I could have done.'

I caught hold of his sleeve. 'Why did you come, then?'

'I was going to take you to Boston with me. To see my mother. But I don't want her to see you.' He pulled away from me and headed out of the glen.

I threw the bits of leaf at him in frustration but they swirled and came back at me. I could hear his footsteps pick up and become a run, and I knew I'd never catch up with him.

If he'd stayed any longer he would have accused, *you still haven't called my mother*. As though it was any easier calling her now I knew what she had suffered at the hands of both my parents. I remembered Aunty Maheen's voice from that first aborted phone call – *Darling, who is it?* – and the sudden ache that made me hang up the phone because it wasn't Uncle Ali she was speaking to. That was four years after the divorce. It made no sense, the strength of my reaction.

Yes, it did.

Yes, it did.

It seemed easier not to see her, that was the truth. It seemed easier not to have to see her and her husband and imagine how Karim must have felt – perhaps still felt – to see them together. Because if I had to imagine how Karim felt about the divorce, I'd have to face how I failed him. I used to walk around all day in those weeks after the divorce trying to shake off the suffocating feeling that came from imagining his hurt, and I felt that if I heard his voice, if I heard him weep, I would break into a million pieces. So instead I told him I didn't know what to say; when he wrote back, I told myself that if he had my voice inside his head to speak to, that was enough. I never broached the subject again in any of my letters. In doing that, I drew a dividing line between us. *I do not want your pain sitting on my heart, boy. Keep it away.*

I leaned against the tree. I had done that, and both Karim and I knew it. When he told me I lived in tiny circles, that I didn't want to acknowledge how I was connected to the outside world, he had been talking about the failure of my friendship to take part of his pain upon myself. Even if he didn't know that's what he had been talking about.

I veered off the path, and half-ran, half-slid, down to the river. I sat there a long time, watching the water flow past. Karim's life after Karachi unfolded in front of me, and I did nothing to stop it, not even when I imagined Aunty Maheen telling him she was leaving. His loneliness then was complete. I stayed by the river long enough to push past tears, past hurt, until what remained was my shame. But I still didn't leave. I stayed, allowing the shame to grow and grow, until finally there was a tiny exhalation, a release.

I stood up then and made my way back to the present. But when I neared my dorm, there were words etched into the soil near where he had fallen when he leapt from the tree: *I'm sorry. I love you.'*

Or was that a soil-speck, not a full stop, between the first sentence and the second?

. . .

In Boston, summer was in full swing. Sunlight glinted off the John Hancock building, glinted off the Charles. A convertible sped past, leaving a smell of ice cream in the air. I glanced down at the directions Aunty Maheen had dictated over the phone.

'At Storrow Drive get into the extreme right lane . . .' It sounded simple enough, but no one had prepared me for the rush-hour traffic of Storrow Drive, the horror of being stuck in the extreme left lane with at least three lanes to traverse and not much time to do it. I emptied my mind of all the rule-bound small-town driving I'd been practising in the last few months, further emptied my mind of the thought that I was driving Zia's beloved black Integra, and reminded myself that I was a Karachiite. Setting my jaw, I slammed on the horn, spun the wheel to the right and, with an utter disdain for the curses that were hurled in my direction, managed to make it over to the requisite lane well before the turn for Aunty Maheen's flat.

When the concierge asked who I had come to see I realized I didn't know Aunty Maheen's last name any more, so I just said, 'Maheen,' and the concierge said, 'Would that be Mrs Ahmed?' which seemed a fair bet, so I nodded and was directed to the eleventh floor.

I thought I'd cured myself of the habit of fidgeting with my hair when nervous, but as I stood waiting for someone to answer her door bell I kept pulling the ends of my hair, conscious that it was much shorter than the last time she'd seen me. I hoped she was alone. When I had finally summoned up the courage to call her and say I needed to see her, I had been unable to think of a way to tell her I didn't want to see the Interloper. Not yet. It had been a strange phone conversation, both of us too aware that I'd been in the US almost four years without calling, and that made unsayable all the truths going through my mind: I've missed you; it's so good to hear your voice; I can't wait to see you.

The door opened. There she stood. There stood a woman who was closer to being family than anyone in my extended family was, and there was that smile of hers which reminded me that of all her child's friends, and of all her friend's children, I had always been her favourite.

'Hello, loveliness,' I said, and put my arms around her.

She laughed as she hugged me, all my failures of communication forgiven, and I saw immediately that for all her years away from home she was still a 'Karachi aunty' in the best possible sense of the term.

'Inside, inside, move inside,' she said when we finally drew apart, taking my coat and hanging it on the clothes rack, off which it promptly slipped. Aunty Maheen moved as though about to pick it up, and then waved her hand dismissively in the coat's direction. 'Floor's clean,' she said. 'Now take this' – she handed me a cup of tea – 'and go and sit down, while I finish things in the kitchen.'

I watched her walk towards the kitchen and couldn't stop smiling. She was a plump woman now, but there seemed something so contented about that. And her walk, her mannerisms, were still so familiar that I wanted to run into the kitchen after her and throw my arms around her again.

I walked across the wooden floor into the living-room area, where the furthest wall had large windows looking down on to the Charles River and on to Boston's skyline. On the console table against the wall were framed photographs. A couple were of Aunty Maheen and her husband, smiling; several showed Karim in various stages of growing up, including a recent one of him and the Interloper doubled over with laughter, pointing at a burning frying pan; the largest of the photographs showed Aunty Maheen in Karachi with eight or ten of her friends – my parents stood to either side of Aunty Maheen and my father had his arm around her shoulder.

How could she ever think back to what he said to Shafiq and not tear up this photograph?

Aunty Maheen walked out of the kitchen with a plate of pakoras, and sat down right next to me, balancing the plate on her knee. 'So have you heard from my son?'

Every day. Every hour. A million conversations, none of them real.

'Raheen?' Aunty Maheen said. 'Have you heard from him since you left Karachi, because, sweetie, I haven't; not that it surprises me.'

'He didn't come to see you a couple of weeks ago?'

She shook her head and handed me a small plate of pakoras. 'He'd been planning to, but I don't know what happened. He'll show up eventually. He always does. Oh, look at you.' She held me at arm's length and beamed. 'Much too much to talk about, so let's start with how is everyone. What are all those scab-kneed boys and girls who my son grew up with doing with their lives?'

'Nothing special. Finishing university, deciding what next. Waiting for proposals to arrive from boys of good breeding who don't care that your father is a suspected drugs smuggler.'

Aunty Maheen patted my hand. 'That was awful. Poor Sonia. Laila told me all about the newspaper announcement. Can you believe anyone would do something so low?'

Such questions are usually rhetorical, but Aunty Maheen looked at me as though expecting an answer. I shrugged. 'Yes, I believe it. It's awful, but I believe it. Just as I believe Zia's father could arrange the police harassment. And I believe all of us just assumed he was guilty. And still do, even though all charges are dropped. I don't like any of it, but I believe all of it.'

Aunty Maheen nodded. 'I would never have said that at your age. That's what it did, you see. Bangladesh. It made us see what we were capable of. No one should ever know what they are capable of. But worse, even worse, is to see it and then pretend you didn't. The truths we conceal don't disappear, Raheen, they appear in different forms.'

I nodded and nibbled on my pakora. I hadn't even spoken to Aba since Karachi, though I sometimes called Ami at the office. She kept telling me to come home.

'Does it get talked about?' Auntie Maheen said, 'The Civil War?'

I shook my head. 'Only in story fragments.'

Speaking of staying up till dawn, remember during the war when we said we'd keep drinking until sunrise, but that was the night they bombed the oil refineries and the smoke covered the sun, so we just carried on drinking until well after noon.

Don't you remember the scandal, when she was engaged to him but he was a POW in Bangladesh so she married the other one instead?

Never throw anything away. In '71, when the bomb fell in the empty plot next door to us, the heat from the blast was so incredible the blades of the ceiling fan in our bedroom curled up like a tulip, and don't you think that would have been worth quite a lot as war memorabilia if I hadn't chucked it out?

'Those are the kinds of thing we hear about '71,' I told Aunty Maheen, and thought to myself, *also, the story of you and my father.*

Aunty Maheen said, 'Also, the story of me and your father.'

'Yes,' I said. 'Also that.'

'I spoke to him a few minutes ago.'

A pakora fell out of my hand and on to the floor, leaving a smear of chutney on the hardwood.

'What are you so surprised about? It's not uncommon for me to talk to them on the phone. You know your mother called me just after both you and Karim left Karachi, to tell me what happened at Asif and Laila's?'

I shook my head.

'Well, of course she did. And then I called Ali. To find out who had told Karim about the way the engagement broke off. Of course, I knew it wasn't Ali . . . or, at least, not the Ali I had known, although it's been a while and people change. I have. Who would have thought my Ali would turn into a middle-aged Lothario?' She looked past me, frowning, not necessarily displeased so much as surprised, perhaps even trying to chart the course her life might have taken if both she and Uncle Ali had given each other the room to turn away from the caricature of opposites that their marriage settled into. 'First proper conversation I've had with him in years. Not just some formal talk to discuss Karim's flight details or school reports. We were never very good at talk, Ali and I. But I think we've improved with age.'

'So was he the one . . . who told Karim?'

'Of course not. Don't be absurd. No, Ali and I did some detective work. Turns out it was Runty. One year when she was visiting London. And a cousin of mine provided confirmation of the details.' She waved her hand. 'But that's not important any more, is it?'

'What is important?'

Aunty Maheen patted my cheek. Her hand was warm, but the rings on her fingers were cold. 'You and Karim. When I spoke to your father just now, he told me what you said to him on the Lady Lloyd Pier. He told me you think you and Karim would be together if it wasn't for Zafar and my story standing between you. Child, that's ridiculous.'

'I know,' I admitted. 'I know I let Karim down. That's the real issue between us. But what I did is made so much worse by the fact that it wasn't just anyone doing it, but Zafar's daughter doing it to Maheen's son. I don't know if he can get past that. I don't know what I need to do to get both of us past that.'

'I think that's why your parents are the best couple I know,' she said. 'You feel they know how to get past anything.'

'But . . .' It seemed a desperate breach of form and manners to say this, but I had to. 'But you and Aba were in love.'

'God, yes,' she said, and smiled in a way I might smile if someone mentioned my teenage crush on Zia. 'But lots of people are in love lots of times. Yasmin and Ali were in love, too, though in a different way. And Yasmin and Zaf were in love, still are. The most surprising thing of all is that one day Ali and I were in love, also, though that came much later. And then, we weren't.' She laughed. 'It would all be very silly if it didn't wreak such havoc in our lives. The issue is not who paired off with whom – I've been trying to learn when to use the word "whom", sweetie, was that correct? – but who was able to make it work and how. Your parents did.'

'So it's not so special, is that what you're saying? What I feel for Karim.'

'Oh, darling. The thought of the two of you together brings such tears of joy to my eyes.' She kissed the side of my head and handed me the entire plate of pakoras.

'I'm really very confused,' I said. 'OK, one question: how do you forgive what he said?'

She stood up and started walking around the flat, hugging her paisley shawl close in the air-conditioned air. 'I thought I was showing courage by staying in Karachi during all that madness, and I'm still not sure I wasn't. But, you see, I was a Bengali. I was born that way. So though people turned away from me at parties, and conversations stopped when I entered the room, and all sorts of things went on that no one should have to live through, there was a certain . . . resignation, almost, in people's attitudes towards me. I was just a Bingo, nothing to be done about it. But your father . . . your father was something much worse. He was a turncoat, a traitor. A Bingo-lover.' She said the words slowly, as if examining them, trying to unravel their mystery. 'That evening – when Shafiq got the telegram about his brother – Zafar had just come back from hospital. Broken rib, fractured thumb, bruises everywhere. He claimed he'd been mugged and beaten, but no one was fooled. There was violence in the air those days, and why should your father have been expected not to get terrified of it? Whatever he said to Shafiq, awful as it was, I don't believe he meant it.'

'If you didn't believe it, you would have married him.'

Aunty Maheen walked over to the window and looked down at a bridge being raised so a boat could pass through. 'You weren't alive in those days. You don't know what you're talking about.'

She had never spoken to me in that tone before.

I walked over to the window. It was certainly pretty, the view of the river and the tall buildings, but I wondered what Aunty Maheen saw when she looked out. Did she see home?

As if she had read my mind she said, 'I don't think I could ever bear to go back to Karachi. First it was because I knew the kind of whispers that would go around about me. I think I was afraid almost – of being shunned, of having backs turn on me a second time round. And now . . .' She ran her fingers over a book on the console table that had pictures of some of Karachi's landmarks on the cover. 'Now, it's changed so much it might break my heart to see it. To be reminded that, after all, after everything, I've ended up a foreigner in that city.'

I put my arm around her, and thought of all my friends who weren't planning to return to Karachi after university. Zia was still trying to convince me that I, too, should stay in America. He had even called up one of his father's contacts who worked in a travel agency in New York and got him to agree to hire me. He meant well, so I didn't tell him it was the kind of thing his father would have done. Besides, I hadn't decided to turn down the job yet. What kind of home would home be without my friends in it?

'I need to find a way to forgive my father. I think you're the only person who can help me do that.'

'No. I'm not. He is.' Aunty Maheen lifted the Karachi book and shook it. A thin blue piece of paper with writing on either side fell out from between the pages. 'This may help; it may not.' Aunty Maheen handed me the blue paper. 'As soon as you called I knew it was finally time to give it to you. I've had it a long, long time. Your father wrote it to me. I'm going down to the store to get something for dinner. You're staying the night, of course.'

She left me alone, and I picked up the paper, and started to read.

Dear Maheen,

Already I'm thinking ahead to how I'll end this letter, and in case you haven't yet scanned ahead to find the answer to that question, let me tell you it will be with the phrase: my love always, Zafar.

I will show this letter to Yasmin when it is finished. She will approve the ending.

You are both reconciled now that Karim and Raheen are born. (You've been too shy, unsure of the new rules of your re-established friendship with Yasmin, to ask about my daughter's name. The 'Ra' is from her grandfather, Rafay. The rest . . .) I have seen you look at your son and then at Ali, and even I'm not vain enough to believe you are thinking of me for even a moment. But I know the first thought you have – will have, have already had, are having even now – of me in conjunction with your child will be: thank God. Because if we had been married your Karim would not have been born, nor would my Raheen – and how can we love the notion of some hypothetical children that might have been more than we love these tiny-fisted creatures who yesterday seemed entirely unaware of each other for fifty-nine minutes of the hour they were together, yet turned to each other in that sixtieth minute, and Raheen – with eyes shut – reached out and put a hand on Karim's cheek, and Karim kept looking at her without blinking.

I picture them already as firm friends. And then I picture them growing up, and, Maheen, what will I say to my daughter when she is old enough to understand the truth and all its implications? Will I stay quiet to protect the image I want her to have of me, or will it already be too late because of this canker that I sometimes think will make me go the way of vicious Bunty and poor, mad Shafiq?

Nothing can excuse or erase what I said. This is not a letter asking for forgiveness. This is not an attempt to gain catharsis. That will come, if it comes, from my daughter and perhaps your son in the ways in which they react to what I say, should I say it, should you allow me to say it.

There: that is the point of this letter. To tell you that if you want me to stay always silent on the matter, I will. But your heart has always been far greater than mine, so let me first – please, Maheen, don't stop reading, and if you do, don't throw this away but keep it until such a time as you might be willing to believe that the moment in which I said what I said was not an indication of who I intrinsically am but just the words of a monster who sometimes lurks in the dark corners of my life. I should tear this up, it makes little sense, but if I wait to write again until I can craft every sentence, I may never write.

What I was saying was this. Let me first tell you why I feel I must speak one day of what happened to make us unhappen.

It is less than two years since Bangladesh was born, and already we in Pakistan have become so efficient at never speaking about it. When we do refer to those events, it's as personalized stories – about that time after the air-raids when we said we'd go out as soon as it was dawn to inspect the damage the bombs had done down the street, but we sat and sat and dawn never came because the oil refineries had been bombed and a cloud of smoke covered Karachi; about that Tony Bennet impersonation whatshisname did that night we sat on the roof, sipping whisky and watching the dogfights in the sky and the fires from the distant areas where a bomb fell on something combustible; about the time she decided to see how fast rumours spread so she started one about plans to bomb the National Assembly in East Pakistan and next thing she knew there were soldiers at her door, ready to take her in for questioning. We tell these stories and make war personal – but not in the way it should be; not in a way that makes it touch us personally. We make it personal in a way that excludes everything and everyone who was not part of that four-line story about the war days that we tell over tea and biscuits.

I don't claim to be better than any of these people – it's simply that my personalized story is you, Maheen, and you will not be contained within four lines and you will not fail to bring with you all the memories of all the things the rest of us try to forget.

What happens when you work so hard to forget a horror that you also forget that you have forgotten it? It doesn't disappear – the canker turns inwards and mutates into something else. In this city that we both love and claim – even though our families' histories lie elsewhere – what will the canker become?

I am terrified, Maheen, because this country has seen what it is capable of, and we should all be spared that on a personal and a collective basis. It has seen what it is capable of, yet not paused to take account, to reach inwards towards that swirling darkness and hold it up to the light.

We should not have kept our name.

Pakistan died in 1971. Pakistan was a country with two wings – I have never before thought of the war in terms of that image: a wing tearing away from the body it once helped keep aloft – it was a country with a majority Bengali population and all its attendant richness of culture, history, language, topography, climate, clothing . . . oh, everything. How can Pakistan still *be* when all of that, everything that East Pakistan added to the country, is gone? Pakistan was a nation with an image of itself as a place that was created because that creation was the only way its leaders saw possible to safeguard the rights of a minority power within India. How can Pakistan still *be* when we have so abused that image – first by ensuring the Bengalis were minimized and marginalized both politically and economically, and then by reacting to their demands for greater rights and representation with acts of savagery? How can Pakistan still *be* when the whole is gone and we are left with a part? (When we are willing to treat a part as the whole don't we fall victim to circumscribed seeing, a thing we can ill afford?) We should have recognized that the Pakistan of dreams died and was buried in the battle fields of '71. Or . . .

Or, Maheen, is it possible to reclaim a name?

It is a name for which I have great affection, great regard. But what must be done to restore it to what it could have stood for? Perhaps our children will answer that question one day, if we give them the tools – the information – they need for that task.

We act as though history can be erased. Who can blame us? The cost of remembering may break our wilted spirits. But if we allow for erasure we tell ourselves that things can be forgotten, put in the dustbin. We tell ourselves it is possible to have acts without consequences. The finger squeezing the trigger becomes a thing apart from the bullet that speeds across the sands, which becomes a thing apart from the child looking down at his blood pumping out of his heart. And that child, that bullet, that finger, they become things way, way apart from our lives, here, in rooms where we look upon our own sleeping children.

I don't know if I've made any sense, and now I'm blotting the ink with these meaningless tracks of tears.

I will – if you allow it, and I'll take your silence as a yes – I will tell my daughter what I did – no, let me not phrase that in the past: I will tell my daughter what I have done – when she is old enough to grasp how unforgivable it was. When she is old enough to look within and around, and understand the canker. And this is the form my own canker will take: the fear, the fear always, that when I tell her she will turn away from me.

I will not cower in self-loathing; there is something in me that both you and Yasmin could love (forgive me the gaucheness of that remark, and of all the other remarks in here. I don't know how else to say it) and to wallow in self-recrimination is an insult to you both. So I will not cower. I will help Yasmin bring up our daughter in such a way that she will

313

have to look at me in horror when I finally tell her the truth of what I said.

There is nothing that gives me more joy these days than looking at you and knowing you are happy.

My love always,

Zafar

• • •

When I arrived back in Karachi that summer, the summer of 1995, he was waiting for me at the airport. Waiting inside the terminal. Uncle Asif's contacts again, no doubt.

I walked towards him, jet-lagged, the strap of my carry-on flight bag cutting into my shoulder. 'I read the letter you wrote Aunty Maheen,' I said.

'I know. Did I sound like a self-righteous ass?'

'Yes,' I said, and then I quoted the letter back to him.

When he put his arms around me, there was a hesitation on both our parts, but although I didn't hug him back I didn't feel the need to pull away either, and that, at least, was a start.

I had read all the papers on the Net, detailing showdowns, stalemates, body counts, analyses, but when I stepped out of the airport and headed home what struck me most was the vulnerability of cars. Glass on all sides, barring neither stares nor fists nor bullets. And was that man criminal, lunatic or immortal angel that he could stand on the pavement, smoking a cigarette, as though life's greatest danger was falling ash?

Electricity failures and water shortages. Humidity that sheened my skin with sweat, seconds after I stepped out of the air-conditioned car. What water there was, was warm. Electricity repairmen needed police escorts to guard them from Karachiites living in dark and heat for days at a time. But what of those areas the police dared not go to for fear of being attacked themselves? To counter the electricity shortage, there was a ban on neon lights. Driving home from the Club at dinner time was like driving through a ghost town – darkness everywhere save for traffic lights, and who wanted to risk stopping at a red light in those days?

'Aunty Maheen, have you heard from Karim?'
'No, darling, just postcards. He's teaching English in Mexico somewhere. Hasn't got a phone, and, frankly, sweetheart, the way things are in Karachi, if I do speak to him I'll do everything I can to dissuade him from entering those city limits.'

Rocket launchers and gunfire in Boat Basin. Sonia's brother, Sohail, was there when it happened. He told us about the incredible illumination of the night sky when the rocket launchers exploded and how the sound of bullets at first resembled firecrackers. How often we'd stopped in that part of town over the years, after school and after parties, scrounging through one another's purses and wallets for money to spend on meals at Chips and Mr Burger and Flamingo Chaat. How could the violence reach somewhere so familiar?
The next day the newspaper gave us the story:

A three-year old son of a custom officer was killed and he and his wife were critically wounded when their parked vehicle was ambushed at Boating Basin in Clifton . . . At the time of attack the assistant collector of Customs, his wife and their son were having food in a wireless-fitted official Land Cruiser at Boat Basin opposite the branch of Allied Bank of Pakistan.
Around 9:00 pm, the armed men came there, two of them stepped out from one of the cars and sprayed customs officer's vehicle with bullets. The armed men then sped away towards main Clifton roundabout.
In Orangi Town, armed men kidnapped two young vegetable vendors, Aftab and Rashid, and killed them.
Two persons were killed in drive by shooting at Manama bakery in the Sharifabad area. The victims were identified as Osama, 25, and Naeem, 14.

In Liaquatabad, Naeem Ahmed, 25, was shot and killed in a targeted attack.

A young man was killed and two others were wounded in Korangi. The victim was identified as Tariq. Police claimed that the victim was kidnapped from somewhere in the city and later he was shot dead on the main Korangi Road. Two pedestrians, Arif and Salim, were also caught in the shooting and killed.

Nine dead that day, in other words. Not everyone's death worth equal column space, in other words. The dead in my part of town more newsworthy.

A three-year-old boy dead.

'Why don't you just stop reading the papers?' Zia said to me on the phone from New York.

There were mornings when that was a tempting idea, but I found I could no longer say to the world, *there's nothing I can do to change this, so why think too hard about it?* I still didn't think there was anything I could do to change the situation, but now it felt like an abomination to pretend to live outside it.

At my father's office, the accountant announced he was selling all his possessions and leaving Karachi with his family to move to Sydney, Australia, where his brother had a shop. His son was so excited he went around all day parroting out the latitude and longitude of Sydney.

'I don't even know Karachi's latitude and longitude,' Aba said.

The accountant had driven around burning tyres and shells of charred buses to get to work that day from his part of town, but he smiled broadly and said, 'Complete latitude in all things if you have the right connections. Little chance we'll live to be long-in-tooth, so don't even worry about that.'

From *Dawn* newspaper:

June 23: Twenty-four people were killed and several others wounded in targeted attacks, sniping and gunbattles between rangers, police and armed youths on Friday, raising the month's death toll to 204.

June 24: Twenty people were killed and many others wounded as widespread violence paralysed the city on Saturday. Two policemen, two MQM workers, two truck drivers, a PPP activist, and a police informer were among those who fell victim to the shooting spree.

June 25: At least 32 people lost their lives and many others were wounded as the city witnessed one of the worst days of violence on Sunday, marked by several rocket and grenade attacks.

June 26: 23 people were killed and many others wounded in the city, which remained in the grip of armed youths.

June 27: Fourteen people were killed on Tuesday as the city tried to limp back to normality

Every night, the Ghutnas gathered, and though there were interludes of revelry, in the end every evening's conversation was ultimately unchanging. 'Haalaat bohot kharab hain,' they would say, again and again, as if English could not encompass just how bad the situation was; and then the conversation varied in its unvarying way from wondering if those accused of the killing were really guilty or just being set up; and how big a part did the ubiquitous Foreign Hand have in all of this; and could the city fall apart in such fashion without some government involvement; and were drug wars part of the reason for the violence; and which businesses had decided to start working through the strikes called by the politicians; and could the 'talks' actually achieve anything or were they merely occasions for both sides to pretend to talk peace while really recouping their losses and getting ready for the next round of firing; and could this city – my city, this ugly, polluted, overpopulated, heartbreaking place – retain its spirit after all this battering? And finally, inevitably, someone would say: It's like 1971. Except that the army will decimate us before they allow Karachi to break away. And it always fell to my father to say. 'No one wants civil war. Don't say it's like '71. Don't even think it.'

In *Newsline*, the sentence ' "What we are seeing today in Karachi is a repeat of the East Pakistan situation," maintains a senior security official.'

'Is that true?' I asked Ami,

'Ask Maheen that. She'll tell you never to compare Muhajirs to Bengalis. Being pummelled makes it easy for us to wring our hands and forget all we're guilty of. We left India in '47 – we left our homes, Raheen, think of what that means – saying we cannot live amid this injustice, this political marginalization, this exclusion. And then we came to our new homeland and became a willing part of a system that perpetuated marginalization and intolerance of the Bengalis. No, Karachi is not a repeat of the East Pakistan situation.' She pressed a red rose petal between her thumb and forefinger. 'But.'

'But?'

'But there are certain parallels. History is never obliging enough to replay itself in all details. Not personal history, not political history. But we can learn how to rise above the mistakes of the past, and that we haven't done. As a country we haven't. Not in the slightest. Your father's letter to Maheen seems to have more than an element of prophecy in it, isn't that so?'

'Yes,' I said. 'You were right. He looked the country in the eye.

And then, he found a way still to want to stay.' I rested my head on her shoulder. 'That's sort of remarkable.'

I could see his shadow outside the door; I knew he was listening when I said that.

Sonia's father was more popular than ever in the wake of the dropped drug charges, thanks to the aplomb with which he had sent out poppy-shaped invitation cards to a magnificent party, just after he got back from Umra. Karachi is a city that applauds spunk, so the Ghutnas clasped the Lohawallas to their bosoms for the first time and Sonia's mother's dressing table collapsed under the weight of all the party invites. No one mentioned that the proposals for Sonia's hand had dried up completely.

But Sonia had to live with the memory of all that had happened, and with the news that our friend Nadia, in London, was on the verge of getting engaged to Sonia's almost-fiancé, Adel Rana, and I knew she would never tell me how she felt about it all, because I'd always believed her father was guilty and I hadn't tried very hard to hide it from her.

'Uncle Ali, have you heard from Karim?'

'Of course. He's very good at scribbling postcards that say nothing. He's due back in London in September to start work with the family, but until then, who knows. But, sweetheart, I wouldn't expect him in Karachi if I were you. I don't understand why your parents allowed you to return.'

Zia was in New York, working with an investment bank; Nadia was in London on an extended holiday, telling everyone that Adel Rana had nothing but good things to say about Sonia but of course he couldn't be expected to marry into a family accused of drug smuggling; the twins were on the west coast of America, one working at an architect's firm in LA, the other immersed in Web design in San Francisco; Cyrus had joined a multinational in Karachi, primarily so that he could get a foreign posting within a couple of years, and he never said a word about Nadia, whom he had loved and been loved by, but to no avail because he was Parsi and she was Muslim; Sonia's brother, Sohail, was just a few months away from starting college in New York, and there was talk of Sonia going to New York at the same time to visit family, which meant she was to be shown around to eligible Pakistani boys on the East coast, though her father had emphasized that she was to steer clear of Zia. And Karim . . .

Squash courts were my refuge that summer. We played every evening, a motley group of ten or twelve of us, arriving at the courts at four and staying until eight, returning home too exhausted to think of much beyond dinner and a video and sleep. Cyrus's sister confided in me, 'I love the squash courts. There are so many places to hide if gunmen break in.'

Zia came home briefly. His father thought he was dying, though the doctors insisted it was chronic indigestion. His father gave him a spare key to his filing cabinets, which were overflowing with incriminating evidence and rumour and supposition about everyone we knew. 'Burn the files,' I told Zia, but Zia said I'd lost my chance at having a say in his life. He didn't call Sonia at all.

Aunty Laila's cousin came to town, searching for brides for her son. Sonia found the piece of paper she dropped on her way out of the Club one day, and we both giggled at the heading PROSPECTIVE DAUGHTERS-IN-LAW. Below were a series of columns with headings as follows: name, age, lineage, school attended, reputation, misc. Then came the final list, subdivided into four columns: the four Fs of beauty – features, figure, fairness of skin, feet. 'How does she collect the data for the final entry?' Sonia laughed, and we both pretended not to notice that her name was on the list with a large cross in the 'lineage' column and the word 'DRUGS' in the 'misc' column.

At the airport, we were told our flight to Lahore was delayed, but the airline was offering us complementary breakfast in the lounge. 'But it's only cheese sandwiches, and I want halva puri,' I told the airline official. 'Sonia, call your car back and let's go for halva puri.'

The airline official said we couldn't go. 'It's not safe, wandering around town, two girls. Stay here and I'll call my wife and tell her to send halva puri over with my son.'

'You're just afraid we won't come back and the flight will be delayed because of us.'

The man shook his head and held out his car-keys: 'If you must go, here, take my car.'

I thought, I must tell Karim about this man. I must tell Karim so much.

In Lahore, I met Uncle Chaperoo, now a government minister. 'Are you heading south soon?' I asked him.

'What? To Multan?' He tilted his large head to one side.

'South of the country, not the province,' I said.

'Oh God, Karachi. No, of course not.'

Not really so long ago that Uncle Chaperoo's was the face I imagined when I imagined Romeo; not really so long since he'd cut the romantic figure of a man defying convention by marrying outside his tribe. And now he said the problem with Karachi was that it was such a mishmash, no good could come from rampant plurality. His wife was not around when I saw him. They weren't divorced, just indifferent.

'Multan! South! Such circumscribed seeing,' I said to Sonia. 'This holiday isn't doing much for me. Let's go home,' and we took the next flight out. On my way home from the airport I remembered that was a phrase from Aba's letter: *Circumscribed seeing, a thing we can ill afford.*

*

The Prime Minister told reporters the country was doing well. When asked about Karachi, she said Karachi was only ten million people.

Aunty Laila gripped me by the elbow in the doorway to the chemist's and hissed, 'We have to get out of here. Act casual.'

Numb could be mistaken for casual. I let her pull me out, my eyes sweeping the area for the glint of sun on trigger. Perhaps we should say something, warn the other shoppers. On the ground, a package. I tumbled into Aunty Laila's car and ducked low in the seat. Still unable to speak, I gestured to her driver to step on it.

Aunty Laila opened the back door. Slowly, so slowly.

A man reached down to pick up the package.

Aunty Laila put a hand to my forehead. 'There's a journalist in there. I don't want tomorrow's papers announcing SOCIALITE BUYS SUPPOSITORIES.'

The man pulled a kabab roll out of the bag, and began to chew.

I heard Aba and Ami talking to Aunty Maheen on the phone. They sat right next to each other, his arm around her shoulder, with the phone held between them. They were both laughing.

I was supposed to be looking for a job, but what did I want to do with my life?

The memory of his throat beneath my mouth, the sting of aftershave in the cut on my lip . . .

A nomad from Uncle Asif's dune begged Uncle Asif to get him a job in Karachi. Even now, even at this time, it was still a city that beckoned. Uncle Asif said that nomad was little older than I was, and I wondered if among his few possessions were a pair of marbles that looked like the eyes of a goat.

'Why are there no parties, why are there no parties?' Aunty Runty wept. 'I can't bear all this sitting at home, I can't bear my own imagination.'

Sunsets were still beautiful, and you could always find boys playing cricket on the street.

Naila hadn't appeared with her coconut oil at anyone's house since early May.

Orangi, Korangi, Liaquatabad, New Town, Golimar, Machar Colony, Azizabad, Sher Shah . . . violence in all those parts of town whose unfamiliarity still felt like a blessing. But then, six died in Kharadar, including a beggar girl. As I read through the newspaper article I saw, between one word and the next, images of bullets and bodies, the wounded weeping for the dead, crushed and broken sugar cane kicked aside by fleeing feet; balloons burst around me and the ground outside the white-tiled hotel rushed up to meet me. Gravel bit into my skin. A man cradled a boy's blood-dark head in his lap, whispering, 'Ocean, oceano, samundar, mohit, moa shoagor, umi, bahari, valtameri . . .'

Sonia called me late one night. 'Just so sick of it. Everyone is gloom and doom and harpoon happiness. But just listen to what happened to me this evening. Ama and I had gone to my grandparents' house for dinner – Aboo's in Islamabad, and who ever knows where Sohail is these days? – and as we were walking to our car to leave, this man, real chichora type, leapt out of the shrubs, caught Amma's wrist and said, "Give me your car-keys." '

'No!'

'Yes, na, I'm telling you. So Amma became suddenly hysterical and she's trying to find the key in her bag but the clasp is so complicated it takes real techknowhow to get it open, and even when she finally manages to do that her hands are shaking so much that she can't really find anything, so then the man starts to put his hand down his shalwar and said, "Hurry up and give me the keys or I'll take out my TT." And Ama went completely mental and started throwing the contents of her bag at this guy, yelling, "No, no, anything but that," and the man got such a shock, what with Ama and also the neighbour coming to see what the commotion was all about, that he ran away. I turned to Ama and I said, "You know, a TT is a kind of gun," and she said, "Oh, thank God, I thought he was going to show us his privates." '

I reminded Sonia that before this summer we used to be able to laugh without consciously thinking, *Now I'm laughing. Now the suffocation is gone from my lungs for a moment.*

She reminded me there hadn't been much cause for laughter in the winter either.

All mobile-phone services had been suspended because there were strong indicators that such a mode of communication aided terrorist activities.

My car developed a flat tyre when I was driving home from the Club. When I got out of the car to check it, a Suzuki van stopped and three men got out. A cyclist pulled over beside me. A fruit seller walked across the street towards me. I knew why they stopped, I knew what they were going to do. They told me to sit back in the car, with the air conditioning on. It was a hot, sticky day. They changed the tyre for me, and then they all left.

It was exactly the sort of thing you'd expect unknown men to do in Karachi.

I walked into Zia's room as he was packing to return to New York. He lugged his suitcase off his bed, making room for me to lie down. But I felt awkward, said I should leave. He said he wasn't planning to come back to Karachi and who knows when he'd see me again. So how much did it really matter what happened between us, this once?

I said, 'Let's go for a drive. I don't feel comfortable here, having this conversation, with your parents maybe walking by on the other side of the wall.' We drove out in his Integra, though all summer I had kept my movements confined to houses and squash courts as much as possible.

I felt no pleasure, no anticipation, as we drove, just some numb sense of inevitability. Zia's face unreadable. Where were we going? How deserted the streets were, so soon after sunset. Near the submarine roundabout he turned off the main road. We were going to one of Sonia's father's offices, the one closest to home. Desk, phone, fax. Makeshift work space for days when it was too dangerous to head to offices in other parts of town. Green carpet. Nothing of real importance there, no caretakers and guards keeping watch. Years ago, Sonia had showed us we could unlock the door with a penknife. Zia swerved, without slowing, around a stalled car blocking the road. A man stepped out from behind the car, right into the path of Zia's car. Zia spun the wheel. Braked. The man, uninjured, pointed a gun through the window.

'It must be fate,' he said.

It was the car thief.

He directed us to get out of the car.

'I'm sorry, I'm sorry, we'll get you a job. I thought my friend had arranged it.' Zia was sweating in the still night air.

The man shook his head. 'Your friend did arrange it. Loha-walla Sahib tracked me down, found me a job. I owe him a lot. But my brother's been shot. You don't need to know details, but he's been very angry, done a lot of foolishness. Still, he's my brother. And if I don't get him to the hospital he'll die. But if I try driving from here to there, the police will stop me, and then they'll recognize him. They won't stop a car with a girl in it.'

He opened the back door of the stalled car. The brother lay there, unmoving. The first-aid box from Sonia's father's office was open next to him, its contents strewn around the car. Zia's expression passed from fear to something more complicated, something that had to do with the shadows he'd always lived among. He took the man's arms and started to pull him out. 'Help me, Raheen.' The car thief still had his gun trained on us. I caught the brother's feet as Zia pulled him further and further out of the car. That wasn't sweat, as I had first thought, on the man's shalwar-kameez. We put him in the back seat of Zia's car and drove to the government hospital. The private hospitals wouldn't deal with a gunshot wound. There were Ranger vans everywhere, but no one stopped us.

Outside the hospital, the pavement was covered with bodies, all lined up side by side. The car thief – Mohommad – laughed to see me cover my eyes when I saw them. 'They're sleeping,' he said. 'They have relatives in there, and they don't have money for hotels or even transportation. So they sleep here at night, and in the morning they'll see their family members, or find out if they've died.'

In the emergency ward, chaos. So many people there was no room to bring a stretcher through. Zia and Mohommad carried in the brother, conscious now, and slumped him against a wall. No beds available, not even a chair. Not nearly enough doctors. I find myself moving away from the three men, even though I should be telling Zia we can go home now. I am moving among groans and cries and sights I will never forget. Surely someone should be moving faster. Surely the world should be moving faster. A man is talking to a woman who has a crying toddler in her arms. The man is holding a syringe, though he is clearly not a doctor. But he speaks to her and she nods. When he empties his syringe into the child's vein, pain eases off the child's face. The woman holds her arm out, too. The man leans very close to her. Some sort of bargaining will go on. A man in a white coat pushes past me. I hear him say, 'We've run out of blood.' Another replies: 'Scrape it off the walls of the operating theatre.' A sleek cat pads past me. This, more than anything, makes me want to throw up. Zia catches my arm. I say, 'We should give blood.' He tells me we can leave. I open my mouth to say yes, but a doctor has overheard my previous comment, he's asking me what blood type I am. I tell him. He asks Zia. Zia pretends not to know, but I know that he's lying and I tell him so. He pulls his blood-type card out of his wallet. The doctor says we're both needed to give transfusions, immediately. But shouldn't someone test our blood first? A patient lying nearby says, 'Test for what? Fatal diseases?' There is much laughter around him. I have lost sight of Mohommad and his brother. I think of them as my allies now. No sheets on the bed I am made to lie on. The needle plunges in while I am looking away, and I panic: was it sterilized? Was it new? No one has time to answer me. A man I don't much like the look of is in the bed beside me. He's been in a shoot-out. I hear someone say he's killed people. 'Was it sterilized?' I keep asking and someone says, 'Yes, yes,' but the tone is impatient. What can anyone do about it now if it wasn't? Zia comes to find me. His head is spinning. They took more blood, he thinks, than is safe. I ask him about the needle. He hadn't thought to check. We dare not think about it. We ask about Mohommad and his brother. No one knows. But we don't leave. We ask every doctor and orderly who passes by about the man with the bullet in his abdomen. Someone tells us Zia's blood couldn't save the girl on the bed beside him. My man, they think, will live. His mother is at the hospital. She finds me. She tells me I might think my blood has gone to waste, because it is a certainty, not just a probability, that sooner or later, probably sooner, another bullet will find its way to her son's heart. 'Then your blood will be spilled on the streets of Karachi. But for every day of extra life you've given him, I thank you.' We see Mohommad at last. His brother is dead. We offer to stay. He shakes his head. He asks me, 'Where's that hero friend of yours? America or England?' I say I don't know. He asks me the hero's name. I say, 'Karim.'

His name is like cool water in my mouth.

Zia drives us back to his house. We lie on his bed together, and hold each other close, trying not to strain our ears for the sound of some infection coursing through our veins.

That night, I dreamt Karim and I were walking through Karachi's streets. When the gunfire started we were right near our old school, so we ran inside, making our way across the open playing fields and towards the crowded car park. Dust rose around our feet as we ran, and rose around the bullets kicking in the dust, left and right of us, harder than hail. Bullets smashed against my spine, and between one twinge of agony and the next there was time to hear all the cries of the wounded on the other side of the wall. Karim turned. Turned, his arms spread wide. And then I couldn't run on, so I looked back at Karim and at the bullets arcing over the wall towards us. Except, they weren't bullets.

They were diamonds.

No, Ra, they were frozen tears.

There are two ways to escape suffering [the inferno where we live every day]. *The first is easy for many: accept the inferno and become such a part of it that you can no longer see it. The second is risky and demands constant vigilance and apprehension: seek and learn to recognize who and what, in the midst of the inferno, are not inferno, then make them endure, give them space.*

Italo Calvino

Karim,

There's a street in Karachi that follows the moon.

Near an Imam Baragh, there's a line of houses, with back and front doors and no boundary walls. When the lunar calendar enters the month of Muhurram, Shia women make their way to the Imam Baragh daily. There is a back door to the Imam Baragh for them, for the ones in purdah, and to reach that back door without being gazed upon by strangers in the open streets they walk through the neighbourhood houses. Back and front doors are flung open, and the women walk through from the hallway of one house to the hallway of another until that alley within houses takes them all the way to the door of the Imam Baragh. It is an alley without name, it is an alley that ceases to exist when the moon disappears, but it is an alley all the same and one that says more about Karachi than anything you'll find on a street map.

Your mother called the other day to say she's given you a copy of my father's letter. In it he speaks of Karachi's war stories that are personal in a way which excludes everything outside the story. I understand now, at last, what this has to do with street names. I've always thought it wonderful that everyone I know in Karachi gives directions in terms of landmarks and stories – go to the submarine roundabout; turn into the lane where the car thief accosted Zia; drive until you come to Sonia's father's office. Such familiarity, such belonging, wrapped up in every set of directions. Don't deny there's something remarkable about that; we belong to a city invested in storytelling. It is in our blood. But you can only be familiar with those you know well, you can only know the stories of those to whom you've bothered to listen. What happens to all those streets that hold no stories for us? Do we simply stay away from them? I've lived my life in such limited circles and it's your voice I hear now, telling me the limited can be so limiting.

But what has this to do with us? You think my limited life excluded you before, will exclude you again. Karim, I can't deny I've been selfish. Your mood has always been so infectious, no antibodies in my blood to keep me immune from the way you feel. So I've always wanted to make you laugh and see you laughing instead of having to weep your tears. I thought you knew that. How could you ever think it was lack of caring that made me turn away from the sight of you in pain?

Am I trying to say my selfishness is a mark of love? How can selfishness and love coexist? Ask the city we live in.

Karachi at its worst is a Karachi unconcerned with people who exist outside the storyteller's circle, a Karachi oblivious to people and places who aren't familiar enough for nicknames. What I've sometimes mistaken for intimacy is really just exclusion. But Karachi is always dual. Houses are alleys; car thieves are the people to help you when your car won't start; pollution simultaneously chokes you and makes you gasp at the beauty of unnatural sunsets; a violent, fractured place dismissive of everyone outside its boundaries is vibrant, embracing, accepting of outsiders; and, yes, selfishness is the consequence of love.

No simple answers in Karachi. Just when we decide that

intimacy is exclusionary, a man at the airport turns round and gives us his car-keys, a motia seller calls us 'sister' and adorns our wrists with flowers, families fling open their doors and avert their eyes and help us make our way to places of worship; at its best, Karim, Karachi is intimate with strangers.

If I am truly to call myself a product of this city, how can I not find it in me to learn that much easier lesson: how to be intimate with my intimates.

This is not an epiphany, it's just the start of an attempt to be brave enough to think about certain things that terrify me. There's a letter we've both read which urges me to face the terror. What my father said and what he wrote were part of both our pasts, and to pretend the matter can be easily discussed and resolved is to deny how deep in our marrow consequences are lodged. We have to every day live with the truth and every day find a way towards unblinking, unsentimental compassion that renders forgiveness irrelevant. And compassion has to wheel all about us, in concomitantly widening and narrowing circles. To look at waves and understand that when they break they start to re-form, that seems crucial, though perhaps I'm getting my metaphors all tangled up.

I love this place, Karim, for all its madness and complications. It's not that I didn't love it before, but I loved it with a child's kind of love, the kind that either ends or strengthens as understanding grows.

I can see you, out there, reading between the lines.

Come home, stranger.

Come home, untangler of my thoughts.

Come home and tell me, what do I do with this breaking heart of mine?

. . .

'Aba, tell me what happened.'

1971

Zafar gritted his teeth in pain as he walked to the door. Ribs, face, fists. Everything in pain. He'd thought it would end when the war ended, but what if it never ended? What if time only exacerbated people's wounds, intensified their madness? What if he and Maheen would be driven out of Karachi by the attitudes of their friends? Only a handful, a tiny handful, of people had come to see him in the hospital. And, of that handful, only Yasmin and Ali asked what had really happened.

How much easier life would be if I wasn't engaged.

Where had that thought come from? Zafar shook his head to clear it away. Couldn't let all the whispering get to him. His cousins, friends, even his mother in her veiled way, all telling him they understood his sense of obligation, 'but at times one must be selfish'. Telling him it was clear to everyone that Maheen wasn't the same person she'd been when he asked her to marry him – 'not a criticism, darling, just a fact. How could anyone stay the same under such circumstances?' Telling him, 'Can you imagine raising Bengali children in such an atmosphere?' Telling him he wasn't cut out for a life that wasn't uncomplicated, so why pretend? Telling him that of course he wouldn't admit to himself that he wanted to break the engagement, but was it fair on Maheen to marry her for the wrong reasons?

Telling him all this, and pretending they said it because they cared about him. Telling him all this, and infecting his thoughts.

Zafar opened the door. It was Shafiq.

'You're going to marry one of them. You're going to let her have your children. How?'

Sheer craziness in Shafiq's eyes, more violent than anything in Bunty's face when Bunty had pummelled him again and again in the squash court. Maheen was in the kitchen. If Shafiq saw Maheen . . . What was that glinting in Shafiq's hand? Was that a knife in Shafiq's hand? Had to get him out of here before he saw Maheen. Don't argue, get him out of here.

The kitchen door swings open.

Zafar knows what to say to placate Shafiq and get him to leave.

Zafar knows what to say, so unforgivable, to make Maheen leave him.

He says it.

He has succeeded.

He has succeeded.

He turns to look at Maheen.

He will give up anything – this city, his friends, his personality – just to erase that look from her eyes, just to get her to stay with him for ever.

He opens his mouth to explain.

But which thought was it, which of the two thoughts, that made him say what he said?

If one, he can explain it.

If the other, he has lost her.

He doesn't know.

He'll never know.

• • •

I was in Uncle Asif's study, in Rahim Yar Khan, when Aunty Laila told me there was a phone call for me. I looked at my watch. My mother had three hours to her deadline for an article on the Orangi Pilot Project, which had turned one of the most troubled spots in Karachi into a haven of high literacy, effective sewerage, tolerance among communities. Listening to my mother talk about the people who worked there I had begun to imagine a possible future for myself, though I'd be lying if I didn't admit that a lot of the time it seemed much more appealing to imagine myself sitting in a comfortable office in Aba's ad agency, drinking tea and discussing slogans. But now I knew it had to be my father on the phone, asking me why I had travelled up north and left him alone in the house to face the dread YUD: Yasmin Under Deadline. Somehow over the course of the summer, Aba and I had learnt to laugh together again. I wouldn't say I had forgiven him; more to the point, forgiveness was no longer an issue. He had to live with his failures, just as I had to live with mine. And if I hadn't known what he had said to Aunty Maheen, I would never have believed that I needed to be vigilant for the serpents and abysses that could slither into or open up in any soul, not just the souls that were housed within obvious monsters.

But for the record, I had told him. *I think you said it to save her from Shafiq.*

I picked up the extension in the study. 'Has she started sticking paperclips in her hair yet?'

'Do Aunty Laila's ceramic bowls still have purple and green dye stains?'

'Karim.' I stood up and the suddenness of my movement

336

yanked the telephone jack out of its socket. 'Don't hang up,' I yelled to anything that might possibly transmit that message to Karim. 'Don't hang up.' I went down on my hands and knees and fitted the jack into the socket. 'Don't hang up,' I yelled into the handset.

'Wouldn't matter if I did. Continue to yell at that pitch and I'll hear you in Karachi.'

'You're in Karachi?'

'Yes. I've decided I really do want to make a map. I need your help. That's why I'm calling.'

'That's why you're calling?'

'Yes. You're the one who gave me the idea. With your mention of the lunar street. I'm going to make a map on the Internet.'

I leaned back in the leather desk chair, watching the clouds outside the window gather and darken. He'd read my letter, and it had given him an idea for a map. It was worse than if he'd never acknowledged the letter.

'Are you listening to me? You gave me the idea yourself. We'll make an interactive map on the Internet. You start with a basic street map, OK, but everywhere there are links. Click here, you get sound files of Karachiites telling stories of what it's like to live in different parts of town. Click there, you get a visual of any particular street. Click again, the camera zooms in and you see a rock or a leaf or a billboard that means something to that street. Click, you see streets that exist seasonally, like your lunar street. Click, you see which sections are under curfew. Click, you hear a poem. Click, you see a painting. Choice of languages in which you can read the thing. Sound files in all kinds of dialects. Strong on graphics for people who are illiterate. Just wait, Raheen, this is going to be amazing. And don't tell me most people can't afford computers; you just wait a few years and an amazing number of people will have access to one even if they don't own it themselves. This is a lifelong project, Raheen, in a city that's always changing. Too exhausting to contemplate doing alone. You'll help me, right, you'll join me? We'll do this together, right? You'll write something; we'll include links to all kinds of text about Karachi. Write something about the city, the Karachi you know. You always could write well. We'll be Eratosthenes and Strabo working hand-in-hand. Have you disconnected the phone again?'

'No.' I looked across at the globe on its axis, which stood on a table by the window, and wanted to throw something at it. We'd be Eratosthenes and Strabo. So this is how it would end. Each of us learning something from the other, sharing ideas, making a map. We'd tell people what a wonderful working relationship we had. After all, we'd been friends all our lives. And if anyone asked us about the time we'd been young and in love, we'd have to pause to draw up those memories of how it had been, how we thought it would be. Sometimes, late at night, when no one else was around, each of us would sit alone and wonder how it would have worked out if only . . . But we'd never think about it too long, or too seriously.

The thought was unbearable.

'Will you do it? Will you write something? Write a story or something. Write about the motia-seller and the car thief and Zia and Sonia and falling in love.'

'What exactly should I write about falling in love?'

'Write, "There was a boy called Karim who never fell in love." '

'He never fell in love?'

'No. There was no falling. He was born in love with her, and he was borne by love all the way back to her, even though there was a period of total stupidity in between.'

I bowed my head. The grace of this moment. Remember this always.

'You keep going silent on me.'

I pressed the phone as close to my ear as possible. 'Karim, you bastard, I'll kill you.'

He laughed. 'What? You really thought I called you up to tell you to help me make a map?'

'Stop being obnoxious. Say something sappy.' From Uncle Asif's collection of seashells and fossils, I picked up a cuttlebone and traced the outline of my hand with it.

'Maple syrup.'

'Are you feeling kinky?'

'It's made from sap.'

'I'm going to hit you. Should I fly back to Karachi or will you come here? Which is faster?'

'I'll come there. Supposing I was being kinky, how would you have responded?'

'When you get here, I'll tell you. When's the next flight?'

'Hang on, girlio. I can't make the next flight. I really am going to do this map thing, you know. 'Cause you know what I realized? There's bound to be a map somewhere. The police, the Intelligence Services, maybe even the post office, they have got to have a street map of Karachi.'

'I guess.' I couldn't help laughing at how we'd come full circle. Rahim Yar Khan and maps and the two of us. But how far we'd travelled to get back here.

'Don't guess. It's true. Zia's father spoke to someone – one of his shady contacts – who said he'll get me a map. So Zia's father is coming over right now with a police escort to take me to meet this guy and get the map. I'll bring it to Rahim Yar Khan and we'll start thinking of ways to use it as the basis for our Internet map. But we won't worry about that in a hurry. Right? All the time in the world.'

'Karim, no.' Despite my happiness, I felt a shiver of apprehension. 'The worst way to start a project like this is to start it with Zia's father's help.' I couldn't bear to be in the same room as him now. The man who still hadn't cried over his son's death. His grief mutated past redemption.

'I'm going to start squeezing toothpaste from the middle of the tube. We're obviously just searching for things to argue about.

Oh, car's here. I'll call you from the airport with flight details, OK? Hey, one last thing. Your name. How come you never told me it means "guide"?'

When he hung up I stayed as I was, phone pressed to my ear. 'Karim,' I said. 'Karim,' I whispered, tasting his name in my mouth.

I turned the cuttlebone around in my hands. Why didn't he take the next flight? Why wait to be taken somewhere with Zia's father? No good could come of any interaction with Zia's father.

I pictured Karim sitting at the desk, pencil poised above a sheet of paper, eyes consulting base maps and aerial mosaics, one arm resting on the desk, palm up. *Clifton, Defence, Gizri, Sea View, Bath Island* . . . I said, wrapping my fingers around each of his fingers in turn, learning by touch the length of each digit. I dipped my thumb in ink and ran it over his palm: heart line, fate line, Mound of Venus. *Boat Basin*, I said. I unbuttoned his cuff and rolled up his sleeve. With the tine of a fork I traced his vein, from wrist up to elbow. *Mai Kolachi*, I said. He held the tip of my ring finger against his elbow joint, moving the fingertip back and forth along the groove: *The Beach Luxury Hotel Road*, he said. I pushed the shirtsleeve further up his arm, and ran a fingernail down a raised and knotted scar. *So then, what would this be?* I asked. He turned his map towards me and pointed out Napier Mole Road. *Can you handle these logistics?* he said.

If I can't handle, then I'll toothle them, I said, and bit his bicep. A drop of blood glistened on his skin. My tongue curled around it.

Hey, that's mine, he said, laughing. *Give it back.*

I gave it back. He ran his inked palm over skin, under cloth, in between teeth, leaving imprints of his destiny all over my body, and I returned the tattoo, his heart line passing from palm to cheek to abdomen to hip to crisscrossed paths to routes unmapped. Our sweat smelled of unwritten words. Ink tastes different on the skin of the man you love. Strange hieroglyphics of desire. The rain drummed down on the long, long windows, leaving streaks that were roads and veins, arteries and arteries.

I stepped away from the desk; it really was raining. I pushed open the windows, back arched and mouth open to catch the liquid sky on my tongue. My hands rested on a globe by the window; mountain ranges embossed on its surface, embedded in my skin. I twirled the cuttlebone. Thought of everything that had led us here. I am so sure now that as I stood there I knew something of what was happening on the dusty streets of home. The rain clouds moved towards Karachi, where Karim was getting out of a policeman's Pajero, collar unbuttoned, sleeves rolled up, veins on arm and throat pulsing blue in a drab landscape. The sky was low, pressed down by rain, clouds impaled on lightning. I pulled off my clinging shirt, rivulets running down skin, tributaries and waterfalls at my shoulder . . . Karim pushing open a door, Zia's father carrying keys to filing cabinets behind him . . . Zia in New York turning an identical key over and over in his hand unable to consign it to fire . . . fireflies dancing around me in rain . . . opposing thoughts dancing through Sonia's mind as she looks from burning matchstick to the slip of paper with Zia's New York number on it in my handwriting . . . Zia twirls the key . . . Sonia twirls the matchstick . . . the globe spins off its axis and careens towards the window . . . armed men charge through the gaping doorway . . . Arabian Sea leaps out to slap my face . . . glass from broken window everywhere . . . glass from bullet-shattered window everywhere and nothing the police can do but fire blindly . . . through the noise of bullets Zia's father screams that every stranger is an enemy . . . Karim watches pools of strangers' blood spread across maps . . . pools around my feet . . . the globe still bouncing . . . world spinning round me . . . spinning round, the only gunman still alive points his weapon at Karim . . . one final mindless act with what strength he has . . . Zia's father cries, *my son, my son* . . . he throws himself between gunman and boy . . . a bullet carves an alley through a heart . . . one object consigned to fire, one not . . . Zia's father's twenty-four-year-old tears unfreezing, falling, drowning him, me, everyone . . .

and I can only dimly understand the startled peace when the boy closes the man's sightless, tear-rimmed eyes and the globe hurls all its oceans at us,

     wave

          after wave

               after wave.

. . .

In Karachi's streets even the mourners turn their faces skywards to the rain and falling leaves. Between sheets of water, indistinct figures dance together.

I take Karim's hand and pull him into the music.

'Follow me,' I say. 'I know the way.'

A NOTE ON THE AUTHOR

Kamila Shamsie was born in 1973 in Pakistan. Her first novel, *In the City by the Sea*, was published in 1998 and shortlisted for the John Llewelyn Rhys/Mail on Sunday Prize. In 1999 Kamila received The Award for Literature in Pakistan and in 2000 published her second novel *Salt and Saffron* to critical acclaim. In 2001 Kamila was selected as one of Orange's 21 writers for the 21st Century. Kamila lives in London and Karachi.